G                                                                          ·k
w                                                                          le
sʃ                                                                         ɔe
eɪ

P

ʻ

ʻ

7

F
TAY

e.ʼ

(

ʻ                                                                          rd
ʰ

ʻ

ʻA compelling and dark-edged fantasy . . . highly recommend-
ed.ʼ *Independent*

# The Curse of Salamander Street

## G. P. Taylor

*faber and faber*

First published in 2006
by Faber and Faber Limited
3 Queen Square London WC1N 3AU
This paperback edition published in 2007

Typeset by Faber and Faber Limited
Printed in England by Mackays of Chatham plc, Chatham, Kent

A CIP record for this book
is available from the British Library

ISBN 978–0–571–23254–3
0–571–23254–X

2 4 6 8 10 9 7 5 3 1

To Hannah, Abigail, Lydia –
the source of my inspiration

# The Curse of
# Salamander Street

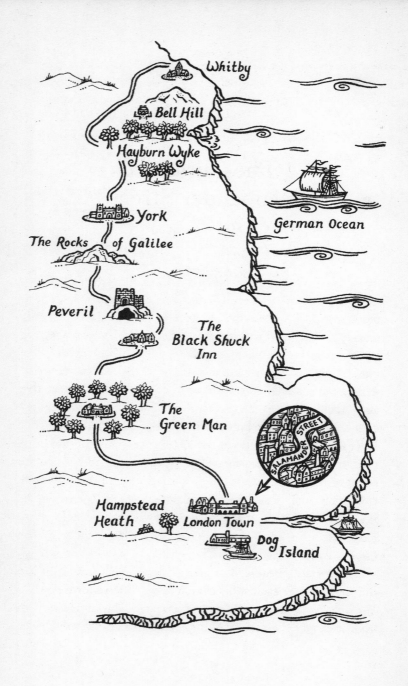

Whitby

Bell Hill

Hayburn Wyke

York

The Rocks    of Galilee

Peveril

The
Black Shuck
Inn

German Ocean

The
Green Man

SALAMANDER STREET

Hampstead
Heath    London Town

Dog Island

# Pergrandis Cetus

IT had been three days since the ball of fire had crashed into the earth, somewhere far to the south. The sky had burnt blood red and turned the sea to a boiling cauldron. Beadle stumbled, half-mad with rage, as he cupped his bleeding cheek in his torn hands and licked the blood from his fingers. The dark of the wood clung like a blanket to the ground, and a fine white mist hovered above the stinking earth. From every tree and every branch came the screeching of small birds as they coughed and chattered mournfully in the cold evening air.

Beadle looked up and saw the light of day fading through the thick fingers of the growing eaves that locked together like the struts of a vast cathedral. The drip, drip, drip of the last of the storm fell to the forest floor from the twisted wooden spindles that beat against each other in the wind. Beadle held out a bloodstained hand to catch the drops that spat coldly against his skin.

'Never mind, Beadle,' he said softly to himself as he splashed the chilled water against his bloodied face. 'On yer own now . . . Yer own man, and not a minute too soon.' He spoke as if to calm his anger. The sound of his voice danced from tree to tree like the whisperings of a wood elf. Beadle laughed. With one hand he pulled the woven scarf up around his face to dampen the wound that throbbed and chided his skin. He wiped the back of his sleeve across his brow and commingled blood and sweat with evening dew. 'Soon be at the sea and then on to the path – never look at Demurral's face again, never hear another lie from his lips.' Beadle said the words in a voice just above a mutter, fearful that the trees could hear his proclamations and the reeds would whisper and a spell be made.

He had trudged wearily for many hours along the twisting path that snaked across the heath and into the forest. To the west, the sky had wept bitterly, washing the moor until the track had run like a small river and babbled over the cliff edge and into the sea. Now, as he strode quickly on, Beadle could smell the ocean. It came to him in the fragrance of seaweed and dead fish. He stopped for a moment and looked about him. To one side the path fell away into a warren of dark gorse and bramble. Above him, cut into the shale crag was a stack of narrow treads that went this way and that amongst the trees that had grown from the cliff. Where the paths crossed the steps spiralled like a stone staircase of a vast cathedral. He stopped and looked to the sea below. Then he looked up to the high cliff that seemed to grow above him as if the earth moved upwards minute by minute with his every breath.

Beadle rubbed his chin and panted hard. The thought of climbing the steps onto the high peak daunted him. If he took that way, he knew he could be seen from the tower of the Vicarage. In his heart Beadle knew that Demurral wouldn't let him go that easily. It had been too simple: Beadle had just walked away from his old life. Here in the wood that clung to the shale cliff, he thought he was safe. The trees and fallen winter leaves made reassuring sounds that reminded him of brighter days. Again he looked up and then down. Beadle stood in the middle of the crossed paths unable to make up his mind and wondering if Demurral had invoked an invisible creature to follow his every move.

'Wouldn't let me go that quick,' he said to himself in a croaked voice as if he was unsure of his own words. 'Can't be just running off – don't know which way . . .' He looked to the path that swept into the arch of gorse and shook his head.

'Never simple, never simple . . . Chin up, chest out, heart full of pride . . .' he said as he looked back and forth, unsure as to which way he should go. 'Down? Dark and easy – but up?' He paused, scratched his bloodied nose and sighed as he thought.

Beadle took two paces up the flight of steps that led through the trees to the light above. He stopped again and looked up, listening to the sounds of the forest that rose up before him. From far off came the splintering of wood as if someone or something had taken hold of a small tree and split it in two.

'Down,' he commanded himself quickly. The call of his tired bones had won the battle of his will. 'And down it will be.' Beadle shuddered uneasily and looked about the dark wood, his eyes searching out the blackness.

Step by step he walked on into the gorse tunnel that formed a canopy above his head. Beneath his feet the mud squelched and moaned with every fall of his foot as it clasped to his worn boots like sticky fingers. In ten paces he was back to night. The gorse tunnel rustled and shivered with every breath of the wind. Spines of bramble sliced to his left and right like sharpened swords, as the shrill whisper of the dying gale leapt from the sea and through the forest.

He wrapped his bitter hands in the soft dampness of the tails of the neck scarf, muffling them against his worn-out jacket. Beadle smiled to himself as he saw the cut from the dagger that had slivered through the cotton warp of his frock coat, just missing his skin. It had burst open just above his heart, but the

5

knife had glanced against the unread prayer book that he had carried for years like a talisman.

'He'll never do that again, not to Beadle,' he grunted as he walked, wiping a tear from his eye as he thought of a time before.

Beadle had stood in the remnants of the Vicarage high above Baytown. The cannon of the *Magenta* had torn down every ceiling and mantel. When the world began to spin and the sky explode, Beadle had hidden in the cellar and listened as the stones crashed to the ground and what was once such a proud place was shaken to rubble. When he had emerged later that morning, all was in ruins. It was then that he knew his life had gone. What had been a reluctant home was now no more. With the falling of each stone, so had his life crumbled. He had no desire to serve his earthly master. All he knew was that his heart commanded him to take the road to London.

Beadle knew that Demurral would come for him. Demurral had once vowed that it would be futile for Beadle to think of leaving and that no matter where his footsteps led him, he would be there. It was a thought that had plagued Beadle all that night. He had hidden from his master and had taken a small knapsack and packed what meagre items he owned and fastened the brass catch. He had then slung it over his shoulder as he slammed the large wooden door to the empty house. In twenty paces he was in the stable. The night sky had quaked and the world shook. Beadle buried himself in the thick straw and, unable to fight off the hands of sleep, he quickly slumbered.

'BEADLE! BEADLE, COME OUT!' Obadiah Demurral shouted three hours later, the sharp words stabbing Beadle from his sleep. 'NOW!'

Beadle had dug deeper into the straw, hoping not to be found as Demurral had trudged the stone courtyard searching for his servant. He had listened as Parson Demurral had smashed his walking cane against the stones and demanded his presence like an angry child.

Demurral had then slumped to the ground and sobbed. 'Humiliated me, Beadle, humiliated,' he squawked, weeping between each word and beating the ground. 'They tricked us . . . A trap . . . Power beyond belief. Imagine, Beadle. They had an angel – and not even Pyratheon could withstand his wonders. It brought the Ethio back from the dead and took death from him in an instant. I fear he will come for me. I am as good as dead and for me there will be no everlasting life. This is my curse, my future. I have taken on the powers of Heaven and I have been crushed beneath their feet. HE CHEATED – BROKE THE COMMANDMENTS AND TWISTED HIS OWN MAGIC! I must leave this place.'

Demurral panted pathetically as he sobbed and as he spoke it was as if another spoke through him. 'My only consolation is that the Ethio boy was snatched from the ship by Seloth and dragged to the depths. Saw it with my own eyes as the ship. They came from the sea like a ghostly choir of dead souls and snatched him from the ship. They moaned and cried until it deafened the world to their lament . . . Beadle, come to me. Beadle . . .' Demurral had then wailed even louder, moaning into the palms of his hands and sighing like a dying dog.

Hiding his knapsack, Beadle crawled from the straw, crossed the yard and warily approached his master.

'Beadle?' Demurral whimpered, looking at him through tear-stained eyes. 'Is it really you? I thought you were gone, abandoned me like the rest, never to be seen again.'

'Still here.' Beadle whispered his reply as he held out a hand to Demurral. 'Just waiting for you to come back. I hid from the sky-quake and fell asleep.'

'SLEEP?' Demurral raged suddenly as he grabbed Beadle by

7

the arm and pulled him towards him. 'You slept and I died, that's what you did. Stole from me while I lay in the grave and made your escape. I can see it in your eyes. Shoes for the road and two coats for the night. You weren't waiting, you were going. Weren't you, Beadle?'

Beadle nodded, his arm gripped by fingers that burnt his skin. He pulled to run away as Demurral twisted his cane with one hand and slipped the sheath from a long blade hidden within.

'No, Mister Demurral. I would have waited, I promise,' he wheezed fearfully as Demurral held the blade above his head ready to strike.

'Why should I believe that? I took you in when no one wanted you. Nursed you, fed you, and this is what you do to me? Was I not kind?' Demurral asked.

'Very kind, sir. Too kind for my own good. Beadle was so ungrateful for your kindness,' he replied as he cowered from the blade.

'Then let this be a sign of my kindness, a cut for the cutting of my heartstrings.' Demurral took the sword and slowly pulled it across Beadle's face. 'There,' he said calmly, stepping back from his servant. 'A slice of my benevolence and one you'll never forget.'

'Forget?' Beadle screamed as he lashed out in pain, knocking the sword cane from Demurral's hand. 'Forget?' he screamed, kicking Demurral in the leg. 'No more, Mister Demurral, no more. This is the last you'll see of me.' Beadle kicked his master again and again as the priest scrabbled to be away from him, the dark shadows pressing in around them as if to hide what would come to pass. As Beadle scurried from the courtyard, all he could hear were Demurral's curses.

'I will find you, Beadle. I know where you will go to hide. My heart is your heart, my thoughts will be your thoughts, you will never be free of me. Remember the blood and the hound of love that pursues you . . .'

In the gorse and bramble, Beadle shook the dream from his head as he listened to the grunting and whining of a distant beast. The words of Demurral echoed relentlessly in his mind as if they were spoken time and again. 'Never did like this place,' he said as he hobbled even faster. In the remnants of the storm, the dribbles of rain pierced the thick shelter of the gorse. 'Blast, bother and boiling blood,' he chuntered, cursing the mud and squelching onward as the mire was transformed to a soft brown soup that covered his feet. 'Not staying . . . He'll never see me again. All them years wasted looking after a monster. Sold his soul so many times he's forgotten who owns it.' Beadle rubbed the rain from his brow. 'He'll never find me in London. Crane will help me. Three days and I'll be there – no matter what will befall me . . .' He spoke the words as if they were a prayer, knowing that the *Magenta* would sail to the south.

In the distance, Beadle could hear the gentle rolling of the waves upon the shingle beach. The sound dawdled in his mind like a dose of melancholy, stealing his wits from thoughts of Demurral. As the last drops of rain slithered through the branches of the gorse he wiped the blood again from his face with the scarf. He blundered deeper into the darkening tunnel until he walked in a muddy night, far away from the evening brightness. In the distance, at the bottom of the slope he could see a faint patchwork of light as the gorse and brambles thinned and the path ended.

Beadle allowed himself a single chuckle, which soon exploded into a beaming smile. His mind raced faster than his feelings. Thoughts of freedom were tinged with sadness and foreboding. What had been his world had crumbled with the meeting of a boy and the melting of a heart. Now, fear and exhilaration twisted together and spurged his guts like the salt washing of a frothed beer barrel.

As Beadle walked the last few yards through the tunnel of gorse and bramble, a faint scent of rotting flesh began to seep in from all around him. He shuddered and shook, then looked this way and that, his eyes trying to catch as much as they could from the half-darkness. It was as if someone was near – he could hear the wispy breath and the faint sighs and, more than that, the slathering, chomping and gnawing of bone. A yard ahead, just as the gorse tunnel dipped to the beach, was a hole in the tunnel roof. It was as if the gorse had been parted, and when Beadle looked more closely he could see that each thong of growth had died back and rotted. There at his feet was a pile of meatlets, small fragments of bone and strips of skin. Beadle nervously jigged two steps and, looking upwards from the shadows, saw the feet of a hanging man.

'Blast, bother, boiling blood,' he said in a whisper as he drew his breath sharply. In the wood, by the side of the path, was what was left of a man. The body hung from the long branch of an oak tree, the rope so stretched by the dead weight that he trailed upon the ground. Clinging to him like a heavy knapsack was a gruesome black creature that bit into his shoulder and chewed the flesh. The beast was the size of a large dog and covered in thick black hair that appeared to be stretched from bone to bone. Upon its back were two thick blades of shoulder bone like gargoyle wings that pulsed with every heartbeat. As Beadle watched, the creature stopped gnawing the bone and stealthily picked a piece of flesh between its lips, pulling a strip from the meat and then spitting it from its mouth. This was the beast that he had often spoken of but never dreamt he would meet. It was a nightmare of children, brought to life, a dark and distant memory or wicked thought made flesh. It was a creation of evil that had been conjured long ago when Demurral had first taken to his alchemy. It was said he had taken a child and merged its flesh with a dying wolf.

'Not possible,' Beadle said to himself as a quiet breath. 'Cannot be . . . not never . . .' The fearful words were choked in his mouth as he saw the beast gazing down at him and squinting through two red eyes that glowed in the darkness of the wood. It licked its teeth as it sniffed the air and two black, pointed ears twitched from side to side.

Since he was a boy, Beadle had heard of the creature. The story of its coming to those parts had been told every Beltane for many years. Some had said that it lived in the wood below the Vicarage and from this creature that place took its name – Beast Cliff. In all his time as servant to Obadiah Demurral he had been kept from the wood for fear of the beast. Its power had lain deep within the imagination. It would grow in force from generation to generation as the horror would be retold, its terror increasing with each telling. Mothers would warn their children that if they were not good then they would be left in the wood for the beast to find them. Every cow that disappeared, every slaughtered lamb or fox-snapped gosling, was blamed upon the creature.

It was said that at night, the creature would sit upon the milk churns and turn them sour or dance through the corn so it would die of mildew. Its shape was carved and placed upon the high spire of St Stephen's, though it had never been seen for many years. From dream to dream it would plague the lives of children and keep them to their beds for fear that its clawed feet would dance upon their hearth and snatch them from their slumber.

Now the creature chewed the dangling corpse, occasionally looking down as if it were aware of Beadle's presence but unable to see him. It ripped at the flesh and took another mouthful of meat, then dragged the corpse into the darkness.

Beadle waited no longer and edged back into the shadows of the gorse tunnel, careful to make no sound as he tiptoed through the mud. Soon, he found himself upon the shingle beach of Hayburn Wyke. He looked up and scanned the sky, wary that the creature could be above him. He felt like a mouse scurrying from the corn and awaiting the pounce of the falcon from the sky.

Walking close to the foot of the cliff, he tottered through the rocks and boulders that littered the cove. Eventually, Beadle came to the waterfall. It gushed from the dark of the wood and into the light, falling twenty feet to a large pool gouged from the shale. This was the place where Demurral had conjured the Seloth to attack the ship that had brought Raphah to the shore. This was the place where he had seen the madness take over his master and turn him from man to beast. Beadle slumped wearily on a large stone that was cut by the waves to the shape of a human hand. He looked to the sea as he soaked his muddied boots in the water and struggled to keep his eyes from closing. His eyelids flickered heavily as he fought the need to sleep.

Reaching into the depths of his pocket he dragged out a solitary boiled egg that smelt of sulphur. In two cracks he had smashed the shell and he peeled it with one hand, holding it to his nose as he sniffed its green skin.

'Quite fresh?' he asked himself, keeping his back to the cliff and glancing up for the beast. Beadle peered to the distance, mindful of the way he would have to go. The path would lead to the south; he would cross the fields and find the way to York. From there he knew he could take the coach to London and find Jacob Crane. This was the safest way – it would keep him from the high moor, keep him from the prying eyes of Demurral and all the creatures in his power. The roads were open, the lanes broad, and he could easily see if he was being followed.

This was a thought that nagged him. It was as if a voice told him that Demurral would not be far behind.

Beadle's feet ached in anticipation, the blisters already twisting like sore burns against the wet leather boots. He stared down at his shimmering reflection in a pool. The wound to his cheek had dried, pulling the skin against the bone. He bathed his face in the cold water and washed away the blood. It burnt bitterly in the salt water. A sudden breeze glistened the pool. Beadle waited until it stilled again, then looked long and hard at the wrinkled face that peered back half-smiling and proud of his escape.

He shivered as he pulled his feet from the frozen pool and brushed flakes of ice from his soaking boots.

'Not good,' he muttered to himself with a shudder of his shoulders as he chomped upon the fusty egg. 'Can't be having things like this. Can't freeze, not now . . .'

Beadle looked to the trees that edged the high cliff above him and he heard the cry of the beast.

'Best be off,' he said to himself in his most reassuring of voices. 'Long way to York and then to London, and my feet won't wait for me. Time and tide, time and tide . . .' He wrapped the scarf around his head.

And then a sudden and painful desire leapt into his mind. A voice shouted from deep within. 'Look into the pool . . . Look again,' it bellowed time and again as if it would not let him leave until he had peered once more into the icy water.

Like a bristling hedgehog, Beadle slowly edged his way towards the pool. He scanned his reflection inch by inch taking care to enquire with his eyes of every chin wart and nose hair that he surveyed.

'Getting older and not much wiser,' he said as his stare fixed gaze-to-gaze, looking dreamily into his own eyes. A warm vapour rose from the pool, misting his reflection and swirling like a newborn cloud about him. Then the reflection of his face suddenly changed. What was once *his* brow and countenance had in an instant become that of Obadiah Demurral. Gone was the wound to his cheek and blood-covered brow, gone the wrinkled jowls that hung like a mastiff dog. Now, staring back, bold and blue-eyed, was his master. Obadiah had chased him in his imagination and was now before him, a thin smile cast like grim steel across his lips.

Beadle quickly closed his eyes and put his hands across his face for double measure to shield him from what he saw. 'NO!' he shouted. 'I won't see, can't be . . . Not here, not now . . .'

Slowly he opened his fingers and peered through the cracks. There was Obadiah Demurral glaring up through the water as if he stood on the far side of a glass window.

'You'll not go far, Beadle,' the vision said as it looked upon him. 'Wherever you go I will find you.'

'Not never . . . Not now,' Beadle shouted back, his face contorted to a grimace as the vision of Demurral's face slowly disappeared as the wind ruffled the water. 'Never!' he screamed. 'I won't go back.'

The sun broke through the grey clouds. In his hand was the freshly peeled egg that stuck to his palm like a bald head. He shuddered as he dared to peer again into the glistening water, looking for Demurral's contorted face.

'Alchemy, must have been alchemy,' he croaked as a trickle of spittle rolled over his chin and onto his shirt.

The waves broke lazily upon the shore as if they had to drag themselves from the sea. A green farrago of stinking seaweed had been washed upon the stones in large mounds as if gathered into stacks along the strand. Beadle looked to the distance where the dark sea met a darker sky. There, on the far-off beach, was the wave torn body of a great fish the size of a small ship.

# The Magenta

KATE looked from the aft of the ship to the quiet and misty water of the estuary. It swirled in small whirlpools as the *Magenta* rocked with the powerful incoming tide. Above her head, the sails on three masts, gustless and empty, hung like drying palls against the reddened evening sky. The ship creaked and groaned as it was led on by the flood that rolled up the Thames towards the glow of the city of London. High on the stern mast, Thomas rang the fog bell and called out. The trees of Dog Island reached towards him as long thin fingers, stripped of life. All around the murk grew thicker, then cleared for a time as the vapours danced upon the water. It would then press in, unexpected and cold, like thick ice against the side of the ship.

Pulling her coat about like a warm mantle, Kate thought of Baytown and her father. She had left without a farewell. She knew he would think she was lost for good; his mind always looked that way and saw darkness even in the brightest of dawns. He would fear her gone in the sky-storm that had torn through time and spun the sun around the earth, turning day to night and back again as Kate had counted the chimes on the church clock.

As they sailed on she itched the flea bite upon her leg. It dribbled a single stream of blood to her ankle. It reminded her of home and how she would watch her father pick the nits from the hairs on his arm and crush them with his fingernails. In the time since leaving Whitby, she had seen the comet cross the sky and every night had wanted to return. As she had looked upon the cold waves of the German Ocean, she knew she would never see the town again. In her heart she had said goodbye. Knowing that she could never return as long as Demurral lived was a curse from which she felt there would be no escape.

Kate felt alone. About her the crew busied back and forth. They turned rope, stowed sail, shouted and hollered from the high mast, but it was as if Kate sailed upon a ghost ship, lost on the sea of her wits. The bell chimed again as the slopping water lapped against the wooden hull. To her right, Jacob Crane barked like a sea-dog at the crew, laughing between each command and wiping the sweat from his brow.

'Hold her fast,' he bellowed. The tide was pushing them on as if the *Magenta* was a bobbing cork. 'Soon have to come about. Can you see the tower?' he shouted to the lookout high above.

'Nothing but the dragon's breath,' came the dull reply, deadened by the fog that had grown thicker. 'Tanner's chimney a mile to port and nothing more.'

'Take in sail,' Crane bawled to the crew as they scrambled to run the rigging like giants climbing into the clouds. 'Keep deep water to the port side and away from the shore.'

Kate half-listened, her mind lost to wistful thoughts. She stared at the black, churning swell that lapped against the ship. Frantically, she searched for some sign of Raphah in the deep and gloomy depths. She ever hoped that he would come from the water, saved, alive.

'Thomas,' Crane shouted. 'Keep a lookout for ships, should

be all about us. Tide's running fast and we would cut them through if we caught one amidships.' He spoke quickly, his words bold and unfaltering as he paced up and down the deck knowing what each man should do.

Something greater than distance now separated Kate from Thomas Barrick. In the days that had followed their escape from Demurral, Thomas had spoken to her less and less. He had sought out a place far away, sleeping in the crow's nest high above the deck. He would wrap himself in an old oilskin, twist himself around the mast and sleep on. By day he would look to the far horizon and keep his words to himself. Neither she nor Thomas had spoken of what had happened to Raphah. It was as if his presence in their lives had been a dream and that in the short time they had known him, he had visited them like a ghost and then left for another world.

After the Seloth had attacked the ship, Jacob Crane had rubbed his chin with his hand, turned to her and smiled. 'Least they didn't take you,' he had said in words that brought no comfort. 'Came from the sea and now the lascar has gone back to it. Can't be moping over him, life is to be gotten on with.'

Kate had scowled as Crane had walked away. He would have cared more for a dog lost to the waves than Raphah, she had thought as the *Magenta* had crossed the bay and sailed far out to sea. Days had passed and with each rising moon Thomas had drifted further away. She had watched him change and had reached out in comfort, but was shrugged away with a nod of the head and the sharp glance of an eye. In his grief he had hidden from her and turned his face to the sea. Kate thought there were no words left for him to speak and anything said would be useless. Raphah was gone and so was their old life. Nothing would be the same again. Life would roll on to death and Kate believed in her heart that she would not find its purpose.

'Ship ahead!' Thomas hollered, and he rang the fog bell again and again, bringing Kate back from her dream. 'Off to the portside, I can see the mast and . . .' His voice faltered as if he had seen something he couldn't describe.

'What is it, lad?' Crane asked as he held to the rail of the bridge and strained to see what lay ahead in the growing gloom of evening. The mist chilled the air; all was silent but for the running of the tide. The faint glow of the setting sun weaved its way through the fog. It was as if they had suddenly sailed into another world.

There before them, growing out of the mist, was a tall sea-ship. In fine gold letters, painted next to a figurehead of the wolf, was its name: *Lupercal*. It had one mast half-rigged with ropes that hung like tattered hair to the deck. It looked as if it were a November hedge webbed in dew, decked for a spider queen and glistening in the fading light.

Crane stood fast and stared as the *Magenta* drew alongside. Everyone to a man looked up as the two ships sailed slowly by. There, hanging from the yardarm, was the long-forgotten body of a man. In the sullen fog that surrounded the ship he could see that the sails had been torn through and burnt upon the masts. The deck was strewn with smouldering rocks, the remains of the comet that had exploded in the sky. As the ship drew closer, Crane began to smell the scent of death.

'Make to!' Crane shouted, as the crew stared on, not wanting to move. 'The ship's adrift without a crew and ours for the tak-ing. Salvage, lads, salvage!'

The words brought his men to life. Kate looked at the high yardarm and the dangling corpse on the empty ship that some-how made progress against the tide.

'How can it go the other way against the sea?' Kate asked quickly as Crane drew the cutlass from his belt.

'It can't, lass, that's what makes it our quest to find out.'

Crane sniggered, raising one eyebrow and creasing his lips with a thin smile. 'Heave her to port and tie her on.'

From above her head, two men swung from the mast across the open water, landing upon the other ship. Quickly they threw several ropes back to the *Magenta* and within minutes the two hulks were strapped together, drawn closer by a bevy of smugglers spinning the capstan.

'Search it from end to end, every door and cabin. If you find anyone, bring them to me.' There was the slightest hint of trepidation in his voice. Kate sensed his throat growl upon the words as if even Captain Jacob Crane expected the worst. 'And cut him from the yardarm – dead men often tell the most tales.'

Thomas went with the crew, clambering from the *Magenta* over the makeshift ramp that had been strapped across the divide between the two ships.

'Captain,' came the voice. 'Best be seeing this for yourself.'

Crane looked at Kate, sensing she could feel his foreboding. 'You better stay here, lass. Can't have you getting yourself into trouble.' In three strides he had crossed the bridge and jumped from the steps to the other vessel. Kate followed and gawped through the fog at the gathering upon the far deck. She could hear their whispers as they glanced this way and that, unsure as to what could be listening.

'Search it well,' she heard Crane mutter as he looked back and forth, cutlass in hand. 'Go stay with the girl, keep her safe.'

Pulling up the collar of her sea-coat, she held on to the side rail as Crane's first mate jumped aboard the *Magenta* and sauntered towards her.

'What's the fuss?' Kate asked as he got near, resenting Crane thinking she couldn't take care of herself. 'Don't need *you* to nanny me.'

'If you'd seen what was over there you'd be glad of the company,' he replied as he took the pistol from his belt and half-cocked the hammer.

'Then let me look – I've seen worse. I once saw a drowned man who'd been dead for a month, crabs had . . .' She was stopped short as the man quickly put his hand to her mouth.

'You've never seen death like that,' he said quickly, in a hushed voice. 'Whatever killed him wasn't a man, nor a creature I've ever seen. There's an empty ship in the middle of the Thames, the lamps are lit below and captain's table set for two and not a soul to be found. You best be keeping your words to yourself and holding on to your breath for as long as you can.'

'Empty ships don't sail themselves,' Kate snapped as she tried to push by him.

'Don't be thinking you're going from here, lass. Crane told me to keep you on the *Magenta* and that I'll do.'

'Then tell me what's going on,' Kate protested as she pulled on his coat and kicked her feet against the bulwarks.

'Let her come, Martin,' shouted Crane from the deck of the other ship. 'If she's a mind to see the state of this man, then let her be. Set three men on watch about the *Magenta*. Tell them to shoot at anything that comes near. Whatever did this is not far away.' His voice echoed through the eerie silence. It was as if he stood in the middle of some great, empty hall and whispered his words for all to hear. 'Come and stare, lass. Gawp at the dead and tell me of what palsy this man died to leave him like a dry canvas and every ounce of juice gone from his veins.'

Kate struggled to cross from the *Magenta*. The two ships twisted about each other as if in a dance as they slipped in the swell that spun them up the estuary towards the city. With a firm footstep, Kate planted herself upon the deck of the ship and stood beside Crane. She looked for Thomas. Crane saw her glance.

'Thomas is searching the ship,' he said in a whisper, without moving his lips. 'Whatever did this could still be aboard.' He pointed to a bundle of rags that littered the deck just by the forward hatch. 'If it's still on the ship, we'll soon find the beast.'

Kate glared at what was once a man, lying on the deck empty-eyed and parch dry. He wore a scarlet tunic with gold braid with a large medal pinned to his chest. She could see that the skin of his face hung in jowls as if the fat had been boiled away to leave him like an empty sack.

'What did this?' she asked without thinking.

'Well, he didn't die of a broken heart,' Crane snapped as he looked up to the high rigging, then realised he'd spoken tersely and tried to smile. 'You've seen him now, best be back to the *Magenta*. I don't have a good feeling for all this, Kate. '

'Captain,' came a voice from below, followed by a long groan. 'There's one alive.'

Crane stepped into the hatch and quickly went below the corked and polished deck that looked as if a foot had never sullied its gleaming boards. Kate followed, wanting to stay as near as she could, fearing that something stalked the ship and secretly trusting Crane for her protection. Nothing appeared out of place. A row of fine, neatly trimmed oil lamps lit their way, the like of which she had never seen before. Crane led on as the shouts and the mutter of gathered smugglers came again and again, calling them nearer.

They pressed on through a glistening corridor of polished wood and shining brass that stank of whale oil and gunpowder. Small cabins, all neatly trimmed and turned, led off to either side, each one lit by a small lamp pinned to the wall on a sea-rocker. Kate looked as she passed by: upon every bed was the body of a man. Each was dressed for sea, each looked as if he had slept the river of death and had never known of his crossing. All looked the same: bodies dried with folds of skin that hung from their bones as if the fat had been boiled from them.

'Here, Jacob,' came the shout again from the midst of the gathering that filled the captain's cabin. 'He's dying.'

Crane barged his way down the long corridor that led from the hatch ladder to the cabin at the back of the ship. It opened into a long galley strung with hammock beds, neatly tied and ready for sea.

'Aside, lads,' Crane shouted as he stepped into the room with Kate on his coat tails.

The gathering parted. There before Crane was a young man. He was slumped in the captain's chair near to death, his head propped against a large table covered in rolled charts with a ship's clock bolted to the wood. Behind him, two of the cabin's windows had been smashed open. They hung from threads of wire as they gently swung in the night air. Kate could see that he was not much older than herself. He was dressed in the coat of a junior officer. He slowly raised his head from the table and tried to smile at them. The skin hung from one side of his face, but the other side appeared quite normal. To Kate, it looked as if he were two men in one, the first young and fresh, the other old and sagged.

'What became of the ship?' Crane asked, as the lad appeared to struggle for his breath.

'A comet crashed from the sky. It exploded above us. We had just left the dock. It was as if the world was on fire. I could smell the burning as we were bombarded. I saw them die, one by one. Their flesh fell from them . . .' He spoke quietly, then slumped back to the table as if the words had taken from him all his strength.

Crane took hold of him by the mop of thick black hair and held his head to the light. For several moments he looked at the lad's face; then, taking a handful of skin, he tugged his flesh. 'What did this to you?' Crane asked as he pulled a stretch of skin away from the lad's face.

'There was a scream – I came in and . . .' He gulped his breath, his eyes flickering with each re-lived moment. 'It was the dust from the sky, it burnt as it came to earth. Everyone it touched melted, the fat dripped from them.' As he spoke there was a sudden creaking of the deck as if a goat had dropped from the rigging and had run from stem to stern. 'We will all burn,' he moaned as Crane let him go and ran to the door.

'Quickly,' Crane said. The officer was melting before them, the fat soaking from his ears and trickling across the floor.

No one dared move. Crane stopped and looked back at his men. They stared wide-eyed at the lad and then at Crane. 'It will kill us too, Captain. The dust is everywhere,' one said as he stepped back from the door.

'We will not die from this,' Crane replied sharply as he raised his cutlass and pulled the pistol from his belt. 'Leave him, he's as good as dead. I care for the living and this is a trick of hell. People don't melt like wax dolls.' Above his head the ship creaked again as if she would split in two.

'I set a charge in the magazine,' the lad moaned. 'Strapped it to the gunpowder, long fuse, it will explode on the hour.' He slumped against the table. 'I couldn't do anything else, had to sink her before we reached the sea. I didn't want to die of this, I didn't want to die away from the city. It's always been my home . . .' He gasped for breath as more of his bile seeped from his skin, soaking through his coat. 'I always thought I would die from a Frenchman's bullet and that I would stare into the eyes of the coward as he pulled the trigger. That's how the old sooth said I would see my death, staring into the eyes of a coward.'

'What hour was the charge set for?' Crane asked.

'When the hands strike midnight, we will be gone. London will never see such an explosion again and the name of the

23

*Lupercal* shall live on forever,' he whispered. 'I thought no one would come for us. We were anchored in the river for three days. I cut the ropes and set us adrift.'

'I've heard enough,' Crane shouted. 'Get every man from the ship, there is but two minutes before this madman has us all in hell.'

'Save the *Lupercal*,' said the lad in his last breath. 'You could cut the charge.'

'And die trying?' Crane shouted as he pushed them all to the door. 'To the *Magenta* – we must be free of this place! Run!'

'We've been through this before,' Thomas shouted to Kate as they all began to run. He dug his fingers deep in the palm of her hand. Kate looked towards the hatch as she ran. Taking two short paces, Crane peered up the narrow flight of steps and into the night. Kate could hardly swallow – her mouth was dried to a crust, her lips charred by a sudden desire to escape her own pounding heart. Strangely, she could taste the scent of salt and feel the chafing of the wind.

For what seemed to be a whole watch of the night they ran. Crane pushed Kate from the galley, his eyes fixed on a square of sky that flooded through the narrow opening onto the deck. He knew that in the hold of the ship, far away in the dark depths was a charge that would soon explode.

'We can make Rotherhithe by morning. There are no ghosts here.' Crane shuddered like a dawn cockerel and ran a hand through his hair. 'Be off and set the *Magenta* free – save her.'

'You can't leave him,' Kate shouted as the chief officer dragged her across the deck.

Every man was for himself. They ran across the decks like rats with no care or concern for their compatriots. The chief officer took his sword and cut the ropes that bound the ships together. He jumped the widening gap that swirled with deep black water. Kate was the last to run the gangway from the *Lupercal* as it fell into the water. Thomas swung the gap on a long rope that stretched from the high rigging.

'Where's Crane?' Kate shouted, unable to see him in the crowd of smugglers who dived from one vessel to the other.

Looking back, Thomas saw Crane coming from the hatch of the ship. He held a pistol in his hand, the hammer fallen and barrel smoking. Thomas realised what Crane had done. The lad would not see his beloved destroyed – he had died close to the city he cherished and, as the seer had foreseen, stared into the eyes of the man who killed him.

'Run, Jacob!' Thomas shouted as the gap between the two ships widened by the second. Crane strode across the deck of the *Lupercal*. The divide was now too wide to jump and the river was bubbling beneath.

'If we fail, find *The Prospect of Whitby*, the Devil's Inn – and there we shall meet,' he shouted from the *Lupercal*, as if his men knew what he meant.

From the guts of the ship came a sudden boiling sound that began to split the timbers and spit each nail from every wooden board.

Thomas swung from high above and as the *Magenta* rolled in the tide swooped to the deck of the *Lupercal*. He screamed to Crane as he sped like a black cormorant towards him.

'Crane, Crane!' he shouted as the rope took him closer.

Jacob Crane looked up as the boy swung near, then, looking to the waves and then to the rope, he dived into the smoke-filled air. Thomas reached out as the cable trailed behind him. Crane missed his hand but as he fell he grasped the rope as it passed by. Together they swung towards the *Magenta* as the *Lupercal* drifted further away, its boards splitting as from deep within came the sound of the growing explosion.

A ball of fire lit the night sky. The mast fired into the heavens as rigging exploded across the river. The fire burst from the ship. splitting it in two as it spun on the tide.

Thomas jumped from the rope, falling to the deck of the *Magenta*, and Crane clutched to the side of the ship as a ball of fire billowed above his head. There was yet another explosion. Splinters of wood were blown through the air, and then all was silent. The burning hulk of the *Lupercal* drifted on like a Viking grave-ship.

# Orcus Gravatus

**B**EADLE stood in the foaming shingle, the waves washing his feet, and looked to the sky for fear of the beast. Far away, high up the cliff in the dark of the wood, he heard its cry – in amongst the murky branches, covered in dew and rot, the beast wailing like a sea-siren wanting to drag mariners to their grave. The frit-hairs on his neck whispered to Beadle that he was being watched. He swallowed hard, fearing the beast could see him against the sky, then ran towards the stranded fish that humped against the shore like an upturned boat wrapped in seaweed.

'Glory, glory,' he said in a daze. 'If it isn't a whale! No greater fish have I ever seen. How such a beast should be found in this way . . .' A sudden wave fell upon the shore, knocking him from his feet. For several moments he lay there silently, his head peering from the surf just above the water like a fat seal pup. He leapt to his stubby feet, water pouring from his pockets and the neatly sewn comfort flap of his breeches. He walked on towards the great fish, soggy-booted and brushing the wet sand from his face.

'Bathed,' he said sarcastically to himself. 'First time in a year have I had a bath.' He scorned the great fish as he slapped his chest, sure that something was writhing in his waistcoat. 'Look at you – sally-eyed and land-drowned. Not much of an exemplar to us, are you, fish?'

To his surprise there was a dull groan from the belly of the whale. Beadle listened again, sure he had heard his own name muttered from its bowels.

With an outstretched finger he prodded its thick skin. It was cold, hard and felt like candle wax. Beadle looked into the creature's glazed grey eye as a large black gull landed upon its back and began to peck at a long tear in its flesh.

'Scuppered,' he said out loud as he mulled his own fate. 'What brought you to these shores from the far north?' he asked.

The whale writhed slightly as if it were shuddered by a wave. There was another low moan just within the realms of hearing. Beadle placed his head against the side of the fish and listened. Again the groan came from the lifeless creature.

'But you're dead,' Beadle said. 'Fish don't speak and men wouldn't listen if they did.'

He stopped momentarily, then opened the whale's mouth with both hands and looked deep inside.

'Hello,' he said slowly, rubbing his chin against its large, hairy tongue. 'Can't see how you can speak – unless you're a spirit.'

Suddenly a dark hand darted from the throat of the fish and grabbed Beadle by the collar. In two tugs, it pulled him headfirst into the creature's mouth. He was held fast by row upon row of stiff hairs like a curtain of baleen teeth. Beadle could smell the stink of rotting flesh and the dank fermentation of the whale's last belched breath. His head was pressed against the inners of the creature's throat and all was dark. Within the blackness he could hear the shouting that came from within. It was as if his name was being said again and again in a voice that he had heard before.

The hand twisted his shirt around his neck in a grip that would never be freed. It choked the wind from him as he kicked and struggled to be liberated.

'Leave me be, spirit,' Beadle groaned.

The hand pulled tighter through the death-stiffened opening of the whale's gullet. 'Beadle, it is I – Raphah,' came the half-drowned voice from the stomach of the fish.

'But you're dead. Demurral told me,' Beadle screamed, as he panicked and pushed against the fish and fell back onto the sand. 'Said he saw you picked from the *Magenta* by the Seloth and thrown into the sea.'

'That I was and if I'm not out of here soon I'll be drowned on the next tide and gone for good,' Raphah cried, his voice muffled by the tightening inners of the whale.

Beadle stared in through the open mouth of the sea-beast and looked at the glistening black face of a lad he knew well. 'It *is* you,' he said as he pulled the mouth open wider, tilting his head to one side so he could gain a closer look. 'How?'

'Swallowed, completely whole – a miracle of miracles,' Raphah replied, forcing a laugh. 'Cut me free before I die of the stench.'

Beadle reached into his pocket and took out the knife he always carried. With both hands he cut again and again into the side of the whale. Skin and blubber parted as the sharp blade went deeper, until it suddenly spilled open like a broken keg of herring.

Raphah slid like a breech pup into the surf, surrounded by black treacle that oozed from the whale as if it were birthing water. For a moment he covered his eyes as he sat in the waves, then as the water cleared he dived beneath the surface and rolled in the gentle swell.

'Free again and by what miracle,' he said, washing gut mucus and bloodied blubber from his face and running his finger through his long dreads. 'Never thought I would see the light of day.' He stopped and looked at Beadle as if startled by his presence. 'Your master saw me?'

'So he said, but he's not my master. He and I have . . .' Beadle paused. 'Parted company.'

Beadle attempted to smile as the sea salt stung the wound across his cheek.

'You're hurt,' Raphah said as he saw the man holding his face.

'A mark for my memory. I'll never forget Demurral now. Every time I look into a glass I'll remember the night he gave this to me. A parting gift for all my years of service.'

'And your journey now?' Raphah asked as he looked to the dark wood.

'London. I know a man who would love a servant like me. A scientist and a scholar, lives in Bloomsbury Square. I once heard Demurral talking of him. Either that or I'll find Jacob Crane and put to sea with him.'

'Then I'll walk with you, share the journey. I search for Kate and Thomas. I know that Demurral will want them dead.' Raphah went silent and looked again to the wood as if he could hear something far off. Beadle saw the look in his eyes but kept silent. He too had heard the distant wail of the beast.

'I'll go alone, if you don't mind,' Beadle replied as he turned to walk away. 'Wouldn't be good for you to be yoked to one like me. Not you . . .'

'Do you forget what happened, Beadle? A friendship forged in adversity is not to be given away lightly. You helped us escape from Demurral. It was you who saved us.' Raphah held out a hand towards him.

'That were then. Needs must and I couldn't see you killed.

Not another one – there's been too many,' Beadle replied as he looked to the wave-washed shingle. 'I travel alone, Raphah. It'll be safer for you. Don't forget who I am. I will never be free of that or my old master. If you came with me he would find you easily. I'm not the Keruvim, you are . . . I'll be off. Soon be dark and best be out of the woods.'

'I know a cave, a Hob-hole. It's not far. We can have a fire and food. You can tell me of your plans and I of mine,' Raphah said hopefully. He pushed his palm closer to Beadle.

'Not tonight. Another time. The further I am away the better I will be. Demurral has a way of reaching you that grows wicked by night. Don't want to close my eyes again until I am far away. Demurral can see things to which mortal eyes are blind. He can see the future and visions that are beyond the sight of men. Wouldn't be surprised if he weren't watching us now. Head to the north, Raphah – he would never think you would go that way.'

'I'll come with you and watch you whilst you sleep,' Raphah insisted.

'No, I walk alone. Take my advice, head for York. Take a coach to Peveril and there change for London. That's where you'll find the *Magenta*. Jacob Crane always boasted that the finest berth in the world was at Rotherhithe.' Beadle spoke urgently and looked nervously about. 'Perhaps I'll see you there, but better you travel alone.'

'So mote it be,' Raphah said, resigned to Beadle's wishes, 'but a handshake for the journey?'

Tentatively, Beadle reached out and took hold of his hand. He looked at Raphah's shining black face and as he held his bright white palm, felt its warmth.

'Best be gone. Want to be out of the wood before sunset.' Beadle chuntered his words half-heartedly. He held on to Raphah's hand and continued to smile, searching his face for some flaw or sign of disgrace. 'You'd best be getting to that Hob–hole, soon be dark.'

'It wasn't by chance you walked this path, Beadle,' Raphah said as Beadle turned to walk away across the shingle beach. 'I asked Riathamus twice for a saviour. Once I was sent a great fish and then I was sent you. There is a power at work in your life that you will never escape from.' But Beadle was walking further away, not turning back. 'Nothing happens by chance. There is a plan to prosper and not to harm you . . .'

Raphah's words faded on the wind as Beadle took the mud-died path across the shingle to the shale cliff and into the wood. It rose steeply up a dirt slope and twisted in and out of clumps of trees that gripped the rocks. As he crossed a small mound close to the cliff edge, Beadle turned to look back to the bay. He could make out the shape of the whale in amongst a glutton of seagulls that bobbed and dived upon its carcass. There on the beach was Raphah, now almost indistinct in the fading light. Beadle stopped and gave a half-wave. Raphah lifted his head and smiled.

'Poppycock and balderdash,' he said to himself as his feet squelched through the mud. 'I can go alone, now is my chance,' he said again and again to mark each step. As he walked on, he thought of what he had become. From somewhere in his head, the memory of a Christmas came to mind. He didn't know where or when. All he could see was a great fire stacked in an old hearth and upon the hearth a weighty stocking that swung in the first light of the morning. Beadle could smell the memory: a burning pine log scented the room, and in the pot mug that steamed by the fire was brandy and fresh tea. Then as now it filled him with great happiness. Joy replaced his desperation and fear – 'A merry Christmas,' he said out loud as he walked along, 'and many of them.'

Beadle pressed on as the brambles pushed in on either side.

The wood grew thicker and branches pulled at his coat. Somewhere near by, he could hear the call of the beast as it brooded, high upon the moor. He fiddled with his collar, muttering as he walked, hoping he would not cross its path.

The track climbed speedily towards the high peak that grew from the sea to its stark summit. In his heart he knew that once at the top he would be able to see a castle far to the south and the pasture lands that led to York. Beadle picked a long staff that lay across the path and peeled the dry bark as he walked, deep in thought.

'Good for villains,' he said out loud, dreaming of being attacked by footpads and beating off an attack. 'Beadle the brave – not one left standing, aha!' He laughed as he dreamed brave dreams and lashed out at the overhanging branches. 'That would be me, given the chance. All would be gone as they saw my shadow, not a single footpad or rogue in the county and all down to Beadle.' He sighed a contented sigh as he mused on another and more adventurous life.

As he walked on he licked his lips and patted the pocket of his coat and felt for another hen–boiler. 'Best be walking on faster,' he muttered. 'Best head inland and get a coach in the morning. Five guineas in my pocket, enough for bread, beer and a seat on the roof with plenty left over for the rest of the way. London calling – to a far away town, as Uncle Joe would say.'

Just ahead, in a dark shadow in the wood, came a sudden cry that raced through the twilight. It screamed from his right and then his left. All around was the echoing sound of the beast. It shook the branches of the trees like a winter wind, and the air around him grew fetid as if filled with the breath of a stinking dog. His neck suddenly blistered with large goosebumps that rushed along his hairy arms. Beadle swallowed what spit was left in his arid mouth and gripped the staff in his hand.

33

The howling of the dog-beast came again. It echoed about the rotting tree trunks and moss-covered branches as it ran swift footed through the forest. Beadle peered into the failing light, wishing he had invited Raphah for the journey. There in the wood he wanted a companion.

'Stupid old fart,' he said to himself in a devilish whisper. 'Fear of Demurral stopped you asking him to come with you. Now look what you've done. Humph!'

He weighed in his mind whether he should scream and call out for the boy. But he knew he had walked too far and anyway, he thought, why should he come?

The shriek of the beast was suddenly distorted into a low, angry growl coming from the undergrowth to his right. Beadle walked faster, dragging his leg the best he could as he beat the stick against the ground.

'Not frightened of you, not never,' he shouted loudly, hoping against hope that the beast couldn't smell the fear that dripped in beads of sweat from his brow. 'You won't get a meal from me – far too scrawny.'

Beadle peered into the shadows, knowing the creature to be near. Something leapt suddenly from the shadows and quickly vanished into the black canopy of an old yew. It groaned as it went, then chattered its teeth as if the frost had taken hold of its skin. The night fell silent. Beadle sighed and rubbed his strained eyes with the back of his hand, muttering slowly under his breath.

'Nothing to be frit of. Beast won't come. Not for Beadle, the old feckwit . . .' He laughed as he hobbled faster. He cast a wary eye behind him with every third step and strained his ears to the sounds of the wood. Far ahead, the path came to the peak. The glow of the evening sky greeted him like a welcome friend.

As the sunset faded into the black of night, a bright star hung beneath the moon. With every yard the trees gave way to tall grass and deer shrub. Tufts of thick heather gripped the peat between the washed-out paths. A craggy outcrop lined with veins of pyrite glistened at the top of the peak, held for the last thousand years by the twisted roots of a stumped tree.

Beadle looked behind for the last time, certain the beast had gone, then cast an eye upwards at the star. Far to the north he could make out the thin wisps of chimney smoke that spiralled up from the alum works. The glow of the burning slag was crescented against the black of the sky. It was a place of darkness and desolation, of smouldering mounds of stinking slag – a dark factory where the cries of children went unnoticed. The alum works were a cluster of houses that gripped the steep cliff, a debtors' prison where Demurral was the master. He thought of Raphah and how he had been held captive and the boy he had healed of his deafness.

'Never see that place again and so be it,' he said, as if it were the ending to an answered prayer. 'Never again . . .'

With a firm arm he planted his staff against the shale path and tottered on, chortling a merry song as he forgot the night-beast. The lane fell away to the undulating vale that continued until it faded into darkness. Scattered across this dark veldt were the lights of farmsteads that glowed like warm candles against the night. As he strode on, he imagined every hearth: in his mind he could smell the morrow bread cooking in the black oven pots hung over the flames of a hot fire, and he saw the faces of the children gathered in straw beds and wrapped like sleeping butterflies, their tired eyes gently resting in the soft warm glimmers of fading embers. Beadle felt even more alone, friendless and miserable. The more he thought of what joys were entertained before the fires of the distant houses, the more his heart ached.

'Bless the lot of them,' he exclaimed as he lifted his dreg-leg over the stile that crossed from lane to field. 'Should have asked *him* to come. Shown him the way. Demurral would never find us, not now. Too busy licking his wounds like an old cat.'

The lane picked its way from field to field. A large solitary oak sprouted from a mound of stones in the centre of a pasture, standing above the terrain like an island.

Beadle picked his way under the cover of its branches and sat facing the south as he tried to count the lights of the houses below. Instinctively he pulled his cloak about himself and, turning up the collar of his coat, snuggled down for the night. The mist rolled down from the high peak like dragon's breath. His eyes shut, he twitched his nose, picked a hair from his ear and slept on, unaware that he now rested on an island above the fog.

There was no warning as a heifer screamed as if it fought to the death. Beadle woke suddenly and looked about, unsure if he dreamt what he had heard. He listened hard as the night again fell silent and the sea of fog swelled back and forth like a rolling tide. There was not a sound.

He breathed heavily, panting in alarm as his eyes searched for what had made such a deathly sound.

'I'm armed!' he shouted, his empty words echoing across the land.

It was then that it came, rising silently from the mist as it crawled upon a moss-covered heel-stone and licked the cow-blood from its lips. The beast turned to Beadle and raised an eyebrow, staring through glowing eyes that cast a red light upon him. It growled as it slowly chewed a fragment of skin that it had ripped from the heifer.

'You'll not get far with me,' Beadle shouted nervously, pointing his staff towards the creature.

The beast jumped from the stone into the fog. Beadle could see the blaze of its eyes glimmering as it circled the old burial mound from which the oak had sprouted. It stopped momen-

tarily and looked up, its head just above the crest of the mist. It
barked eerily, then ducked beneath the mist and slowly crawled
towards the mound.

Beadle stood his ground, back to the oak, staff in hand. His
fingers trembled as he tightened his lips across his teeth and
waited for what he knew would soon come. And then the creature climbed from the fog and sat before him. It stared at him
and gave what he thought was a half-smile. The ponderings
and fears from Beadle's childhood leapt through his mind as
one by one each of his fingers froze in fear. Every story that he
had heard of the creature churned in his head, and the words of
the teller were now again in his ears. 'No one can survive the
beast,' he heard the voice say as it repeated its warning: 'Once
it sees you – done for . . .'

The beast growled and barked as it stood before him with
blazing eyes. Beadle waited, ready to make one valiant wallop
with the stick, knowing he did not want to die without a fight.

'Give me the staff,' a soft, dark voice said by his side.

'Raphah?' Beadle asked as the beast growled in discontent.

'You are not a hard man to follow and I *never* take no for an
answer,' Raphah replied quietly. 'Friends shall always be
friends no matter what . . . Give me the staff.'

Beadle handed him the oak staff as Raphah stepped before
him.

'Go, creature. Leave this world be and do no more harm.'

The beast snarled and bared its teeth like an old dog as it
clawed the air, about to attack.

'Very well,' Raphah said as he held the staff towards the
beast. 'So be it.'

The mound began to shake and every limb of the oak tree
started to tremble. Mud and stone quivered beneath their feet
as a power welled up from the earth through Raphah and into
the staff. The beast stared at Raphah. In that instant, the staff

began to shine and glisten. What bark was left turned quickly into scales as the staff was transformed to a spitting serpent that danced back and forth in Raphah's hands.

'Take him!' Raphah shouted as he threw the serpent towards the beast.

Beadle screamed and buried his head in his hands and huddled deeper in his coat as the sound of the attack burst through the night air. The creature shrieked at the edge of hearing as the snake took it by the throat and wrapped itself around its limbs and choked from it what life it had left. It writhed and tore at the beast, falling into the mist. The creature screeched as the snake pulsed venom into its veins with every bite.

'Is it gone?' Beadle asked as Raphah sat by his side and cradled the man in his arms.

'Soon,' he replied.

There was a final ear-splitting howl that shook the trees and swirled the crows from a far-away roost to circle the moon. The beast shook the snake from its neck and turned and ran into the night. Then all was silent. Raphah stood, picked the staff from the ground and handed it to Beadle, who cowered by the oak tree. He held it in his hands and looked at the dry wood. A single scale was all that remained of the snake – that, and the faintest outline of a serpent's head in the grain of the wood.

'It has gone,' Raphah said.

'But will it be back?' Beadle asked warily, sure the beast would return.

'Where it has gone, it will not stay forever.'

'What was it?' Beadle asked.

'A Diakka – a creature created through magic, sent by an *old friend* to haunt me.' Raphah smiled.

'The oak staff – was it transformed by magic?'

'No,' Raphah said. 'By a power that we can all know.' He sat next to Beadle and held his hand. Together they looked out

38

across the vale towards the lights of the castle and the sea beyond.

'Will Demurral follow?' Raphah asked.

'He will,' Beadle said. 'He will not be content until we are all dead.'

'Then we find Thomas and Kate and live or die together.'

'The *Magenta* will be in Rotherhithe by the morning,' Beadle said, as if he knew the lad's thoughts. 'It'll take us four days if we travel fast enough. We could get to London before Demurral.'

'*Us?*' Raphah asked.

'Best we travel together, lad. Can't have *you* coming to any harm.' Beadle laughed. 'After all, that golden statue you carried must be worth a pretty penny.'

'The Keruvim?' Raphah asked.

'The golden creature that Demurral had.'

'It's lost,' Raphah said as Beadle began to dream by his side. 'Dropped from the ship and given to the depths. It was my task to return the Keruvim to my homeland. Now it is gone – but I will wait for a sign. There is a power, Beadle, that speaks through the rising of the sun and the dew upon a blade of grass. Soon it will reveal what I am to do. One thing is certain: as long as Demurral has breath he will seek us all. His desire is to see me dead and my spirit captured to be used as trinkets of divination. I know it will not be long before I see him again.'

# The Great Chain of Being

THE morning breeze carried the chimes of St Martin's clock down the Thames. The water to the east of London Bridge was crowded with ships of every size. It was as if every vessel in the known world had sought sanctuary as close to the broken and battered tower of St Paul's as they could berth. From the bridge of the *Magenta*, Jacob Crane peered into the growing dawn through a long, brass telescope. He rested his arms upon the side of the ship as he bent his knee and strained his back to direct the heavy lens back and forth along the quayside.

He had not slept but had paced the deck as he had watched the *Lupercal* burn her way towards Woolwich. The ship had turned on the tide as smoke and fog had twisted together and then, when the blazing magazine had exploded, it had quickly sunk. As the first light of dawn had come upon him, he had tried to rid his mind of the thought that somehow the disease from the ship had survived the pyre and was somewhere in the world of waking men. Crane cast his eye to the entrance of Billingsgate Dock and shouted for the *Magenta* to be turned to starboard and eased slowly into its awaiting, stinking birth.

The whole of London appeared to crowd the quayside. Beggars, barons and mountebanks jostled and tugged as cutpurses snatched moneybags and fob chains and ran into the throng of the morning market. The barking of mad dogs echoed through Darkhouse Lane and on to Lyon Quay as the Militia fired musket shot after musket shot, in the way they had done every morning since the coming of the comet, in a vain attempt to quell the madness that gripped every dog in the city. Packs of these discarded creatures had stalked the graveyards, digging into the ground and dragging bits of corpses through streets. So crammed were the burial grounds and so shoddily had the bodies been interred that many were just given a loose covering of earth. In the panic to leave the city when the comet had come many of the dead had just been left in the street. These became a veritable feast for the howling gangs of dishevelled and mis-matched dogs that ran with each other.

Looking up at the Customs House, Crane envied the row upon row of silent white statues on the marble façade. Their blank white eyes now stared down upon the mob. There at the height was old-grey-beard, God himself, universe in hand and the world as a footstool. To his right was the sun and stretching into the distance, chiselled and smoothed in stone, was the great chain of being that captured every creature and beast in the order they were created. A week ago, Crane would have scoffed at the mention of such a creator; now his mind was torn in two with the possibility that such a being could exist.

As the *Magenta* heaved to and came to rest against the oiled hay bags and fenders that hung from the side of the quay like dead, tarred pigs, it creaked and groaned and the keel shuddered. Its sea-worn timbers rasped and twisted against each other, as if the ship were but a bobbing carcass of misshapen ribs and broken bones.

From below the mottled deck, Kate and Thomas peered

upon the teeming quay. Neither had seen so many people. Everywhere they looked was a mass of staring faces. The voices of the crowd gabbled like Christmas turkeys ready for slaughter. The stink of the street oozed over the side of the quay as if it were a pall of smog, carrying its stench to the very depths of the ship.

'We did it, Kate. We got away from Demurral. I'm sure he won't find us here,' Thomas said with an excited smile. 'I've never been further than Runswisk Bay – and now, Kate, we're in London, the capital of the world.'

Kate laughed as she saw the look in his eyes. Gone was the melancholy of the ship, the distant looks and hidden despair. Thomas had returned to her life and as the sounds of the city filled her ears she felt that all was well. With one hand she twisted her hair into a knot and slipped it beneath her triangular hat as she pulled the brim to her ears. 'I wish Raphah were here. He'd know what to do. Less than a week since he was taken. Do you ever think of him?' she asked.

'Every minute of every day,' Thomas replied softly as they stared from the hatch to the deck. 'He'll be well. It'll take more than the stopping of the heart to take the life from him. Raphah may be gone to the depths, but it's as if he's not dead. Funny, really. I felt the same when my father drowned. Always thought he'd walk through the door one day, the same as before he'd left. Still . . .' He paused and looked deep into her eyes. 'Maybe not on this earth but one day, I think, we'll see him, face to face . . .'

Without any command being given, a thin gangway was pushed from the quay and down upon the deck. Kate could see three men dressed like clerics waiting for the ship to be tied to the pier. They gripped each other in close conversation. The tallest held a parchment writ wrapped in a red silk ribbon, clutching it as if it contained the secret of life itself.

Crane gave no attention to these men but checked each line and rope with a careful eye and shouted out a list of commands as if he were a babbling madman. In turn, the three men scrutinised his every action. Crane knew they were not country parsons. From their garb it was obvious that they were in the pay of the King. He knew also, as if this were written upon the lines of their faces, that they came with malcontent.

The smallest, weasel-faced cleric was noting down every word Crane spoke as if the Captain was dictating the mass. When the ship had been finally secured Crane folded his arms and leant back against the rails, smiling to himself.

It was then that the tallest man, holding the writ, set off at a trot down the gangway and onto the ship. Kate and Thomas watched on as Crane bristled, seeing the men step one by one from land to his ship.

Crane detested clerics. He had met so many and realised that they were more often than not the third son of a minor aristocrat who could only find them a living in the Church. To him, they were men who did not know their master nor ever would, and Crane would give them no more time than he would to wipe the foul of dogs from his boots. 'Is it not the custom to ask for permission to come aboard?' Crane asked as he stepped towards them.

'Depends who owns the ship,' chirped the smallest man from his gin-ruddied face.

'This vessel is mine, always was and always will be,' Crane answered as he took a rope-peg from the rail and held it as if he were about to knock an eighth bell from the man and beat him with it. 'Anyway, clerks, no matter how holy their orders, are not welcome here.'

'Clerks on high orders and not holy ones,' replied the writ-carrier caustically as he side-stepped Crane and walked towards the mast. 'Give unto Caesar what is Caesar's and whatever is left to whoever you want,' he said, and all three started to giggle and laugh like cackling children.

'I'll have no games here,' Crane shouted, holding the rope-peg like a club. 'Tell me what tax you enforce and then be gone.'

'MILITIA!' shouted the cleric as he took a hammer from his robes and nailed the parchment to the mast.

Above Crane's head, the crowd parted as a row of brightly clad militia stepped forward and lined the quayside. Each man pointed his musket towards Crane's head and took aim.

'I advise you, Captain Jacob Crane, not to resist what we do,' said the tallest cleric. 'We have it on the highest authority that you are remiss in your duties.'

'In fact you are found out by sin,' chivvied another as he turned his hat rim with long bony fingers.

'What have I done that brings a legion of red-coats and three halfwits to my cabin door?' Crane asked quietly as he nodded to Kate and Thomas to keep under cover.

'Payments and debts for docking in the port of Whitby, leaving without the payment of the aforesaid monies, the carrying of goods without a certificate and . . . abduction of children.' The tall cleric spoke smugly and preened an eyebrow with his licked fingers.

'For any writ you need a complainant. I know no one who would complain against me in those parts,' Crane replied.

'The Crown is your accuser and Parson Demurral is our witness. Are you acquainted with him of whom we speak?'

Crane shuddered at the words. 'Dogs, rats, slugs and priests – I know them all in the order of their creation, and you take his word over mine?' He walked to the mast and read the charges nailed upon it.

'See for yourself, my dear, unfortunate fellow,' the cleric said through pinched cheeks as he tapped the writ with his finger. 'You have twenty-one days to pay the Crown the sum of *two*

44

*thousand guineas* and return the children you took from Demurral's care, or the ship will be lost.' The cleric spoke in one breath and then paused. 'In the meantime, I would be grateful if you take your belongings and vacate the ship.' He paused momentarily and looked about him as if he had just remembered something important. 'We also seek a thief, Mister Crane. An Ethio, who has stolen an item of great value. For him and the gold we will search your – or should I say, *our* – ship. Guards, see that Crane and his men are gone at once and if they refuse I give you permission to kill them where they stand.'

The cleric wrung his hands together, then wiped them on the front of his long black cassock. It was as if he tried to brush away the grime of what he did. Crane eyed the Militia as one by one they marched on to the *Magenta* until they outnumbered the crew.

'Two thousand guineas?' he asked. 'What makes you think I can't just pay you now and have you off the ship?'

'What makes me think?' the cleric asked, half-laughing. 'I know Parson Demurral and on his word have it that you are a chancre, a scullion beyond scullions *and* a villain. But I also know that you are witless, feckless and penniless to boot, and if I were the last man alive and you the richest, it would break your soul to give the money to a mere priest. Am I not right?'

Crane shrugged his shoulders. 'So it is not just for the money that you are here. I know of no children taken from Demurral and as for the African, what is your real interest?'

'It is more what he has taken. Ethios can be bought at a guinea apiece, but the item he stole is of far greater value.'

'Do you have long arms? For where you will have to search you'll be wet up to your elbows. The boy's dead. Went overboard in a storm. Took all he had with him, and it was his to take, not Demurral's, the Pope's or the King's, but his.'

45

'Do you have proof of this?' the cleric asked as his companions clustered around him and grumbled like foxes.

'Proof? What is proof? Tell Demurral that all he seeks lies twenty leagues beneath the waves and will never be seen again.'

'That, my dear friend, is not the news I would wish to convey,' the cleric said. 'Read the writ and bring all I have demanded in twenty-one days or else your precious *Magenta* and everything in her rotting hull will be taken to Dog Island and scrapped. Is that clear enough for you to understand, *Captain* Crane?'

The cleric nodded to his companions and together they filed from the ship as if they followed a funeral procession, heads bowed and hands grasped in pious prayer.

'Search the ship,' the cleric shouted to the Militia as he walked the gangway and stepped onto land, followed by his two assistants. 'You know for what we search, an item of gold that could be hidden anywhere. Search the ship, I say. And when you are done, cast Crane and his vile friends to the dock. Remember, Crane – two thousand guineas and the children or the *Magenta* will be matchwood.'

Crane didn't grace him with a reply. He urged Kate and Thomas to go deeper into the darkness and then slowly followed them as the Militia set about the search. He had known such times before, riches and poverty had always slept in the same bed.

'The day is lost. Remember, *The Prospect of Whitby*,' Crane said to the chief officer as his crew gathered what they could and left the ship. He turned to Thomas and Kate and spoke quietly. 'I know a place where we can go until this *temporary* setback is taken care of. There is a street not far away from here. I have a friend who lives there called Pallium. He'll look after us.'

'Demurral got here before us,' Thomas said as Crane pushed

them into the ship's store and a guard stomped upon the deck above them.

'Faster for the old scroat to get a message to London than for us to sail here,' Crane replied under his breath. 'Thought we were done with him. But don't fear.' Crane smiled. 'Can't say I have ever wanted children, but now I appear to be stuck with you.'

'The Militia are looking for us, how do we get from the ship?' Kate asked as the sound of stumbling boots tramped above them.

'Powder monkeys and sewer rats never get stopped leaving the ship,' Crane said as he reached to a shelf at the back of the store and pulled the stopper from a wooden barrel. 'Smother your face with this grease and take a handful of black powder and do the same. You'll stink and look as if you've come from the bowels of hell. If anyone should speak to you, mumble a reply and keep walking. I'll talk for you. Carry a sack on your shoulders and we'll be from this place without an issue. Mark my words. If they should catch you then you'll be back in Whitby faster than a brig could set sail, and I hold no hope for your future with that madman. Stay here and I'll be back for you and don't move until then.'

Crane left the store, locking the door behind him and slipping the key in his pocket. Kate and Thomas stared at each other. A thin shaft of light seeped into the room from the slatted hatch above their heads. All around were sacks of flour, sides of beef and tight barrels of wine.

Kate plunged her hands into an open sack of flour and held it in her hand. 'We could use this,' she said, looking at the weevils running amongst the rough grindings of corn and stone.

'Or this,' Thomas replied, holding out a small keg of gunpowder. 'Whatever, we have to look older than we are. I don't want be spend another night in Demurral's tower, not with his garden full of graves. Now's the chance to be away from him. Give me the flour sack and I'll show you what we can do.'

Thomas emptied the sack of flour and began to fill it from the shelf around him. Kate packed her bag and made her disguise from goose grease, black powder and a slither of treacle. 'I wouldn't mind going home. I want to see my father.'

'And end up as another missing girl only seen by spirit charmers and drunks as they wander home? Not me Kate. I'll chance my arm with Crane. Whitby is a place of the past and if Demurral wants me, then he'll have to come to London and find me.'

The key turned in the lock of the store and the door slowly opened. Crane nodded without speaking, bidding them to follow. He pulled a sea-sack to his shoulder and buried his face in the side. Kate and Thomas did the same, then went ahead of him from the darkness of the ship into the light of the London morn.

On the deck of the *Magenta* there was no sign of the Militia. 'Below deck,' Crane muttered as he urged them on towards the gangway. 'Looking for the Keruvim.'

'YOU!' shouted the officer of the guard as he stepped from the bridge. 'Where are you off to?'

'Doing as the writ commands, leaving my ship to the care and providence of the Militia,' Crane replied as he pushed Kate in the back to walk on.

'Fancy yourself as quite a wit, do you, Crane?' the officer asked as he drew his sword and came towards him.

'Only with fat, ugly officers of the Militia whose pocked faces go beyond human decency,' Crane growled as he continued to walk on.

'Quite a celebrity, I hear. Captain Jacob Crane is as famous amongst the drunks and low-life as I would ever want to be.'

'As my great friend Montaigne said, fame and peace never

48

sleep in the same bed and I have never seen a greater monster or miracle than myself.'

'Then I will cut off a piece for you to look at and we will see if your great name can protect you from my sword.'

'Cut from me what you will. My life is yours. To fight would mean the gallows for me and if I recant of my good nature and kill you where you stand, then I am done for.'

'Dead if you do and dead if you don't,' said the officer of the guard. 'But you will not leave this ship without being searched.'

'I would prefer to die with a sword in my hand than a rope around my neck. You'll not search me.'

'Very well. Then you die on your ship. Smithson,' he shouted high into the ropes and furled sails. 'Take aim and should they run, kill the lad first.'

From the rigging above they heard the long slow click of a musket ratchet. Thomas looked up and in the crow's nest saw a rifleman.

'RATS! PLAGUE!' Thomas screamed the distraction over and over, his words echoing around Billingsgate Dock, and every mouth took up the cry. Fear of the plague had hung over London since the coming of the comet. Now it was as if God himself shouted it from the echoing stone of the Customs House, and panic swelled the multitude. Thomas pushed Kate and set off to run.

'Run!' shouted Crane as a musket shot rang out from the rigging, missing Kate by an inch and splintering the plank beneath her feet. The sound of the musket rolled from building to building, growing in anger like distant thunder and sending people running for cover as the panic spread like a fever.

'Quickly, every man for himself – *The Prospect of Whitby, Sola the Hermit!*' Crane shouted to his men as he pushed them towards the quayside.

Thomas sprinted along the plank as Kate panicked, threw her sack into the water and frantically gave chase. The three ran from the ship as the rifleman madly reloaded his musket and within a minute had fired another shot from high above their heads.

The three ran panting along the muddied, cobbled streets, their hearts bursting as catcalls and shrieks bit at their heels. It was as if the whole of the city had taken up the cry of the plague. Carts were overturned as those in fear stole what they could and made off into the labyrinth of alleyways that infested the quayside. Madness and mayhem burst from every opening. Shots rang out again as the *Magenta* was surrounded by a crying riot of men and women. They screamed for the ship to be burnt and all who were upon her.

'Quite a storyteller,' Crane said as they slowed to a quick march and looked back to see if they were being followed. 'Thought I would have to kill him until you came to my rescue.'

'First thing that came to mind,' Thomas said as they rested in a doorway of a narrow street that even in the morning light felt as if it was well before the dawn. 'How will you get the ship back?'

'Steal it from under their noses,' Crane said as they walked on.

'Will Demurral come looking for us?' Kate asked anxiously.

'As sure as night follows day. Whatever it is you have about you is certainly very peculiar. Demurral has unfinished business with us all,' Crane said as they escaped along the narrow marketplace.

They trekked through the narrow streets and alleyways by the river. They passed the same place several times, as if the street for which they searched didn't exist. There was no one to ask the way. All the roads were empty of life and as they went on, the streets became narrower and darker as the buildings grew from the dirt to form high caverns.

'Here,' said Crane abruptly after they had walked the hour through a maze of alleyways. Above what looked like a small doorway was a sign cut into a wooden plate. Crane read the words: 'Salamander Street.'

# The Glory Hand

THE crowing of a pheasant called the dawn as Beadle woke from his sleep. He was alone, wrapped in a pile of dry bracken as warm as ten blankets. He nuzzled from the heap like a woodmouse and looked about.

'Raphah,' he called gruffly as an earwig crawled from his nostril and across his chin.

There was a cough from the branches of the mighty oak. Beadle looked up and there in the heights was his companion staring down at him.

'Can see the castle and the sea, ships at harbour,' Raphah said with a smile etched on his face. 'And the road to the west.'

'Then we best follow your eyes,' Beadle replied as he stood up and brushed the dust from his coat. He picked the earwig from his chin and quickly popped it into his mouth with a chirp.

Raphah dropped from the tree and cartwheeled across the grass.

'A stroll to London?' he asked. He strode on, expecting Beadle to pick up the pace and follow.

'A long walk and then a carriage ride and not all easy.' There was trepidation in his voice as if he knew what would be ahead. 'If you keep striding that fast you'll be dead before we get across the field.' Beadle panted, already out of breath. He beat his staff into the ground as he gave a final glance to the oak tree. In the light of the morning he could see that the upper branches were festooned with the ribbons of a prayer tree. They trailed in the breeze as if they whispered to the wind all the desires that had been written upon them.

Every long mile was passed in deep conversation. Beadle set the pace as Raphah told his tales of wonder. Through narrow lanes and across the marshes they sauntered on. With the crossing of every river, Beadle threw a penny from the bridge for the Hob beneath and was scorned by Raphah. In the distance they could see the spire of the great Minster that hung grey against the bright blue of the November sky. They saw no one; it was as if the land had been emptied of all life. Barrenness hung across the long vale that stretched from the coast to the hinterland. All was still.

The dirt track they followed through the day opened out into a winding lane and then to a narrow, muddy road. For several miles they pursued the wheel ruts of a heavy carriage that was some way ahead. Occasionally, as if carried on the breeze, they could hear the baying of the coach hounds and the call of the horn. Then it would be gone far into the distance as it rattled against the thick cobbles that stuck out of the ground like so many dead men's skulls.

It mattered not to Beadle how far he would have to walk. The journey was an opening to a new life, and as he marched on his thoughts of Whitby and fear of Demurral faded. With every word that Raphah spoke of Riathamus, Beadle was taken to a new world. Nothing mattered to Beadle but what was before him. Every concern for the journey ebbed away. It was as if the words of his companion brought hope and comfort and new life. As they walked they laughed, the byways echoing with their mirth. All was well.

With each step, the tower of the Minster drew closer. It was old, dark and craggy against the sky, the best efforts of men to mimic their creator. The road twisted back and forth, as hedges gave way to open ground littered with small clumps of birches and islands of thick marsh grass.

The low sun that had followed their day began to set and shimmer against the shepherd sky. As night drew closer like a blanket, the sound of the coach hounds came again.

'There's an inn,' Beadle said, suddenly remembering the purpose of their journey. 'We can get a coach from there to Peveril and from Peveril to London – that's if…' He stopped and looked to the ground, the joy gone from his face.

'If what?' Raphah asked.

'They may not let you travel inside the carriage. I have the money for two of the best seats. All I have is here, honestly, and I will gladly pay, but . . .' He gabbled the words faster and faster, not wanting to get to the truth behind what he spoke of.

'Because of my skin?' Raphah asked with a smile.

'Not used to it . . . Different . . . I know, but they might not . . .' Beadle choked on his words, knowing what he meant to say but fearing speaking what was so obvious.

'Then I will travel on the roof, as I have done before,' Raphah said.

'And I with you . . . and they will not say a word against you. I will stand for you and speak my mind no matter how gigantic they may be.'

'Brave words, my fellow traveller,' said a steel-bright voice from behind an upturned cart that lay at the side of the road. 'I am glad you would stand and be so bold. Who is this knight of the road to whom I now speak?' the man said as he wrapped a black cloak around his shoulders and stepped towards them.

Beadle eyed him up and down. He was tall, half a man higher than he and Raphah. He was incredibly thin, as if a layer of translucent skin had been draped across his bones. The thoughts of his mind were barely disguised as they glinted through his deep blue eyes. It was as if a storm raged them as they glinted like the beady stare of a wolf through the throngs and spikes of the pure white hair that jagged across his face.

'And you are?' Raphah asked as he took a step back from the man, uneasy at his presence.

'Barghast – Cartaphilus Barghast, if a name should matter at all,' the man said with a hauteur lacking in grace.

'We are . . .' Beadle said only to be interrupted by the man's sharp voice.

'Beadle and Raphah. I am well acquainted with you both, having listened to your ramblings for the last few miles as we travelled together along the highway,' the man said brusquely, pulling the cloak closer to his chest and looking at them through one eye.

'We were alone in our travels. How can you say you heard what we said?' Raphah asked as he began to push Beadle slowly from the man.

'Alas, you were engrossed in your laughter. A whole legion of creatures could have walked in your shadow and you would have known them not. Come . . . It is a mile to the Inn and we should walk together. The sun has departed the world yet again and darkness reigns. I would be found wanting if I were to allow two fledglings to be out at night and snapped up by foxes. It is a dangerous place since the coming of the comet and the sky-quake. Many people lost their lives and so will many more.' Barghast waved his cape back and forth like the wing of a huge bird trying to scoop its prey beneath. Beadle shivered as he tried to smile at the man.

'Then we are pleased with your company,' Raphah said

quickly, before Beadle could reply. 'To the inn,' he continued, hoping not to give the slightest glimpse of suspicion that filled his heart.

Barghast walked slightly before them, his head bowed low as if to stoop to their height. As he walked, Beadle thought the man looked like a gigantic bird that nodded and pecked as it walked.

'From your accent, Mister Beadle, I would say that you come from Baytown?' Barghast guessed as he strolled on.

'Nearby,' said Beadle with a nod. 'Nearby but not too far away.'

'Not a place that I would choose to visit for myself. I once passed through but never again. Had business with the parson. Demurral . . . Have you heard of him?'

'And you, sir, from where do you hail?' Raphah asked as he walked at a wary distance, two paces to his side, and ignoring the man's question.

'Did someone once say, birds have nests and foxes their holes, but I have nowhere to lay my head? Then that truth would be mine. I am a wanderer, always have been and always will be. Never will I rest until I have travelled every road that man has made and then walked them all again.' He paused and gazed at the stars in a melancholic way as he rubbed his long, wolf-like nose with the sharp tip of his finger. 'If I had only given *him* rest, then life would have been so different.' Barghast muttered and then snorted a sly and sorrowful laugh. 'I take it from your direction that you seek a coach to take you to Peveril?'

'We seek a coach and . . .' Beadle attempted to reply before Raphah spoke above him.

'We too are travellers and will go the easiest road to the furthest place.' He tried to laugh but could only give a very unconvincing snigger. 'We'll walk with you until the inn and then our ways will surely part. You look like a man that would only travel within a coach and we're so poor that a journey on the coach roof wrapped in a horse blanket beckons.'

'Then let us walk. Perhaps you will have news that interests me? Since the sky-quake and the comet, things have changed in this world. I passed many a bare hovel and shack. 'Tis as if the whole land has emptied itself for fear of another curse falling from the sky. Met a man the other day that said he would never venture forth from his house for fear of the whole sky falling upon him. He's taken to wearing ladies' clothes and painting his face – sadly he had not shaved the beard from his chin, which gave him a disturbing countenance.' Barghast spoke slowly, his eyes glowing in the night.

Ahead, by the crossroads, the sound of the inn grew closer. Glimmering flag-lights quickly came into view as the three walked silently on. There was something unnerving and yet comforting about Barghast. He reminded Beadle of a man he had once met after a shipwreck in Whitby. The man had travelled from the east of Europe and had been washed ashore during a squall that had sunk his vessel. He and a black dog had been the only creatures to survive the beating of the sea. Like Barghast, he had that gaunt look of one who neither slept nor ate. Also like Barghast he had the same penetrating eyes that shone like two full blue moons set within darkened rims.

As they approached the inn they could see a pack of languid coach hounds sleeping by the stable door. The beasts crowded together to keep out the night cold. Behind them was a smouldering forge from which hot embers were lifted upwards by the breeze like fly-sparks. For the travellers, the scene murmured contentment and peace. A fat, drunken man belched merrily upon a milking stool by the doorway.

'You will have a room for the night?' Barghast enquired of them. Beadle noticed that beneath the long black cloak he carried a leather bag.

57

'Barn will be good for us. Plenty of straw for a night's sleep and why spoil yourself for a fleapit of a coaching inn?' Beadle replied, as if a cantor.

Barghast didn't speak, his gaze drawn to the pack of dogs that now clambered up on his approach. Suddenly, the lead hound bolted to its feet and stared at Barghast, its legs trembling as if before some old adversary. The dog growled and rumbled as it bared its teeth and snarled. One by one its pack followed on, each hound arching its hackled back like a frightened cat and pacing away from the man.

Barghast walked on, ignoring the beasts as their whining changed from snarls to baying howls. 'Dogs,' he muttered through clenched teeth. 'Can't see why such a fuss is made of them. Man's best friend? Good eating, that's what I say.' He cackled, pulling the cloak tighter and lifting the bag he carried with his other hand.

Raphah walked to the hounds and patted one gently upon its forehead. 'If only you could speak,' Raphah said to the hound under his breath as it licked his hand, shaking with excitement. 'Perhaps you could tell us more of this man than we would want to know.'

'Do you have rooms?' Barghast shouted at the drunk as he kicked away his stool and watched him crash to the floor in an ungainly heap. 'Rooms? For sleeping?'

'Full,' said the man awkwardly as he stared up from the ground at the black-clad figure that towered over him like a hawk. 'To the brim. Three coaches from York and one from Peveril, can't fit 'em all in.'

'Then I suggest you go inside and turf someone from their bed so that I can have a night's sleep,' Barghast growled at the man, dropping his bag to the floor and taking off his cape.

'Tell 'em yourself and not one will budge, not even for the devil himself,' the man replied, awash with ale and ready to fight.

Barghast knelt over the man and for several moments whispered in his ear as he held him by the scruff of his collar. Beadle watched as his lips moved and incanted the words and saw a change in the man's face.

'Very well,' the man said feebly as Barghast lifted him to his feet. 'That'll be done.'

It was as if the drink had suddenly left him. Gone was his gurgling of discontentment and venomous face. The man sucked in his guts and tightened his belt as he stepped across the threshold and into the inn. Barghast followed on, dragging his cape and bag behind him.

'We have rooms – at my expense. You will be my guests,' the man said as he waved for them to follow.

'I have money for the both of us,' Beadle protested.

'But not enough when there is no room at the inn,' Barghast insisted.

Raphah nodded to go along with the man as he pushed Beadle forward. 'Don't worry, Beadle. This is no chance meeting. For now we do what he desires,' Raphah whispered, stepping over the threshold.

As they walked into the hallway they could hear the frantic conversations that filled the downstairs rooms. From the large front parlour with its raging fire and strong smell of burning pine needles came the hubble-bubble of a gathering of men who clustered together. They stilled their chatter to hushed voices as Barghast led Beadle and Raphah ever onwards. They traipsed behind the old drunk, slowly leaving behind the night chill as the house warmed them like a garment.

To one side of the hallway was a large kitchen; the door was open and a black oven range steamed in the candlelight. Beadle looked in and saw a maid, who gave a soft smile as she hurriedly pulled a pair of jerkins from the drying rack and folded them neatly. The old drunk beckoned them on; he apologised under his breath for the lack of rooms and said that if he'd realised Barghast was in the district he would have made better the accommodation.

They tramped up two flights of stairs and along another dark hallway until the man took a key from his belt and opened a door for Barghast.

'Hope this'll do, sir. I'll have someone come and take the things away. I'll double the man up in another room. Don't think he'll mind, not if he knows it's you who has taken his room.'

Barghast didn't reply. His eyes scanned the room and then he turned to Raphah and Beadle. 'Only one bed, sadly. I am sure our host will find you a soft resting place?'

The man nodded as he tugged on his belt and pulled up his breeches over a large paunch that flopped like the rump of an elephant. 'This way,' he said as he pushed Raphah back along the way he had just come. 'I'll send up some food, Mister Barghast. We tend to turn in early. If it's a coach for Peveril you want then it leaves at six. Breakfast at four. Three tickets?'

Barghast nodded and smiled as he slid into the room and quickly shut the door.

'Important friends,' said the innkeeper as he hurried them along and pulled the hairs from the wart on his chin. 'Without him *you'd* be in the barn, *if* you were lucky, *and* you'd be walking to Peveril.' His mood had changed and he glared at Raphah.

The innkeeper pushed them along the landing and down the stairs until they came to the kitchen door. Once again the gathering in the parlour hushed their voices to a mutter as Raphah and Beadle went by the open door.

He took them into the kitchen. 'In here and up there,' he said, pointing to a double bed that was framed to the ceiling and hung across the room just below the roof. 'It's warm and too high for fleas, so think yourselves lucky. Eat, drink, sleep and make it quick – not good to be awake when it's dark. Too much goes on that's not the doing of men.' The man gestured for the maid to leave the room. 'All you can eat on the table, the oven's stacked so will keep you warm. *Important friends* . . . Huh!'

'What did he mean, Raphah?' Beadle asked when he was certain they were alone.

'He meant we take some bread and cheese and drink some ale and fall asleep.'

'No, about the darkness and the goings on . . . And what about Barghast? Why did he follow us?'

'It was only when I saw him in the light that I realised who he was. He is more than he says he is. I have heard of him. Cartaphilus Barghast is a collector of antiquities. He searches for that which he thinks has special powers. I was once told that he carried the finger of a saint and that all he desires to find is the Grail Cup,' Raphah said. He picked at the meat that had been left on the table, pulled a chunk of bread from the loaf and filled his pockets with tiny apples that had been daintily stacked upon a white plate. 'I think he knows who we are. It was *not* a coincidence we met on the road.'

'The Grail Cup? Demurral spoke of it often. So what's Cartaphilus Barghast doing here and why does he travel with us?' Beadle pleaded.

'That we will discover my friend, that we will discover,' Raphah said as he climbed the ladder to the high bed and looked down at Beadle from the ceiling. 'This is a good place. A warm night's sleep and then on to Peveril. Soon I'll find Thomas and Kate.'

'But who is he?' moaned Beadle as he warmed his steaming backside against the oven. 'Did you see the coach hounds? Every one of them terrified and he said he'd been with us whilst we walked. What is he – invisible?'

'If Barghast is the one I was told of when I sailed to this land, then he will soon reveal himself and his purpose. Until then, let us keep close counsel.' Raphah rolled himself into the blanket. The heat from the oven had warmed the bed, and it was as if he rested on hot buttered bread. Raphah smiled to himself as he looked down at Beadle, who shuffled and strutted up and down the kitchen angrily chuntering to himself. 'Beadle, sleep.'

'SLEEP?' Beadle asked as he stepped too close to the oven and singed his rear upon the scalding door. 'Sleep? How can I sleep when we have trouble with us? That's what Barghast is – TROUBLE. I can smell it a mile off and it'll follow us all the way to London.'

'And all I can smell is a burning Beadle.' Raphah laughed as Beadle wafted the smoke from his burnt trousers. 'Whatever Barghast may be will not concern us. In the morning we will be gone to Peveril.'

'But why does he follow?'

'That we shall soon discover,' Raphah replied calmly as he snuggled himself into the blanket and closed his eyes wearily.

'Blast, bother, boiling blood.' Beadle fussed as he pulled every item of flotsam from his coat pocket and burnt it in the stove fire. 'Everyone sleeps and Beadle paces . . . Clock ticks on and I'm on my own.' He reluctantly began to climb the ladder to the bed.

Lying next to Raphah he gazed down to the wooden floor far below. With the coming of the night it was as if the house began to yawn and tremble. From all around came the sound of strange groaning. Footsteps beat wearily above his head; far away he could hear words spoken in whispers. The gnawing of rats echoed in the walls and as all in the house fell into dreams, Beadle stared about the room.

In his mind he suddenly entertained the thought that he now missed life with Demurral. He had his place in the order of the world and had walked in the glow of being *the master's* servant. Beadle felt quite alone as his thoughts raced. He wondered how circumstances had come and tattered his life like scoundrels and vagabonds stealing all he had.

Late into the dark hours, Beadle twisted and turned in sleeplessness. He was hot and bothered in his high bed, and itched as if every crawling creature had taken to eating him alive. The house had fallen into silence as all the travellers slept. 'Last to taste sleep,' he muttered. 'Hate it, hate it . . .'

Wide awake, he looked on as a small mouse crawled from a cobwebbed corner of the scullery and climbed the carved table leg. It scurried in and out of the covered plates and every now and then took hold of a crumb in its claws and feasted merrily upon it. The creature then sat, rubbing its whiskers, looking at Beadle. The candles flickered against the whitewashed plaster. To hurry sleep, Beadle counted the slats of the wooden shutters again and again. Half-drowsy, he listened to another set of footsteps pounding the stairs, making their way to the outside privy. Something in their stealthy and somewhat sinister bearing made him listen more intently. It was as if they stopped at every doorway of the passageway above Beadle's head. Time and twice time they walked quietly across the bare boards, stopping and starting and moving from door to door. At every doorway the footsteps entered the rooms above his head, then moments later shuffled their way along the passageway.

He thought for a moment, knowing that this was not just the nocturnal wanderings of a weary traveller. 'Can you hear it, Raphah?' Beadle asked as he nudged his companion. There was no reply. Raphah slept soundly, wrapped in the quilted blanket.

The sound of the footsteps carried on across the landing and then, slowly and carefully, began to descend the wide staircase that led into the hallway. From beneath the scullery door, Beadle could see the flickering of shadowy light. It moved with each pace taken, coming quietly closer by the second.

'There's someone coming,' Beadle whispered as close to Raphah as he dared without being overheard from the hallway. 'Outside – listen.'

Raphah didn't stir. He snored gently, a smile etched in his dreaming like a contented cat filled with cream. The footsteps stopped outside the door. Beadle could tell that whoever was walking the house did so with great ease, not fearing or showing concern that they would be discovered.

The large brass door handle began to slowly turn. Beadle pulled the covers up about him and peered quietly from the bed as he pretended to sleep. Slowly and purposefully, the door opened. Beadle remained silent. He could feel a rising sense of panic begin to grip his throat. Inch by inch the door opened. A hand gripped the wood and gently eased the door wider and wider.

From his vantage point, Beadle could see the bright glow of three candles. Covering his head, he peered below through his crooked elbow. The door opened wider – and it was then that he saw the Glory Hand. The fingers gripped the candles that burnt brightly. Beadle knew it well. It was like the one that his master Demurral had used several times before. It was the hand of a hanged man, severed at the wrist, dipped in saltpetre and wax, dried and charmed by a magical incantation. In its grip it held three candles. Once it was lit, all who slept could not wake and to put out the flame would take blood or the milk of a mothering cat.

A cloaked figure held the Glory Hand before it. With a chank of bagged coins, the hand was wedged between two plates of cold meat and a moneybag emptied on the table. A living hand came from the shroud and began to count the money coin by coin. It stacked them in neat piles, gold to the left and silver to the right. But it was as if the robber searched the bag for something more and that the money was of no concern.

Beadle could not see the figure's face nor recognise by its dress who it was. He was certain it was neither Barghast nor Demurral. The figure was far too small and its hand far too delicate. All he could fearfully see was the thin white hand counting the money.

'Money and nothing more,' the soft voice said.

On the table, the mouse hid beneath the rim of a pewter plate, its long tail trailing from its hiding place. The hand suddenly stopped its reckoning, darted to its left, snatched the mouse and in one loud gulp the tiny creature had vanished into the hooded fiend's mouth. There was the crunching of bones and the satisfied chuckle of contentment.

The coins were placed back in the bag and the hand taken from the table, and without any backward glance the figure left the room.

Beadle counted the footsteps back up the stairs and along the corridor. Again, at every room they stopped until their sound faded into the still night. In the kitchen, Beadle sniffed the air that hung heavy with the fragrance of wild jasmine.

# Salamander Street

CHARRED plaster walls rose up from the muddied lane that was Salamander Street. Thomas looked to the narrow gap between the buildings and the slither of sky that cut through the rooftops. He could see that the street ran out of sight towards the city. There was little light from the sun; even on this bright morning the oil lamps beckoned them as they walked slowly on through the shadows. With every yard, they picked their way in and out of the open sewer that ran its length.

'Good place to stay,' Crane joked as he pulled the scarf around his face like a mask. 'I know a man here called Pallium . . . He's a banker. We'll take a room and see what is to be done.'

'What about the *Magenta*?' Thomas asked as his feet slipped from him, as if the slime beneath him was alive.

'Never give in to those who think they are your betters,' Crane snarled suddenly. 'Priests, kings and excise men, every one of them a rogue by another name. Give me a week and I'll have it back and we'll be away to France. I have a house in Calais away from the customs men. You can stay there and I will return. I have unfinished business with Parson Demurral.'

His words put an end to the conversation. In the mean light they walked on silently. Thomas caught Kate's glance and tried to smile. He could see she looked more and more concerned with every step as they walked forth into the looming cavern.

Crane stopped by a flaking wooden door. The house that surrounded it was stacked against the sky like a rocky outcrop. It had once been painted white and had now dulled to a mouldy yellow. The thick and crumbling plaster was engrained with dirt and the taint of wood smoke. Nailed into the broad oak panel was a lion's head that had once heralded the call of visitors but now its jaws were rusted shut.

'This must be the place,' Crane said as he rapped his fingers against the wood and pulled at a flake of paint. 'Wonder if Gimcrack Pallium is here?' There was unexpected warmth in Crane's voice. His eyes glinted, suggesting he had shared much with Pallium and remembered him as an old friend. 'The most generous man in the kingdom – he came here but a year ago and never a nicer man you would want to meet. If it is within Pallium's power he will get it and if it's in his benefit he will give it to you. But beware – he is the fattest and most gluttonous man in the kingdom. My own age but the size of a whale. Eats like several horses and will pinch the food from your plate.'

Crane banged on the door again as he leant against the wall and looked back and forth along the empty street.

'No people,' Kate said as she followed his eyes. 'Strange for the time of day, it's morning and every house looks as if they still sleep.'

There was no reply to Crane's banging. He rapped again upon the door and, taking the dagger from his belt, punched the panel once more. 'PALLIUM! PALLIUM! ' Crane shouted.

From the dark bowels of the house came the babbling of what sounded like a madman.

'Who wants me?' asked the croaking voice from within. 'No one has called on me before at this hour, it's the middle of the night and I am one for sleep.'

'Pallium?' Crane asked, scarcely believing the frailness of his friend's voice. 'Is that you?'

'Who should want to know such a thing?' came the reply. A small wooden slat was slid open and two feeble silver eyes stared out into the gloom. 'Crane – Jacob Crane? *He* said you'd be coming. All's made ready, all ready. What an amazing thing . . .'

Feebly, the bolts were pulled and the door slowly opened. A frail hand came from within and was held out towards Crane in greeting. Thomas could see that the fingers were covered in sores, and long, uncut nails curled about them.

'Pallium,' said Crane softly in greeting to his friend, looking at his shrivelled body that wore the clothes of a man thrice its size. 'You have changed, my friend. I was telling my companions . . .'

'Changed?' argued the voice as he snapped back his hand. 'I am as I have always have been. Never in finer health and a more robust creature in London will you never find. I didn't expect such an argument in the middle of the night.'

'We seek rest and not discontent, Pallium. My friends and I are in need of a bed. I am without a ship and I do not wish to be without a friend. This is Kate and Thomas, we have travelled from Whitby.' Crane smiled as he spoke, hoping to calm his friend.

Pallium rolled a worn gold coin in his hand as he looked at Thomas and Kate and gave them a slight grin. His mouth was filled with jagged teeth that appeared from the darkness like sharp rocks in a night storm. The man rubbed his chin as he surveyed them both warily.

'*Suppose* we could find you a straw mattress . . . somewhere. Things are not as easy as they once were Jacob, money doesn't grow on trees and I am sure someone has been helping themselves to mine. You never know when you will need all you have. Always death and always taxes, nothing so certain as those two creatures.'

'Since when has concern for the future been a thought for Gimcrack Pallium?' Crane asked as he looked about the cob-webbed hallway with its rotting drapes and tattered rugs. 'The man I once knew wouldn't give a thought for the morrow. Weren't you the one who would tell me never to worry for the morrow, as this day has enough troubles of its own?'

'That was then,' snapped Pallium, pulling his baggy coat about himself as if it were a blanket. 'A year ago I would have agreed, but things change, people change, lives change and with each day in Salamander Street . . .' Pallium stopped short and looked at them all through a screwed-up eye. 'Not short of money, are you? Not here to take what I have, are you, Jacob?'

'If it's money you want I have plenty for us all,' Crane bel-lowed, his temper growing shorter. 'I may be a thief, but I have honour for my friends and from you would I take nothing. If you want me to pay for our lodging then very well, but don't think I'm a thief.'

Pallium shook his head, as if he tried to rouse himself from a dream only to be sucked back into his waking slumber. He stared at Crane and sniffed the dew from his nose, wiping it on his silvered sleeve that looked as though it had been garlanded with mercurial slugs.

'A shilling for the lodge and find your own food?' he offered, slobbering over the amount. 'Each?'

Crane looked at the dust-covered panelling and smiled. 'It would be a pleasure, Pallium. I take it you would then burn some wood to warm this place through?'

'Only enough to take the chill from your breath. Can't have Galphus thinking I am being wasteful.'

'Galphus?' Crane asked as Pallium led them through the long

69

hall and into the scullery. 'I have not heard his name before.'

'A fine man. And my landlord. He has a word for every season and if I'll be blown, it is as if he knows everything. Owns the whole street and deserves every glorious brick and beam. This is the finest place to live in the whole of the city. Never been happier and it's such a place. I'm honoured to live here, honoured, Jacob, and you will be too when you meet Galphus.'

'Where do we eat?' Kate asked, looking around with eyes that spoke of her discontent.

'The Inn, of course,' replied Pallium amazed that such a question should be asked. 'The Salamander by Potter's Yard. No finer place to eat in London, and Galphus dines there.'

'Then that will suit us well for we could eat a whole ox,' Crane said as he stepped into the scullery. 'In fact you will join us and we will all eat together.'

'Can't leave Pallium's Palace,' Pallium sniggered as he held out his arms as if to show them the finery of the scullery. 'Well, that's what I like to call it . . . Never know when someone will come. There's always work to do and so little time and so much to count.'

The three looked about the room. Its cold stone floor echoed the sound of their steps. An empty fireplace stared back at them like a golem's eye, caked in black soot. In the centre of the room was a long candle-lit table that was stacked with neat piles of gold and silver coins. The wood was worn with many times of counting and recounting. By the table was a solitary chair.

'Don't get out much,' Pallium said wearily as he looked at the coins. '*They* need so much work, so much consideration. Just like children, they have to be kept safe. I know each one as if it were my own. I look after them for Galphus and he would not be best pleased if I were to lose a farthing or halfpenny.'

'We'll need a bed, Pallium. Sleep has been a stranger to us these last days,' Crane said as he eyed the sparseness of the room.

'You'll have to share,' Pallium said briskly to Thomas and Kate as they looked nervously about them. 'I have a room for you Jacob, all ready. Fit for a king, some would say an emperor, with a sea-hammock and not a bed. Was told you'd want it like that. Prepared it all yesterday when I knew you were coming.' Pallium rolled the coin in his hands as he spoke.

'*Knew* we were coming?' Crane asked, his sharp eyes searching Pallium's face.

'Yes, Galphus told me yesterday,' Pallium said in a matter-of-fact way as he edged his way closer to his precious coins. 'Came especially . . . Said he had heard that Jacob Crane would come and stay at Pallium's Palace. Never thought he'd be right, but as with everything, Galphus is astounding.'

'I would love to meet a man who knows my thoughts a day before they come to mind,' Crane said suspiciously.

'Galphus is a seer and prophet beyond doubt. He has made me a happy man since I came here. For years I had a melancholy that would never leave me. Galphus soon fixed that – for not only is he a seer, but also a physician. When Galphus said you were coming I didn't question his word. I made up the beds and strung up the hammock. Didn't sweep the rooms. I find dust keeps the place warm and then you don't waste on a fire.' Pallium spoke quickly, pulling on his long brown whiskers and frowning like a cheated cat. 'Didn't tell me *why* you were coming . . . Don't want any trouble, Jacob, can't be having any trouble . . .'

'The last thing I would want,' Crane said as he eyed Kate and Thomas to be silent on all that had happened. 'Just a few days' rest until I get the *Magenta* back and then we'll be to sea.'

'Then,' Pallium grumbled reluctantly and with much chagrin, 'my home is your home.' His eyes flickered from one to the other and back again as if he were a cornered animal.

Thomas stared at the man, wondering why his melancholy

gripped him like a tight glove. Pallium appeared to be nervous of their presence, as if he were hiding some deep secret that he could share with no one. As they stood in a long and uncomfortable silence, Thomas looked him up and down. He thought Pallium to be a ragged man in dead men's clothes. The collar of his shirt was stiffened with neck grease and draped about him like a forlorn noose of grimed cotton. His jacket and waistcoat hung from his body like a horse blanket, his breeches sagged like sash curtains about his spindly legs.

The one thing that gave Pallium an ounce of glory was his shoes. Thomas widened his eyes as he stared at their beauty – never had he seen foot coverings so fine. In the dust and the murk they glimmered and shone like burnished jet-stones. Large silver clasps held them to his socked feet. Thomas could not help but gasp as they glinted in the candlelight.

'A lad who appreciates the finer things?' Pallium asked propitiously, breaking the long silence.

Thomas nodded, and glanced to Kate and then to Crane and back to Pallium's feet.

'Made by Galphus and never taken from my feet in the last year. Prosperous shoes, boots of providence and a charm against the world,' Pallium said, suddenly sparked to life. 'Blessed me with them he did – the finest, most assiduous shoe-maker in the country. Italian leather, fine silver and Mandarin cloth. Warm and soft, lad. Restful for the feet.' Pallium sighed and sat at the chair by the table as he raised a foot in the air for all to see. 'I never take them from my feet. Far too precious to be left for anyone to pick them up. Look but never touch.'

'Shoes are shoes, Pallium. You speak of them as if they have a life of their own.' Crane scoffed, his words tired and angry. 'Does this hammock have a life of its own? Will it be decked in finest Mandarin cloth?'

'No – hemp, and found in the room above,' Pallium snapped

72

as a cloud of gloom enfolded him again. Slowly, his thin smile slipped from his face. 'If you follow the stairs you'll find where you sleep. I won't walk with you. I have to be about my counting. All these interruptions keep taking my mind from the task. If I were lonesome for a year and a day it wouldn't be long enough.' With that, Pallium turned from them and looked to the table and the neatly stacked piles of coins. Ignoring Crane, he picked a stack and began to count each coin slowly and precisely.

Without the touch of human hand, the door to the stairway suddenly jumped from the latch and opened. It blew cobwebs and a cloud of dust from the rafters, showering the room with a crepuscular mist. Pallium nodded as he grunted and cuzzled his words like an old and wizened dog. It was if he had been expecting the door to open as an invitation for them to leave his presence and depart to their rooms.

Taking a candle from the side table, Crane nodded to Kate and Thomas for them to follow. Silently they left Pallium in the dirty scullery to arduously count his coins. He twitched and shuddered with each one, his eyes wide, lips slobbering as he stared at the bright gold.

Kate and Thomas slid by and into the stairway. Crane took the steps two at a time and as he disappeared into the darkness his heavy footsteps swirled the dust about them like a thick fog.

Within a minute they were in a large room that overlooked the dismal street. Crane had kicked open the stiff door with his sea boot and lit the two candle stubs that were on the narrow table by the window. He ignored the scurrying of the mice that ran off into the dark corners and said nothing of their presence to Kate and Thomas.

'I'll leave you to it . . .' He smiled and stepped into the passageway that ran the length of the house. He stopped abruptly in front of a black door that was double-bolted. 'Sleep, and then we'll eat,' Crane said as he took the light.

73

Kate and Thomas stared at each other for a moment and then looked about them. In the corner of the room was an old mouse-eaten leather chair and to one side a *Fortbien* magi-chord. It was propped against the wall like a gigantic flat pyra-mid with four octaves of ivory keys that had tainted with the years. The magichord looked like a grand piano stood on its end. Above it, an elaborate candelabrum hung, webbed and wax-dripped, like the tangled roost of a dawn rook. At the far side, by the narrow window was a small bed, neatly made with fresh but tattered linen, whilst at the fireplace was a day-bed that had been turned down ready for sleep.

Kate smiled as she saw a neat bundle of fire-sticks and a tin-derbox. 'He made ready for us,' she said in a whisper as she tip-toed across the wooden floor and sat upon the bed. 'Do you really think he knew we were coming?' she asked.

'He's mad,' Thomas said quietly as he looked at the magi-chord, eager to press the keys. 'Did you see him? Looked as if he'd shrunk away to almost nothing, and all that money hang-ing about – just asking to be robbed, if you ask me.'

'Thomas . . .' Kate said unhurriedly as she looked at him. 'I keep thinking of going back. I can't get the thought from my head. It's like something's pulling at my insides and telling me to go home.'

'Back? Not now. It's all changed, Kate. The world's gone mad. Have you forgotten what we saw – the creatures in the wood, and the night at Finnesterre's house? I've seen too much to go *back*, my life is away from that place. Anyway – we are villains. Go back now and Demurral would have us dead. Wouldn't be surprised if he wasn't planning to come and find us as we speak.'

'What about your mother?' Kate asked as she lay back on the bed.

'You saw what I saw. That thing was a monster, tried to kill

74

us. Whatever it was is now long gone and my mother with it. That's all I could think of on the ship. All I could see was my mother's face and then that demon coming from her mouth. I couldn't rid my wits of the vision.'

Thomas knelt by the fire and, picking up the kindling, angrily snapped each stick and placed them in the hearth. He felt as if he was breaking every memory of his life – kneeling to abjure his past and renounce who he was. Carefully he placed each thick splinter against the others until they were stacked neatly in the back of the blackened grate. With one hand he reached into his coat pocket and pulled out the torn hankersniff given to him by his mother. It had been the greatest gift he had ever had, longed-for and loved and never used for its purpose. For three years he had carried it with him every day, always the ever-present memory of one close by. Thomas thumbed the darned initials before he screwed it up in his hand. He pushed it quickly into the grate and in his heart whispered goodbye to her. Taking the tinderbox, he sparked the glintings against the hankersniff and watched the fire take hold. It burnt brightly and quickly, crackling from stick to stick as the flames lit the room and warmed his face.

'Not too bad with the fire lit,' he said, wiping his face with the cuff of his jacket to take the fresh glint from his eye. 'If we stick with Crane, things will be right, Kate. What else have we got?'

Kate had been smiling as she watched him light the fire, but now a sombreness had crept through her mind like the chill wind. As the flames took hold she remembered another room only days before where she had slept in a deep dream and been woken with joyful laughter and the calling of children. There had been warmth, comfort and an open hearth in that place. It had proclaimed hope and love and was something she had wanted all of her life.

'Do you think we'll see Rueben Wayfoot again?' Kate asked, remembering his bright whiskered chin and the warm fire of Boggle Mill.

'Not I, Kate. I'm for going on. When I hear that Demurral is dead, then I will return, and not until,' Thomas said, his words determined and edged with hate.

'On that day, will you take me back?' she asked. The thought of again seeing Boggle Mill with its smoking pots and glistening windows was fixed in her mind.

'On that day, I will dance on his grave,' he said sharply, curling his hands into tight fists as he stood and looked at her shadow-lit face. 'He put my mother in that place and conjured that demon. Something in my bones tells me he's not finished with us. He wanted all three of us dead. Raphah's gone and it leaves you and me.'

'I thought that too,' Kate replied with a hint of hesitation in her voice. 'Every time I shut my eyes I see him. Sometimes I think I can hear him whispering to me, calling me back. On the ship, in the night I was sure I heard Demurral calling out. I went on deck and all I could hear was Jacob shouting at the crew to raise the sails and the wind whistling through the rigging.'

'So what's it to be?' Thomas asked brusquely. He opened the top of the battered metal box by the fire, picked out two dried oak logs and placed them on the flames. 'Are we going to see this through?' His voice was dry and harsh and had broken since the coming of the sky-quake. Then he sat upon the day-bed and looked into the flames. Listening to the crackling of the fire, he waited before he spoke again. 'I have you, Kate, and no other. I realised that for the first time when we sailed from Whitby. It never meant anything before, but with every rise and fall of that ship it came to me. I had no one else. No father, mother . . .'

76

'Then we'll stay together till death parts us,' Kate said. She leant against the bolster and closed her eyes as the room warmed.

'Do you mean that?' Thomas asked. He turned to her and in disappointment realised she had slipped into sleep. '*Do* you mean that?' he asked her again in a voice lower than a breath, hoping she would hear him in her dreaming.

Taking more logs from the firebox, Thomas stacked the grate and then leant back in the lounge chair. From a darkened corner he could hear the scurrying of mice. The fire crackled in the hearth and the dancing flames warmed his feet as the dusty, whitewashed panels shimmered in the light. Pulling the old blanket up to his neck, he rested against the back of the chair. A growing sense of unease kept him from sleep, even though his eyes sagged with bleary tiredness.

Thomas twisted back and forth, hoping to find a comfortable place to rest himself against the prickling threads that bit at his skin. As he drifted from the world, he tried to keep an open eye, fearful that Demurral stalked his dreams. He rubbed the black powder away from his eyes with the back of his hand and snuggled in the warm blanket. As Thomas dozed he looked into the flames, which leapt from the grate to the mouth of the chimney.

Suddenly the flames flickered and then faded. Thomas blinked hard to rid his mind of what he now saw. It was as if every strand of fire had come together and just for a moment were frozen in time, and there looking at him from within the flames was the outline of a gaunt, twisted head – lines and contours that in the light looked almost human, eyes that opened with every flicker. Then, as quickly as it appeared, it was gone.

# Ord Vackan's Chair

EADLE was shaken from his sleep as Raphah leapt hurriedly from the bed to the floor of the kitchen below. As Beadle had dreamt fitfully of the sea, so the house had been whipped into a storm. The clock had struck the fourth hour; every traveller had been pulled from their beds and now clustered by the fire in search of enough food to break the night fast.

A cook flustered by the scullery pot as she strangled the last drops of blood from the neck of a dead chicken with one hand, whilst with the other she showered the floor with fresh feathers. All about her ran the skullers, carrying sizzling trays of roast meat and hot bread, screaming at each other as they went. A steaming pot bubbled upon the open fire, filling the whole inn with the smell of boiled cabbage.

Raphah looked up at Beadle, who peered upon the scene through a crusted eye and moaned to himself that he had only found true sleep moments before being woken. From outside came the jangling of a horse harness and the clatter of hooves. It was like the preparation for war as the carriages were made ready and wicker baskets stacked with journey food and wire-corked beer in pot jars. Every corner of the inn shuddered with the sounds of making ready. Coats were warmed by the kitchen fire and hot stones were rag-wrapped for the coachman's feet. Men shouted a morning's welcome as maids bustled back and forth from hearth to table. The clamber was that of a city street or summer fayre, and laughter echoed along the passageway as the joy and trepidation of the coming journey filled all with its excitement.

Standing in the shadows, Raphah listened enviously for a moment. To him, such homeliness had been a stranger since his leaving Africa. Now, all around was the sound of contentment, as all was made ready. Even the candles appeared to burn brightly in their stands as they awaited the dawn and the call of the bugler. No one gave him a bye or leave as he stepped from the kitchen unnoticed and walked the three paces across the passageway and into the parlour.

A long oak table was stretched across the room and covered with pewter serving plates and jugs of warmed beer. They steamed like early morning cowpats, the mist from the porridge, meat and bread quickly disappearing in the growing heat of the fire. A cooked hog's head stared at him as he stepped towards the large fireplace that ran the length of one wall. Quickly the room filled with people, many lost in their own thoughts, some fumbling with small bags that they stowed beneath the long benches.

No one looked at Raphah or bade him any welcome – it was as if he had no shape or form and could not be seen. They gave their welcomes to one another but none spoke to him. He waited by the fire as the seats were taken and the breakfast eaten. Everyone had a place but him. A china plate of rich cooked meat was handed along and as Raphah reached forth his hand, the plate was pulled away by the innkeeper.

He tried to catch the eye of a rotund traveller with a tight golden waistcoat and puffed cotton sleeves. The man instantly looked to his plate and filled his mouth as if he were a starving urchin. Seven men sat upon the bench and ate their vitals. Each one kept their eye to the fire, speaking warmly to their neighbour of the journey ahead.

'Good breakfast,' snorted the fat man as he undid the collar of his shirt and lifted out a flap of skin that had somehow trapped itself beneath. 'The journey will be fine to Peveril. Heard they have hanged the highwayman – now we have nothing to fear.'

There was a rumble of approval as heads nodded on both sides of the table. Raphah looked on, thinking it would be best to keep silent. He leant against the fireplace as the conversation gathered pace, then looked for a place to sit at table.

The fat man caught his eye and gave him a slight smile, curling the corner of his lip and allowing a dribble of meat juice to scurry across his chin.

'Where are our manners?' he said mockingly as he saw Raphah looking for a place to eat. 'The Ethio has travelled a long way to eat with us and we have not made him welcome.'

The gathering bristled silently, spreading out along the benches so there was no room for Raphah to sit.

'Gentlemen, we have a foreign guest who would like to sit with us. How can we make him welcome?' The man spoke between slurps of red wine that he held in a silver flagon by his side. 'Surely there must be one seat in which he can take his meal in such pleasant company?'

Raphah edged his way towards the gap on the long bench between the coachman and the bugler, who was dressed in a leather apron and heavy tunic. As he approached they snuggled together so he could not be seated.

'Sit, my dear friend,' the fat man scolded as he smiled with his piggy eyes and wobbled his jowls. 'I know, gentlemen,' he said quietly. 'There is always Vackan's chair by the fire?'

The bugler shook his head in deep disapproval and whispered to the fat man. 'That would not be a good thing, Mister Bragg, not a good thing.'

'But we could test the chair, see if what is said about it is true,' Mister Bragg replied equally as quietly.

Raphah noticed the large oak chair at the far side of the brazier. It was coated in fire dust and looked as if it had never been a place of rest for many years, or that a hand had touched or cleaned it in all that time. It was unlike any chair he had seen before. Two spindle front legs were turned in dark wood and capped with lion's claws. A large third leg the width of a man's arm followed the line of the chair back to the floor. It was old and ugly, rudely made and dog-gnawed.

'Would you like to seat yourself there?' Mister Bragg asked as he filled his mouth again with food. 'Ord Vackan loved to sit in that place – was taken from it on the last night of his life. Loved it, he did, loved it.'

'And all who . . .' The bugler tried to speak.

'Reserved for special guests, that's what he would like to say, special like you – a friend from far away,' Bragg said, sipping his wine from the flask. 'Please be seated and we will serve you. It is tradition to eat a hearty breakfast before . . .'

Raphah slipped quietly into the inglenook chair that rested on the hearth by the brazier.

All was suddenly silent. Words stopped half-spoken as every head turned and stared. Raphah became aware that all who were gathered were glaring at him. He looked away quickly, staring into the shimmering flames that sucked at a holly log. Everyone glanced at each other, urging with sharp eyes for someone to speak. Silence prevailed, thick, uncomfortable and brimming with anticipation.

With a ruffle of his long black cloak, Barghast walked through the doorway and saw Raphah sat in the Ord Vackan's oak chair.

'Did no one tell him?' he shouted loudly.

'What?' Raphah asked as his eyes went to the faces of the gathering.

'You let him sit in the chair and not one of you came to the lad's aid?' Barghast bellowed again, his white face reddening for a moment.

'We never saw,' muttered a small, shrew-like man with a thin face and jagged front teeth sticking from his mouth.

'Rumour, legend . . .Nothing is for certain, they could have all died by coincidence,' said Mister Bragg feebly as he chewed a slither of liver and sipped the dregs of fine chianti that he had hoarded from the night before.

'What do they speak of?' Raphah asked, unsure as to what he had done and why it should cause such a commotion.

'Vackan's chair,' said Barghast solemnly. 'There is a legend that it is cursed. Whoever sits upon it meets an untimely death. Vackan was a villain of these parts, a cut-throat and a murderer. On the night that Ord Vackan was dragged from here and hanged, he cursed the chair on which he had been sat and said that whoever rested in it would come to an end worse than his.'

'A curse upon a chair? Should I be worried by that?' Raphah laughed.

'Such a thing cannot be shaken from you by laughter. It is well known in these parts and has become more than legend. Too many coincidences have taken place and I am saddened that your fellow travellers should play such a trick,' Barghast said.

'Brevity at breakfast, Mister Barghast,' Bragg snorted as if pleased with himself. 'I never thought for a moment he would take the seat.'

'Perhaps Raphah offended you in some way?' Barghast asked of him.

'I am not easily offended – and was not Church and State

built on the backs of the Ethio? Perhaps I would find it easier to share my vitals with pigs than the likes of him. But we live in a *modern* world and things have changed. One day we might find one as the Minster bishop – and hell shall freeze.' He belched as he spoke, cow-cudding a mouthful of food and picking some pieces of liver from his teeth.

'I have a spell that will break the curse on you, lad,' the shrew-man said above the babble of voices, and he held out his hand clutching a folded piece of linen. 'Take it and it will stop the evil befalling you.'

'I need no magic to break the curse, for that was done for me in ages past – I fear not wooden chairs nor the curse of those who sat in them, nor what lies in a man's heart.' Raphah stood from the chair and brushed the dust for his breeches. 'I will eat my vitals with those who are not afraid of my company and can understand I am a free man.'

'Then sit with me,' said a soft voice in the darkened corner of the room by a far-off window. 'I travel alone and have no concern for curses or Ord Vacken.'

Raphah looked across the room to where the voice had heralded a welcome. In the shadows by the shuttered window, he saw the outline of a figure edged in a dark cloak, the hood shrouding about the head as if to keep the wearer from the draught.

'And I too,' said Barghast as he snatched bread and meat from the table and followed Raphah across the room.

Together they sat and in the half-light Raphah saw that his welcomer was a young woman of his own age. She smiled at him as he sat in a high-backed chair and then nodded politely as Barghast joined them.

'Do you travel together?' she asked as Barghast offered Raphah some meat and then poured some beer from the table jug.

'As of last night, this fine fellow is my companion upon the road. Never a finer fellow to share a journey,' Barghast boasted as he peered at the girl. 'Are you going far?' he continued, an eyebrow raised to top a smug smile.

'Does not everyone travel to Peveril and then to London?' she asked as she looked at Raphah. 'But such a journey will be a trifle to you. For what reason do you travel – friendship or skirmish?'

'Or just the joy of the wayfarer?' interrupted Barghast. 'We could ask the same of you and our enquiry could be unwelcome.'

'That you could, Mister Barghast, and it most probably would.'

Raphah smiled as the candlelight flickered upon her face. 'I travel to London with Beadle,' he said quietly. 'I search for some other friends who have gone ahead of me.'

'Then we share the same journey. I too search for someone. My sister went to the city on *business* and has not been heard of since.' Her voice trembled slightly. 'Some with whom I have shared the journey have not been the politest of company.' She nodded towards Bragg, who continued to fill his face and chomp upon the minced liver as if the meal would be his last. 'He joined the coach with me at Lindisfarne and has been an oaf of a companion along every winding road.'

'Then I will make you my ward for the coach and tell you of the world and all of its complications,' Barghast jested as he held out his hand and smiled benignly.

'That would be a fine thing, Mister Barghast, at least to Peveril. They say that since the sky-quake the coach to London has been stopped as the horses all went mad in the city and had to be shot. I don't know if we shall have a coach to take us on from there.'

'Then I will walk with you all the way and my cloak shall be

84

a bridge to whatever we have to cross.' Barghast smiled again.

'Mister Barghast, I am weary of beer and wonder if you would bring me some milk?' she asked quickly as she coughed.

'A fine pleasure, warmed like a mother cat?' he asked as he stood from the table and walked to the kitchen, scowling at Bragg as he went by.

The woman leant forward and spoke quickly. 'Don't travel with this man. I heard Mister Bragg speak of him this morning and he is not what he appears to be. I have heard much of him and he's not to be trusted.'

'And you are?' Raphah asked.

'More than you may think. My name is Lady Tanville Chilnham.'

With that, Beadle appeared muttering to himself. '*He* sent me with some milk. *He* said I had to bring it. Beadle do this now, *he* said . . . Take it to Raphah, *he* said, I'm off to pack, *he* said . . .' Beadle scoffed loudly as he came to the table clutching a pot jug of steaming milk. 'Gone off to pack, *he* said, and thrusts this in my hand for the *Lady* . . .' Beadle stopped and stared, his eyes darting back and forth from the cloaked figure to Raphah. 'It's you,' he said without thinking, believing her to be the nocturnal visitor to the kitchen.

'Yes, it is I . . . Have we met before?' Tanville asked as she smiled. 'Perhaps you were asleep and you dreamt of me. It would not be the first time that such a thing has happened. When I was a child I once dreamt that my great aunt leapt from her painting upon the wall and her ghost gamed with us all night. I awoke in the morning to find my room was strewn with everything from the cupboards and her picture upon the floor. Was it a ghost or just a dream? Do you believe in such things?'

Beadle was silent. He looked at Tanville's hands and the soft black cotton shroud in which she was wrapped.

'Do you still think you have met me before, Beadle? It is

Beadle?' she said wistfully, her skin glistening like gold in the candlelight.

'Perhaps it was a dream and one in which I thought I was awake,' Beadle said slowly as he stepped away from the table. 'Coach is ready, my friend. Barghast has booked us a seat on top with a double rug and an oiled skin. We'll be snug all the way to Peveril. Barghast travels inside *and* he's booked on to London. From what I've heard we'd have to wait a night at Peveril before we can go on. Word is that all the horses went mad when the comet struck, only five carriages left in the whole of the country.'

Beadle turned from the table and walked away, giving neither Raphah nor Tanville any courtesy of his going. He seemed to be in another world, his mind weighted down with concerns for the morrow as he rubbed his temple and pulled nervously upon the hairs of his brow.

'Your companion thinks much of you,' Tanville said as she poured herself a tip of milk and sipped it slowly.

'Much . . . And much more as each day passes,' Raphah said cautiously. 'Always a good judge of character and always remembers a face.'

'Tell me, Raphah. Do you really not fear Ord Vackan's curse?' she asked.

'I fear not curse, spell or spirit.'

'Then by what magic are you protected?' Tanville asked.

'Not magic, Lady Tanville. Something far more powerful than conjuring tricks with bones . . .'

Suddenly shouting in the hallway broke into the eating room. A sharp, sudden draught of cold breeze rushed through the doorway. Ord Vackan's chair tumbled to one side and fell onto the charring embers of the fire.

'It's the Ethio, I tell you. Who else would steal our money?' shouted Mister Bragg as he leant against the doorway, so fat that he looked as if he was a firkin and a half the size he should be. 'Robbed as I slept – could have cut my throat, to boot!'

'How do you know?' argued the innkeeper. 'Could have been his companion as well.'

'Then bring them both here and we can speak to them directly. Two hundred pounds has gone and they will have it,' wheezed Bragg, red-faced and stricken with anger.

'I am here of my own accord,' Raphah said as he got from the table.

'Thief, laggard and footpad!' shouted the barrelous Mister Bragg as he heaved his stomach back into his bulging coat and attempted to keep the buttons from snapping. 'Give me the money and let's hang him now!'

Raphah was grabbed by the arms and dragged before the fire by the coachman and the bugler of hounds.

'It has to be him – who else could be a thief amongst us? By his very nature and birth he is not to be trusted. That in itself would deem him guilty.'

'Guilty? Of what am I guilty?' Raphah protested.

'Theft, house breaking, robbery,' slobbered the man in a half-breath snatched from the fireside air as he lunged towards him, then held on to the mantelpiece to steady his frame from falling over. 'An Ethio will always be a thief as far as I am concerned. Take him and hang him and the dwarf as well.'

'Dwarf?' protested Beadle as he ran from the hallway to kick Bragg in the shin. 'Call me a dwarf and a thief? At least my stomach tells my mouth when to stop.'

'What is he accused of now?' shouted Barghast, arriving in the hallway holding his bag as the room filled with travellers.

'Your companion is a thief. Last night as we slept, he made into my room and stole my purse. Let him be searched and all will be found.'

'I have nothing and would not steal.'

'Is this what you search for?' Lady Tanville asked, holding out a leather purse and jangling the coins within.

Bragg looked for a moment. 'The very same. See, we have found the evidence. Take him and string him to the oak. He can dance from the same tree as Ord Vackan's ghost – what did I tell you? The curse comes true.'

Raphah looked into her eyes as she held the money before him and smiled. 'I'm sorry . . . It was where you left it,' she said, looking back at Raphah.

'And Lady Tanville Chilnham as a witness,' Bragg gloated almost choking on his own spittle with excitement.

'No – where *you* left it, Mister Bragg. This morning at breakfast before you went about your business. I have just found it upon the bench warmed by your weighty posterior.'

'The case is altered, Mister Bragg, and my companion is free to go?' Barghast asked as the coachman let go of his grip.

'This is not to my liking, Mister Barghast, not to my liking. I smell conspiracy and my eyes will not leave you all for the journey.'

# Digitalis

*A*S the hour halved, Kate woke. The fire still crackled and spat in the grate and Thomas snored. In her sleeping she had heard music, notes tapped auspiciously in quick succession upon the magichord by her side. In the opening of her eyes it had ceased to be and the room was empty, and she felt as if she had been cheated of something wonderful. As she had slept the music had danced through her thoughts. Every note had been like the chiming of a summer bell and though the tune was indistinct, it reminded her of all that was good. In her waking she had thought of the day, months before, when she had stood by the dock-end in Baytown and watched the lasses slicing fish. They had joshed her for her dress – no lass wears men's boots, they had rhymed, as the little ones had jumped rope and watched the elders stripping the fish of their scales. In her mind she sniffed, her senses filled with the scent of seaweed and salt spray. Her eyes imagined looking up to the high cliffs and the swirling seabirds.

Nothing they did offended her. Like mother, like daughter, was what she thought. She had followed the way of her father. Sea-boots, waistcoat, corn hat and a post to lean upon as she looked out to sea. It was always over the horizon that her life would be lived. It would not be the ways of fisherwomen that would fulfil her life. She felt different and knew that within she was. It was as if she had some nagging predestination of what her life would become, and that from an early age she was set apart, different.

Kate rested upon the bed and stared at Thomas. It was then that she heard the jingle of the magichord and sensed someone close by. Every inch of her body tensed, and her breath laboured as she fought the desire to scream. The room was filled with the scent of perfume, strong and bold. It smelt of frankincense and myrrh, Christmas cake and old sherry. There was a sudden and shrill icy blast that took the flame from the candle by her bed and dimmed the light in the room to a soft gloom, lit only by the flames of the fire.

From under the bed came the rustle of dried winter leaves being scattered across the oak beams. A seething breeze squalled through the floorboards like wind through rigging ropes far at sea. The leaves scraped the wood like dead fingers, tapping a tale of grief. From all around the buds of foxgloves fell about her as the odour of the murky, deep wood grew stronger. Instinctively, Kate wanted to close her eyes; she was now unable to move a single limb as the room was transformed into a dark woodland glade. Kate thought she saw the magichord grow into an old oak, gnarled and knotted. The firelight faded, dimming to a meagre glow. The leaves swirled about themselves, spiralling higher and higher as if the wind were breathing long whispers of a half-heard conversation.

From somewhere far away she heard laughter, coarse and cruel. She dare not look to right nor left, but kept her sight fixed upon the bough of the oak that now grew about her. What had once been the ceiling of the room had been replaced with a canopy of dead branches. There was no sky, just a grave thick mist that hovered above them.

In her trepidation, Kate became aware of someone standing near to her. She strained fearfully not to look, hoping against hope that she would be left alone. The music played gently, a flowing hand tracing over the keys like a butterfly breath. A warm voice began to sing the melody, and Kate pulled the covers close about her neck. The singing quickly turned to a child's laughter as a cold hand touched her face. She turned – the room was empty. The forest had gone in the instant. Looking to the magichord she saw the ivory pegs moving on their own, each one tapped out in succeeding notes by an invisible hand. She watched, unsure what to do, more intrigued than frightened as the keys danced back and forth along the octaves. Kate gulped, unable find her voice.

The laughter came again, this time from the window, as suddenly the music stopped and the lid of the magichord slammed shut. The notes jarred loudly. A swirl of dust twisted by the bed as a jagged and unseen finger prodded Kate sharply in the chest. Again laughter, deeper, and groans as if tinged with pain. A shadow crossed the candlelight and for the briefest of moments Kate saw a dim outline of a girl. There was a bustle of skirts and scouring of crinoline as if the ghostly spectre were about to dance.

'Thomas,' Kate said shakily, 'are you still sleeping?' She hoped he would hear her voice. Thomas moaned in his slumber and returned to his snoring by the fire.

'Look at me . . .' came a whisper from by the magichord.

Kate turned and stared.

'No . . . Here . . .' The voice came again from the window.

Kate turned again.

'Or here . . .' whispered the unseen voice from next to her.

Kate couldn't move. She could feel a presence close by and

see an indentation in the thick mattress. And then, inch by inch, a figure began to become visible. First the tips of her fine silver shoes, then the white leg stockings, then the bottom of a pink crinoline dress embroidered with a thousand foxgloves. It was an experience that was stranger than strange, to watch someone appear from thin air. Kate gulped and held her breath as the smell of perfume grew stronger and stronger. Finally, like a Cheshire cat, the face of a girl materialised at Kate's side. She smiled and looked to be quite human, solid and very real. Kate couldn't move. She was more fascinated than frightened. It was as if the spectre were more than a girl and that her features were but a childlike mask that hid someone within.

'I was watching you sleep,' the spectre whispered close to Kate's face as she picked her white powdered nose and sniffed. 'Wanted to wake you up but waited until *he* was away . . .' She gestured towards Thomas who slept soundly on. 'When did *you* die?'

'I didn't – well, not that I know,' Kate replied, unsure what to say.

'I thought the same. Didn't realise I was dead for a week. Kept trying to speak to everyone and no one was listening. I even followed my coffin to the funeral and thought someone else had died. Mother crying, father crying, all of them sobbing. It was only when the priest said my name that I realised that all those morbid tears were over little me.' The ghost paused as if to take a breath, her dark eyes searching the room as she continued to speak. 'Strange thing, death. It's at that time when you find out what people *really* think of you. All those salutations of how sweet, what a pretty face, how charming. If only they had said it to me when I was alive. Even if they were insincere, life could have been so much cheerier.'

'So you are dead?' Kate asked.

'Buried and resurrected.' The girl laughed as she pulled on

her skirt and smiled. 'You shine too much for someone who's alive – sure you're not dead?'

'Alive . . . I hope.' Kate shuddered as a tingle danced a deathly shimmer along her spine. 'How can I see you?'

'Because I want you to – well, for now anyway.'

'I've never seen a ghost before. You're not how I expected,' Kate said anxiously as she looked the girl up and down.

'Neither are you,' the spirit said, then paused and looked at Kate quite strangely as if she attempted to peer inside her head. Kate shuddered as the ghost spoke again. 'I knew you were coming. I listened to old Pallium as he made the bed and stacked the fireplace. It was him who brought me here.' The girl pointed to a flaking portrait locked in an old gilt frame which hung on the plaster wall next to the magichord. 'That's me.'

Kate hadn't noticed the picture before. It was blackened by fire soot, the face nearly invisible in the dark sky against which it was set. At some time, the portrait had been barred into the frame as if to imprison the girl within. The rusted spikes were roughly pinned into the gilt and looked as if they were the bars of a lonely prison.

The ghost caught Kate's stare and knew her thoughts. She turned quickly to look at her; the spectre's face blurred as she moved and trailed a glistening of tiny sparks as if she were on fire.

'They thought it would keep me in, said I was a nuisance in my walking. Got a priest to pray upon the portrait – that it would lock my spirit away. *Somehow* I found it easier to escape.' The spectre looked at Kate and smiled as she touched the painting. 'Zurburan was a master painter – so my mother said. Painted me when I was sick, caught me in the moments of death.'

'Nice,' Kate replied slowly, unsure what to say in conversation with a chattering spectre as she peered at the dim image that hung on the wall. 'Did you live here?'

93

The spirit glimmered as if angered. Her face changed colour as she searched for the words in which to reply. Like a deathly vapour, its image began to fade as she spoke quickly, trying to tell all before she vanished completely. 'Wherever the portrait shall go, so will I be,' the ghost said feebly. The blush drained from her face and she wore the pallor of death. 'That picture is my dwelling place, no paradise for me. I live within the picture. It is my prison and has been sold and resold many times. Some say it's cursed. I listen to them, hear them screaming when I walk from it. Then it's quickly vended and I go to yet another keeper. I'm a long way from home and wish to return. It has been so . . . so . . . long.'

The ghost slid from the bed as if drawn back to the picture. She looked no more at Kate but gazed at her own deathly portrait.

'So where are you from, what's your name?' Kate asked, her lips trembling as the ghost walked from her towards the wall. 'Come back . . . Speak to me . . .'

'*Again . . . Sometime soon . . . Tell no one . . .*' The words were spoken without a movement of the lips, and then she blew a kiss.

'Now,' said Kate, trying to seize her before she disappeared. With one hand she grabbed at the pink dress and for a brief moment took hold by her fingertips.

Her words were of no use. There was a swish of crinoline and a twirl of dust. The magichord shook momentarily as if it too was bewitched and the ghost began to fragment. As if made of melting ice, all her form subsided to nought. With a sudden gasp, the girl was gone.

'*Tell no one . . .*' came the voice again from all around her.

Kate lay back on the bed, staring at the portrait. The dark eyes of the girl stared back to her. She heard a sudden rush of footsteps outside the room that stalked along the passageway. Thomas stirred from his sleep.

'Did you say something, Kate?' he asked.

'It's just Jacob Crane,' Kate said, wanting to keep the ghostly visit a secret for fear of not being believed. Crane tapped on the door and walked into the room.

'Thought I heard you playing that old magichord,' Crane said as he smiled at them both. In his hands he carried a large bowl of steaming water and two folded towels. 'Quite a talented lass when you want to be, eh, Kate? Get washed and I'll see you both in the scullery.'

'I don't like this place, Kate. I saw a face in the fire. It was Demurral,' Thomas said.

'It was a dream, nothing more. He'll never find us here,' she replied.

In a short while, Thomas opened the narrow stairway door and stepped into the scullery. All had changed. Pallium sat at the table, the money gone and the floor swept. A fire burnt brightly in the hearth and the room smelt of fresh lavender. Pallium smiled as if he had been stuffed and then given the expression of a tight grimace. His eyes signalled to the world that despite his waxen appearance he was still alive; they danced across the room, inviting all to see what had been done. Pallium's achievements were but vainglory, as it was Jacob Crane who scurried about the room like a vimful housemaid.

'My dear friends, you look so clean and hungry too,' Pallium said unctuously as he sipped the glass in his hand and swallowed slowly. 'I decided – err, *we* decided – that I had worked for too long and had neglected many things. It was Jacob who reminded me that there was more to life than counting coins.'

Pallium looked disheartened, as if something had been taken from him. His fingers twitched without the coins to count. The half-smile broke at the edges of his mouth and his lip quivered slightly.

'Fine thing you've done, Pallium. A very fine thing. Can't be spending all your life locked in here counting money,' Crane said.

'Good to have you here, Jacob, and I'm sure that Galphus will agree.' Pallium coughed the words as he pulled his coat about him.

'Where can we meet this great Galphus?' Crane asked, putting the brush against the wall and looking at all he had done.

'The Salamander Inn would be a place to start. He will be taking breakfast there. I could introduce you.' Pallium looked at them one by one and smiled again.

'Such a seer of the future would not need to be introduced to the likes of us. He should know our very thoughts before they trip from our tongues,' Crane said.

'That he will, I am sure, for he is not just a mender of soles but a maker of them.'

'What does he do, Mister Pallium?' Kate asked, not wanting to be left out, the thoughts of the ghostly visitor still fresh in her mind.

Pallium waved his arms waving excitedly as he blurted the words. 'Galphus is a man of business transactions and has the desire to prosper. He is cordial, jovial and greatly avuncular. To be in his presence is something beyond the imagination.'

'Then we must meet him,' Crane said, wiping the dust from his hands and slipping on his frock coat. 'I have always wished for an uncle, especially one who is jovial! Perhaps he will take me under his wing, as he has you, and I too may prosper. The Salamander Inn shall be visited with haste and we all shall eat merrily.'

Thomas slapped his hands against his chest and turned to Kate as if he wanted to push her from the house and into the street. He grinned at the thought of food, as his stomach rolled over for yet another time. He was sure that in the distance he could hear the chiming of a church clock.

Kate held her place, unwilling to move. It was as if she wanted to speak, to hold Pallium in conversation for a moment longer. Her eyes glanced quickly from Crane to Pallium and then to Thomas, betraying her agitation.

'Mister Pallium,' she said, her voice croaking with indecision. 'There's a picture in my room – where did it come from?' She asked the question quickly, wanting to rid her lips of the words before she could think of their consequences.

Pallium nodded his head slowly back and forth as if he mulled the question in his mind like a morsel of chocolate. He smiled, then frowned, his forehead wrinkled like the eyelid of a tortoise. He looked to Crane as he began to speak like an excited child.

'Wonderful picture, Galphus bought it for me and as soon as I saw her face I fell in love. Never was there one so pretty, but beauty like that comes at a great price.' Pallium stopped for a moment and thought, his eyes withering within their frames. 'Not a question I would have expected. If you had asked about the magichord I could understand, for it is a fine piano, but the picture?'

'It was that she looked so young . . . And the bars across the frame. I have never seen the likes before.' Kate stumbled in her answering.

'Nor will you again. The portrait is unique. An ageless painting of that which will age no more.'

'Did you know the girl?' Kate asked.

'Not for even a minute of a day. Galphus had the picture delivered. She looked so lost and I wanted to give her a home. I find her entertaining.'

'And I find my stomach screaming to my wits,' Crane interrupted. 'Kate loves to talk, Mister Pallium. It is the finest thing she does.'

# The Delightful Mister Ergott

THE baying of the coach hounds quickly ceased as the wheels of the heavy carriage began to turn slowly through the rutted mud that led from the inn to the open road. The light of the morning grew brighter but was shielded from the earth by thick, dark clouds that glimmered just brighter than dusk. The coach trundled on, gathering speed as the lamps flickered.

Beadle pulled the blanket about him and wrapped the oilskin around his shoulders. The first shards of hail began to fall like teeth of ice, clattering upon the stacked baggage that was strapped to the roof. Raphah and Beadle were perched high above the ground in their one-guinea seats outside the coach, exposed to the driving hail that began to tear at their skin. Together, they swayed on a thin running board above the ground that whisked ever quicker beneath their dangling feet. To the front the driver cracked the whip above the horses' heads and the bugler called the hounds to his side. The beasts ran in and out of the spinning wheels, yelping with discontent; some dashed ahead, snapping at the horses legs' and splattering through the deep puddles of the narrow road.

Beadle could feel a tingle of excitement growing within as the carriage sped onwards. His heart leapt in his chest and he smiled, rubbing his hands. Faster and faster they went, gaining speed with each yard. The hail beat down as the squall from the Fell burst like a dam above them. All was glistening white as hounds wailed and cried, struck by stones of ice, and the horses snorted steaming breath as they lathered on. Relentlessly the coach went on in the dark of morning, buffeted this way and that as it pounded the road. The storm broke harder. Wind whipped the horses with icy fingers that stripped the dying leaves from even deader branches.

Beadle gasped as the breath was taken from him. He pulled the oilskin to cover his face and keep off the gale. Without a word, he and Raphah slipped from their fragile seat to the lee of the cases and huddled together, shaken by the coach.

'Do you think *he* will follow?' Beadle asked Raphah as they were beaten against the baggage and twisted in the oilskin by the rocking of the carriage. 'I keep thinking I've got away. That now I'm on the coach to Peveril, I am free. With every yard of every mile, another step away from Demurral.' He tried to smile, but the happiness of his escape suddenly faded. An uncertain thought of the pursuer began to grow uneasily in his mind. 'Never thought I'd face him again, never. Never thought I'd ever, ever see you – and look at us now.'

Raphah didn't speak. He pulled the oilskin over their heads and braced himself for the journey. Above the sound of the rumbling wheels and the snorting horses, he could hear the heated conversation through the leather hatch by his feet. Bragg shouted with moans of complaint with every stone and rut that jolted him from his seat.

Within the darkness of the carriage the five passengers sat in a haze of thick smoke. In the deepest, darkest corner, snuggled in the leather seat and wrapped in a velvet scarf, was a young man. In his hand he held a large wooden pipe, filled to the brim with roasting tobacco. It flumed from the rim and rolled about the carriage as if heavier than the air.

The man listened to Bragg's moans and complaints as with each rut he was tossed to the side and held his guts as if they were to spill from his pants.

The man never spoke, but puffed on his pipe, his wide, owl-like eyes surveying each person. A weasel-faced man called Mister Shrume picked and plucked thick hairs from his nose one by one. Sat to his right was Barghast. Bragg filled the half of the seat opposite with his fat rump. By his side and pressed into the corner so she could not move was Lady Tanville. Her face was lit by a tallow lamp that jarred back and forth with each roll of the carriage.

'Do you never stop complaining?' Barghast quizzed Bragg as he moaned yet again and contorted his face even further.

'If only they would slow down and transport us in sedation,' he complained bitterly.

'Then we would never get to Peveril and never get to London,' Lady Tanville said quickly.

'I find it delightful, quite delightful,' said the young man as he slurped upon the pipe and mopped his dribbling chin. 'It's as if we are at sea and tossed upon a storm.'

'If I had wanted to be at sea then I would have travelled by ship and not by coach,' spluttered Bragg as he coughed. 'Do you seek the pleasures of London too?'

'I travel on business and that business takes me to many places,' the man said as he tapped the pipe upon his boot then stomped on the burning embers with his foot. From a neat leather bag he filled the bowl with what looked like mouldy dried grain mixed with strings of black seaweed. Without consideration, he leant across the carriage, opened the lamp and lit the brew.

'What is that business, Mister . . .?' Lady Tanville asked.

'Ergott, Vitus Ergott. I am a dowser.'

Barghast leaned forward and smiled. 'Interesting,' he said above the rattle of the wheels. 'And for what do you search?'

'Whatever my wand and I are paid to enquire for. Some would have us look for gold, others water and still more a precious item they have lost. All I need is my clear seeing and diving wand. I express the intention in my mind and allow the spirits to take me to that place. Simple, really, and quite delightful.'

'Do you always find what you seek?' Lady Tanville asked.

'Is that a request for my services?' Ergott replied with a raised eyebrow and a smile as he puffed on his pipe through withered lips.

Lady Tanville didn't speak, but ruffled herself within her coat as she put a hand to her face.

'Peradventure, Mister Ergott,' Barghast said as he leant across Shrume and tapped the man on the arm. 'Does your divination take you to the city?'

'Delightfully, yes. All paid for and a first-class seat. Apparently I am highly recommended.'

'And will you tell us of your quest or does it have to be a secret?' Tanville asked as she smiled at him.

'I search for lost children. Taken without consent and sold into slavery. With my wand I will find them, for that is sure. My *employer* has given me an element of each child and therefore I know I will be drawn to them.' Ergott spoke in a matter-of-fact way as he tapped the side of his pipe and looked at Barghast and then to Lady Tanville. The coach fell silent and even Bragg stopped his moaning as all the inhabitants thought on what he had said.

'And when you find them?' Tanville asked.

'They will be liberated from their captor and he will be put before the Crown.'

'You speak as if you know who has them,' Barghast said.

'That is my only clue. I only know the name of the man who I search for. A man so vile and sinister that I would not mention his name in such company. When I took on the adventure I sealed myself never to speak his name until he was fettered and being dragged to Tyburn.' The look on Ergott's face changed suddenly as if the quarrelsomeness of his thoughts marred his youthfulness.

'I have met many wicked men, Mister Ergott. Perhaps I could help you in your task?' Barghast asked, reclining against the leather seat as the coach rocked violently.

'Delightful, and kind. But I work alone. In all my investigations I find it better to keep close counsel. I even try to hide the conclusions from my own thoughts as there are creatures that can listen to whispering wits as if they were shouted from the rooftops.'

'How childish,' Lady Tanville said, her voice cold.

'Far from it. Who is to say that all we have not said has been eavesdropped by some creature right now,' Ergott said.

'With the noise of this troublesome carriage they would be driven deaf, Ergott,' Bragg replied.

'In my dowsing I have seen many things. I once heard of a man who could transform himself into a dog. It could even be you, Mister Bragg.' Egrott pointed his pipe towards the fat man and smiled.

'Preposterous!' Bragg squealed like a pig.

'But possible,' Ergott said, returning comfortably to his pipe as he pulled his velvet scarf about his neck and lifted the collar of his coat against his neck. 'Tell me Bragg, what is it that takes you to London?'

'I am a collector of fine art and ancient artefacts,' Bragg replied.

'And you, Barghast?'

'I am just a traveller, always have been.'

They were the last words spoken within the carriage. It gathered even more speed as they travelled the toll road to Peveril. Within the hour the storm had given way and the clouds parted. The sun rose from behind the hills to the south and lit the long road that wound its way across the country. Each beast settled into its canter. The carriage trundled on and on. The hounds barked and gave chase.

Beadle peeked from beneath the oilskin where he had slept. From his pocket he took a boiled egg and cracked the shell. Breaking it in half, he shared it with Raphah as they sat upon the high bench and look towards the forthcoming hills that loomed in the distance.

In the midmorning they stopped at an inn and changed the horses. Raphah watched Barghast and Mister Ergott in deep conversation by an old yew tree. Bragg had stamped and complained as Shrume strutted up and down looking for fungi amongst the blades of sheep grass. For the rest of the day they travelled. Mile faded into mile, each one dull and giving nothing to the memory. By late afternoon the hills to the south loomed above them. With each passing hour they appeared to get no closer, but grew even higher.

'Are we nearly there yet?' Beadle shouted to the driver.

'Three hours to Peveril,' he shouted above the rattle of the carriage. 'Two before we get to . . .' The driver stopped as if he didn't want to say the name of the place. The bugler elbowed him in the ribs and nodded his head to tell him to say no more.

'To where?' Beadle pressed.

'To a place where we might need this,' the bugler said, pulling the butt of a blunderbuss from its long leather sleeve and showing it to Beadle and Raphah. 'The Galilee Rocks. Not a place to be as darkness falls. Full of lepers and madmen. They'll attack the coach given half the chance.'

'What about the Militia – won't they protect us?' asked Raphah.

The bugler laughed. 'The Militia are more frightened than we are – see the madman and you'll know why.'

'See him?' asked the driver without turning his face from the road. 'You'll hear him from three miles. Screams like a dying dog. Why do you think we run with hounds? Only thing that'll keep him away.'

'But he's never stopped you?' asked Beadle as he pulled the oilskin about him.

The driver laughed warily. 'Some have gone to Galilee Rocks and never come back.'

'Can't you rush the horses through and out the other side?' Raphah asked.

'Only if you could fly. Imagine a hill that stands before the entrance of a deep valley. There you'll find Galilee Rocks. The road takes you to Peveril but it twists down the side so steep that the brakes will hardly keep the carriage from rolling on. It's as if a knife has cut the hill in two and sliced out the rock. Trouble is, we have to stop the carriage and all walk down the rise as we hand-brake the wheels. Far too dangerous to drive down with passengers. Too steep. That's where we'll take our chances.' The driver tapped the large wooden hand-brake on his left.

'And the madman?' Beadle enquired nervously.

'Will be somewhere waiting for us. Thinks he owns the place and doesn't like visitors. Would take an extra day if we went by Casterton. So we face the madman and hope for the best.' He laughed.

Beadle watched the sun as it tarried towards the west. He tried to count the hours as he watched the horizon. Raphah seemed unconcerned and slept quietly on, wrapped in his blanket.

The two hours passed slowly. In the journey they had

stopped only once. Beadle was cramped and stiff. His muscles ached and he wished he were in a warm bed having drunk three quarts of beer. He held the thought in his mind and tried to remember what it felt like to be drunk, but the cold wind took whatever warmth he got from his remembering.

There was no conversation from the carriage for Beadle to be distracted by. All he could hear were his own anxious thoughts as they raced through his mind. If he closed his eyes he could see the face of Demurral peering at him in the darkness. The wind that blew from the hills seemed to whisper to him to return, to go back and face his master.

Within the mile the carriage began to slow. About them the coach hounds grew anxious and grumbled to each other in low growls. The road twisted up the side of the hill. Far in the distance, Beadle could see Galilee Rocks for the first time. Strewn across the horizon were mounds of outcropped limestone. They had fallen year on year and littered the way with vast upturned boulders that gnarled from the earth like dragon's teeth. In amongst the stones grazed a herd of thin pigs. They squealed upon the approach of the hounds and disappeared amongst the wizened trees that could barely grow from the ground in the face of the wind that sought to uproot them.

Raphah woke from his slumbering to the sound of Bragg shouting in discontent. 'What a man thinks in his heart, so is he,' Raphah said as the moaning from the carriage went on.

'I'm frightened,' whispered Beadle as he shuffled closer to his friend. 'What will become of us?'

'They're pigs, Beadle, not monsters from hell,' Raphah joked.

'What of the madman? We have to get from the carriage and walk. What if he attacks?' he asked, his voice quaking with fear.

'Then the bugler will use the blunderbuss and the hounds will see him off. Fear not,' Raphah said.

'But we are on the outside,' he protested.

'So will Barghast and the others be – we will walk together.'

The carriage slowed to a crawl as the sun set and the shadows grew longer and darker. The wind worked through the spindle rocks and moaned and called across the moor. It wailed like a woman giving birth as it called to the night. The evening was lit by a burning red that edged the rushing clouds with a scarlet hem. The horses' pace slowed even further as they pulled the carriage higher towards the peak.

Beadle could see the road vanishing into the gloom. The glow of the carriage lamp lit the thick strands of spartina grass that grew in coarse lumps from the bog at the roadside. Tufts, like the spikes of a strange creature, shadowed themselves in dark patches across the moor, warning the traveller of the mire beneath.

Then it came – first as a distant sound like the call of a buzzard, then again like the screaming of a child. The bugler slipped the blunderbuss from its case and rested it across his knees as the horses twitched and danced nervously. They clattered their hooves upon the metalled toll road as they passed another milestone.

'Peveril within the hour,' said the driver hopefully.

'When do we walk?' Beadle asked as the wailing came again from the high tor.

'As soon as we've gone through Galilee Rocks,' the bugler, pulling the hammer upon the gun.

'Why Galilee?' Raphah asked as he pushed the oilskin from his knees and looked towards the craggy outcrop that appeared from the gloom.

'In the morrow you'll see the lake. A man once said it was like the Holy Land. Built his house up there. Nothing but ruins now. Crusader, they said he was. A knight of knights. Carsington's his name. He brought the sickness. Every generation a

Carsington goes mad and ends up living in these rocks. As soon as he has a son it strikes him down. It's been amongst the people here ever since. The last one was the keeper of the coaching inn.'

'Cursed as a misguided fool,' Raphah muttered quietly to himself. 'A war for God and the murder of innocents.'

'Does no one seek to help him?' Beadle asked as the coach reached the top of the road.

'It carries on from generation to generation,' the bugler said. 'Every descendant of the man has one of his kin to take his place. The madness strikes within the hour. One moment they are about their business, the next they are ranting and eating grass. They leave Peveril and come and live amongst the rocks. They can look upon their town but never return.'

'Enough of your legends,' said the driver as he pushed the braking handle. 'Time to walk.'

Beadle looked nervously at Raphah. The sound of screeching and clattering of iron fetters came again from beyond the marsh grass. 'He's out there – the madman.'

'And that's all he is, nothing more,' Raphah said as they stepped to the road.

'If only it were true, my friend,' said the bugler as he gathered the hounds about him, feeding them with dried meat. 'If he were just a madman then we wouldn't need the hounds. Some say the madness makes him change into a beast. Saw him once upon the rocks and it was no man that I saw.'

It was then that the screams came again. They echoed from all around as if a legion of creatures joined in the baiting of the travellers.

# The Salamander Inn

JACOB Crane dragged Pallium from the house. His friend was desperately trying to hold on to the doorknocker as if he were a rogue seeking sanctuary. Kate and Thomas stood and watched as Pallium wrestled with the doorknocker. He double-locked the door and wrapped the keys in his hankersniff, muttering all the while that he would be robbed and laid bare of all he had.

'It must be locked and bolted,' Pallium protested as he was pulled from his feet towards the Salamander Inn. 'Who knows what would happen if I were to leave it open?'

'It would be still here when you got back,' Crane said. He thought that his friend looked like a starved chicken and that under his drooping clothes was a bag of bones. 'This is the first time in the year you have left the place and it shall not be your last. You need to eat and eat you will.'

'I need to eat,' said Thomas. 'Beef, bread and gravy.'

Crane pulled Pallium across the muddy street to a patch of cobbles that stood like a dry and deserted island in the froth of the sewer. He protested loudly that a venture into the street would dirty his shoes and that they were not to be sullied. He jumped from toe to toe as he tried to keep his precious shoes from the mud.

Thomas tried to hold back his laughter as Crane lifted Mister Pallium from the cobbles and carried his meagre frame along the street, tucking him neatly under his arm like a roll of French carpet. With every step Pallium would kick and protest and shout so loudly that his words echoed far into the distance.

There was no one to hear. All was as night. The street was empty. The clock of a far church chimed the hour. In Salamander Street the only light to penetrate the darkness was that of the tallow lamps that hung next to each door. They burnt brightly, each freshly trimmed by an unseen hand. It was as if the place were the seat of some vast cavern and they were setting out to explore its depths.

As they journeyed on, Salamander Street began to change. Although darker by the yard it grew cleaner and more polished. The closer they got to the inn the more respectable the road became. Walls were newly painted, timbers oiled and doors garlanded with wreaths of holly and mistletoe. The sound of music came from behind several of the doors. High above, the roofs of the tall houses met to form a continuous arch that blocked out the sky. From each window, lamps like tiny stars flickered and lit the street below.

Still there was no one to be seen. Ahead, the door of the Salamander Inn stood open. From inside came chattering, it was as if the night had come for some great event to be celebrated.

'Do they spend all their time drunk?' Crane asked as he carried his friend along the street.

As they walked on, Kate could only think of what she wanted to eat. She was sure that she could smell the faint aroma of milk pudding, melted cheese and roast apple. It hung about her like a garland and rumbled her guts with longing.

Pallium did not reply. He moaned as with one leg he tried to hang on to his captor and keep himself from falling.

'You're a *Mackem*, Jacob Crane, and may you be eaten by magpies . . . '

'As long as they serve me with breakfast I shall not complain,' Crane said as he dumped Pallium on his feet upon the brushed cobbles.

'Is it safe?' Kate asked as if she sensed something sinister. 'Won't we be asked who we are?' The image of the ghost stuck in her mind, bold as the portrait and haunting as the apparition.

'Tell 'em nowt,' Crane said as he brushed the dust from his coat. 'Let me speak – *if* there is any speaking to be done. We shall eat, drink and then carry Mister Pallium back to his abode so he doesn't dirty his prize shoes. Tonight will be a good time to decide how to get the *Magenta* back and find the crew. But first, breakfast.'

'And you're paying?' Thomas asked.

'Payment for your sailing, boy. Your life belongs to me,' Crane replied with a smile and a wink, the light from the door reflecting from his face. 'Onward – the Salamander awaits. I shall have two herrings and a boiled egg.'

Kate stumbled into the bar of the Salamander Inn. She shielded her eyes from the glare of the lamps that lit every corner and dark place. Blinking several times, her eyes slowly became accustomed to the light and she saw what was before her. The inn was a place of warmth and light. Music played loudly, people sang and danced on the polished wooden floors, and like the rest of the street the inn was incredibly clean, with not a speck of dirt to be seen. It was packed with tables and at each sat four or five people. She was aware of Crane, Pallium and Thomas following on, but her mind was taken up by something more incredible. For the first time that she could ever remember Kate suddenly felt totally happy. It was as if every care in her life had gone, forgotten in the bewitchment of the Salamander Inn.

A gigantic fireplace warmed the room and everywhere she looked there were happy, shining faces. People of all sizes and ages talked merrily. She could not make out what they said, all was babble, but that did not matter. This was not the discord of the gin-house but the open conversation of friendliness. It was not like the dirty drinking houses that lined the quayside at Whitby. No one seemed to notice them as they stumbled in. All appeared lost in the chatter with their companions. The hosteller looked over the crowded, noisy room and gave his welcome, nodding his whiskered face to four seats in the corner by the fire.

Kate looked upon the walls that glimmered with gold and silver paint all edged in bright blue. The wooden floors were polished, scrubbed and dowsed in sawdust that smelt strangely of lavender.

Pallium led them on, shrugging his shoulders as he looked back to the door. 'Shouldn't be here,' he mumbled to himself. 'Should be at home with the money.'

'Nonsense,' came a loud voice from a table by the lighted window. 'This is the place you should be, Mister Pallium. See, I have saved you a table and a seat for each of your guests.'

Mister Pallium suddenly changed. He quickly stood upright and puffed out what chest he had left. His hand speedily smoothed his hair and rubbed his cheeks, and then spinning on his fine shoes he turned in the direction of the voice. 'MISTER GALPHUS!' he exclaimed as he threw open his arms as if to welcome a long-lost friend. 'It is you . . .'

'Of course, dear Pallium, it is me . . . What a pleasure to see you again.' The man stopped speaking for a moment and stared at Jacob Crane and then at Thomas.

'Jacob, Kate, Thomas, come and be seated and we shall drink together,' Galphus said. He raised his hand to signal to the hosteller, who immediately arrived at the table, followed in turn by two servants who carried large trays with silver warming tops.

Kate looked at Galphus sitting serenely in a high-backed oak chair by the window. He wore a small green felt cap upon a bed of neatly cropped hair. Galphus wore the suit of a trader with a thick green tweed coat that came to his knees. At the elbows and the cuffs it was sewn with leather patches.

It was then that she saw his hands. Upon each he had five fingers and a long thumb. *Boggle*, she thought quickly to herself, hoping that Thomas would see it too – She remembered Rueben Wayfoot at Boggle Mill and the morning they had taken breakfast together. He had the same hands, and in so many ways looked just like Galphus it was as if they could be brothers.

'Kate,' Galphus said softly as he noticed her staring at his extra fingers. 'A quirk of nature and a cruel joke upon me,' he mocked, changing his face to a sad expression. 'Tell me – what brings you to Salamander Street?'

'Our mutual friend, Mister Pallium,' Crane interrupted. 'I have known him a while and he said that should I be in London then I was to call.' He looked at Galphus. 'Then again, from what he has said to us, you already knew we were on our way.'

'Another cruel joke of a cruel creator,' Galphus laughed. 'I have been dogged with seeing what is to come. I dream. Practically live in the sleeping world, and whilst there I experience what is to come. That, and a device which helps me to focus my dreams so that everyone I choose can see them also.'

'How can you do that?' Kate asked, forgetting that Crane had told them to be silent.

'Kate, it is a great mystery. Mankind can travel to the farthest out places of the world and discover whole continents. Yet within us all there is a galaxy just waiting to be explored. It is an inner universe. But I feel as if it is not just within but without.' He looked at the food that had been placed upon the table under the silver warmers. 'If I am correct in my assumptions then what is on each of your plates is what you all really desire to eat at this very moment.'

'Then you would not be a man to gamble with,' Crane said as he lifted the silver lid from his dish. There on a white china plate were two perfect fried herring. By the side of each had been placed a fresh, soft boiled egg that had been meticulously peeled.

Kate gasped as she lifted the lid upon her breakfast. There was a bowl of steaming milk, curdling cheese and roast apple. The smell of nutmeg swelled from within and brought to her the memory of her mother and the coming of Christmas.

Thomas laughed as the eyes of the gathering fell upon him. There was great expectation, as if he were the last piece of a puzzle about to be placed. 'You could never guess what I desire,' Thomas said as he slowly lifted the lid, his eyes widening in disbelief.

'Beef slices upon crusted bread and smothered in gravy?' Galphus asked.

''Tis true,' Thomas replied as he cut the meat with his knife and then ate it with dramatic celerity.

'Very good, dear Galphus,' Crane said, looking at Pallium as if he had somehow informed upon them. 'Not only did you herald our arrival but you know what we would eat. Is there any point in conversation? For you will know what we are to say before the words appear upon our lips.'

'Party tricks, Jacob, party tricks. I know nothing of your thoughts and am but shown portions of the future. I dreamt of the ship coming and of your food. What good is that in telling the future? That in itself will not change the course of history.'

'No food for you, Pallium,' Crane said. 'Galphus must know you have lost your appetite.'

'But I do know where the *Magenta* is berthed,' Galphus said quietly.

'By another dream?' Crane asked.

'By street gossips,' Galphus replied. 'It will be taken to Dog Island, the rigging chained and a charge of gunpowder placed in its belly. It is the news of London. A plague ship full of rats – that's what they say. It is also said that two children were stolen from their master in Whitby.' Galphus spoke quickly. He looked directly at Crane. 'If you were to be caught they would hang you for kidnap, Captain Jacob Crane. Think on that as you swallow your herring.'

'Then you'll turn us in?' Crane asked.

'Luckily for you it was made very clear in my dream that you were to be protected at all costs. Whatever you are running from is coming to find you. At least in Salamander Street you will be safe.'

'Even with a price on our heads?' Thomas said.

'There would not be enough money in the world to make me give you up.' He spoke quietly, his words stern. 'This is not by chance that you are here, not by chance.' Galphus smiled as he picked a fishbone from Crane's plate and began to clean his teeth. 'I would betray a friendship. Someone whom you have met. I too have the acquaintance of Abram Rickards. I believe he was known to you in Whitby and helped in your escape.'

'You're well connected, Galphus. News travels fast,' Crane said. He rubbed the fish oil from his chin with the back of his hand. Kate and Thomas could not contain their exhilaration.

'Have you heard from Abram?' Kate whispered as the raucousness went on around.

'Not in a long while. I hear he is in London. He was seen some nights ago by London Bridge just before the sky-quake.'

Galphus became sullen and drew them close as he leaned towards them and hushed his voice. 'I have known him many, many years and I know he will be very surprised to see me again.'

'So, Galphus,' Crane said. 'You say we are safe. I say I'll wake up and find a Militia man standing at the end of my bed if I stay here.'

'Still don't trust me?' he replied. 'Look about you, Jacob. Everyone here is just like you. They have run from their past, left families and fortunes so they can be free. Yet to a man they all trust and believe in Mister Galphus.'

'Never trust anyone until they prove it.'

'Perhaps I can do just that,' Galphus said as he picked a long thin silver cane from the side of the chair and twizzled it in his hands. 'I have a party trick, a way of entertaining my guests,' he said jokingly. 'Gather round and see what is to come.' With that, Galphus took the cane and held it before them all. It looked to be made of solid silver and was tipped with a round glass globe that shone milky-white.

Galphus pulled up his chair and stared into the crystal ball. He mused for a while, his thick eyebrows twitching up and down, then coughed slightly to clear his throat. He looked solemnly at each one of them before he spoke.

'Wonderful, amazing, marvellous . . .' he said as he looked into the glass and then tutted as if he saw something he had expected. Kate stared into the crystal; she saw nothing but the reflection of the fire and the many people who by now had gathered around them to see Galphus's performance.

'There is a rumour in the world of my dreaming that someone close to you will be seen again. Someone you thought to be lost and long gone – do you know of whom I speak?' Galphus asked with a dramatic smile. 'I can see him travelling, walking across the windy moors.'

Kate jolted a glance at Thomas, daring not to say the name. He stared back at her and then at Galphus, his look urging him to speak.

'I have lost many people in my time and can't recall . . .' Crane said, his face telling the children to be silent.

'You are wise not to mention his name or where he is from. But I can tell you he is alive. He searches for you with a desire that can overcome death.'

Kate felt as if she would explode if she didn't say his name. She had to know the truth from Galphus. 'Do I know the one of whom you speak?' she asked, talking as she ate.

'Not only do you know him, but you have spent much time with him. From what I can see in the crystal, he is on his way to London.' Galphus touched the tip of her nose with his finger. A spark cracked from the tip as if a minuscule bolt of lightning had jumped through the ether towards her.

'Another one of your dreams, Galphus?' Crane said as he leant forward. 'Was it picked from slumber and chewed like cud? Don't give them great expectations, Galphus. These kids are in my care and I don't take lightly to them being made fools of.'

'I tease not, Jacob. Within the crystal, news travels faster than the horse and outruns the mortal messenger. These matters are of heavenly importance. For as your friend seeks you, so does another – an adversary. I can see him in the stone; he hides his face like a spectre in the candlelight. You all know his name and it doesn't need to be repeated.' Galphus rambled as he stared at the walking stick. 'You are being hunted by your friend and news is but two days away.'

'So what is your place in all of this?' Crane asked. 'You speak as if we were brought here for this very purpose.'

'Believe me, Jacob. This is the safest place for you to be . . . for the time being. All I can say is that Salamander Street will grow upon you. It will become like a haven of rest. Wait with me three days and all will be made clear. Stay in Salamander Street and you will find your friend and you, Jacob, will be on your ship again.'

Galphus turned to Thomas and held out his hand. 'I see you're the son of a fisherman. How would you like to make shoes? I could teach you myself this very day. You could be my apprentice. Jacob and Kate can take old Mister Pallium back to count his money and you and I can make shoes. Whatever you make you can keep. How does that sound?'

Thomas nodded, his mouth filled with food. 'Can I go?' he asked Crane as he swallowed quickly.

Crane smiled and gestured for him to go. 'Go and make some sea-boots. If Galphus is right then we will soon be sailing again.'

Then Galphus got to his feet. Kate hadn't noticed before how tall the man was. As he stood, he seemed to tower above them. Crane stood with him and held out his hand.

'Come, come, Thomas,' Galphus said slowly as he made to walk to the door. Then he stopped and turned. 'I'll bring him back tonight. We can talk again, Jacob. Perhaps I can help you free your ship.'

With that Galphus stepped from the Salamander Inn and disappeared into the street with Thomas following like an obedient dog. Kate shrugged to herself, not wanting Crane to see her anger at being left behind.

'Do you believe him?' she asked Crane.

'Of course he believes him,' said the silent Mister Pallium as if suddenly stirred from a trance. 'That is Galphus you speak of. Didn't he amaze you with what he knows of your lives?' he asked querulously.

'We've seen much in the past days. Enough to last a lifetime, Pallium. It's only right she should ask,' Crane replied.

'But it's Galphus. He's a seer and knows the future. The man has the finest leather factory in London – some say he has a thousand silver guineas. Imagine all that wealth, and he ate with *us*.'

'Can't you see, he's so much like Rueben Wayfoot in every way,' Kate said, remembering the time at Boggle Mill. 'He talks the same, looks the same. It's as if Rueben were here amongst us.'

'Whoever Rueben is, he must be a fine fellow,' Pallium chuntered as he nodded his head fretfully. 'Let the man be, Jacob. By his fruit is a man known.'

'Exactly, by his fruit. I feel as if we stand on the verge of winter and there has been no harvest and a thorn tree cannot bear a fig.'

# The Rocks of Galilee

WITHIN the minute they were all on the road and walking with the carriage as it began to descend the steep and winding hill. The bugler walked ahead, his faithful hounds packed close to his feet. The hairs on their backs stood bristled and each bared its teeth and uttered a low growl. The man carried his blunderbuss at the ready as he looked about him. To the east, the sky rumbled with the approach of a storm that flashed against the dark sky.

The travellers huddled together, jostling to be inside the group, not one of them wanting to be on the outer edge. All was quiet, except for the distant rumbling of thunder and the growl of the dogs. The madman could not be heard amongst the rocks, and as they walked a sense that the danger had passed came to them.

Bragg sighed, out of breath and with a sense of relief. Behind him, Mister Shrume scurried on like a little mouse, his legs at a trot to keep pace. It was Raphah and Beadle who had been pushed to the back of the gathering. They walked on, Beadle constantly looking over his shoulder with every distant peel of thunder.

'How far do we keep this up?' puffed Bragg discontentedly. 'The hill can't go on forever and I paid to be carried, not to walk.'

'Just a mile, sir,' muttered the coachman, pulling the brake even tighter as the carriage pressed hard against the horses.

They quickly descended into what was a vast open cavern with steep sides, littered with dark, jagged boulders. Pigs grazed on the sparse grass between the rocks. They were silent, their small sharp eyes reflected in the light from the carriage lamps.

'In daylight, it is said that you can see for miles from this place,' Ergott advised the gathering as they walked. His hand gripped the wand that he kept within his coat.

'I prefer the inside of a hostelry, with a warm fire and hot food,' Bragg snapped.

'Then you better keep walking or else we shall never see such a place again,' said Barghast, his long cloak flapping like a bat's wing.

For a while the road became steeper. The horses slipped their footings and the carriage rocked back and forth. The light of the carriage gave a meagre glow that surrounded the travellers. Not one would step away from the glow of its paltry flame. Like moths they were drawn closer to it step by step, as if it would provide them with some protection. Outside the rim of its defence, the blackness was so intense that the travellers could not see a hand's breadth in front of their faces.

'We're like sheep,' Beadle said as they shuffled even closer together, as if herded by an unseen shepherd. 'Ready for slaughter.'

'The hounds say we are alone. They show no fear,' the bugler said as he cocked the blunderbuss.

'They're dogs, what do they know?' Bragg argued again.

'They can see and hear that which we cannot,' he replied. Suddenly one of his beasts began to growl.

'My guts tell me different, my guts . . .' Beadle said. His guts were rumbling and gurgling like a sewer.

'I think we are all aware of what your guts are telling us, Beadle,' Barghast said as he made a loud snort.

From the outer darkness came the babbling cry of a young child. The company gathered closer to the carriage as it squawked and squealed with every turn of its wheels. Beneath their feet, the road fell away steeply. The coachman held the brake tightly until it smoked against the rim. The cry came again, high and shrill, this time from the far side of the valley. The hounds growled and jumped about their feet. They pressed in against their human companions to form a frightened pack.

'There's someone out there,' Beadle said as they walked slowly on.

'Not for long,' said the bugler as he aimed the blunderbuss into the darkness.

The screaming came again. It echoed around the walls of the valley and upwards to the thunderous sky. A blanket of lightning flashed from horizon to horizon. In amongst the rocks the shadow of a gigantic man was silhouetted against the stones.

Quickly, without taking aim, the bugler fired his gun. The shot rang out just as the storm began to explode upon the moors. Falling to his knees, he reloaded the weapon.

The carriage horses reared up in panic. Lady Tanville screamed, and from somewhere near came a loud growl as if from a tiger. The lightning flashed again and a creature leapt from the road and disappeared into the night.

'It's taken Barghast, he's gone!' she screamed. She held his cloak in her hands. 'He was here and then the creature took him.'

'Then we are at war,' Ergott shouted as he pulled his diving wand from his jacket and held it like a short sword.

'Thought you'd have a bigger one than that,' Bragg said snidely, stepping towards the carriage light. 'Take more than a twig to frighten off the creature out there.'

'Keep your panic to yourself,' shouted the bugler. He sounded the alarm, blowing several times upon the small cow horn that he kept on a red rope around his neck. The hounds hollered with each blast, sensing that a chase was about to take place.

'The screaming came again. It pierced the air like the shrill cry of a dying lamb. As the night sky lit up with a crack of lightning, the shape of a man could be seen upon the tor. For the briefest moments he was as clearly visible as if in the brightness of day. His hair blew in the wind; a beard covered his face. He raised his hands to the sky as if he wanted to catch a lightning bolt as it crashed to earth. His arms were bare and about his shoulders was tied a tattered cloak. From each arm dangled a short, broken chain of iron fetters, manacled to his wrist.

'*Mad Cassy!*' screamed the coachman as he fought to control the horses and battle with the brake.

The bugler took aim and fired into the night. The barrel of the blunderbuss exploded with a flash of double-charge so bright that it dazed and blinded the travellers. In the darkness there was a languishing moan.

'You got him!' shouted the coachman as the hounds barked.

'And I'll have him dead,' shouted the bugler, double-charging the gun yet again.

'He's wounded,' Raphah called as the moaning turned into a scream. It was shrill and harsh and pierced them to the bone. From peak to peak it sounded like the dying of a mad dog. 'You've got to help him.'

'Kill him, lad. That's the only thing good for him,' the bugler said as he rallied the hounds to set off on the chase.

'But what of the creature that has taken Barghast?' Ergott asked.

'Your duty is to protect *us*!' screamed Bragg as he desperately tried to mount the carriage and hide within.

'Can't let a chance like this go by,' the bugler replied. 'Could be my making.'

'Could be your death. What if the madman takes you like he has taken Barghast?' Ergott asked. He waved his wand frantically in the shape of a star and muttered under his breath.

'Then it'll get some lead as well,' the bugler said excitedly as he stepped from the toll road and began to make his way slowly upwards through the steep rocks.

'We can't let him kill the man,' Raphah said quietly to Beadle.

'Oh yes we can,' Beadle replied, burying his face in his hands. 'The man's got a gun and can do what he likes.'

'Then I'll go with him,' Raphah said, breaking rank from the gathering and jumping from the road. He ran through the stones and into the darkness. In the blink of an eye he was gone from sight as if he had entered death.

Beadle ran up and down the road shouting for Raphah to return as the carriage was pulled to a halt. Bragg screamed in protest from inside the coach. He locked the doors and slid the window shut, leaving the rest of the travellers to await the approaching storm.

Mister Shrume, fearful of the night, took up a place under the coach. Holding the axle in both hands he hung on from beneath, so that he could not be seen by whatever had taken Barghast.

Ergott had rooted himself to the ground and mumbled a malediction time and again. He clutched his wand with both hands and stared into the darkness that surrounded them. The tallow lamp that hung from the outside of the coach began to fade. Slowly its light became softer and reached out less and less to banish the night.

'Let us in!' screamed Lady Tanville, banging on the carriage door. Reluctantly, Bragg slipped the lock and edged it open to allow her to enter. The travellers ushered each other inside as Shrume appeared from his hiding place, quivering with fear. Beadle took hold of the handle and stepped upon the mounting plate. The door was pulled tightly shut and locked before him.

'You paid for the roof,' Bragg said. 'And the roof it'll be.'

There came a shuddering howl from the ridge above them as if one of the coach hounds was being torn to pieces in the darkness. Beadle jumped quickly from the road and pulled himself to the driver's seat.

'Take this, use it if you must,' the driver said, handing Beadle a small flintlock pistol. 'It's not right here, they should never have gone.'

On the far side of the valley, they could hear the hounds making their way up through the rocks. With every flash of the storm they could see the bugler followed by Raphah, clawing their way higher. The hounds bounded on in the brief but blinding flashes and then were gone as ink-black covered their tracks.

'What took Barghast?' Beadle asked the coachman anxiously as he pointed the pistol into the blackness.

'Hate this place, hate it. Knew we should have gone faster and made it in daylight.' The coachman nodded his head and steadied the horses. 'There's talk of a hound, a hellhound. Comes from the fell and uses a storm to take its victims. They say that the madman feeds the beast and in return it keeps him safe. The Ethio is a brave fool.'

'Do we stay?' Beadle asked.

The driver stared him in the face and wiped the sweat from his brow. 'I'll be gone before they come back. Peveril in the mile. I'll run this coach down the hill and take my chance.'

'Give them time,' Beadle insisted.

The howling came again, this time closer. It sounded like the call of a wolf and the growling of an old bear that had somehow come together to make a cry so terrible that it shuddered the bones. The horses jerked upon their hooves and danced upon the road as if it were hot coals. They steamed and groaned, panting short breaths and eager to run.

'I can't hold them much longer,' the driver said, gripping the reins tightly in his gloved hand. 'There's something that they can see and we can't. If it comes closer they shall be from this place like the devil were chasing them.'

'Just a time longer,' Beadle pleaded.

'Go on man, go on – think of your passengers,' screamed Bragg from within.

'You can't leave them,' shouted Lady Tanville. She tried to open the door, only to be pushed back by Mister Shrume, who now quivered violently as if he would fall apart at that very moment.

There was a crash of glass from the far side of the coach as something smashed the window. The carriage swung to the side as if the weight of a beast fell upon it.

For a moment, in the flash of lightning, Beadle thought he saw a beast. Full of fear and trembling, he tried to aim the pistol. He closed his eyes as he squeezed the stiff trigger. The hammer fell suddenly and the plate ignited. But there was silence. 'No!' he screamed as he realised that it had no charge.

'Not loaded?' shouted the driver . 'I never thought . . .'

The coach rolled like a bobbing ship and Mister Shrume screamed like an old hag. And then the lead stallion bolted, its black mane streaming like silk fingers as it took off from the road. The other horses gave chase and the carriage was dragged at speed down the hill. The driver held them fast with one hand as with the other he pulled the screaming brake. But the carriage got faster and faster, the wheels clattering ever quicker.

Beadle gripped the iron rail that ran the width of the carriage seat as he was pounded up and down. Inside, Ergott, and Shrume were buffeted from their seats and heaped upon the unconscious Bragg. Lady Tanville held tightly to the fading lamp, her hands burning upon the metal.

From the darkness the roar of the beast came again as if it gave chase. The horses were spurred faster, not caring that they raced to death.

'I can't hold it!' screamed the driver as the reins began to slip from his gloves.

Lightning flashed again. For a moment Beadle could see the road ahead. It twisted and turned, flattening out as they approached Peveril. At the turn in the road he saw a vast expanse of water.

'Galilee!' shouted the driver as he battled to pull the sweat-lathered horses to a halt. 'We'll never make the corner.'

Beadle let go of the rail and grabbed the driver's hand. With all the strength he could summon he took hold of the reins and began to pull.

'By Riathamus, we will not die!' he screamed at the night. Cries of terror from the carriage were all he could hear. The carriage rolled on, out of control. Beadle feared he would soon be dead, tossed from the coach and down the rock-strewn valley. He gripped the reins for all his life, desperately trying to pull the horses back. A shard of bright blue lightning hit the lake and appeared to jump from the water, hitting the clouds and then in the blink of an eye firing to earth. The explosion was so intense, so loud and powerful that the sound knocked the wind from Beadle's chest. It was like the final note to some great concerto. All fell silent. The storm was over.

Beadle gripped the horses' reins with both hands, knowing his life depended on it. They began to slow. Yard by yard, step by step, their pace changed from a mad gallop to a canter and then to a trot. He pulled harder, unable to speak a word, his mouth clamped with fear. The driver leant upon the brake, holding it fast as the leather and wood braced the wheels and squealed.

Far ahead Beadle could see the lights of Peveril and the mouth of the cavern in which it was built. Upon the hill was the dark outline of a large castle. Scattered all around were the smoking chimneys of the houses. To the west was the vast entrance to a large cave.

'You did it,' said the driver, panting hard and drawing his tight breath. Beadle turned his head and looked away. 'I'd lost my strength couldn't find it in me to hold on – but you did it.'

'I fear it was not I but the lightning that saved us,' Beadle said, his teeth still chattering with fear. 'What of the bugler and Raphah?'

'Pray they are not lost to the madman,' the driver said.

The lights of Peveril beckoned them onwards.

# The Mender of Bad Soles

GALPHUS walked nimbly along Salamander Street and then, without saying a word, turned into a long, narrow alleyway. Thomas followed, wondering what awaited him. The alleyway was darker than the street, with only a feeble lamp at the far end that gave a sombre glow. There was no light from the sky. It was as if the whole of the district had been placed under a pudding bowl and the world that Thomas knew was no more. The further that he walked from the Salamander Inn, the dirtier the streets became, and here was no exception. With every step, the alley began to fill with the flotsam of London life; at every doorway some unfortunate huddled silently in the gloom, holding out a hand for an offering of grace.

Galphus strode on, oblivious to all around him. He never stopped or looked back to see if he was being followed. Pace after pace, he prodded his cane sharply to the ground. Step after step he walked boldly through the dark. They followed the alley until it turned into another and then another. Left and right, faster and faster Thomas followed until they walked through what was nothing more than a crack between the buildings. He knew not if he travelled north or south or how far they had come as their route twisted back and forth through dank, mouldy alleyways that stank of the sea.

'Mister . . . Mister Galphus,' Thomas said as he attempted to catch the man, nearly breaking into a trot to keep pace with his steps. 'Where do we go?'

'Onwards, ever onwards. Questions, always questions,' Galphus barked with a swagger and a clatter of his cane as his coat appeared to sparkle in the lamplight..

'Mister Galphus,' Thomas belched breathlessly. 'How far do we go? We have walked for miles.'

Galphus stopped suddenly. He turned and looked at the boy. 'So, Thomas, you think you know we are far from Salamander Street?'

'We have been walking for the hour. I came to make shoes, not wear them out.'

'Shoes? Did I say you would make shoes? Then we must go back to Salamander Street at once.' Galphus made a small side-step and vanished from view. 'This way,' he said curtly, his voice echoing from the darkness.

Thomas realised that Galphus had slipped into yet another part of the labyrinth that he was being dragged through. Quite lost, he dutifully followed, trying to catch up with Galphus. The man strode on at the speed of a horse. Thomas ran to catch up before he completely lost Galphus from view.

Soon they came to a place where there were no street lamps. Thomas felt his way forward by holding out his hands to both sides of the passageway and touching the cold stones. He could hear the clatter of the cane and the sharp tap of Galphus's shoes a little distance ahead. The passage made a sudden turn and opened out into a neat and well-lit yard.

Galphus stopped in the light of two wall lamps that stood like sentinels by a large green wooden door. It had an ornate handle and a knocking plate moulded in the shape of a lion's head. Above the door was a large carved shoe. It was painted in what had once been bright red, but years had taken away its shine and glory. Now it hung there, waiting. Thomas could see no other way from the place. Only the route they had followed had brought them to the door and he wondered how this place could be chanced upon or how it could bring any trade.

With his left hand, Galphus raised his cane and struck the door three times. He turned to Thomas and tried to smile. 'We are not but a minute from where we started, Thomas. This is the Salamander Factory,' he said proudly, nodding with contentment and rubbing his angular chin.

'Factory?' Thomas asked, unsure what he meant.

'A place of business, a building containing equipment for manufacture. Have you never been to a factory?' he asked. Thomas looked even more puzzled. 'Then you shall have a great delight. I see factories as the palaces of the future. The people shall live at the place they work. Their beds can be next to their anvils. Gone the squalor and the roughness of life. This is fair trade. Mankind shall do what it was meant for – work and sleep, Thomas. Work and sleep.'

Galphus puckered his lips to kiss the air. The door to the factory opened and he stepped inside.

Thomas followed, not knowing what would be in this factory. He turned to see who had let them in and there in the shadow of the door was a young child barely five years old. He did not know if it was a boy or a girl. It wore a regimental suit of grey wool with a jacket of the same cloth over a clean white shirt. The child had short-cropped hair and upon its head a neat round skullcap that gripped tightly to its forehead.

Thomas smiled at the child, who neither spoke nor acknowledged that he was there. Galphus pressed on, not speaking to anyone as he entered a busy hallway with a spiral staircase of rough wood that spun upwards out of sight. On every side of the hallway, people all wearing the same clothes busied themselves. From every corner came the sound of hammering and industry. An overpowering smell of tanning leather burnt Thomas's nose and caused him to cough with the fumes. Galphus led him onwards through rooms and passageways that seemed to go on forever. The factory was brightly lit. No one looked at him nor spoke to him or Galphus, all went about their business as if they couldn't see him. They carried boxes from one place to the other, climbed the stairs to the rooms above and descended to the depths through a door in the far wall.

It was as if Thomas had stepped into a gigantic anthill where a multitude of similar creatures carried out tasks without being asked. All just knew what they had to do and how to do it.

'This way,' Galphus said, leading Thomas up the staircase to a higher floor. Thomas followed on and undid the collar of his shirt. 'There is much to see and you cannot become a shoemaker until I have shown you everything. I take it that is why you have come to Salamander Street?'

Thomas didn't know what Galphus really meant. He remembered Crane commanding them to say nothing, so he just said *yes* – but quietly, in a whisper, hoping it would not be heard. It was easy to say and fell from his lips without any concern.

'Sorry?' asked Galphus.

'Yes,' Thomas said again.

'Then before we go another step let us sign the contract of employment.' Galphus laughed and then, as if he were a fairground magician, a quill pen and piece of parchment appeared in his hand. 'Here. This is for you. A job for life and your life for the job. All will be found and you will be found wanting . . . nothing. I even have something that will make you smile with merriment. Sign and we will be friends and the teaching will begin.'

'But . . .'

'There are no *buts* in life, Thomas. Do you think I would have got to my station in life if I had said *but* all the time? Seize the moment and every opportunity that comes your way. Say a brilliant *yes* to everything and the world will open like a clamshell, nay, an oyster, and there inside you will find the most precious thing of all. The pearl. Sign. Quickly.'

Galphus thrust the pen into his hand as they stood upon the landing in front of another large door. Thomas felt a compulsion to run as an inner voice screamed to him. But Galphus grabbed his hand and in the flick of the wrist, Thomas saw his name scrawled in black upon the paper. He read his name clearly printed upon the contract and then fine large letters that he could easily see. As he read on they grew smaller and smaller, until by halfway down the page they were like tiny dots that looked as though they moved across the parchment of their own volition.

'DONE!' Galphus shouted as the door in front of them opened. 'See, Thomas. When you say *yes* to something doors will open.'

'I would like to go back and see Captain Crane,' Thomas demanded. He had suddenly realised that what he had put his name to was an indenture of employment. 'He will want to know where I am if I do not return. This is *not* why I am here. I came for a day, not a lifetime.'

'Thomas, Thomas, Thomas – ever doubtful and kept in the dark.' Galphus stooped to him and took a hankersniff from his pocket and put it into Thomas's hand. 'I am sorry, lad. I now realise he didn't tell you. I knew you were coming because Crane told me. He sent word days ago before he left Whitby. Crane said he would bring two young people who were without work or family. I paid him his usual fee as agreed and met him in the Salamander Inn as requested. We couldn't say so at the inn, but our meeting was arranged. All has been pretence – Crane could neither care for you nor help you in your future. You are every bit the young man he said you would be. You will be happier here than in Whitby and safe from Obadiah Demurral.'

'Demurral? How did you know?' Thomas asked.

'My old friend, Jacob Crane. He told me everything, everything. Don't worry; Kate will be here within the day. Couldn't have you both coming here at once.'

'Crane would never do this to us, he would have said. He never mentioned a factory or work. Told us we would have a new life with him, that he'd look after us,' Thomas protested as he looked about for a means of escape. He felt hoodwinked and betrayed, and for a moment he believed Crane to be a liar.

'And that he has. Crane has looked after you in the best way he could by bringing you here. I in turn will keep my bargain and give you an apprenticeship. From now until you are twenty-one I will encourage you as a craftsman and then on that day you will be free to leave and set up for yourself.'

Thomas felt uncomfortably numb, lifeless and without feeling. He could hardly take a breath for the panic that filled his chest. Something stuck in his throat and twisted his neck. He wanted to run, to jump the staircase and fly away. He tried to recall the twists and turns that had brought them there. In his mind he went over and over the maze through which they had travelled. Somehow it had all been a misunderstanding. 'I can't stay that long – I'll be old,' Thomas said, his mind spinning with what was happening to his life.

'Old, but wise,' Galphus said as he took him by the arm and led him onwards.

They stood on a large gantry overlooking a vast factory floor. Each anvil was the same. By each one stood a worker dressed in grey with a white shirt. As if keeping time they all hammered the leather and smoothed it flat. On the far side, lit by strong lamplight, were row upon row of sewing lads who needled the threads through the leather to form the shoes. They moved as in a dance, the thread slipped through with a twist of the elbow and wrist and back again and again.

'Look, Thomas. This is the future. One day the entire world shall be like this. Gone the squalor and the hunger. A worker is worth his keep and while he shall work he shall live.' Galphus pulled a fine timepiece from his pocket and looked upon it. 'Did you know that a lad of your age need only work for ten hours a day to be profitable? Think of it, Thomas. That gives you fourteen hours of your own time.'

'Then I can see Crane, once I have worked?' he asked.

'Crane has gone by now. I paid him the money he needed for his ship and now he is gone. Kate will stay the night with Mister Pallium and then she too will come and be *indentured*. I will find you rooms nearby and you can share a fireplace and a hearth.'

'Tomorrow?' Thomas asked, as what Galphus had said began to take hold.

'And you will stay?' Galphus asked, placing a warm hand on his shoulder. 'And not try to run away?'

Thomas nodded in a daze as he stared at the factory and the hundred people in neat rows all hammering in time and sewing frantically. Not knowing what had happened, unsure if he were in a dream, he tried to gather his thoughts. It all began to take shape. Crane had been so adamant to come to this place, Thomas thought. Of all the inns and lodging houses in London, Crane had brought them to Salamander Street and had given him to Galphus.

'How much did you pay him?' Thomas asked, his mind twisting in sudden anger towards Crane.

'Not as much as you are really worth as an apprentice. I know

134

someone who would give far more for you than I ever would,' Galphus replied sweetly. 'Then again, I shall have each day's work from you. And Thomas, with my help, all this could one day be yours. I have been looking for an heir. Marriage is beyond me and I would like to hand all this to someone I can trust. Could you be that man, I ask myself?'

Thomas didn't reply. He still couldn't think; his wits were screaming to him whilst he tried to control his body and not let it shake. All around, the sound of hammering went on and on relentlessly. No one spoke; eyes were kept to the floor as the workers went by each other.

'I will take you to your room. Every new boy has a companion who will teach you all that you need to know. Remember, Thomas, I am always here. Look upon me as a . . . father.'

Galphus lead Thomas down the stairs and across the factory floor. He could see that here all the workers were about his age. None of them looked at him, spoke or even smiled. All of their concentration appeared to be upon the anvils and the leather that they pounded and softened with what looked like felt hammers.

Together they crossed the room. Galphus marched at his usual pace, pounding his cane to the time of the hammers. It was as if they were inside some gigantic clock and the hammering was the signal for time to move on another second. Eventually they left the factory floor and stood in the entrance to a large room with rows of neat, clean beds. Each bed had a small locker by its side with a new candle in a pot-holder. At the far end a lad swept the floor with a brush that rasped against the wood with its thick bristles.

The lad turned, put down the brush and stood to attention. Thomas could see his face. At best he looked as if he were a pugilist, at worst a murderer. The lad appeared to be the same age as Thomas but was of an incredible size. His face was that of a beaten stick, battered with a broken nose that made him look like a pug-dog. The lad looked to the floor as Galphus approached and said nothing.

'Aha!' Galphus said brightly as if he had seen the lad for the first time. 'Thomas, meet Smothergig.' The lad nodded as Galphus spoke again. 'We only know his last name. Tattooed upon his back by a *caring* blood relation. I think his friends call him Smutt . . . Doesn't speak much, but sweeps well. He'll be your companion.'

Smutt nodded again and looked Thomas straight in the eye. His own were dark and edged with black. Smutt looked mean and cold, with not a glimmer of warmth in his heart. Galphus looked at them both, slapping them on their shoulders. He turned to Thomas, took the contract of indenture and tore it in two. 'This is for you. I will keep my half until you are twenty-one. Then you will be free to do as you wish. Smutt – Thomas is in your care, do well for him and you will do well for me.' He spoke the last words very slowly as he stared at the lad. Smutt nodded, picked up the brush and continued to sweep, saying nothing to Thomas.

'And I stay here?' Thomas asked Galphus as he began to walk off the way he came.

'No, Smutt will take you to your room and you will be given all you need. It should be there, waiting for you.' With those last words Galphus walked away. He whistled as he went, tapping his cane against the floor merrily.

Once he was out of sight, Smutt put down the brush and looked at Thomas. He stared him eye to eye then began to take off his grey jacket and roll up the sleeves of his shirt. The boy made a fist of his hand and pushed it slowly to Thomas's face.

Thomas could see the broken knuckles and scars upon the skin. Smutt said nothing and nodded his head slowly as if to invite Thomas to do the same.

136

'I'll not fight you, Smutt,' Thomas said as he stepped back. 'Solves nothing. I would be your friend.'

'What do you need friends for?' Smutt asked through clenched teeth. 'These is me friends,' he said, holding up both his fists and jabbing the air. 'So do you fight or do you give in to me?' Smutt growled.

'Neither,' Thomas said as he walked away and looked about the room as if he didn't care.

'Brave talk or just a fool?' the boy asked.

'I want no fighting. I just want to go from this place to my friends,' he said.

'I can make that happen,' said Smutt. 'Step onto the punch and you'll see more than your friends.'

'Don't make me fight you,' Thomas said. 'I've had enough fighting to last me all the days of my life.'

'Then you'll have one more,' Smutt screamed as he lashed out at Thomas, missing him by a hair's breadth. The lad danced from toe to toe, jabbing the air and snorting like a bull. Thomas looked at the dance and slowly put his hand behind his back.

Smutt jabbed again and Thomas moved his head to the side. The blow glanced against his cheek and snapped in the air like a thunderclap.

'I don't want to fight,' Thomas said.

'Then I'll knock you to the floor and prove to them all I'm still the lord of this place. I fight everyone who comes here. It's the only way.'

'It doesn't have to be like this,' Thomas said.

'This is my way, my rules and my workhouse. I fight everyone and when I win you do what I say.' Smutt screamed like a madman as he lashed out again at Thomas's face.

Thomas's hand flashed from behind his back and the blow pierced the air like a pistol shot and smashed into the lad's face.

It knocked him from his feet and sent him spinning to the floor. Blood splattered the boards. All was suddenly silent and the lad saw no more. He lay in a crumpled mass, unable to move. It was as if every nerve and sinew had lost consciousness. Somewhere he could hear the tap, tap, tapping of the leather hammers but nothing more. He was vaguely aware of footsteps coming towards him. He knew in his heart that they were those of his adversary. He tried to move his frozen limbs and get to his feet. All was numb. There was no pain, just a rising panic. On the cold floor it was as if he knew that the one who came had power and dominion over him and would be Lord.

# The Devil's Arse

'NO bugler and no hounds?' asked the hosteller as the carriage pulled up in the yard of the inn at Peveril.

'Gone after the madman at Galilee Rocks,' the driver said. He climbed from the seat and opened the door to the coach. 'There's been trouble, more than we expected. Could have been a wild boar or a wolf. Never seen the likes of it before.'

'A shuck?' the hosteller asked, his eyes raised in alarm.

'Don't go saying the likes of that,' said the driver as Beadle got down from the coach. 'No one will ride with us if they thought that Ord Shuck was out.'

'It was a vicious beast. If we had not fought it off then we would have all died,' Bragg boasted as he woke from his dreams and lolled about the carriage like a lairy animal.

'Are the Militia here?' the driver asked. 'I have need of them. We lost a passenger – well, two passengers. One went after the madman, the other has disappeared.'

'In front of our very eyes,' Bragg said loudly as he stepped down from the coach and pulled his coat about himself. 'Give me your best room. I was injured when I fought off the beast. I need to sleep.' The hosteller took Bragg by the arm and led him away as Ergott and the others stepped to the ground.

Ergott followed on as the coachman set about loosening the horses and fixing the broken door. The inn loomed above them like an old castle keep. It was made of ancient stone with a small bridge that went over a deep moat. On all sides were high stone walls that surrounded the courtyard. Everything was finally made safe by two large oak doors that kept out the night. The courtyard was brightly lit by burning tallows, the walls ran with deep green ivy and above the door was the sign of the inn. It hung from a metal brace and swung with the wind. Upon it was painted the head of a man with the face of a dog and underneath were the words: The Black Shuck Inn.

Beadle scanned them quickly as he followed on. He saw that upon the wall in a high tower was a watchman. He carried a musket and had a sword in his belt. Throughout his years he had heard stories of Peveril. They had been told late at night when good men should be sleeping but Beadle would always listen, intrigued by the treachery of the place and of its importance in the world. He never thought he would ever stand in the courtyard of the Black Shuck. He had been told that it had once been a castle that had stood over the town and governed Peveril and that now the only safe place for the traveller to stay was within its walls.

He had only heard the story of the Black Shuck mentioned once in a song – a hawker had chanced upon Baytown and to earn his rest by the fire had sung of a beast so terrible that it defied nature. The man had sung again and again of the beast that had come from the night and killed a priest. The marks of his death could still be seen upon the church door. It was a beast that would howl as it ran and then would snatch its victim without a sound, so quickly that they couldn't even scream. Beadle shook the thought from his mind as his eyes were warmed by the open door and the glowing hearth within.

'We owe you our lives,' Ergott said to the driver.

'Not I, but your companion, Mister Beadle. If it were not for him we would have perished,' the driver said as he pulled Beadle forward from where he was skulking in the shadows.

'Then, Beadle, I will buy you dinner,' Ergott insisted. 'In fact I think we should all eat together and talk of what is to be done.'

'Kind sir,' said Shrume as he stumbled across the cobbles. 'I will be away to my bed. It is late and the things of the night do not concern me.'

'Then that leaves Lady Chilnam and Mister Beadle, or will you both be running away from me?' Ergott asked.

'I cannot eat, Mister Ergott. I will drink with you, but until I know what has happened to Raphah and Barghast my stomach will be empty,' Beadle said.

'I too, Mister Ergott,' said Lady Tanville as she walked towards the door of the inn.

'Then it will be drink and nothing more and in the morning we shall find out what has driven this world to madness. My father once said, call a girl Agnes and she'll be mad by thirty. Strange – every girl I knew with that name was as mad as cheese.'

Stepping over the threshold, Beadle saw Bragg and Mister Shrume walking up the long staircase that went off to the right and then galleried the room. The inn was empty but for an old table and several chairs that filled the space by the fire. Ergott sat as close as he could to the flames with his face in his hands. Lady Tanville warmed her cloak by the fire as servants brought them food and drink. She folded it neatly and left it upon the back of the chair.

Beadle felt uncomfortable. He looked for the way to his room, hoping that someone would point him to the barn.

Ergott looked up and smiled. 'Mister Beadle, our saviour,'

he said as he laughed and held out a hand in welcome. 'To this fire and to my company you are very welcome.'

'And I to my sleep,' Lady Tanville said as she bowed to Beadle and went the way of Bragg and the others.

'Then it is you and I,' Ergott said as he poured Beadle a drink. 'We shall toast the night and the finding of your friend. Tell me, Beadle. Do you know Whitby?'

For the next hour, Ergott talked of nothing but the town. It was as if he were being circumspect, not wanting Beadle to believe he enquired too much. He spoke of the pubs, the ships and even of Baytown. Beadle watched the long case clock by the staircase. It seemed to drag each minute, and each minute appeared to be as long as an hour. All the time, Ergott would tease with his wand, rubbing it with his hand. He would tap out the words of each sentence and draw pictures in the air. Ergott held it by the fork and had it dance in his fingers. It was only when the flames of the fire began to fade and die that he asked Beadle a final question.

'I hear that Whitby was ravaged by a smuggler, Jacob Crane I believe?'

Beadle spat the beer from his mouth as he choked on hearing the words. 'I believe also,' Beadle said, caught like a rat upon a trap.

'Then you know him well?'

'I have had acquaintance . . . Once or twice,' he muttered sheepishly in an unconvincing lie. 'Every man jack knows of Crane. The King and Crane, one king of the land the other of the sea.'

'I would like to meet him, talk with him.' Ergott asked if, by chance, Beadle could arrange such a meeting.

'He's gone, left Whitby by sea, bad business.'

'That I know,' Ergott replied cautiously. He put the wand back into his pocket and stood from his seat. He took a small cloth from the table and wiped the beer from the corner of his mouth. His face was sullen and gone was the smile of a fellow well met. 'I saw the madman, Beadle. In the darkness on the moor. I have seen many things and never had that experience before. These are strange times. Let us hope that in the morning we will have an end to all this and be away from Peveril.'

'I'll stay until they find Raphah, or what's left of him,' Beadle answered.

'Raphah – the Ethio. Doesn't he do *healings*? Isn't he accused of witchcraft – healed a blind boy, or was he deaf? Stole Bragg's money and then put it back, by magic . . .' Ergott took a long splinter from the fire and lit his freshly stoked pipe. It crackled and spat as the black strands caught fire and smouldered in amongst the festering rye seeds. With each inhalation, Ergott began to snigger. His eyes glazed and reddened as he stared at Beadle. 'Amazing how news can travel in the right circles. My uncle lives close to Whitby. Lord Finesterre – have you heard of him?'

Ergott didn't wait for a reply. Like a small child, he spun on his feet and danced across the wooden floor. He took the stairs two by two as he warbled to himself. Upon the landing he turned and looked angrily at Beadle as if in that instant he had been transformed.

'I am an eagle, swooping down upon my wings to pick you from the ground like a hare, Mister Beadle. Never forget that, an eagle, always watching. Even when you can't see me.' Ergott slobbered his words and stared in a melancholy fashion. 'Do you know . . . Do you know, you are the ugliest man I have ever seen? If I were you, I would wear a bag upon my head or cut off my face. Promise me one thing, Mister *Beagle* – never, never have children. One monster in the world is enough.' Ergott sniggered again as he clutched the pipe and stared down through bright, wide eyes. He stood for a minute and then as the clock struck the first hour of the morning, in a twist of his coat tails he vanished along the landing.

Beadle counted Ergott's footsteps as he staggered along the corridor above him. He listened to the creaking of the door and then the clumsy turning of a lock as Ergott took to his bed.

For another hour he brooded like an old hen. Beadle stacked the fire, piling the logs as high as they would go, and nestled himself upon the hearth. Taking Lady Tanville's cloak from the chair, he wrapped himself in it. He nuzzled his face into the cloth and sniffed the heavy scent of wild jasmine. No one came to show him a room and very quickly the house fell silent. He dozed, half dreaming, half waking. In the distance he heard the innkeeper locking the doors and sliding the bolts to keep out the night. The cold wind whistled outside. Beadle felt safe, knowing that upon the walls an armed guard waited.

No matter how hard he tried to dream, his mind was brought back to Raphah. All he could see was the lad's face as he went off into the night. Beadle found himself doting on the lad, fretting as to what had become of him.

The old pig-candles that lit the hall waned with time. They flickered grimly in their holders. Some died away in the shallow breeze that swirled up the landing from the gap beneath the oak door that led to the courtyard. Beadle watched intently as he angrily mulled over Ergott's words. Finally he felt the onset of sleep as his eyes grew heavy and the light began to fade.

'Don't care if I look like a dog,' he moaned to himself as he closed his eyes.

There was an unexpected and sharp footfall from the gallery, as if someone had danced across the floor in a room above. Beadle sat bolt upright. All was in darkness but for the glow of the fire. The sound came again and then he heard the soft voice whispering above him: '*Sleep one sleep all . . . As the night shall fall . . . Sleep once, sleep twice . . . Bed-bug, lark and mice . . . And all shall dream, and all sleep well . . . Until the dawn shall break the spell . . .'*

There was a swirl of blue light, like that of a will-o'-the-wisp. It seeped under the door, took the form of a burning orb and then took flight about the house as if summoned by the spell.

Beadle pulled the cloak tightly about him and hid himself, pretending to sleep. The footsteps came closer, walking across the landing of the gallery and then onto the staircase. One by one and step by step they drew near. Beadle held his breath as he tried to peer out through his wrinkled eyelids and feigned dreaming.

From the corner of his eye he could see the dark figure coming towards him and carrying the Hand of Glory. Upon the stairs it was held aloft and then motioned in the sign of a star as the words were chanted again: *'Sleep one sleep all . . . As the night shall fall . . . Sleep once, sleep twice . . . Bed-bug, lark and mice . . . And all shall dream, and all sleep well . . . Until the dawn shall break the spell . . .'*

The candles that were within the hand spluttered and winced as the blue orb circled around it and then vanished. Beadle pretended to snore. He gulped the air and moaned, hoping that he would be left alone. The footsteps came closer and closer and the smell of wild jasmine became stronger. A hand reached out to his neck and took hold of the hood of the cloak.

Slowly and steadily Lady Tanville gently pulled the cloak from him. Beadle carried on in his profession of dreaming. He had heard the spell and knew her to be a witch.

For Beadle, witches were dangerous creatures. Once he had visited the witch of White Moor. He had gone with a single wart upon his chin. She had given him the cure of crushed spiders, elm root and nettle. Within the hour he was unable to speak and his head had swollen to the size of a summer cabbage. What were once his eyes had shrivelled to that of a newt. Witches were all the same, he thought. Pay them good money and await your prickly fate.

Beadle knew that the Hand of Glory was not a commonplace object. Whoever had it in their possession was not to be trusted and it was only by chance that he too had not been controlled by its charm. For those who slept would remain asleep and those awake when the spell was uttered would keep awake.

He listened as Lady Tanville took the cloak from him and wrapped it around her shoulders as she walked away. Now he knew what she was. In his heart he had known it, and now he was sure. With one eye he followed her as she walked towards the far end of the room. By the side of a large oak panel, Lady Tanville stopped and from a small bag unfolded a piece of paper. She studied this map for some time and then pressed the wooden panel in front of her face. The oak parted and she stepped inside.

Beadle waited, then got to his feet and followed. Something inside, a cold dark voice that defied reason, told him to go onwards. He reached the open panel and just as he stepped across it the panel slammed shut, pinning him to the wall with the force of a landslide. He squealed momentarily as he tried to grasp his breath. Then he heard the footsteps coming back out of the darkness towards him.

Beadle was trapped, his head in the hall of the inn and his body inside the passageway. The footsteps came even closer. There was a click of the secret lock and the panel slid open. He breathed a sigh and slid down to his knees. It was then he found a knife at his throat.

'You're supposed to be asleep,' Tanville said as she pressed the blade against his flesh.

'So are you,' Beadle grumbled as he tried to speak without opening his mouth.

'How long have you known about the Glory Hand, Beadle?' she asked quietly.

'Since the night before. I saw you counting the money, Bragg's money.'

'And you said nothing?'

'You helped Raphah. I know not why. It would have been easy for you just to let him hang and you would have the money still. No one would suspect you,' Beadle said.

'He was innocent. I wouldn't let him hang for me.' She took the knife from him and pulled him within the passageway, shutting the oak panel behind them.

'What are you searching for?' Beadle asked looking around the dark passageway that was illuminated by the Glory Hand.

'Bragg is an art dealer, an expert on all things literary and artistic. Oh, he would want to write but has not the faculty. So he collects, or should I say he hoards. Books, pictures, anything of beauty. He took a picture from my family and now I want it back. He sold it to a merchant in London. It was Bragg who sold the Glory Hand to my uncle, exchanged it for a piece of the true Cross. It's what he does best, magical artefacts.'

'Can't you just buy the picture from him?' Beadle enquired as he rubbed his neck and stared into the flames of the Glory Hand.

'I am following Bragg to London. He takes something to the merchant, something that I believe to be hidden in the cave beneath us. Bragg will take me to the portrait and then I will kill him. Now, Beadle, tell me secrets of yourself or I'll have to kill you.' Tanville put the knife to his nose.

'I am Beadle, I have no secrets,' he said nervously.

'Then how do you know of the power of the hand?' she asked.

'My master . . . He used the Glory Hand many times.'

'And who is that?'

'Obadiah Demurral. But I have run from his service,' Beadle muttered, hoping that he would never have to say the words again.

In the passageway the shadows cast by the hand loomed about them as if they were to hold them in their grip. A shrill breeze whistled from the depths below. It sounded like a thousand children weeping in their graves. The walls dripped and the water splashed upon the steps to form a small stream that trickled out of sight. The cold shivered their bones as Beadle stared into the Lady Tanville's bright eyes.

'And you say you have no secrets? He is a warlock and knows Bragg well. I would say we are equal in our skulduggery. Swear an oath on this knife that you will say nothing.'

'Swear,' said Beadle.

'Then follow me. You are now in *my* service. Bragg hid an item here the last time he travelled. It will tell me all that I need to know.' Tanville led Beadle down the passageway and over the rock steps to a cavern below.

# Uninvited Guests

'SMUTT, Smutt, wake up,' Thomas said urgently as he began to lift him from the floor.

'Never before,' Smutt moaned and tried to focus his bleary eyes on Thomas's face.

'I tried to tell you. It could have been different,' Thomas said quietly.

'You hit me so hard . . . I never saw you.'

'You'd have hit me, if I'd given you a chance.' Thomas looked at the lad. 'Why do you fight everyone?'

'Always have, what I do best,' Smutt said cautiously as he held his face. 'It's my job: keep the lads in order. Top dog – that's what Galphus says. He always brings them to me and leaves me alone with them and I give them a good beating and tell them the rules of the place.' Smutt swallowed hard and looked at Thomas. 'It'll be your job now – best bed, best food and all that goes with it. Here,' he said, pulling a bunch of keys on a brass ring from his pocket. 'You'd better 'ave these. I was on lock-up. No one would ever argue with me. When they find out you beat me they'll all wanna 'ave a go.'

'Keeps your keys,' Thomas said as he helped Smutt to his

feet. 'Show me my bed and keep yours. I'm not planning on staying here. I was tricked into this place, signed against my will and I'll be off by the morning.'

'They all say that, every one of them. Within the day you'll be just like the rest. Those that try to escape get *shoed* and then they can never leave,' Smutt said pugnaciously as he picked the bloodied snot from his nose.

'Shoed or barefoot, I'll still be going, every day, even if I was caught a hundred times I won't be staying. I've a score to settle and my blood boils.' Thomas spat the words as he thought of Crane's betrayal for selling him to Galphus.

'If you get *shoed* you can't leave. Once they're on your feet, Galphus will know where you are every minute of the day. If you ever did get out they'd come alive and stop you. If you run they trip you up and if you hide they shout out. No one has ever got away from this place. Once you hear the bell, you'll know what I talk of.'

'Who's heard of shoes that do that?' Thomas said. He suddenly remembered Pallium's magnificent shoes.

'I've seen them. Galphus makes them. They stick to your feet, become a part of you, can never take them off. Does it to people he wants to *control*. Seen it with my own eyes.'

'Then you'll see me jump from them and from this place.'

Smutt hit the wall with his fist. 'Been here three years and hate every minute. Said those words myself. All I know now is fighting. Fought the lad who had this job before me and will fight everyone who comes to keep it. A hundred kids look to me as boss – all this landing and half the one above. The only people I answered to were Galphus and his Druggles.' Smutt dropped his head. 'You were the first to beat me, it's yours now – them's the rules – get beat, get lost. That's what Galphus said.'

Thomas noticed the chequerboard of cuts upon the lad's

arms. They crisscrossed back and forth across his skin in ribbons of cut flesh. Smutt saw him looking and quickly rolled down his sleeve to hide the marks.

'Who did them to you?' Thomas asked.

'No one, did 'em meself. What else is there to do?' He spoke half-proud, half-ashamed, his eyes cast to the floor.

'What for?' Thomas pressed him.

'When you've been here three years, let me see *your* skin. It's what we all does . . . Part of the apprenticeship – cut yourself, cut out the pain and the misery.'

'Then I'll be gone by the night – coming?' Thomas asked.

'What makes you think I won't tell Galphus?' Smutt asked.

'Because I would beat you every day to within an inch of your life and enjoy doing it,' Thomas said coldly. 'You can keep your job and your keys. If anyone asks, I'll say you beat me. Treat me like you would a new lad, treat me bad. Do that and I'll be gone and no one will ever know different.'

Smutt paused for a moment. It was as if you could see his mind whirring as he thought out the consequences. Slowly a smile came to his face. 'I could help you get out . . . You could go now. Galphus would never think you'd make a break straight away.' He kicked the heels of his boots as he sprung to life. Thomas didn't notice the glistening leather and the golden soles that shimmered radiantly as Smutt walked on.

'We go now?' asked Thomas.

'Right now, before anyone suspects. Galphus will think I am showing you the room where you'll live. I know a place where there is an open window, from it you can get onto the roof and from there into a courtyard and across the city. It's the only way. Every door is guarded and the only things that leave this place is Galphus's shoes.' Smutt seemed excited as he spoke and thought at the same time and, amazingly, was able to walk as well. 'It won't be easy – if we get stopped tell 'em I'm showing you the place. We won't get far until you get out of them clothes and into your kit. This way.'

Smutt led Thomas down a narrow flight of stairs. From all around he could hear the pounding of the hammers that punctually beat out the seconds. The longer they walked, the darker the staircase became. Smutt went ahead until he stopped by an open door with a warm light that bled into the passageway.

'Here,' he said. 'You can get fixed up. If we get caught, you'll get banged up for a week and then Galphus will have you *shoed*, no questions asked. Them's the rules, so let's not get caught.' Smutt's eyes darted around the narrow room. 'Get garbed and make it quick.' Smutt pointed to a rack of dreary clothes hanging from a rail. Puritan white shirts hung next to grey jackets with dull trousers, drabber socks and black, dowdy boots.

Thomas changed and in an instant looked just like the rest who drudged and moaned about the factory. Smutt laughed to himself, already knowing what was to come. Thomas reached for a pair of fine black shoes that looked to be his size. They were different from the others and looked inviting.

'No,' said Smutt as Thomas was about to slip his foot into the shoe. 'Them's the ones I told you about. One toe in that and he'll have you for life. Take these.' He handed Thomas an ordinary pair of black lace up boots. 'I've changed my mind,' he said capriciously as he took Thomas by the hand. 'I'll come with you. Had enough of life here, going nowhere, might as well get out of the place.'

'Then we'll flee together. I have one thing to do when we escape and then I'm heading for France – come with me if you want, I could use a mate like you.'

'That's right – I'm your *mate*, always will be. Right to the end.' Smutt rubbed his fist in his hand as the bruise to his face began to ache. 'Ten floors higher and then we can get out of this place. There's a window in the tower.'

They set off together, Smutt slightly ahead and walking at the same pace as everyone else. The factory seemed endless, as if it was built like a city within a city, standing outside time and space. They walked for several minutes, Smutt stopping to point out the work stations, water butts and the feeding hall. Each doorway was guarded by a boy not much older than themselves. They all held a thick cudgel behind their back. They stood deathly still, faces cast like stone, eyes dead to the world. Smutt smiled at each one in turn and they duly nodded and let him by.

'They're the Druggles,' Smutt whispered. 'Get picked by Galphus to keep an eye on us. None of them is any good – keep 'em sweet by giving them your food.'

'Do you not get paid for what you do?' Thomas asked.

'Galphus keeps it until you're twenty-one. What do you need money in here for? You can't spend it. Sixpence a week and all found. Free boots and a shirt for your back. 'Tis luxury beyond dreams,' Smutt said sarcastically.

Upon the seventh landing they were stopped by a guard who asked Smutt his business. He nervously explained that he was under Galphus's orders to show the new lad the factory and they were let by without further question. They walked through another workshop that appeared smaller than the rest. In its centre was a large platform and upon the platform was a metal sphere encrusted in gold and hanging from a wooden frame. In the centre of the sphere was a hand-painted dragon with an eye that seemed to follow Thomas wherever he stood.

Thomas stopped and stared.

'It's a gong,' Smutt said, as if he knew what it was. 'Only heard it once – they use it when someone gets *shoed* . . . Dragon's Heart, Galphus calls it. No one gets out if they hear the Dragon's Heart.' Thomas stared at the Dragon's Heart and wondered what power it contained and how the beating of the gong would stop anyone from escaping from Galphus.

Smutt took Thomas higher and higher. Each floor was identical: on each level a Druggle, each Druggle staring in the same manner. All wore the same boots that looked as if they were a part of their bodies. They were made of thick black leather with deep wooden soles. Thomas noticed that the colour of the bootlaces changed. 'Why are they different?' he asked Smutt as they walked by another Druggle.

'Red for the Druggles and black for the interns – Galphus calls us apprentices. Indentured for life and only leave when you die.'

'But you can go when you get to twenty-one,' Thomas said. 'It's in the contract, Galphus showed me.'

'Galphus lied. Look around you – you won't find a man of that age here. Come eighteen they all vanish and no one knows what happens to them.'

'And you would have stayed?' he asked.

'I wouldn't live that long. Not here. After a while you give up caring. Living or dead – what's the difference?'

Two Druggles approached as they walked the corridor. Smutt looked swiftly to the floor, his face coloured to glowing scarlet. Thomas stared straight ahead as if they weren't there.

'Sweeper boy,' one said, taking hold of Smutt by the collar. 'What you doing here?'

'New lad,' Smutt said his voice wavering as he spoke. 'Galphus told me to show him the factory – top to bottom.' Smutt put his hand to his face to hide the bruise.

'Someone smack you, did they?' asked the Druggle mockingly.

'He fell, brush hit him in the face,' Thomas said as he stepped towards the Druggle and held out his hand. 'I'm Thomas, a new apprentice, Mister Galphus picked me himself.'

The Druggle stepped back and looked at him. He was older than Thomas and taller, with the first fledge of hair growing on his face. His chin was blistered with a deep red pox that broke the skin like the surface of the September moon.

'New apprentice, eh? What would you like to apprentice for, my lad?' the Druggle asked. 'Sweeping, like young Smutty?'

'To be a Druggle, that's all I want, for that's the best there is,' Thomas replied mellifluously.

'So it is, so it is,' said the young Druggle as he stared at him. 'Shall we let them pass?' he asked his companion, who smiled a toothless smile but had not the wits to answer such a complicated question. The Druggle waited for a moment. His eyes fixed sharply on Thomas. He looked him up and down slowly, as if he took in everything about the lad. 'On your way – I'll see you later.'

'They know,' Thomas said as they walked off as calmly as they could, fearing to look back. 'I could tell by how he stared at me so.'

'He does it to us all – it's in his nature. A dangerous creature and a vile bully. He was a Mohawk before he came here. His family fell on hard times. Father lost all their money – a gambler, so I hear. Galphus paid five pounds for him, cheap at the price.' Smutt scoffed in a low voice for fear the words would carry far.

'And how much did Galphus pay for you?' Thomas asked.

'I was given to him. Not worth a penny. Hate it here, but it's home. One day want to run, another want to stay and another wish myself dead. Better here than on the outside, some would say. All them wars and fighting, things falling from the sky, earthquakes and misery. Galphus tells us at prayers. I saw the sun once. It burnt my eyes. Prefer the dark, better for you. Hides many things.'

'But you'll come with me?' Thomas asked again, unsure if Smutt would follow him to the outside.

'Half my head tells me to stay – if I was an honest lad, which I'm not. Don't know what to do. See what happens when I get to the window. Take a look and see, eh?'

Smutt took him higher. They very soon left the uppermost floor of the factory and began to spiral higher and higher as they walked the steps to a tower. Thomas could hear the wind beating against the side and shivering through the shingles. The noise of the hammering faded with each step. Every window had been painted black, and some had been boarded shut. On every landing was a small candle set beneath a glass hood. They cast long shadows as they approached and then were cast as giants upon the ceiling as they went by. Smutt didn't say a word. He kept his head down and his face motionless. Thomas could hear his breathlessness as they walked the stairs together.

Eventually they came to the top of the tower. Here was a room with no doors. To one side was a tall window that nearly came to the floor. Like a thin door it was locked with a bolt and bracket. The glass was blackened, all except for a small square which had been etched away by eager hands seeking the outside world. Smutt saw Thomas looking at the scraped paint.

'Some come here to see the world. Makes 'em sick for it. A bad thing, I says – best forget and just work until the day you move on.'

'How do we get out?' Thomas asked as he looked for a way of escape.

'The key. Simple, really, had it with me all the time, didn't know until last week,' Smutt replied.

Thomas peered through the scraping. It was a black, dark night. The sky blew a London gale that blotted out the sky yet did not move the thick smog.

'There,' Smutt said, taking the key from the brass ring and putting it in the lock and opening the window. 'A few feet below

is a roof, beyond that the alley and further still the river. Freedom, Thomas.'

'How do we get down?' Thomas asked.

'Just hang from the ledge and let yourself drop. I'll keep
watch, then follow on.' Smutt tried to be convincing, looking
Thomas in the eyes for the briefest of glances. 'Do it quickly –
the Druggles will come and check this place and we have to be
gone.'

Smutt seemed agitated and his voice trembled. Thomas
looked from the open window into the pitch night. He could
hear the distant cries of the town. Far to the east a ship's bell
rang out. In the fog-driven dark he could see nothing but the
raven black. Thomas looked below. It was as if he stared into
nothing. The mist whirled thickly about the tower.

'You sure about the roof?' he asked.

'Sure. Trust me, it's just a short drop – you won't feel a
thing,' muttered Smutt as he looked away.

'Then you go first, I'll follow you,' Thomas said, and he
pushed him towards the window.

Smutt panicked, his eyes flashing to the lamp and then to the
stairs. Thomas could see he had set his mind to run.

'Give me the key,' Thomas demanded. He snatched it from
the lock and threw it through the open window. There was no
sound of it clattering to the roof. 'One . . . two . . . three . . . four
. . . five . . . six . . . seven,' he counted and just as the last word
left his lips the faint sound of metal dashing against stone
echoed through the mist. Smutt held his breath, knowing his
malevolence to be discovered.

'It was a way out of this place,' Smutt snapped in panic as he
saw the look of anger upon Thomas's face.

'It was a way to my death – you tricked me, Smutt.'

'Tricked yourself – should have let me beat you. Things
would've been different. Never be beaten, that's what Galphus

says. You knocked me to the ground once, but *I* would have listened as the ground swallowed you up.' Smutt spoke like a resentful old man, his face contorted with bitterness. 'Let me pass, boy. I've shown you the way out – now go. If you dare,' he taunted.

'Then I go alone.' There was a crack of the wrist as all that burnt in Thomas's heart exploded through his fist, knocking Smutt from his feet yet again. Thomas stood over him and kicked him in the chest with the tip of his boot. Smutt's head lolled across the wooden boards, limp at the neck. He moaned, not knowing where he was or what had happened. 'Could have been so different, Smutt,' Thomas said as he snatched the brass ring and keys from his belt and ran off down the stairs, hoping to find a way to escape.

# Vere–Adeptus

**B**EADLE followed Lady Tanville as she ran up the steps from the cave, along the passageway and through the oak panel to the inn. There was a sound of barking hounds and a frantic pounding at the great door. Beadle and Lady Tanville hid quickly beneath the stairway as he slid the panel back into place to seal their escape from the passageway. With long, nimble fingers she took a vial of milk from her bag and extinguished the flames of the Glory Hand. She looked at Beadle with his ruffled hair and wild eyes that spoke of years of misery and gave him a half-smile.

'The spell is gone, they will soon hear,' she said as the sound of the banging grew louder and the dogs barking more insistent. The noise chilled her spirit, reminding her of a white stag that had had its life torn from it by a pack of her father's dogs.

'Quickly,' screamed a voice from above as the barefoot innkeeper ran the length of the corridor and stumbled down the stairs. 'Are we robbed?' he shouted, half-sleeping, the dreams still running through his mind. He got to the door and fumbled with the lock. Tanville wrapped the Glory Hand within the folds of her cloak.

The door opened and in spilled the night mists. Hounds leapt into the hall looking for food and a place by the fire. They stank of heath and moor as they shook the mud from their backs and shivered with contentment. The bugler stepped within and grabbed the innkeeper by the shoulders, shaking him as if he were a rag doll.

'To see it, to see it!' he screamed as he shook the man even more. 'Carsington is made well. The madness . . . Gone . . .'

The innkeeper dropped his arms to his sides and took a step back as if he had been given dire news. 'Carsington – well?'

'Tonight on Galilee Rocks I saw it with my own eyes. They are coming now, here,' he babbled quickly.

'Who comes here?' the innkeeper asked as the hall filled with the barking of hounds.

'Carsington and the Ethio that was with me.' The bugler stared with his wide eyes as if he couldn't believe his own words. 'It's true, they follow on. I shot Mad Cassy in the leg as he screamed from the rocks. I went to finish him off but the lad got there first. He took the madness away and if I dare to speak, he's as sane as you . . .'

'But what of the inn? I took it from him. It belongs to Carsington,' said the innkeeper.

The man had just finished his words when the doors opened. Raphah stood before them, drenched with the storm, his hair dripping with sweat and rain. He smiled when he saw Beadle by the fire. 'All is well,' he said as he pulled Carsington in from the night and walked him to the fireside. A second dark figure followed on, skulking into the room like a scolded dog that edged the walls and kept out of sight. Barghast held his hand tightly to his side as blood trickled from his fingers. 'Bring sage, water and cloth, he is injured,' Raphah shouted to the innkeeper.

Soon the Black Shuck had come to life, as from every corner

of the inn came people to stare at Carsington. Raphah sat the man by the fire and pulled the rotting fabric from his leg. It covered the wound of a musket ball that had split the skin. The man didn't speak, his eyes glaring at the fireplace and looking about the room. He hunched himself, as if he were unsure of his surroundings and the people who stared at him.

The innkeeper brought Raphah all he had asked for and sat and stared at the man. Taking a pair of shears, Raphah began to trim back the hair from the man's face. It hung in thick clumps, matted by dirt. From its midst stared two bright eyes. Slowly his face began to appear. Soon he looked like a man and not the beast that had plagued the moors.

'So long,' he said, breathing the words. 'So different.'

'What did he do to you?' the innkeeper asked.

'He spoke words and held him by the throat, I saw it all, everything,' said the bugler as he enacted the deliverance. 'Raving one minute, like a lamb the next. The sky burst open and it was gone.'

'Truly healed?' the innkeeper asked again as he wiped his hands upon his nightshirt.

'Truly,' said the man.

'Then you know this house.'

'Well, I know it is mine.' Carsington stopped and looked at the innkeeper. 'From the look of the place, you have kept a better house than I.'

'Then it shall be yours again, for I took it in your madness and gave you nothing,' said the innkeeper. 'I watched you eat grass and thought only of my gain.'

'We were once friends and will be again,' said Carsington as he held out his hand. 'I have back my wits and the Shuck.'

'And what of Barghast?' Lady Chilnam asked as she warmed herself.

Barghast sat against the far wall clutching his hand. The

innkeeper took Carsington up the stairs and smiled at Raphah. 'We have a lot to be thankful for,' he said as they went.

Barghast sniffed and gave a sly look. He wanted not to talk and held his gaze to the distant fire.

'We thought you to be dead,' Tanville said as she saw his wounded hand. 'There was a madness in the storm – we all saw it . . .'

'I saw nothing – fell in the dark, that is all. Woke in the ditch and then heard the hounds coming from the hills. There was no beast, only dogs and pigs.'

'And your hand – it's damaged?' she asked.

'A slight wound from the fall. A night's sleep and it will be gone,' Barghast mumbled.

There was a clatter of fat feet from above as Bragg and Ergott chased along the corridor.

'What is this? What is this?' Bragg shouted as if to wake the dead. 'Barghast alive?'

'Very much so,' echoed Ergott, wand in hand. 'Survived the moor and only a scratch, the maid has just left my room and . . .'

They stopped at the landing and looked down at Barghast.

'Never thought . . . Never thought I'd see him again,' wailed Bragg as he held in his belly with the rope of his night coat. He turned and looked at Raphah. 'And you, sadly more life than a Rotherhithe cat,' he scolded as he walked down the stairs, flanked by Ergott. 'To think, Mister Ergott, we worried our-selves to sleep over Barghast. I thought you had been taken by a beast on the moor, Barghast – the least you could have done was to be eaten by it.'

'There was no beast. Your eyes cheated you,' Barghast growled. 'I was the one lost, not you, remember that.'

'And I was the one who nearly lost my life in that carriage.'

'All is well and everyone is safe.' Raphah shouted. 'Is it not time for you all to sleep?'

'The Ethio has elected himself our leader, one miracle and he becomes the saviour. Whatever next, Mister Ergott?' Bragg said as he pulled the cord of his coat even tighter.

'The boy's right. Best we all sleep. Goodnight, Mister Bragg, and may your money be as comfortable to sleep on as the fat on your backside.' Barghast got up from his seat and crossed the room to sit by the fire. 'Sleeping here, Beadle?'

Beadle looked at Raphah. 'They have nowhere for us to sleep, so I pitched myself here. Good supply of logs and I did have a cloak for a blanket,' he said as he chomped his lips and made a sound like a horse.

Lady Tanville laughed and held the cloak tightly. 'I'll bring you blankets and some food,' she said, and she followed Ergott and Bragg up the stairs.

The three sat in silence, Barghast staring at the flames and Beadle trying to doze. Raphah stared at a cobweb that floated on an updraft. His mind thought of Africa and his heart called him home. *Fulfil your desires*, his father had said the night he left the village. He searched his heart,, knowing no more what he really wanted. The night he had set off he had known so clearly what he had to do. He touched the golden Keruvim with his fingertips and felt its power filling his bones. It was as if it spoke to him, gave him strength and made straight every path. Now he sat alone. He was tired, empty and far away, and all he knew was that he wanted to see the faces of Thomas and Kate. As with everything he knew he could not strive to find them, but circumstances themselves would lead him onwards.

'Here,' said Tanville as she carried a bundle of thick woollen blankets and dumped them on the floor by the fire. 'I'll leave you to the night. The driver said there will be little chance of comfort on the roads, so sleep well.'

'That's if we sleep at all,' Barghast replied as she walked away. 'There's more to her than can be seen at night,' he said in a whisper as she turned the landing of the stairs. 'She runs from something. I knew her grandfather well.'

'For a man who can seem so young, you have lived such a long time,' Raphah said.

'Is this the time for honesty or does the game continue?' Barghast asked.

'My father told me to be honest but only trust a man when he had saved your life. I trust no living thing. We are all fallen from goodness and our hearts can turn on a silver coin.'

'So when will you trust me to tell you a story?' Barghast asked.

'It is the night and a time for stories. Beadle sleeps and I have no need for that distraction. I would be cheered by a lullaby.'

Barghast moved closer and wrapped himself in a blanket as he threw another log onto the fire. He looked to Raphah and then to Beadle and listened intently to the sounds of the house. Barghast hesitated before he spoke, his eyes fixed to the fire. There was something about the lad that intrigued him. It lay deeper than his broad smile and bright eyes. Something shone from within him, something Barghast desired, and a look he had seen once before.

'There's an old legend of a man who is cursed to live forever,' Barghast said very slowly. He stooped towards Raphah, drawing him closer with each word. 'He was once a money-lender, a wealthy man who in the eyes of the world had everything. On a dark Friday on the way to a hill of execution, soldiers were dragging a beggar to his death. In his poverty the beggar asked the man for water. He had the chance to help the beggar, but turned his face. All that was asked of him was one sip. Instead, he tipped the water to the ground at his feet. All the beggar said to the money-lender was, *"I will go now, but you shall wait until I return and walk every path until you find me."* Little did the man know that the beggar was a king in disguise.

On that day, at the time of the execution, the beggar cried out and then as the thunder roared he died. In his dying, he took away the power of death.

'From the man, the beggar took the gift of dying. Years passed by, his family grew old and died; yet the man stayed the same. In anguish, he threw himself from a high cliff. Instead of finding death, his broken body healed itself. He threw himself into the sea and the water cast him to the shore, even though he had given up the will to live. Neither flame, nor frost or fire of hell could take his life.' Barghast recounted the story slowly as he looked at the flames.

'It was such a simple request – water for a beggar,' Raphah said.

'Simple, yes. But it was fear and not a lack of charity. To show the beggar any favour would have meant death. His captors would have seen to that.'

'And what of the man now?' Raphah asked.

'He went in search of the beggar to ask his forgiveness and be set free. Upon every road he walks until he has trod all the paths of the earth . . . until the day the beggar returns. It is a futile search. Every road he has walked has led to despair and loneliness. The beggar is not to be found.'

'Is not the beggar already here?' Raphah asked.

'You speak as if you know him.'

'I think I have met the foolish moneylender,' Raphah said as he took hold of Barghast's hand. The skin was newly formed over the wound as if no injury had befallen him. 'Your prophecy about your healing was truthful, though several hours too soon and before a night's sleep.'

'Had I have slept and not entered into foolish stories you would never have known,' he replied.

'So was meeting us a coincidence?' Raphah asked.

'Like a moth to a flame I seek the beggar and his people. I

could feel it in my bones, something stirred within the earth. I knew that Riathamus had returned, but was too late. The night of the sky-quake and then the comet – all were signs of his return and the world saw them not. I followed my heart and upon a barren road found you.' Barghast spoke quietly as if the walls listened to them. 'Tonight you showed yourself on the moor – powerful magic, healing a madman. I quite expected the pigs to rush into the lake and drown themselves . . . Then again, you are not the beggar, only his lackey.'

'And you're the carcass that can never die,' Raphah said as he gripped Barghast's hand until he called out in pain. 'I would not expect a man who can cheat death to cry like a dog.'

'Nor a prophet who heals to bring pain,' Barghast said as he snatched away his hand.

'So you follow us?' Raphah asked.

'Don't flatter yourself. News of your arrival spread amongst my *associates* . . . Soon, everyone was talking about the healer. If Demurral hadn't caught you there would have been others far more powerful than that meddler. I searched you out for selfish reasons.' Barghast moved closer to the fire. 'I hunt for the last road on which my earthly feet will walk. I have looked for it many times but it can't be found. It's as if it only appears to invited guests, those whose fate it holds in its hands. You are the key I have been looking for.' He leaned closer to Raphah as if to bring him in to a deeper secret. 'There is another who travels with us who seeks the place also. Somewhere in the city is . . .'

From the room above Lady Tanville screamed in horror. It pierced the silence of the dark night. Beadle jumped from his sleep as Raphah and Barghast ran to the stairway. He followed, not knowing why he was running towards the screams when his wits told him to flee.

The landing quickly filled with the guests at the inn. Merchants, soldiers, mountebanks and laggards ran from their sleeping. Barghast kicked open the door. In the centre of the room was a large black dog the size of a man. Lady Tanville cowered against the end of the bed, candlestick in hand as she screamed and screamed.

The dog turned and looked at Barghast and growled. He stepped forward into the room as Raphah tried to hold him back. The dog hackled and snarled, spitting blood from its teeth and shivering with anger. It stood its ground, its head darting back and forth as it looked from Barghast to Lady Tanville. The creature panted as it stood, its breath phosphorescent in the meagre light.

'Stay away,' Barghast said quietly as Carsington attempted to push by.

'It's Black Shuck, he's returned,' the man cried as he caught a glimpse of the dog. It bristled with fear and repugnance at the smell of humankind, and coughed as if it choked on the blood that dripped from its mouth.

Lady Tanville trembled as the creature paced the room, its head swaying. The breeze blew the drapes at the open window. The dog settled back, its eyes glowering as its stench filled the chamber.

Slowly, inch by inch, Barghast moved closer, his eyes fixed upon the beast. It glared at him as it bared its teeth. There was a sudden cry from the passageway as fearful voices spread the word of Black Shuck.

Without warning, Carsington ran into the room and dived upon the beast, grabbing it by its throat and attempting to wrestle it to the floor. Lady Tanville ran from the bed as Black Shuck twisted and spun with Carsington gripped in its jaws.

'A gun, bring a gun!' Beadle shouted as he pulled her from the room.

Barghast slammed the door behind her and locked it from within, barring it with an old chair.

Raphah banged against the door, shouting to be let in. From inside came the screams of Carsington and the howling of the beast that ripped at him in frenzy. A soldier smashed at the wood with the butt of his musket. Raphah and Beadle kicked and punched the wooden slats. The door held fast as the pandemonium within grew louder. It was as if two beasts pitched themselves to the death. The floor trembled like the opening of hell's gates. There was a roar of a wind that sealed the room and pushed the door against itself. The wood bowed into the hallway. Raphah stepped back as the noise grew more intense. The sound of the howling dog filled the Inn and shook the windows, and all who heard it trembled.

There was then complete silence. Raphah kicked at the door again and heard the chair slide to the floor. He looked to the soldier who stepped back, his face saying he would go no further for fear of what was inside. Beadle held Lady Tanville as she wept beside them.

With one hand Raphah turned the handle and pushed against the door. It opened slowly. He looked into the room. Gone was the beast. Carsington lay like a cloth doll in a pool of blood. Raphah took a pace inside. He listened for any sound of the animal. All was still.

Inside the chamber was the heavy smell of blood. It had the stench of a charnel house. By the window lay Barghast, his face ripped open as if a wild animal had gorged upon it.

As he looked on, Raphah saw what should have been Barghast's hand. The flesh was ripped from the bone.

'Let no one see,' Barghast said as he laboured to speak. 'I thought that it would kill me and for a moment saw death. How cruel this curse,' he whispered. 'It was the hell-hound, but not the one they speak of. There is a changeling in our midst, a beast of hell that wants to see us all dead.'

# Quondam Discomfit

THE moment Thomas stepped upon the factory floor, the sound of screaming rang out. Far away he could hear the cries from the tower. It was a voice he knew, the voice of Smutt. The lad screamed for help, his wailing carrying down the open tower with its spiral staircase and through the halls and galleries that made up his world.

'He's escaped!' Smutt screamed loudly. 'A killer, he's escaped . . .'

Like the wail of a far-off sea-horn, a susurrating voice rumbled in a low moan that echoed throughout the workhouse. 'Rooms – back to your rooms!' It repeated again and again, louder and louder, drowning the cries of Smutt to a whisper.

From every floor came the sudden sound of a stampede. Footsteps clattered on wooden boards as hundreds of feet dashed to their lodgings. Thomas hid in the shadows, wondering what to do next. Two Druggles ran by, each with cudgel and red-laced boots. They dashed up the stairs of the tower, following the sound of Smutt's cries for help.

Thomas knew that somehow he would have to retrace his steps through the countless passages and workshops until he found the doorway out of Glaphus's workhouse. For the moment, he hid himself in a dark corner of the stairwell and tried to think. Smutt's screaming grew louder and closer by the minute as the boy shouted of how Thomas had tried to kill him by throwing him from the tower.

He could wait no longer – he would have to run. Darting from the blackness like a bolting fox, Thomas made for the workshop. All was still. No one was to be seen. It was eerily silent. Upon every anvil was a leather hammer, and over them a neatly folded apron. Gone were the rows of workers who had tap, tap, tapped the seconds of the day. Now, there was just Thomas.

As he looked on, he became aware of a set of footsteps prowling in the darkness. Thomas moved quietly along a narrow aisle between cold anvils. He kept as low as he could, just peering out to see who followed him. From the murky corridor appeared a Druggle, cudgel in hand, tapping it on his palm in time with every footstep. As he walked, he searched for Thomas, looking along the empty rows and listening with each step.

Thomas crouched behind a rack of heavy overcoats, hoping to cover himself and not be seen. They rubbed against his face and made him want to cough. He held his breath, hoping that the Druggle would turn and go back the way he came. But footstep after footstep, he came closer to his hiding place. Thomas knew he couldn't move or he would be discovered.

It was just one boy, he thought as he choked on his breath. One boy and that was all, not much older than himself – he could take a chance, take him by surprise. He waited until the Druggle came to within an arm's length. Thomas stood as still as death, his lungs fit to burst, and then in an instant he thrust the coat rack upon the lad. Its wooden spikes cracked against the Druggle's skull. Thomas kicked out with his boots as he grabbed the cudgel. The fearless lad seized his leg and held fast with brawny hands.

Without thinking, Thomas lashed out with the cudgel as hard as he could. There was a head-bending scream as the lad's arm snapped. Thomas ran. On and on he blindly stormed through the building. His feet clattered, banging out his place in the world for all who could follow. Left – right – back and forth. Corridor after corridor.

From behind feet chased him. He turned as he ran but could see no one. He could hear them running above him until he reached the stairs, but Thomas ran faster. Down a level. Across a landing. Into unfamiliar places. Panic gripped him tightly with unwelcome arms. His breaths burnt his chest, his heart pounded, his feet ached and blistered within the ill-fitting boots.

Then the sound of the Dragon's Heart beat out from some-where very near. It echoed from hall to hall, shaking the build-ing with each beat. The sound went on and on until all the notes merged into one long continuous pitch. The sound pierced Thomas's ears until his mind was blinded, numb. His heart began to ache as his guts shook and shook with each wave.

Thomas ran as fast as he could to get away, but upon his feet the boots came to life. They seized his ankles, squeezing his feet to bursting and stopping him dead. The louder the Dragon's Heart, the greater the pain. It was as if they had been brought to life and fought against him. The boots became as lead weights holding him to the floor and stopping him from running. He dragged his feet clumsily across the wooden boards, scraping them as he went. Hiding in a dark shadow, he tried to untie the laces. They became like tiny snakes in his fingers, snapping at him to leave them be as they coiled about his ankles.

The boots twisted and pulled, turning his feet until he fell to the floor. Thomas dragged himself across the workhouse until he came to the stairs. He slid face-down down several flights, loose nails biting at his skin. All the while he could hear the

Druggles coming closer. The demon boots gripped him until tears came from his eyes and blood flowed from his ankles.

Pulling himself into a tight ball, Thomas attempted to roll from flight to flight. The treads of each stair bit at his back as he fell downwards. High above him the beat of the Dragon's Heart went on. It shivered his heart and quivered in his guts, vibrating them from him. He could feel his insides dance, and as he breathed his lungs had the air beaten from them like a springtime carpet. The boots crushed his feet to breaking as he tumbled into the black hallway.

Ahead of him was a light. He could see the lanterns that had welcomed him to the factory. There was the green door, its paint flaked from the wood like dead skin. The Druggles had gone. Thomas was alone. He got to his feet, dragging them as if he pulled the world behind him. He screamed with pain as he reached out. His boots were rooting him to the wooden floorboards as he clutched the brass handle.

Incredibly, the door fell open as the beating footsteps of the Druggles thundered down the stairs. Thomas fell into the dimly lit yard. The sound of the Dragon's Heart faded. He was free.

The boots loosened their grip as he got to his feet and began to run. He ran towards the blackness of the alleyway and then – a cane snapped across his legs, knocking him to the ground. Within two paces, Galphus's hand gripped him by the throat and held him to the floor. As he looked up he saw that Druggles surrounded him.

'Take him to the cell and teach him a lesson,' Galphus said eagerly as Smutt appeared in the doorway. 'You did well, Smutt. For this you will be rewarded.'

Smutt bowed, grinning at Thomas who was arm-gripped and dragged past him. Smutt cracked him one to the face and then the chest as quickly as he could and laughed out loud.

'Even,' Smutt said as he spat in Thomas's face. 'Pray they keep you in prison for I'll be waiting.'

Thomas was pulled back inside the factory and down a flight of stone steps to a basement room. It smelt like a converted sewer with iron bars across the grates. In the corner was a wooden bed held against the wall by two iron chains. There was no light. From all around came the sound of running water and the damp dew of an icy underworld.

'We meet again,' said a young Druggle with a grin upon his face. 'I'll be back to give you a lesson myself. I won't say when I shall come or what will be done. Waiting is half the pleasure. First we'll see how you like the dark.'

With that Thomas was left alone as the light was shut out with the closing of the door. He closed his eyes tight shut, wanting to keep the memory of the light within him. He sat upon the bed in complete darkness and took off the boots. This time there were no snakes to bite at his fingers and they slipped easily from his bruised feet. The power of the Dragon's Heart was finished when the gong ceased its ringing.

Above him he could hear Galphus barking angrily at Smutt for allowing Thomas to get that far. There was a sudden crack of a cane and a shriek of pain. Thus, Smutt was given his reward. He could hear the lad's tears as he cried over his treachery. 'Take him,' Galphus said to the Druggles. 'Do unto him what he would have done to another.' Thomas thought of his own punishment and what the Druggle would do upon his return.

He waited in the dark. The green door slammed shut and footsteps echoed along the alley above. The sound of Galphus's footsteps filtered through the drain from the street. Thomas could taste the strong and vile air. For a moment he opened his eyes and the light from inside vanished – now he felt dark within as without. He tried to remember what was in the cell and where the door was. In the thick black, he was mouse-blind. He reached out to the wall and followed the stones until he found the door. Now he knew from where the young Druggle would come.

Thomas didn't know if he had slept at all during his waiting. One thing was in no doubt: his dreams had escaped him. All he was aware of was another presence in the cell. It was as if he had woken from sleep to find someone staring at him, someone he couldn't see. He knew they were there. They could be felt close by. Thomas could neither hear them breathe nor feel their heat, but in the night-black he knew he was not alone.

As a young boy he had once awoken from a nightmare. In the dark of the cell it came easily to mind as if he were there again. His room was dark and the sky jet-black and starless. The night sweats wetted his head as if he had slept rolled in damp seaweed. All he could recall was that as soon as he opened his eyes, he was aware of someone near. Half-dreaming, he had called out, and his father had answered, telling him to fear not and all was well. Thomas had lain back against the pillows and in that complete trust had drifted again into sleep.

All of a sudden a noise of screaming came from outside. It called from far away, then grew closer by the second and then stopped. Thomas could hear nothing more. The cries carried on in his mind, and he knew it was the sound of someone falling.

Within the darkness of the cell, the cold presence came even closer. Thomas sat against the wall, believing something sentient to be near to him. He could smell the scent of wild jasmine that overwhelmed the stench of the sewer. As he sat upon the bench he could feel someone sit next to him and then touch his face. Thomas sat completely still, wondering if by some strange means the Druggle had returned. He said nothing as a swish of crinoline swept the floor and there came a sound of faint laughter, and then all was gone. He held his breath to listen, but all he could hear was the pounding of his own heart.

From the alleyway above, Thomas heard the tap, tap of Galphus's cane. It seemed speedy and urgent and matched his steps. He rattled a door with a heavy turn of the key and entered quickly. All went quiet. The door opened to a room above Thomas's head. He could pick out the sounds easily as they filtered down through the sewer. There was much talking and heated conversation that babbled and babbled.

'Get the boy and shut him up. I have been followed – we have *visitors*,' Galphus belched at the guard.

From outside in the alleyway came shouting. 'Galphus! Galphus! I know you're near!' Crane screamed loudly as he stormed the labyrinth of passages like an incoming tide. 'I want the boy and the boy comes now.'

There was a scurry of feet from the stairs outside, the door to Thomas's cell opened quickly and two Druggles grabbed Thomas from the darkness. They bound his hands and feet, gagged him tightly and then threw him to the floor.

'Say nothing, make no sound, we have uninvited guests,' one said as he slapped him around the face and left the room. Thomas lay in the darkness and listened as Crane beat upon the factory door.

'Mister Jacob Crane – I am glad you have come at my wishes . . .' Galphus fawned as Crane pushed his way into the factory. 'Did my messenger find you?'

'Don't treat me like a fool, Galphus. You promised to bring the lad back. I've just seen the writ of indenture upon the door of the Salamander – the boy's name is upon it.'

'So it might be, a hasty decision on his behalf and one I warned him against. But sign he did, all legal and irreversible, Captain Crane.'

'Just like death?' asked Crane.

'Sadly, just like death. And that is the grave matter of why I called you.'

'Then I suggest if you wish to delay yours then you bring the boy to me now and give me the indenture. I promised him a future and your sweet ways will suit him not.'

'If only that were possible. Were you not told?' Galphus paused. 'I sent word to you, Jacob . . . Life is so cruel,' he said as he sat at the desk in the cold room that he used to store his goods. 'There has been an accident. A fall from the roof, a stupid mistake, and poor Thomas is . . .'

'No, Galphus, more lies?' Crane asked.

'Look at me, Jacob, look at me. These are not lies, Jacob. He is dead. Believe me.' Galphus looked at Crane as he turned his head to the side.

'Then you killed him and I will not rest until I have seen him for myself.'

'I would advise you as a friend to remember him in life,' Galphus said slowly as he breathed deeply. 'He fell from the tower, Jacob, and like any Jack has broken his crown.'

'You lie, I know you lie,' Crane said as he felt for the knife on his belt. 'I will see him and speak to any who saw him fall. One hint of treachery and I will split your face from ear to ear.'

'And I will willingly allow you to do it. Look at me, Jacob. There is no treachery here. It was an accident. You can speak to anyone.'

Crane was taken aback. He looked at the guards and then to Galphus, unsure what to believe.

'So he's dead?' he asked, dropping his hand from the handle of his knife. 'Fell? From the tower? How?' Crane spoke as if the possibility of such a thing taking place began to simmer truthfulness.

'He was looking across the city, he slipped and was gone.' Galphus sighed at each word as if he were the grieving father. 'Such promise, such a waste of life.'

'Then I will see him. Who was he with?' Crane asked.

'It was I,' smiled the young Druggle as he slyly doffed his cap. 'I will never live with myself. I should have . . .'

'What we all should have done in life is not to be wept over,' Galphus said. 'I have taken the steps of providing him a place of rest in our garden. It's the least we can do.'

'I should take him back to Whitby, bury him there,' Crane said as he thought of the night they stood on the headland and the world stood still. 'It's near to his home.'

'Unless he was salted or waxed it would not be wise to do such a thing, better leave him to us. Take Mister Crane and show Thomas to him,' Galphus commanded.

'It's not possible, an accident?' Crane murmured, his heart still not believing what he had been told.

Crane followed on like a broken horse. He walked the dark corridors of the factory two paces behind the guard. All the while he thought of Thomas, and of how men are made by the lives they lived and the hurts they carried. Crane felt bitterness in his heart, it tainted his mouth and he could smell its stench as he breathed. He couldn't believe Thomas was dead and yet everything around him spoke of death.

They stopped at a small broken door that led into a narrow room. Inside was a table, and upon it the body of a boy covered in an old blanket. The light was dim, barely above the gloom.

'Let me see him,' Crane said, breathing heavily and squeezing his hands into fists.

'There's not much to see,' the guard said as he lifted the blanket from the lad's face.

In the darkened room, Crane looked at the bloodied corpse. There was the lad he knew so well. The body was draped in a shawl so that all he could see was what remained of the head. He could barely see any of its features; the face was battered beyond recognition. For a second, Crane thought it didn't look like Thomas. He stepped closer, only to be pulled back by the Druggle.

'Galphus would not want you to touch him,' the Druggle said. 'He has been prepared for the burial and the balm would poison you.'

Crane wished that for one moment he would be able to see Thomas's smile again. Taking the knife from his coat he cut a lock of the lad's hair, twisted it into a knot and buried it deep in his pocket. He closed his eyes and bit hard upon his lip. He was lost for the words that his heart cried out for him to say.

Footsteps came from the corridor and Galphus stood by the doorway.

'Look at me, Jacob, look at me . . . All I can say is sorry.' He held out a small bundle wrapped in brown paper and tied with string. 'His clothing and all that was his.' Galphus said sombrely as his eye twitched and blinked. 'We will say goodbye to him at dawn. Join us Jacob, bring Pallium and the girl – you were his family, you should be there.'

Crane nodded, his hand clutching the lock of hair. 'I've seen many die and killed a few myself. Never thought I would ever feel this way. He was a good lad. Doesn't feel like he's dead. Didn't seem like him.' Crane tried to smile at Galphus.

'It is Thomas – there has been no other death today. Look at me, Jacob. Grief makes the mind bleary, after the funeral it will all make sense.'

'I had you for a different man, Mister Galphus. Could have killed you myself when I came here. Now I know you're a man of good intent. Forgive me,' Crane said as if bewitched or mesmerised and finding the words hard to speak.

'Forgiveness is never necessary and too esteemed. This is just life and we are but men.'

# Irrefragable Mister Ergott

N hour later, the moon still burnt brightly. Beadle stood in the doorway of the inn as the hall emptied of people. They all were desperate for sleep, heavy-eyed sluggards wanting to rest but fearful of the night. None of them dared go to their rooms alone. Two by two they dwindled away, agreeing to share their lodgings to be safe from the beast. Twenty of the Militia had taken to the road and set off on foot to scour the hills in search of the hell-hound. They had taken lanterns and muskets and every hound they could find, leaving the inn without defence. Lady Tanville sat by the fire, Barghast to one side, now totally recovered. Raphah walked the courtyard in the moonlight, looking at the stars and thinking of home.

'What was it?' asked Beadle as he came near. 'Do you think it was a dog from the hills?'

'Was a creature, but not one that this world knows much of,' Raphah said, only half-thinking of his reply, his mind caught up with what had happened. 'It was the beast that attacked you at the tree. I saw the look of its red eyes and knew.'

'Will it come back?' Beadle asked.

'Has it ever gone away?' Raphah replied as he strode towards the door and barged past him into the inn. 'Who was it?' he asked Barghast as he approached the fire and turned to warm himself.

'It wanted to kill me, I could tell,' Tanville said as she looked anxiously about her for fear of the beast's return. 'It came in through the window.'

'It left by the window, but I am not sure if it came that way,' Raphah said.

'Then how else did it come?' Barghast asked.

'The door,' he replied

'Opened the door with its clawed hands?' Barghast jested.

'You are one to speak of such things – how would you do it?' Raphah asked, knowing he betrayed the confidence.

'It's not possible even to dream such a thing,' Barghast said as he got to his feet. 'No one can change from man to beast.'

'What?' asked Tanville unsure as to what was being said.

'The creature was a changeling, someone who can turn into an animal at will. Someone who wished either to frighten or kill you,' Raphah said as Barghast stared at him, not wanting him to say any more.

'I agree with Barghast. No such thing,' Lady Tanville said, the thought of a changeling shuddering her mind. 'It was a dog from the moor, that's all. Why should it want to kill me?'

'Perhaps it has some interest in this quest of yours to find your sister in London,' Raphah said.

'My private affairs are of no concern in this matter,' she said, most discontent that he should talk of such a thing. 'It was a hound. Something from the fell. There are legends of these creatures throughout the north. This is not an uncommon belief. It is not a man who can change into a wolf – that is for fairytales.' She said this hopefully, as if speaking to convince herself. 'It was just the savage hound, nothing more.'

'When the hound struck, who didn't you see?' Raphah asked her.

'Mister Ergott, Mister Shrume and Bragg, I never saw them,' she said as she thought of who had not been in the passageway. 'But the inn is full of people from all parts of the land – why do you ask?'

'Then we visit Mister Ergott, Mister Shrume and Bragg. They're in rooms next to yours, are they not?' Barghast asked, showing more belief that the beast might be a changeling. He got to his feet and ran to the stairs. 'Come Raphah, let us see if one of them is the beast.'

Barghast ran up the stairs and Raphah followed. Lady Tanville prodded Beadle, who eyed the world like a harvest mouse woken at Christmas, and eventually they followed. By the time they had climbed the stairs and crossed the landing, Raphah and Barghast were at the door of a room and were listening intently.

Barghast turned the handle and slowly pushed the door open. It slid silently ajar. Upon a table in the corner was a candle. It flickered as the drapes moved in the wind. The room was dark. There was the stench of blood and the faint odour of a dog. Upon the bed lay Mister Shrume. Barghast took a pace closer, stopped and then turned to them.

'No further, Lady Chilnam. We're an hour too late,' he said. Shrume was dead and lay in a pool of blood. 'It was the beast.'

'How do you know?' Raphah asked, looking about as if the creature still lurked in the room.

'See for yourself, there is no question of it. We must find Mister Ergott and then Bragg.'

'What kind of a beast are we looking for – a fat one?' Beadle asked under his breath.

'A beast that snaps the necks from the living and then makes off into the night, Beadle. A beast that would make a meal of you and take you like a morsel,' said Barghast as he examined the body closely. 'He died instantly. Strangely, he was not killed here, but by the window. His body is arranged like a Viking funeral.'

From the high fell came the crying of a beast that called out to the moon, howling like a lost wolf. It cried as if it searched for others of its kind.

'Black Shuck?' asked Lady Tanville, as the vision of the creature from her room burnt in her mind. Beadle hid behind her, not wanting to see anything.

'The creature is closer than that. He will show himself by his surprise to see me alive,' replied Barghast as they left the room and walked along he corridor.

It was Raphah who was the first to enter the room of Mister Ergott. All was neat and clean, the bed unruffled. Taking a tinderbox, he lit the candle, shut the open window and cast the bolt in place. He took a moment to look through the glass, across the moat and towards the fell. The cry of the dog came again, this time closer. It was as if it called from the thick wood. 'It gets nearer,' he said softly as he tried to make out the flickering lights upon the moors.

Raphah chided himself for thinking the worst of Barghast. Suspicion and mistrust had covered his eyes. His looks alone had made Raphah feel that Barghast was baptised in wickedness – the gaunt white face and searing blue eyes, capped with a mop of jagged white hair, were everything Raphah had come to despise. In knowing Barghast, Raphah had lost his suspicion. He had thought him to be a threat, an enemy, a stalker with a heart of misdeeds. Now he saw him as a lost traveller, a wayfarer like himself.

'The Militia search the moors,' Raphah said.

'And we are alone,' said Lady Tanville anxiously as she and Beadle stayed close by each other. Beadle gently held her hand, more for his own comfort than hers.

'All we need see now is Mister Bragg. If he is there, then it is Ergott who is our devil-hound,' Barghast said.

'Don't like Ergott,' Beadle sniffed. 'Said I were ugly, as ugly as a dog.'

'Then he only sees the condition of his own heart and not how you are truly seen,' Lady Tanville said.

'I go first, Raphah,' Barghast said as they left the room and went along the passageway.

As they approached the door they could hear the sound of talking. Bragg was boasting to himself. In one breath he sang and with another other he scolded. He was drunk, and from the noise that came from within he was trying to get even drunker.

'Worse than a fool is a drunken fool,' Lady Tanville said, following the procession closer to the door.

'But at least it will loosen his tongue. Leave us and we'll talk with him. Watch the door and beat upon it should Ergott return,' Raphah said.

'You leave us here, alone, with a mad dog roaming the inn?' Beadle asked nervously. 'Rather face Demurral,' he said, forgetting who was with him.

'It *is* you . . .' Barghast said, as if he knew of Beadle from long ago. 'I have been searching my mind as to when and where I saw you before. A face like yours should never have been forgotten. My mind must vex me in my dotage.' He pointed at Beadle with a long finger. 'The servant of the master, of course . . .'

'Can't say I remember you,' Beadle stammered, knowing full well of the night that Barghast spoke of.

It had been ten years before. Demurral had grown in his desires to follow his dark heart. Beadle had grown a beard and long whiskers. He had seen a picture on a rum bottle of an old sea-hawker. The man had beard and chin-wings, which Beadle thought gave him charm; they were waxed and looked like the tusks of some great ocean pig. In the weeks that followed Beadle had grown the beard, even though it came to contain more food than his platter and became the nesting place for several earwigs and a host of fleas. He had waxed and curled it until he looked like a mad sow with deranged spikes of bristle. The dark hairs made his eyes stand out as if they were on stalks and hid his jowls so that he looked like a walrus.

It was the eve of the summer and the night was light even though the hour was late. As he had answered the ringing of the bell, the long clock had chimed the quarter hour after eleven. The sun had set beyond the sea at Whitby and a red glow engulfed the whole of Baytown.

The visitor had called and demanded to see Demurral. Beadle now knew the man to be Barghast. He had called unannounced and entered the house without being made welcome. He had sat in Demurral's own chair. Whilst waiting he had lit the fire and poured himself a glass of wine. All this he had done as Beadle had scurried forth for the master.

What had then taken place had mystified Beadle since that day. Demurral had gone into the study and had bowed to the man, taking great care not to look him in the eye. The visitor didn't speak but held out his hand as if to receive a gift. In return, Demurral had gone to his safe-chest, taken out a silk bag and placed it in the man's hand. The man had then finished his wine, nodded to the parson and walked out without any farewell.

No mention was ever made of the strange transaction. Later that night, as the moon had risen from the sea, Beadle had listened at the chamber door as Demurral had sobbed like a child. He had been troubled for his master, knowing that something was deeply wrong. Even though in his heart he despised the man, it pained him to hear him blubbering. Beadle had thought of the times when he had been left to cry. Even though Demurral had beaten and scolded him, all that Beadle desired was to open the door and show him some kindness. Yet it had been from that night that Demurral had changed. In handing the silk bag to Barghast it was as if he had become like a madman, and Demurral cried out of anger for the giving of a possession to someone more powerful than he.

'You must remember me?' Barghast asked again quietly as they stood outside Bragg's door.

'I haven't the memory to bring these things to mind,' Beadle said as he looked away.

Raphah tapped upon Bragg's door. Not waiting to be summonsed within he pushed the handle as he and Barghast stepped inside.

'Mister Bragg,' he said loudly. 'We thought by your conversation you were entertaining.'

Bragg was slumped in the chair by the fire, a flagon of wine by his side and a half-pint mug in his hand. He was slow to look up from the flames, as if he cared not who spoke to him.

'Ah, Barghast – fresh from the hunt. What news of the beast that stalks our lives? Is it the one at Galilee Rocks?' Bragg said as he sipped his wine.

'Neither,' Barghast replied. 'Shrume is dead. Killed like a farmyard chicken, not fifty feet from this room.'

'Dead? How can he be dead? I heard nothing. I have sat by the fire and entertained myself. Since the hound ran from the inn all has been quiet,' Bragg said.

'And what of Ergott? We need to question him,' Raphah said.

'Who could have done such a thing?' Bragg replied, ignoring Raphah and looking to Barghast.

'Why do you travel to London?' Barghast asked.

'I am a collector of fine objects, and I take something to a

185

customer. He buys many things from me and I offer a personal service. Why should this concern you?' he asked.

'Did you know Mister Shrume before the journey.' Raphah insisted.

'You should keep better company, Mister Barghast. There is a curse on the Ethio's head. Remember – he was the one who sat in Ord Vackan's chair. Look what has happened since. You vanished, Lady Chilnam attacked, Shrume dead and Ergott nowhere to be found.'

'Ergott? Did I say Ergott?' Barghast asked Bragg. 'I only mentioned Mister Shrume.'

'A mistake, a presumption, a conjecture, a . . .' Bragg flustered and sweated before the fire. 'So Shrume is dead – the tragedy . . . Who will be next?' He gulped his wine eagerly and tore off chunks of bread from a loaf. He swallowed hard as his eyes flicked like a snake from Barghast to Raphah and then to the window.

From the high fell came the calling of the hound. It cried to the moon as it ran.

'There, that's your hound. Came from the hills, Black Shuck, got in through Lady Tanville's window and did the deed. You know what you'll have to do. Bury Shrume before dawn, face-down or he'll be back. Once a hell-hound has killed you then you'll return – you of all people should know that, Mister Barghast. A man of your travels will have heard every tale.' Bragg rambled, his piggy eyes widened to the rims.

'That's all they are, fireside tales,' Barghast said.

'Look at what's happened since the Ethio joined us. Hell has come a-calling. We should make him walk to London. Don't want to travel with a *Jonah* on the carriage. Who'd be next? There's too much good eating on me and whatever is following us has only appeared since *he* arrived.'

'Raphah's money is as good as yours,' Barghast argued.

'Then he should take it and spend it somewhere else. The man's a Jonah, bad luck, misfortune, death on two legs, that's what he is.' Bragg grizzled with discontent as the wine slobbered over his lips and down the front of his nightshirt.

'One thing,' Barghast asked as they turned to leave. 'Mister Ergott – are you and he . . . *friends*?'

'No time for the man, he is a charlatan. Believes he's a diviner and a dowser. Why would I need an acquaintance like that? Who would keep company with a man who plays with a stick? Rather have a dog for a friend, at least the dog can bark . . .' Bragg laughed, pleased with himself. 'Listen to me, Mister Barghast. You'd be better off ditching the Ethio and mixing with us. Taints a man, bad company, it corrupts good character and I can see nothing good in your dark shadow – even if he can heal the sick. Think I'd rather be dead than let him touch me.' Bragg seethed as he spoke, cringing his shoulders and shuddering at the same time.

'I have that feeling myself,' Barghast replied.

'Really?' said Bragg astonished that someone should share his view.

'Usually for fat old drunks who find their own company *pleasurable*,' he said as he turned and followed Raphah from the room.

The door of the chamber closed quietly and Bragg sat in his own company before the fire. The soft light flickered against his face. He lifted the mug and drank from it again. He waited as he heard the footsteps walk along the corridor and down the stairs.

Bragg broke the bread and dipped it in the wine before taking another bite.

'Safe to come from your hiding place my dear little hound,' Bragg said as the creature crawled from beneath the bed. 'They believe you to be Black Shuck . . .'

The beast curled itself by his feet, warming against the fire. Its dark fur bristled as it sniffed the air. Bragg stroked its long nose and looked into its red eyes.

'To think that they would want to hurt someone as sweet as you,' he said.

The beast grumbled a low growl at the edge of hearing. It sounded as if it purred softly, its large dog-ears listening to every word spoken in the hall below.

# Funeral

T dawn, as a far clock struck the hour, Smutt's body lay beside a damp sepulchre. The tomb had been hewn from thick clay and dug out of indolence to three shovels' depth. Like the rest of Salamander Street, the garden – if that is what it could be called – never saw the sky. It was a bare patch of earth surrounded on all sides by the factory, in a lost corner where the eaves of two buildings came together. Upon the dirt lay the body, wrapped in grey rags and tied with hemp cord. Looking down upon it was Galphus. He waited impatiently, tapping the head of the corpse with his cane and listening to the dull thud that it made.

From the flaking door of the factory stepped Jacob Crane. Kate held Pallium's hand and clutched three flowers. She followed him slowly and wept as she walked. Crane kept a hard stare, straining his lips across his teeth to stop them from trembling. He kept his eyes from looking at the body as he nodded to Galphus in welcome and nervously rubbed his hands together. In his heart he felt as if he had come to bury his son. Looking at Kate, he remembered Demurral's house. The garden there was bright and faced the sea. He had fought to keep

Thomas from a grave in that garden. Now he looked around to the bare stone walls and crumbling brick that surrounded him.

From inside the factory, two of the Druggles came and took hold of the body. Upon a quick stamp of Galphus's cane they picked it up with the straps and clumsily dropped the body to the grave. There was a gentle spatter as the water that half-filled the tomb overwhelmed the body. It floated momentarily and then slowly slipped deeper and deeper. Everything was grey and without colour. The cloth soaked up the water and the lamp above them flickered on the grey earth.

Kate could restrain herself no longer. She screamed in pain as if her heart was being torn from within her. Crane held her to him as the harsh shovelling of clay splattered against the carcass. Soon, Thomas was gone, no words said, dust to dust.

'Short life,' Galphus chirped as they looked at the pile of earth. 'Makes you think of wasted time.' He tried to smile at Kate and took her by the chin, holding her as if she were a doll to be inspected. 'Salamander, Jacob?' he asked as he turned to Crane with the offer of a drink. 'Never too early to taste a fine wine.'

Crane looked to Kate who held out the flowers. 'Let's give her some time to say goodbye,' he said. He took Galphus by the arm and walked towards the door, and Pallium followed.

'When she has finished her mourning bring her to my room, we'll wait there,' Galphus said to the Druggles who stood in the shadows with their muddied shovels. Crane took a final glance as Kate sank to her knees in the dirt and pressed the flowers into the stinking clay of the grave. He brought the words of goodbye to mind but knew they would never reach his lips.

Galphus led Crane from the courtyard and into the factory. They walked silently through the workrooms until they came to Galphus's study.

It was a windowless room stacked with shelves and wooden boxes. There was a large desk lit by several candlesticks. To one side was an old skull and several discarded teeth. Crane looked about the room. It smelt of cabbage and old women. The plaster was falling from the walls in several places and the door had been gnawed by rats.

'Tell me, Crane,' Galphus said, 'how much would you need to free your ship?'

'Enough and enough again,' he replied.

'On my desk is a bag, take it and pay off what you owe. Take it from me as a gift, and from you I'll take a third share in all you make from now on,' Galphus said.

'What else will you take?' he asked.

'Just a third, nothing more. Reasonable and honest for the amount in the bag. I know that when you pay the release there will be more than enough.'

'Signed for or shaken upon?' Crane asked. He looked at a thousand glass jars neatly placed upon the shelves in tidy rows; each one was precisely labelled with a name and date, and underneath this inscription were words that differed from jar to jar in a tongue he could not comprehend.

'The offer is there and I will not shake or sign. Let us say that it is just for the taking.' Galphus saw that Crane was staring at the jars. 'They are interesting, are they not?' he asked as he lifted one from the shelf and held it before Crane's face.

'Empty jars – interesting?' Crane asked.

'More than that. They are the finest collection in the world.'

'Of what?' said Crane.

'The last breaths of those who have gone before. Aristotle, Caesar, Pythagoras and there,' he said, pointing to a larger jar at the end of the shelf, 'King George the First.' Galphus smiled and spoke excitedly, all thought of the funeral now a distant memory. 'I know it may sound strange, but to me it is an interest and one that not many people may entertain. They are my *pneumamorte* . . .'

'So why keep them?'

'I believe that they possess a power, that in the last breath the soul jumps from the flesh. Within the world there are some of us who know this. This is glass made from the sand beneath an Italian volcano, Capacious Alta. It has the power to trap the soul. That soul can give us vigour. Think of it, Jacob – wouldn't you like to live forever?'

'I would like to die old and in bed,' he said.

'I have summonsed a man to bring me an implement so that I can partake of these breaths, hear the last words of those who died and take on their lives. As we speak I am being brought a cup, and from this I will drink my eternal life. I tell you this as a fascination. I know you have seen much and now that we are partners I can tell you more.' He smiled.

'Kate,' Crane said as she stepped into the room with a tear-stained face. 'Galphus and I were . . .'

'I heard. Pity his implement was not here to give Thomas life,' she said angrily.

'Come, have breakfast with us, we can mourn your friend over a drink,' Galphus invited her.

'I have Thomas's things for company – Crane gave me a par-cel of clothes, they are all I need for company.' Kate scowled and looked to the floor. Her face was set like stone. 'I'll go with Pallium, he said he'd take me back. I need to sleep,' she said.

'Jacob and I have some business. I'm sure he'll be along later.' Galphus held out his hand. Kate turned without speak-ing and made off along the corridor to where she had left Mister Pallium.

Together they made their way from the factory back to Sala-mander Street and Pallium's home. He offered her chocolate and milk, but Kate refused and asked that she could sleep some more. As it always did, the door to the stairs opened on its own. Taking quick strides, she leapt up the treads two by two and turned into her room. The morning fire still burnt warmly and the bed where Thomas had slept was still in its place, the covers not touched since he had last been there.

Kate looked for the parcel that Crane had given to her. She pulled open the string and ripped the paper. Inside were Thomas's clothes. They were cold, damp and stank of shoe leather and glue. She took the shirt and warmed it by the fire. It was soon soft and warm and smelt of Thomas. She held it to her and smothered herself within as she tried to picture his face.

The room fell cold. Snowflakes flurried across the ceiling and stacked against the far wall. Leaves blew about the boards and the scent of the forest grew stronger. The sound of the magichord began to play softly.

Kate looked to the wall. The picture had gone, the wall had gone. There stood the entrance to the forest. The magichord was still in place. She waited and waited as she clutched Thomas's shirt.

'Saw him fall,' a voice from beside her said. 'Right from the window of the tower. Looked as if he were already dead.'

Kate sat still with fear, not daring to look at the girl. 'How would you know that?'

'When you die your soul jumps from you and goes off. Some disappear and are never seen again. Others, especially the ones who don't know they're dead, hang about. Get up from the body and look around. When your friend hit the ground there was nothing. So I went looking . . .'

'And?' Kate asked as she buried her face within his garments and sighed.

'Couldn't find him, not a trace. Looked everywhere – called

out to him and everything. No boy. Just the body. Strange thing is, I found someone in the cellar, very much alive. Looked like Thomas.'

'But I've just buried him. Saw it myself. Jacob Crane saw him not an hour after he was dead.' Kate screwed up her eyes and covered them with her hands. 'Leave me, you do nothing but torment.'

'Typical,' said the girl with a tut. 'Try to help the living and all you do is complain. When will you realise that death is not the end of life? How many spectres will you have to see before you believe?'

'But I don't believe. You're bad meat, a dream, madness of my mind,' Kate shouted.

'Then look at me. Look at me if you're not afraid,' the girl asked as she touched Kate on the face.

'NO! Leave me alone.'

'But if I am just a figment of your mind then you are alone, Kate.'

The words made her drop the hands from her face and stare at the spirit. Like before she wore the crinoline dress etched in foxgloves. She looked younger, fresh of face.

'Am I mad?' Kate asked the spectre.

'Why ask me? I'm dead,' the girl replied, giggling to herself. 'So why did Galphus bring you here? Does he want you in the factory or will he steal all of the man's money?'

'What?'

'That's what he does. You're not the first and won't be the last. Pallium gets them here and hands them on. That's how he's paid. He'll have you in that factory before the morning. He'll convince your friend to leave you here and then you'll be snatched, vanish from the face of the earth. Had a parson here. He would sell him children, came from the north. Not particular, our Mister Galphus.'

'How do you know? Thought you were trapped?' Kate said angrily as she looked intently at the girl who appeared as real as she was.

'I listen, never eat or sleep but listen. Walk the street and listen, as they work I listen. Kate, you can't leave this place.'

'I'll leave when I want,' Kate said.

'Do it now, go, see how far you get. Follow the street and you'll come to a dead end, a blind alley. Whatever way you choose you won't get out. Galphus made this place and he's an alchemist, a magician. Look on a map and it doesn't exist. There is no Salamander Street in the whole of London. I heard them, Kate. Listened to the screams of children trying to escape, they soon find out they'll be here forever.'

'I'll go now,' Kate stammered.

The spectre bent forward through the leather chair and whispered in Kate's ear. 'Mister Pallium is listening to you from outside, thinks you're talking to yourself. Thinks you're mad.'

There was a gentle knock at the door, then the latch slipped and it opened slowly. 'Couldn't help hearing you, Kate,' Pallium said kindly as he peered at her. 'Must be a great shock. Mister Galphus will make it better, always does.' Pallium stepped into the room. It was as if he was unaware of all that was around him. He could see neither the spectre nor the forest that lay beyond the wall. In his eyes all was as it should be and nothing had changed.

Kate glanced to where the wall should have been. There was the glen that led to the river. She could see it clearly. A fawn ran through the wood and in her mind she could hear the sound of birds calling.

Pallium stared at her. 'I think you should rest. Galphus will come soon and all will be well.'

'I want to see Jacob,' she said suddenly.

'How can I say this, what words will suffice to calm you on such a day?'

'Words? I want to see Jacob Crane and I go now,' Kate said as the ghost vanished before her.

'I have bad news – he's gone. Didn't want to say. Left you in my care. Knew I would look after you. Galphus and I will be your guardians. Took the money offered by Galphus and went. He wasn't going to drink in the Salamander, he was going to get the money. He's gone for the *Magenta*.' Pallium spoke breathlessly.

'He would have told me,' Kate said.

'He couldn't – too hard and too hurtful. That's old Jacob. Like a nut, but crack the shell and he's so sweet.'

The girl appeared again by the fireplace and shouted to Kate. 'He's gone, Kate. Your friend is neither at the inn nor anywhere in the street. Galphus drinks in the Salamander but the smuggler is no more.'

'Gone?' Kate yelled. 'How can he be gone? What have you done to him?'

Pallium reached out a hand to touch her brow.

'Don't trust him,' the spectre whispered, Pallium unaware of her presence. 'I've seen this before, he has a knife.'

'Where?' Kate screamed, not knowing whom to believe.

'You're tired – it's the shock. I have some tea, I'll bring some for you,' Pallium said as he hurried from the room.

'Gone for Galphus and his men, that's what he always does,' the spectre said as the latch snapped on the door and the locked turned. 'See – bolted and kept within, you won't get out.'

Kate grabbed the door and rattled the lock. It stuck fast. Below, she heard the door open and Pallium dash into the street. Kate ran to the window and saw him scurrying like a rat into the darkness.

'What will he do?' she asked the ghost.

'He gets Galphus and they'll take you away. Then he . . .'

'What?' Kate asked.

'Just escape, that's all you have to do. That or cheat them.'

'Cheat them, how?' Kate asked.

'Come with me into the forest – we could live there together. I wouldn't be lonely and you'd be free.'

'But you're dead.'

'So could you be. It's like taking a step from the world to another.' The spectre sat on the bed and put her face in her hands and looked Kate in the eyes. 'Just walk into the glade and all will be well. Quickly! Galphus will be here soon and I can't say what he'll do to you.'

'I'll hide.'

'They'll find you.'

'Run . . .'

'You're locked in – how will you escape? Come with me, Kate,' the spectre pleaded.

'Not my time, not for me to decide. Raphah said there was a time for everything, living and dying, and it wasn't for us to choose. Belonged to someone else. There's always hope – no matter what your circumstance.'

There was a cry in the street. Torches came through the darkness as Galphus and three Druggles made their way towards the house. Pallium followed on, dragging himself in his baggy suit through the dirt. From the window, Kate could see their approach.

'They come for you,' the spectre said as she stepped towards the glade. 'Come with me.'

Kate hesitated for a moment and looked to the street. Galphus walked quickly, his cane beating out the pace as the Druggles in their grey cloth coats and black boots came closer in the twilight.

'You have but the minute and then you'll be theirs forever.

The smuggler won't come back – he'll never find the place again. It's easy this way. Just take a breath, Kate. Trust me.'

'I promised my father I'd always be there,' she said, feeling her feet slide closer towards where the wall should have been.

'Three more steps, Kate. It will all be over. Quickly, follow me.'

'But I promised him,' she pleaded.

'The threshold, Kate, and death will come quickly.'

'I want to stay. I want to live,' she said as her voice grew fainter against the sound of the forest. As she looked it was as if the world began to fade. The room blurred and the fire dimmed. The glade grew in its power and presence. As she got closer, the magichord chimed by itself, dancing notes that came forth from within it and could be seen in the air like tiny moths. As they flew by they sung in chords together, filling the room as the light faded. Kate reached out and gripped her hand upon the bed as her feet were dragged from her. 'Let me stay,' she shouted as the spectre took hold of her from inside the wood and tried to pull her into the forest. And her death.

# The Black Shuck

THEY had spent the night camped by the fire in the hallway, taking it in turns to keep watch. Raphah had not slept a single wink. His mind was filled with discontent, the thoughts of Africa stronger than before. He felt alone and helpless in a land where so many people hated him. The inn was like a great ship at sea. It creaked and groaned as timbers rasped against the stones. The cold night air shivered its bones. Raphah thought again of Africa and fought the voice within that told him to run and leave these people to their own desires. He had come to their land to find the Keruvim, which had been stolen from his people. It was something so old, so powerful, that in the hands of evil men it could change the course of history. As they slept, warmed and lighted by the flames of the fire, Raphah looked at their faces.

Beadle snored, his jowls flapping as his head lolled from side to side. Raphah thought him to be honest, but was crushed by his fearfulness. Barghast was motionless as if he rested in death. Lady Chilnam sat serenely in the chair, wrapped in her long black cloak.

The inn grew silent as the night went on and by the dawn

was perfectly still. Barghast woke early and as Raphah dozed had gone to tell the innkeeper of what he had found during the night. Silently and without fuss, the body of Mister Shrume was taken from the inn and buried face-down beyond the walls. Barghast returned as the house came to life, his boots still wetted by the dew, the fog hanging from his clothes.

In the great hall, a meal was set. Bragg, smelling the scent of meat and hearing the clanking of plates, appeared from his room. Ergott was still nowhere to be found. Raphah checked his room and returned with news that the bed had not been disturbed and Ergott had not returned.

Bragg didn't appear surprised as he sat at table and stuffed his mouth to bursting. 'Likes to take the air,' he said.

'But he didn't return at all. We checked his room last night and he was gone,' Barghast replied.

For a moment, Bragg was silent. He looked about the room as he chewed upon the gristle, then pulled it from his mouth and dropped it to the plate. 'Could have been taken himself – had you not thought of that? We sit here filling our bellies and Ergott could be dead. What people are we to leave a fellow traveller?' As he spoke, his eyes disappeared into the depths of his skull and his face quivered.

'So you say we look for him?' Lady Tanville asked.

'If he is not here then where can he be?' Bragg said, somehow convinced by his own concern.

From the courtyard came the cries of the Militia. In the still morning air, their voices carried from the gates. The innkeeper flung open the doors as a musket-man dragged the carcass of a large black dog up the steps and into the inn.

'See,' he said proudly. 'The beast is dead.'

The inn filled with excitement as all gathered round. From every room came people to gawp at the large dog that lay upon the cold stone floor, staring with dead eyes. The vaulted ceiling of the hall with its panelled staircase and mullioned windows echoed with all their apprehension.

'Caught it upon the fell. Heard it calling and then shot it from the crag,' the man said with a broad smile upon his face.

'It's not the hound,' Barghast whispered to Raphah. 'Not big enough and not enough teeth.'

'Say nothing to them,' he replied quietly. 'Let them think it to be the beast. Our coach leaves at dusk – we have until then to find the animal.'

'Or man,' Barghast added.

The innkeeper roared with excitement as he looked at the hound. He beat his chest in merriment and gave beer to all, and the inn sang out with the celebration. Beadle took his part, dancing on the table, his face covered in froth as he sung of the dead beast.

Raphah looked on as he and Barghast sat by the fire. Bragg had disappeared in the throngs of the glee and was nowhere to be seen. Men danced and jabbered. They kicked the dead creature and beat it with sticks.

'I shall look for Ergott,' Raphah said as Lady Tanville came to the fire. 'He has to be found.'

'Taken by the dog – or is the dog,' Barghast said.

'But they have the beast – we saw it,' Tanville replied.

'That wasn't the creature, Tanville. That was a wild dog, a wolf and not a changeling.'

'Where do we look?' she asked.

'Somewhere close by, somewhere . . .'

Tanville quickly interrupted. 'The cave – there is an entrance from the inn. I showed Beadle last night when you were on the moor. I have a map. It was stolen from Bragg a year ago. I bought it at great price from the thief.' She looked towards the panelling on the far wall.

'Within?' asked Raphah trying to guess her meaning.

'Deep within, third panel from the floor, second to the left.'

Beadle continued to dance upon the table as the hunters dragged the kill from the hall and into the courtyard. They hoisted it from a gibbet in the corner by the tar-splashed walls and let it dangle in the wind. Some of them came back and continued to drink. They spoke loudly, brutal talk for brutal men. The wolf swung in the breeze. Its bloated tongue stuck from its mouth as the rope stretched its neck.

'We wait,' said Raphah as the merry-making began to still and each man found a place to rest his drunken neck. 'They will soon sleep and we can search for Ergott.'

Barghast nodded in agreement, knowing the hunters had been gone all night. The beer would swell their tiredness and sleep would soon come to them. He had been strangely quiet as he looked about him, his eyes searching each face.

'They have it!' exclaimed Beadle as he slumped from the table, his song complete and his belly full of beer. 'We can travel in peace, find Kate and Thomas, and Demurral won't find us,' he said foolishly.

'So you look for someone and someone looks for you?' Tanville asked.

'Some people we know – that we will visit,' Raphah said without thinking as he tried to cover Beadle's mistake.

Barghast stared at the floor, his gaze fixed upon a broken claw that had been shed by the wolf. 'Your mistake was to find me upon the moor,' he said to Raphah as Lady Tanville walked with Beadle to the kitchen in search of food. 'I know the man who pursues you and the rumours of why he needs to find you. I took something from him, a shard of wood touched by the hand of Riathamus. What did you take from Demurral?'

'That which belonged to my family. That which he would have used for magic. I took the Keruvim.'

'So it is true. The Keruvim is real and he had it all along. I

202

heard a rumour that it had come to this land. When I first saw you, I knew,' Barghast said, his eyes still fixed upon the claw. 'Lives entwined like hemp rope. You in search of your friends and me a beggar. Find you and find the beggar. Eh, Raphah?'

'You could be from Demurral,' Raphah said with narrow eyes.

'That I could. But on this journey I have to trust you and you me. There is a creature that since your arrival has begun to kill. Any one of us could be its intended victim. I've made many enemies in many years and now Bragg is one of them.'

'So I just trust you? As simple as that?' Raphah asked.

'Thought trust would come easily to someone like you,' Barghast said as he picked the piece of claw from the hearth. 'Interesting,' he said, looking upon it. 'There is little wear upon it – not a beast that travels far, more a house dog than a monster from the fell.'

Beadle slumped by the fire. The sleeplessness of the night was brought heavy upon his brow by the light of the day. He stacked the hearth with more logs and leant back against the warm stone. The hall became quiet. The Militia drifted away, leaving only those who had joined the hunt from the inn to sleep by the flames. It became like the night-time. Peace was on all, there was no fear, the beast was dead – it hung from the gibbet with the first raven picking at its skin.

Raphah looked to Barghast. 'Time?' he asked.

Barghast looked about him. 'Time indeed,' he said with a shivered smile.

'I come with you,' Lady Tanville insisted.

'Would be best for you to stay and . . .' Raphah tried to insist.

'I am coming and you cannot make me stay. I have something that will bring a blessing to our journey.' She said as she walked quickly up the stairs to her room. When she reached the landing she turned and looked at them. 'Be here when I return, understand.'

Raphah laughed with Barghast. 'We have no choice – she would have us for bodice stays if we went alone.'

Tanville soon returned. In her hands she carried a black silk bag the size of a dead cat. It was strung about her with a long twine handle and buttoned with a gold clasp. She nodded to them both and walked to the far end of the hall. Barghast and Raphah followed, checking to see if all the hunters were asleep. Beadle groaned and snored, kicking out his legs as if he were having some mad dream.

Barghast pointed to the stone floor. By the wall was a single paw print etched in blood. 'We are not the first to go this way,' he said quietly. 'The beast goes before us.'

'This is it,' Tanville said as she tapped the panel with her hand. It opened slightly. The door slid quickly to one side and the three entered in. Inside was complete blackness.

'Keep awake, don't close your eyes,' she said as she undid the clasp and brought out the hand.

'This is not a good thing you have,' Raphah said, sensing its presence but unable to see the Hand of Glory.

There was the striking of a flint and the burning of tinder. A glow filled the stair chamber. The hand burnt brightly as each finger flickered with a purple flame.

'What a surprise, my dear girl,' Barghast said as he chuckled to himself. 'A Glory Hand. I took you for a lonely traveller, not a witch. Will you not entice us with the spell?'

'We don't need magic,' Raphah insisted. 'Leave magic to those who don't know a greater power. If we must suffer this contrivance, then let us have only the light from its fingers, without any so–called *magic*.'

'But it will make them all sleep,' Tanville said eagerly.

'Sorcery and wickedness are the same word. The drink will be enough. I have known the spirit of this same hand before. It will bring you no good.'

'So it was *you* who stole Bragg's money,' Barghast said to Tanville.

'And nearly got me hanged,' Raphah said.

'It was not the money I wanted. I was looking for a key, the key to his trunk. Bragg stole a painting that once belonged to my family. Some time ago he sold it to a collector in London. I follow him, for wherever he goes I know I will find what he has stolen. On the day my father died, he commanded me to get the picture and bring it home. Since it was taken a curse has come upon us.'

'All I hear of in this country is curses,' Raphah said angrily as they followed Tanville's light down the steps into the cave. 'When will you learn to be free of the curse?'

'When faith vanquishes superstition,' Barghast said. 'Even in this time of great science, does not the chemist by day become the alchemist by night?'

'Then they are as mad as the lead they work with,' Raphah grunted. 'The sun shines in their faces and they turn to darkness. They worship the stars and not the one who created them. I met a man aboard a ship who would not get from his bed until he had read the dregs of his teacup . . . Fools.'

'They take it seriously, Raphah,' Barghast said as they walked deeper into the cave.

'Then they should wake from their slumber and you also, Tanville. Whatever curse is upon your family can be broken.'

'Then help me find the picture,' she said angrily, her hand shaking the light of the Glory Hand. 'Unless it is in the castle it will cause great harm. It is the prison for a spirit.'

'Your great-aunt Lady Isabella?' Barghast asked. 'The ghost painting?'

'How did you know?' she asked.

'Let us say I have an interest . . . I heard the story of how she was painted, a likeness captured from the grave. She haunts wherever the picture hangs? I have heard that she is prone to much trickery for a ghost.'

'Isabella has done more than that,' Tanville replied as she stopped in the vault of the stairway and looked to the passage below. There in the dust was a further paw mark upon the stone. 'My father heard that she had taken to killing those on whose wall her picture hung. Just a rumour, when he tried to find her. Lady Isabella will not be at peace until she is back at Chilnam Castle.'

'Then I will search for her and she will have peace. How can you allow the spirits to walk the world of men?' Raphah asked, at the edge of his temper.

No one replied. As the glow of the hand lit the stone about their feet, his words echoed ahead of them. Raphah looked up. High above his head was the glistening roof of a gigantic cave. It shimmered in the light from the candles that were gripped in the fingers of the Glory Hand. The steps that had come from the inn had brought them to a vast cavern. A wind blew against their faces like a sea gale. It beat against the candles, the light flickering but unable to be extinguished until the spell was spoken. The cave belched and bellowed like a rumbling gut. Far away was the sound of rushing water.

'Here,' Barghast said, pointing to the shadows that lined the floor. 'The creature came this way.' There were distinct marks upon the wet sand that lined the floor. 'It went deeper in.'

Lady Tanville shuddered. She looked at the cave roof and wondered what kept it from falling. The thought made it hard for her to breathe. Leaning against the wall, she held out the Glory Hand, hoping that it would somehow hold back the rock that she thought would fall on them at any moment. The vast emptiness of the cavern made her wits reel. It reminded her of the castle she had left and the reason for her journey.

Abruptly, she was taken from the cave as a vision flashed

across her eyes. The fear in her mind sped her back in time to a cold, foggy morning. The light had not yet come, the dawn still far off. It was the morning of her eighth birthday. The ghost of Lady Isabella had dragged her from the bed. She chased her playfully from the nursery in the spire of the castle. Through chilly, unlit corridors Tanville ran as fast as she could. At first she laughed – a game they had played before. Then something had changed. As they got to the stairs, Lady Isabella grabbed her by the hair, her ghostly hands twisting themselves coldly in her long locks and winding the strands tightly in her spectral fingers. Isabella then dragged her down each flight, faster and faster, Tanville's feet not touching the treads but missing the steps as she ran breathlessly. It was as if the ghost wanted her to fall.

Tanville had looked up – the ceiling darkened and yet spinning above her head, the walls pressing in upon her as if they would collapse at any moment – and had reached out for balance as she screamed for Isabella to stop. No one came. Tanville screamed even louder and Lady Isabella twisted her faster. The castle faded and all around them was the great hill. There stood Isabella on a high crag, spinning Tanville as if she were a top. Every twist took her closer to the edge.

'Hold out your arms and fly, Tanville,' Isabella had sniggered. 'Then we can play always.'

Tanville had done as she had said and just as she had reached the precipice she slipped. The dream was broken. She was balanced precariously upon the top of the stairs, her feet at the edge. She looked at Isabella, who laughed, 'Jump!' she said, as Tanville stared at the floor far below. Then Tanville had stepped from the banister as two arms snatched her from the air. She could never forget the smell of her father, holding her close and banishing Isabella.

The next day the priest had scourged the spectre. He had

poured holy water upon the picture and nailed iron bars across the frame. With his withered fingers he had laced it with henbane and holly leaves. For many nights the castle was sleepless as Lady Isabella gripped the bars, screaming from inside to be set free. For a year and a day the picture had been turned to face the wall so that she could not escape. Lady Tanville Chilnam never slept alone in the house again. She was glad that the picture had gone. Now, the dying wish of her father, spoken in his madness, had caused her to search for it again. 'As I die,' he said, 'bring Isabella home again to rest with me.'

Now, inside the cavern, Lady Tanville held out her hand and forced her mind to think only of the flames. Barghast, knowing something was wrong, took the Glory Hand from her and held it above his head to cast the light as far as he could. He could sense that she was troubled. Her eyes looked empty, her face vague.

'What troubles you?' he asked as they walked towards a place where the tunnel narrowed and stalactites hung down like teeth.

'It's the cavern – it presses in upon me, takes my breath,' she said.

'We have nothing to fear,' he said softly.

'And what of Ergott?' she asked. 'Is he not to be feared? You think him a man who can change to a beast.'

'Whatever Ergott may be is no cause for us to fear him,' Raphah said. 'I'm certain Barghast will make sure of that.'

They gathered pace as they walked. The passageway grew narrow and low, causing them to crouch as they stumbled on. The sound of water grew louder, and the gusting of the wind was like the eerie farting of a gigantic animal. Barghast continued to find the tracks of the creature. Every now and then it had stopped and scraped the floor as if it searched for something in the sand. He knew it to be near. The cavern dripped with water that filled the icy pools all around them.

In his senses he could feel the beast close by, watching them as they walked on. In the outer limits of the darkness he knew it waited for them. Barghast stopped, held the Glory Hand even higher and peered into the blackness.

'Ergott!' he cried, the words coming back to him. 'Where are you, man?'

From far in the distance came a scream – half man, half dog. There was then the sobbing of a child and then the scream again.

'We can't go on,' Lady Tanville said. 'It's the creature.'

'We must find him before he finds us,' Raphah said, knowing that the beast was nearby.

'You must go back – take the Glory Hand,' Barghast said.

'What is it, Barghast?' Tanville asked as she took the Glory Hand.

But Barghast was running off into the darkness.

'The hell-hound – it's here!' Barghast shouted back as he vanished into the shadows.

# Scrofula

THERE was a banging upon the door as Galphus and his men burst into Pallium's house. They ran through the hall and into the scullery as the door to the stairs opened for them. Kate's screams filled the upper passageway and made their steps even more urgent. In the room upstairs, Kate held on to the bedpost as the spectre pulled her towards the forest glade. Galphus led on as Pallium struggled behind, out of breath and holding his spindle neck.

'She escapes,' Galphus cried as he ran across the landing and unlocked Kate's room. There was Kate, holding fast to the bed, her fingers white-knuckled, gripping the post as she slid across the floor, pulling the bed with her.

Neither Galphus nor the men could see the power that had hold of her. All they knew was that before them was a girl who levitated in the air. Pallium stumbled into the room and then stood aghast as Kate's feet began to disappear into the solid wall.

'Help me!' Kate screamed as she felt the first chill of death touch the tips of her toes. 'She has me and takes me to her world.'

Galphus could see no one but Kate, who had by now disappeared up to her knees into the glade. 'Who has you?' he shouted. He ran towards her, grabbing her hands and pulling against the force that would have her vanished through the daub walls.

'A spirit takes me, she came from the picture,' Kate moaned as she felt the grip on her legs tighten to breaking point.

'Get the picture,' Galphus commanded the older Druggle, as if he knew what would stop the spectre. 'Take it and throw it to the floor.'

The Druggle grabbed the frame and threw the picture to the floor. Kate was catapulted back into the room and fell upon Galphus.

'She would have me dead,' Kate said.

'And I will have you alive,' Galphus muttered to himself as he got to his feet and held her by the arm. He looked at her, not sure as to what he had just witnessed.

It was then that the ghost appeared to Kate.

'I wanted to save you,' she said as she stood by the window with her arms folded and brow vexed. 'They'll only kill you. Ask him what happens to all his indentures.'

'I don't believe you – you wanted me dead,' Kate shouted.

'I want no such thing,' barked Galphus, believing Kate spoke to him and not the ghost. 'We came to save you.'

'She's by the window,' Kate said. 'The ghost is there.'

Galphus looked at her as if she were quite mad. He nodded to the Druggle to draw his stave and then to Pallium, who silently slipped the door bolt and stood before the entrance.

'I see nothing,' Galphus said, his eyes searching for a trace of the spirit.

'You could have set me free, but wanted to kill me,' Kate said to the ghost, who smirked at her maliciously.

'You speak to the ghost or me?' Galphus asked, believing he was witnessing the ranting of someone quite mad and still unsure that he witnessed the workings of a spirit.

'Both of you have the same desire,' Kate said as she looked at the bruises upon her wrists. 'I want to see Jacob Crane, he will take me from this place.'

'Jacob has gone, took the money and went for his ship. As soon as it was offered to him, you became the least important thing in his conversation. Jacob has entrusted you to my care and for that I paid him well.'

'I want to leave and will never work for you,' Kate screamed, as the ghost chattered in her ear as to how she had warned that this would be the case.

'Look into my eyes, Kate,' Galphus said slowly. 'There are ways and means . . . Some give in willingly. Others need to be *encouraged.*' Galphus spoke in a matter-of-fact way as he took a pair of thin black gloves from his pocket and slid them with difficulty on to his fingers.

'He'll poison you,' said the ghost. 'Offer to give you *gaudium-auctus.*'

No sooner had the spirit uttered the words than Galphus brought a silver pyx from his pocket. He nodded to the Druggles, who without further instruction took hold of Kate and held her by the hands and feet. She struggled violently, kicking out in an attempt to break free.

As if it mattered, Pallium crossed the room and drew the shutters across the windows. He rubbed his hands and danced his tiny feet upon the boards nervously. With one hand he covered his face, then went and made busy by stacking the fire and checking the tinderbox.

'As good as dead,' said the ghost cheerfully. 'Should have come with me, at least you would be free.'

'Don't think Jacob Crane will like this,' Pallium said, backing away to the door. 'Liked the girl, he did. If he ever found out, Mister Galphus . . .'

Galphus looked at Pallium as he rubbed his jaw. He slowly

unscrewed the cap of the pyx and, grabbing Kate by the chin, dribbled several drops into her mouth. '*Gaudium-auctus* . . .' he said, smiling at her. 'It won't be long before you are begging me for more and will do anything to please me. Still see the ghost?' he asked. 'If you do, then please inform her that soon she too will work for me. I have not lived these seven lives just to take capture of the human spirit. I would like to have my very own haunting. My friend, Obadiah Demurral, often promised me that, but nothing came to pass.'

'Demurral's a pork-hedge, a babbler, a murderer,' Kate screamed. Suddenly she realised who this man was who had her at his mercy. The spectre was still by the window, gazing at her and shaking her head. 'I could have escaped – if you had given me the chance,' she said to the ghost, as the Druggles let go their grip and allowed her slump to her knees. 'Can't you do something?'

'Does she talk to us?' Pallium asked.

The ghost thought for a moment, and then with a sudden twist of her hand sent a fire-stick spinning from the grate across the floor towards Kate.

'Take it and fight, you have but a short time,' the spectre said. Galphus jumped back as the metal rod spun at his feet and stopped suddenly by Kate's hand.

Without hesitation, she took the rod and smashed it against Galphus's leg. Jumping to her feet, she hit out at the two guards, beating them upon the arms as she ran to the door. Galphus fell to the floor, the sound of the ghost cackling in his ears. He looked up towards the window and for the first time in the candlelight could see the apparition.

'There!' he shouted, pointing to the ghost who looked at him coolly, sangfroid, realising she was visible. 'I can see the spirit.'

Kate wasted no time. As the Druggles came to her she beat them again and again. She slipped the lock and ran to the stairs.

Pallium went after her, begging for her to return, his feeble voice chasing her footsteps.

In a minute, Kate was at the door. She took the key and locked it behind her, then threw the key to the mud. She looked in the direction of the Salamander Inn, then turned away and began to run. Far behind she could hear the door of Pallium's house being kicked from its hinges as the Druggles beat their way from the house. Kate ran faster. She followed the road back towards the river. Far away she could hear the sound of the quayside and the city. Yard after yard she ran, knowing soon she would be free.

One way led to another until she found herself having doubled back. Every way she took looked the same. There was no one to ask, no door upon which to knock, no hiding place to rest and think. Street after dreary street with no light from the morning sun. Kate ran through the mud, knowing that Galphus was not far away. Salamander Street went on and on forever.

She wanted Thomas to be there – he would know what to do, how to hide. From being the youngest of children they had gone through life together. They had fought, loved and caused bedlam. They were known from Whitby to White Moor and in their mischief were always together. Now he was gone, as dead as the ghost that tormented her, and he would never be seen again. From behind she heard the steady footsteps upon the stone and voices calling for her.

Kate ran again, ever faster. She hoped that she would see the way to the city and find Jacob Crane. From corner to corner she ran, sometimes stumbling in the mud. She thought that Galphus lied. Crane would never leave them – it was a scam. He'd promised in Whitby, and smugglers don't break their promises . . . She thought over and over of how she had been wary of Crane when they had met at Boggle Mill.

She had told Thomas of every evil deed given to the man. Now, in the short time since then, her mind was changed. He had done so much, risked everything. Crane confused her. He could be dark of heart and filled with gloom and then in the blink of an eye be bright as day. He would shout and scream and yet be tender. He conformed to no pattern of man and nothing was beyond his desire. Kate fixed a picture of him in her mind: it was a hope that she would hang on to. She wanted him to be around every corner and in every dark place. His face was her only safe thought.

She turned into an alleyway that was lit by tallow sticks. The yellow light shimmered against the dirty white wall and stinking mud that covered the cobbled road that lay beneath. Kate stopped and took her breath. For some reason she found it hard to walk each step. Her feet were an encumbrance, a tiresome burden that slowed her to a snail-pace. She leant wearily against the wall, her eyes stinging and wanting to close. The spectre appeared beside her.

'It's the *Gaudium-auctus*, it will make you feel as if you are without blood in your veins. Then your feet will not want to move an inch. Worse than all this, it will take the bile from your gourd and dry you like a wizened apple. *Such joy . . .*'

Kate tried to focus her eyes on the girl. The world became comfortably numb. It was as if her feet had disappeared and her hands changed to sheep fleeces. Gone were thoughts of Crane and Thomas – all she could see was the vivid outline of the ghost as the light faded. 'Name,' she said dreamily, 'I need to know your name . . .'

'Isabella . . . Isabella Chilnam . . .'

'Isabella,' Kate said, and then she felt something upon her wrist and jerked from the floor as if to run. The chain that held her hand stopped her. It manacled Kate to the wall. She didn't know if she dreamt what she saw. Kate was in a room, Galphus's room. The wall was lined with glass jars. She was in the corner and she cared not. All she could feel was the smile upon her face that stretched her lips from side to side and creased the skin into rough wrinkles. Kate breathed deeply, savouring each breath as if it were her very first. Wherever she was and whatever had happened held no importance for her. All that mattered was the glowing smile that filled her with a deep sense of joy and the vibrant light that seemed to flicker all around.

The door opened and Galphus walked in. He looked shorter than before, his head far too big for such a small frame. Kate began to laugh to herself. It started in the depths of her stomach as a tiny voice that giggled and squawked. Then it grew, twisting her gut until it shuddered her lips and broke from her mouth as if she were a tiger. She couldn't stop. Her belly hurt. Tears trickled down her face. How could a man go through life with the head the size of a horse, she thought, as she dared to look at him through one eye.

This made him look even stranger. He leant towards her, his eyes growing to the size of the moon that glowed with their own light. His nose appeared vast and cavernous. She flinched for a moment as she stared within: it was lined with a million hairs that looked as if they were a coppice of trees. Kate felt that should he come any closer she would be swallowed by it. Then laughter came again – she cared not. It bellowed forth as she rolled on the floor, kicking her feet as if she ran in the air. She danced like a dying fly upon its back, screaming with joy as she cried and cried with laughter.

Galphus smirked as he took a jar from the shelf and examined it carefully.

'See,' he said as he looked at the green mould that lined the jar. 'You are enjoying my *Gaudium-auctus*.'

Kate knew not what to say. She continued to laugh. As Galphus turned to sit at the table she thought she saw several black slugs make their way across his face and vanish within his ear. She looked again and they were gone.

'I won't work for you,' Kate said. 'When Crane hears of what you have done, he will kill you. I know you tricked him. He will look for me.'

'And he will never find Salamander Street. Only those I desire to see can ever find its entrance. They do not find me, I find them. Who is to say that Crane himself is not a prisoner just like you?' Galphus paused and looked at her. He could see the *Gaudium-auctus* had turned her veins purple and reddened the tips of her fingers. From its seduction she would never be free, he thought. 'You're right, Kate. I tricked him. Gave him a bag of worthless copper and convinced him it was enough gold to pay off his ship. That was all he could see, charmed to believe lead was gold. Trouble with greedy men is they see gold in everything. I merely fulfilled his desires and told him what he wanted to hear.' He began to laugh.

Kate giggled and moaned, her sides fit to burst from laughter. In her heart she knew of Crane's discontent, which made it even funnier. She could hear Galphus, but his voice had changed. It was as if he were a fat mouse that squeaked and squeaked each word. She hollered even louder, wiping her face with the cuffs of the grey suit in which she woke.

'I was so much like Crane, then I changed. I found the meaning of life and pursued it with vengeance. Within the hour, Kate, you will be crawling upon the walls and begging me for another dose. That is the way of *Gaudium-auctus*. I intend to give it to the world. First it shall be free for everyone and then, when it takes hold, it shall be like a pearl of great price – impossible to find. Men will sell their children, priests will steal and murder, the Monarch himself will hand over the kingdom. There will be no surprise in the depths they will plummet to have one drop. Good will be called evil and evil good. Look at

Pallium – once as fat as a pig. Now his only desire is to count what little money he has left and give me whatever I want. I once found him trying to work out how long he could live and still pay me for the *Gaudium-auctus*. I intend to charge him a penny more each day and see his life shrink even more.' Galphus laughed.

'Then I would rather die,' Kate said.

'And that you will – or should I say, and *that* you'll fear. For that is the price you pay. *Gaudium* keeps away the fear – without it the slightest object becomes an obsession. You could no more kill yourself than I set you free. I surprise myself . . . Found it by accident. I wanted to make glue for the leather that would not rot. I took some Persian poppies and boiled the seeds. Within the day all who used it were singing merrily. Sadly they also died singing – they didn't seem to mind at all. One moment in the midst of a tavern aria, the next dead upon their anvils.' He laughed and Kate laughed with him. 'You, dear Kate, are blessed. For you are the first one to take part in my experiment. The *Gaudium* I have given you is far stronger than any I have made before and far more addictive.'

'Then let me die and be with Thomas.' Kate blurted the words without a trace of joy. She felt a sudden stab in her emotions as her heart missed a beat. A cold thread ran through every vein as if her blood were ice. Within a breath, her lips had tightened, her mouth dried and thirst gripped her like a maddened dog.

'You shall be with him, but he is not dead. Again a deception for the benefit of Mister Crane. He took it so well – his grief soothed by the promise of money. Thomas is alive. He is my servant, a replacement for young Smutt who had a terrible *accident*.'

'It was right what she said, the ghost – she told me he was dead before he hit the ground. You murdered him!' Kate screamed, all joy gone. The floor swiftly crawled with all kinds of creeping insects. She stared as they ran about her feet and over the boots in which she had been encased. 'Do something, Galphus!' She screamed in panic as a large beetle appeared from the crack between the floorboards and the wall and walked towards her. As it came closer it grew in size to that of a small dog and upon its head it appeared to wear a Frenchman's hat.

'What troubles you, Kate?' Galphus asked, as if she had a minor malady.

'A Frenchman dressed as a beetle. Kill it Galphus, kill it now!' She screamed as it appeared to come closer.

'There is nothing there but your dream – the *Gaudium* is leaving you.'

'Then let it be gone and the Frenchy with it.'

Galphus banged his cane upon the floor three times. The door opened and the Druggles entered and without a word took hold of Kate. She had no strength; whatever she had been given had emptied every bone of fortitude and now she hung like a cloth doll in their arms. Within her wits she could see another dimension where a tragedy played out with herself the only guest.

'Take her to the upper warehouse and put her in the cell,' Galphus said. 'She would like to see Thomas, so bring him as well. Give her what she wants. And leave this outside the door.' He handed them the pyx of *Gaudium-auctus*. 'She will want to know it is nearby and I will hear her scream when she would like to try it again. I am expecting a visitor from the north, an old friend, tell me when he arrives.' He gave a slight wave as he pulled a silk hankersniff from his pocket and dabbed his nose. 'One more thing,' he said softly, as if he only wanted her to hear. 'Kill Thomas – and I'll let you keep the pyx and the *Gaudium* for yourself . . .'

# Capacious Alta

'LEAVE me,' urged Lady Tanville Chilnam as Raphah took the Glory Hand to see where Barghast had gone. Ahead was a narrow tunnel through which came the ferocious roaring of a running torrent of water. 'I'll go back,' she shouted to him, half-wanting to follow.

'He is just ahead,' Raphah said. 'We must get to him before he discovers Ergott, he will kill him.'

'What is he?' Tanville asked.

'A wandering Aramean, cursed to live forever.'

'Is he human?'

'And something more . . .' Raphah said as he took her by the hand and led her on. 'What goes on within him is against the authority of nature. Barghast needs our help.'

From somewhere in the dark cavern came the sound of footsteps clattering against the stone. A shovel sounded as it was dragged across the wave-cut rock. Dimly at first, a light came into view.

'We're followed,' whispered Tanville as she and Raphah stooped through the tunnel and into another cavern. They walked up a narrow row of hand-cut steps that led to a high stone gantry. Each one still bore hurried chisel marks. The steps took them higher, almost to the ceiling. They stood in a large cave, its roof garlanded with stalactites that dripped and dripped cold, echoing water. To one side was a vast heap of rock that looked as if it were a flow of frozen magma spewed from the centre of the earth and then petrified.

Lady Tanville took her cape and shielded the Glory Hand within it as the chamber was plunged into darkness.

'What if Bragg is found by Barghast?' Tanville asked as they followed on.

'Then our job will be done for us. Bragg must know more than he says.'

'He was the last one to hold the picture of Lady Isabella – sold it to a man named Galphus. I follow Bragg to Salamander Street. I read a letter when I took the money from him. Galphus wrote to Bragg saying it would be good to meet him in person and not by courier. Bragg has an old goblet that Galphus has bought from him.' She spoke urgently, holding on to Raphah's coat as they stumbled up the dark passageway. 'You promised to come with me, Raphah – did you mean that?'

'I promised,' Raphah said. 'That is enough.'

'Then I will tell you this. On the night the dog attacked me, I had listened at Ergott's door. I heard him talking to someone, a man. He spoke about the journey. He too spoke of this man, Galphus, and two children. He told the man about Bragg and a chalice.' Tanville stopped for a moment and then went on, speaking even quieter. 'Ergott argued with the man in his room about finding children. Ergott had asked the man what he would do with them and he'd said they had to die – I know these are the companions you seek.'

'How did you know?' Raphah asked, sure that she could not have discovered this by mortal means.

'It . . . It was Beadle. He didn't want to tell me but . . .'

'Beadle?' Raphah laughed. 'The first sign of friendship and he cannot control his tongue. Beer and good companions. Did he tell you everything?'

'For an hour, as we searched the cellar and the edge of the cavern. Beadle told me about your *magic*. He thinks much of you. It was *you* who changed his heart.'

'I'm a stranger to *magic*. Beadle changed himself. He had lived under the curse of his master and when he was free he found himself,' Raphah said.

'You never take praise, always give it to another.'

'Why seek praise?' Raphah said.

The sound of the water torrent beat louder as the light of a travel lamp below lit a glow around a pair of feet.

Neither of them spoke as Bragg came into view. He was carrying a shovel and lamp. Strapped around his capacious frame was a linen bag. He muttered as he walked, swinging the lamp back and forth and unaware of their presence. Bragg walked as if he knew the caves well and his stride said that he walked to meet someone.

He left the chamber and continued on through a narrow passageway that led upwards. Raphah and Tanville walked on, close enough to hear the tap of his step but far enough to whisper to each other without being overheard. They followed the light of Bragg's lantern as it disappeared ahead of them.

They kept three coach lengths from Bragg. The path went on forever. It climbed high and circled a large vault of a cavern. Old ropes hung from the ceiling. Coils of loose hemp were spun on the floor. By the entrance was an old hut built of rocks piled upon old wood. There was a doorway the size of a child. Raphah looked inside and saw the remnants of a fire long since dead and covered in the dust of a hundred years. He thought about who could have lived there. A house in perpetual darkness, in amongst the dripping cold stone.

It was a whole world beneath the ground. Coated with black soot from a thousand fires, the ceiling dribbled the cold drip of limestone water. From the heights above them hung what looked like stone gargoyles, etched through the years by flood water.

The wind gusted stronger as they neared the entrance to another passageway that led from the chamber. The air vibrated and moaned as it was sucked into the narrow opening. Raphah thought it strange that such a storm should blow this far beneath the earth, and wondered if miners had cut some kind of air channel to bring the breeze to the depths. Upon the ground were several footprints: two from passing animals and another from a man.

'This way,' Raphah said as they stooped through the entrance of the narrow opening and made their way onwards. From the footprints in the sand he knew it to be where Ergott, Barghast and now Bragg had trod. A little way ahead they heard the sound of digging, of metal clashing with stone.

In the shadow of the lamp, Bragg sweated as he dug at the earth. When the spade was no use he got to his knees and dug with his hands. Raphah couldn't make out if Bragg was digging something up or burying an item so that it would never be found. Bragg wheezed, golem-like as he slathered his breath, spittle drooling from his jowls. In the shadows of the cave he looked like a dog slobbering over an old bone.

High above him in the arch of the cavern, Raphah crawled to a ledge to gain a better view. Lady Tanville waited in the passage-way. She shielded the flickering light of the Glory Hand with her coat. From where he hid, Raphah could see Bragg scrab-bling in the dirt, his face lit by the smouldering wick of the old lamp that he had wedged between two large stones. The cave was filled with shadows. Bragg dug even deeper.

Raphah watched as Bragg fumbled with a small chalice that

he was trying to wrap in a black cloth. Bragg wiped the remnants of dirt from its rim and sniffed the cup. He looked about, as if he knew he was being watched. Then he shrugged his shoulders and with one hand pulled the collar of his coat to hide what he was doing. Picking his way through the stones, Raphah climbed higher. Far below at the bottom of the cave, Bragg took the vessel and wrapped it in the black silk.

Without any fuss he took the bag that was wrapped around him and put the cloth within it. Like a pedantic gardener, he placed the bag upon the shovel and then began to fill in the hole he had created by hand. The chalice hung on the handle of the spade, wrapped neatly in its sack. Every now and then he would look up and smile at the hidden cup. Quite neatly, he placed several stones in the hole and then covered them with the fine sand. With a fat hand he then scrubbed out any trace of his presence.

Raphah looked on from the shadows as Bragg turned to face the lamp and pick it from the floor. His face changed: he began to smile, and a word of greeting formed on his lips as if to welcome someone he knew. Bragg's eyes then changed, widening with disbelief as he took a pace backwards. It looked as if he was about to scream or shout out when . . .

There was a sudden rush. Something glistened as it flew. A knife spun through the air. Raphah cried out as Bragg clutched his chest. He staggered forward, looking for his bag as if he was quickly losing his sight. Raphah clambered down the rocks as Lady Tanville dashed from the hiding place, her clothes torn as if a beast had set upon her. She screamed as she ran, looking for Raphah.

Bragg stared at her. The smile came back to his face. 'Capacious Alta . . . Consanguineous,' he said as the blood dribbled from his mouth and down his chin.

Bragg fell backwards like a crashing oak, his hand flailing

about him as he desperately tried to hold on to life. Upon his face he carried the grimace of a frightened child. As Raphah scrambled towards him, he could see that the man feared death. Bragg pouted like a dying fish gasping for air.

'Capacious Alta . . . Consanguineous,' Bragg said again as he reached out to Lady Tanville. Without a word, she walked to him and pulled the knife from his chest. Bragg gasped, muttered to himself and then fell, face to stone.

'He came from the tunnel – I didn't hear him. He attacked me . . . Then this,' she said between each breath. 'I never saw his face, but it was a man – that's what I think he was . . . He threw the knife.'

'I saw no one, just Bragg, I thought he had seen you and that's why he smiled.'

'Smiled at the one who killed him. There are others here. We must leave now,' she said as she shivered, cold as an arctic monkey.

'Not without Barghast,' Raphah said.

'Then I leave alone and take the Glory Hand.' Tanville panicked, looking frantically about the cave for some sign of the killer. She held the knife in her hand and dripped the blood to the floor. 'Why did he kill him?'

'For this?' Raphah asked as he picked the bag from the shovel and took out the cup. 'This is the goblet, hidden here for safekeeping. This is the cup that Galphus wanted.'

'A pot mug, why should he want that?' Tanville asked.

'More than that, much more than that,' Raphah said. 'If I am right then this has not been seen for many years.'

'And should never have been seen at all,' Barghast said as he limped into the cold chamber holding his arm. 'Ergott has gone, nowhere to be found,' he said wearily.

Raphah held the cup in the light of the Glory Hand. The hand dimmed suddenly in the presence of the chalice as if it demanded reverence. He and Barghast stared at the goblet. It was meagre and bare and quite ordinary. All that set it apart from a fireside drinking pot was the silver rim inlaid into the clay. Years had hardened it to stone that felt as strong as metal in Raphah's fingers. 'Do you know of this?' Raphah asked.

'I have heard of the Grail Cup,' Barghast said in awe as he looked at the simple goblet of fire-hardened clay. He reached out and touched the inlaid silver rim. 'I met a dandy who dined out on telling the tale. Said it was buried beneath a rose by an abbey wall. The entire world was captured by his ramblings. And to think, they have searched the codes and all the time it was here at Peveril, in a cave below the old castle.' Barghast wanted to laugh; his neck felt too weak to hold his head. 'I'm weary, Raphah. It is a good feeling,' he sighed. 'The beggar is near, I know it. One more road and then I'll taste the sublime slumber.'

'What will you do with the goblet?' Tanville asked as Raphah put the bag around him.

'It is a morsel to catch a rat,' he said as he lifted the lamp from the floor and stared at Bragg slumped in the dirt.

'What of Bragg?' asked Barghast.

'Killed by a knife,' he said.

'Then whoever did this is not far. In fact they could be in our midst,' Barghast replied. 'I will tell the innkeeper. He will not want another death. We'll put Bragg in the grave with Mister Shrume. There is no reason to lament his loss. He shared a carriage with Julius Shrume – now he can share his grave.'

From somewhere high above came the moaning of an agonised man. Barghast sniffed the air as if to scent from where it came. The sound of the carping echoed through the caves. It was quickly followed by the noise of heavy boots scrambling upon the rocks. It got closer and closer by the second.

Raphah looked to Barghast. 'Bragg's assassin?'

Barghast listened intently, his eyes searching the cavern. 'Ergott,' he said slowly.

Holding the lamp higher, Raphah looked towards the pathway that led from the floor of the cave, up through the scree of broken rocks to the entrance to a higher chamber. Like a blundering blind man, Ergott stumbled from the pitch black and into the paltry glow of the lamp.

'Bragg? Is it you?' he asked. His hand covered his face to shield it from the brightness. 'I've been lost, man, for many hours. Lamp burnt out and have stumbled my way back. Bragg?' He spoke the last word as he looked down from the path and saw the humped body of Bragg face-down on the dirt. 'What have you done to him?' he asked, not daring to come any closer.

'Not us, but another,' Raphah said.

'You stand above him like witches at a cauldron and you expect me to believe your lies?' Ergott said, not desiring to take another step. 'Look, that *is* a dagger I see before me . . . and something is rotten in *this* kingdom.'

'We didn't do this, Ergott. It was your disappearance from the inn that brought us to this place,' Raphah said. 'What are you doing in the cavern?'

'I could ask the same as you,' he snapped. 'I was lost, went for a walk in the fields and found my way in here. The lantern burnt out and I couldn't find my way. Why should I explain myself to you?'

'Because Julius Shrume is dead and Lady Tanville was attacked by a hell-hound,' Barghast said.

'And am I responsible for both?' he replied coldly, looking at Bragg. 'Do you take me for the hound?'

'Your excuse is not one that can be easily proved,' Raphah said.

'So choice, coming from a thief,' Ergott said coarsely, and he began to move away from them. 'And how will you explain the demise of Mister Bragg – self-inflicted wounds? I will have my account to give.'

'I trust the magistrate will not take too much notice of a man obsessed by magic and whose habit of smoking, shall we say, *clouds* his understanding. Then we shall see,' said Barghast as he searched the pockets of Bragg's coat.

Within them were many things: balls of string, empty shells of various snails, a large monocular spectacle and the dried tip of a woman's finger. In one pocket was a silk ribbon and attached to that a thick brass key. Sundry papers and bills of sale lined the other pockets, and nothing to incriminate Ergott or indeed Bragg could be found. As he was finishing his search, Barghast had almost given up when his finger struck upon a small piece of metal. He picked it carefully from the lining of Bragg's coat and pulled it into the light.

At first glance it looked nothing more than a large button cut with three rectangular holes. It was only when Barghast put it to his mouth and blew sharply that it made a distinctive high-pitched sound just at the reach of human discernment.

Ergott appeared to grow more and more uncomfortable. He itched his neck and twitched his face as he fumbled with the wand in his pocket. He muttered to himself and rubbed his chin.

'A wolf whistle,' Barghast said as he put the metal to his lips again. 'What was the rhyme?' he asked and then went on. 'Once to call from mountain range, twice the wolf to man will change, thrice will change him back again, once more for luck and see him then – is that how it should go, Mister Ergott?'

'I have no idea, Barghast. Silly children's riddle and of no meaning. Why Bragg should carry a wolf whistle is beyond me. Perhaps he had a desire to see if there were any such beast left in the country?' He stuttered uncomfortably and panted like a dog. 'Now that I have found a light I will take it and be gone, I have been without sleep and need to rest before the journey.'

'I play games,' Barghast said. 'It's been a long time and in a different land that I last saw one of these. Used to call a man-wolf from the hills by its master.'

'Master?' Lady Tanville asked, never having heard of such a creature.

'There is a belief that when a man or woman is charmed by a magician they can be turned into a creature of their desire by the playing of an instrument. In the case of the wolf it is always a silver whistle. These are highly collectable and very rare. To blow it in the presence of a man-wolf would render it trans-formed immediately. This is something to keep should we need to find the beast.'

'Then I wish you luck,' Ergott said. 'I am a dowser and not a magician. My art is a science and as I have said I search for that which is lost – not that which wets against the trees and chases sheep. So if I can be excused?'

'We will walk with you so that the assassin does not strike again,' Barghast said.

Raphah knelt upon the floor and, putting his hand upon Bragg's head, closed his eyes and stilled himself. In that moment all were silent. No one dared ask what he had done. All knew that he had sealed Bragg's passing.

'One more thing,' Barghast asked of Ergott. 'Your uncle is Lord Finesterre, I believe?'

'What of it?' Ergott snapped.

'He sent you on this quest to search for two lost children?'

'That he did. What concern is it of yours?' Ergott asked.

'Your uncle and I share a common acquaintance,' Barghast replied.

'And who would that be?'

'Obadiah Demurral.'

Ergott did not reply. He stood and stared, the shadows flickering upon his face, his brow twitching with every heartbeat. Slowly and carefully he licked his lips and swallowed hard, trying to bring a smile to his face.

'Really?' asked Ergott. 'Then upon my return I shall seek him out and give him your favour.'

No one saw the figure of the man who looked down from a high balcony cut by long-dead hands into the rocks above. He watched intently as they left the cavern, taking the light with them. Once they had gone, he took a silver bowl from the leather sack that was strung around his neck and scooped water from a nearby pool of lime-water. The man crouched in the darkness and struck a flint against a burnt rag and then lit the lamp by his feet. Long shadows flickered against the high walls as he took a small knife from his pocket, cut the tip of his finger and dripped seven drops of blood into the bowl. With the blade of the knife he stirred the water and watched as it turned to solid ice. As the liquid froze a vision appeared in the ice. The man watched as Raphah and Barghast walked through the cave. It was as if a floating eye followed their every move.

'Never shall they be from my sight,' he muttered angrily as he looked upon the vision that danced in the ice. 'From the day I first saw him I knew he was the key to the world. Seven drops of blood will fill the Chalice around his neck and bring down the kingdom of heaven.'

# The Quondam God

IN the upper warehouse of the factory, thick ice had frosted the windows. It patterned the brittle glass, causing the moonlight to cast crystal shadows upon the wooden floor. By the window, wrapped in rags, was Kate. She was imprisoned in a large cage that had once been the home of Galphus's chickens, now long since gone. Outside the cage, on a tall stool and set upon china plate, was the pyx. Inside the pyx was fresh *Gaudium*. In the hour that she had been imprisoned she had heard the comings and goings of the factory below. The light of the London skies had faded to afternoon grey and soon had left the room dressed in a fading blue. From within her prison, Kate looked out towards the door. It was at least fifty yards away across the warehouse. Scattered throughout the warehouse were various large wooden boxes, many of them empty, some containing old shoes and shards of leather.

The only thing that mattered now to Kate was the small silver pyx sitting tantalisingly upon the plate, two arm's lengths from where she now sat. At first she hadn't thought of it. The French beetle had followed her from Galphus's laboratory up the stairs; it had smiled a melancholy smile and had then vanished into the floorboards. Galphus's nose had shrunk to its normal size and the thrashing pain in her guts had subsided. The candles that lit the warehouse did seem to shimmer differently from any she had seen, but apart from that all seemed normal. But with the passing of every second from then on, the desire to hold the pyx had begun to grow and grow.

At first, she thought the feeling was just a desire to quench the burning thirst that cloyed her tongue to her mouth. But as the moments passed, the desire grew. It became like the burning sun scorching the ground. It fixed in her mind alongside the memory of her father and the reccurring face of Obadiah Demurral that grinned at her. Her thoughts of Obadiah had always been the same. She had known him since she was a young child and had never felt comfortable in his presence. It had been his ranting that had made her believe that if there were a creator, then he had forgotten that the world existed. From what she could read in Demurral's holy book, this great power *loved* her. But in her life there was no evidence of this. Her mother had died; her father had turned to smuggling and drink. Until her meeting with Raphah she had only believed in what she saw. Now she wasn't so sure. Over the days since Raphah had gone she had begun to speak to Riathamus.

She had no idea of what to say or how to say it. How does one address the creator? She asked herself again and again. Within an hour she had decided just to speak and hope he was listening.

Now as she looked through the bars of the chicken shack, she spoke to him again. She had learnt a prayer as a child and in her jumbled mind a few of the lines stuck out like a rugged outcrop.

'Give us bread, give us bread,' she kept on saying, the words flowing like a mantra.

The vision of Demurral came and went again and again. The

urge to hold the pyx grew stronger with each word she spoke. In the barren room, devoid of any beauty, the silver pyx shone brightly. Kate knew she coveted it, had to have it, had to take it from the chair and possess it forever. It became everything in her world. All her thoughts became focused upon it as her eyes examined its every inch. She tried to count the impressions around the rim. Followed the Corinthian swirls on its side and guessed and re-guessed its height. But she knew that what was important was not the pyx but what lay inside.

As the *Gaudium* was sieved from her body, it left a dull but gnawing ache. It was as if she was being dried like a fig and that her very essence was evaporating. Her skin felt as if it were becoming crisp, her lips were dry and bruised. She tried to form the words to speak. All that came from her was a harsh cawing, as if she had become a dying rooster calling its last dawn. Kate tremored with each cackle of dry breath, not from the cold without but from the icy grip within. She looked to her hands: they were thinning before her eyes and the veins stood from her flesh.

The factory churned beneath her feet. From the floors below she could hear the thud and thump of the felt hammers. They smoothed the leather and beat in time with the turning world. It was as if they had become attuned with a deeper rhythm which continued relentlessly like the ticking of a clock, never sleeping, always going on.

Plugging her ears with the tips of her fingers, she sat upon the wooden box that had become chair and bed. She tried to keep out the noise from below and fill her head with sublime thoughts. This failed. She could see nothing within but Demurral. He sat upon a horse, making his way across the moors – relentlessly getting nearer, coming to take her home.

There was a sudden hissing that sounded like a thousand mocking tongues. Through muddied eyes, Kate was sure that she could see a snake in the corner of the cage. She looked through the gloom and could make out its dark head as it bobbed back and forth, silver-eyed. It remained in the growing dark that the candles could not keep at bay. Then, in the blink of an eye, it was gone.

Kate looked again, unsure that the vision had completely disappeared. Hovering two feet from the dirty wooden floor was the snake's head. It stared, half-gone, through one eye. All the time it fragmented, slowly disappearing, bit by bit, until all that was left was the spitting tongue. It silently flickered in the gloom, the light from a nearby candle reflecting off the moist tip. There was a snap in the air, and from the blackness came the death-white fangs of the creature as it lurched towards her. Kate screamed. The snake grew to the size of a dog's head, reappearing from the blackness. It bit again and again about her head, fangs sinking into her flesh. Then it was gone.

She held her face in her hands to feel for the blood. Her skin was dry and crisp, with no sign of any attack. And then her head began to buzz. At first it was like a distant ache. It was as if a wasp were alive inside her head. It was as if the creature had crept in whilst she was asleep and now made its home within her head.

Kate screamed again. She shook her head from side to side, remembering the time as a child when her dog had bitten the brittle paper of a wasps' nest that hung in her father's barn. It had taken an hour for the dog to die. Now the wasp was contained in her head, and she banged her skull against the bars of the cage. It would call for others to come and take residence within and she would be powerless. They would share her head and she would have to listen to them talking, whispering about her as they searched the world for flower-dew.

The far door rattled and shook as it was pushed quickly open. A solitary Druggle dragged in a boy, his head covered in a flour sack and tied about the neck. The boy walked slowly, led like a dog across the warehouse towards the cage.

'Friend for you,' the Druggle said. He tugged the rope that held the boy fast, then he turned the key and opened the cage door and in one movement had thrown the boy inside. 'Take off his bindings and his mask. Here,' he said as he handed Kate a small knife with a silver blade and bone handle, 'use this.'

With that he locked the door, placed the key on a table by the wall and left by the way he had come.

The boy didn't speak. He held his head down as if he didn't know which way the world had turned. Kate took the knife and cut the bindings and then sliced the knot that held the sack to his head. The boy shook it from him, showering the floor in a fine rain of white powder.

'Thomas?' Kate asked, unsure if he was real or another delirium.

'Kate . . .' he said thinking that something had changed within her.

'Galphus said you were dead. I went to your funeral – then he said it was Smutt.'

'Smutt?' answered Thomas. 'Dead?'

'I saw you dead, put flowers on the grave.'

'And Jacob?' Thomas asked.

'Gone . . .' Kate sagged as she thought of him leaving, not knowing if she had been tricked or if he had deserted them.

'Galphus told me. Said he had sold me to indenture until I was a man. He has them all on indenture, never pays, then they all die.'

'We need to escape. He'll come back for us and do the same,' Kate said.

'What's that?' Thomas asked, his eyes taken towards the stool and the silver pot that sat unnaturally upon it.

'It's mine,' Kate said warily. 'Remedy . . . A linctus . . . For me.' She held the knife in her hand, the words of Galphus repeating constantly in her head. 'I need it, but he won't let me take it. Left it there to laugh at me.'

'You'll be fine, Kate. We'll get from this place. If Demurral couldn't keep us locked in his tower, then we can escape this place.'

'Demurral,' she said nervously. 'He's coming for us. I see him when I close my eyes. On horseback. Coming slowly, mile by mile. Nearer by the day. He'll finish what he started. I have to have the silver pot, Thomas, and have it now,' she pleaded.

'Give me the knife and I'll force the lock,' Thomas said.

'We'll never get from the building and then he won't let me have the linctus,' Kate moaned. 'Let's wait, see what happens. I know another way. Sleep on it, Thomas. I'm tired, don't want to run.'

'What's wrong, Kate? We can't stay here.'

'Wait until the morrow and then we'll be gone. Just let me rest until the middle night – we'll try then. Galphus will be sleeping and the Druggles busy.'

Thomas slumped himself into the corner of the cage and looked at Kate. He knew she was stubborn. It would be pointless to argue. He would wait. Sleep first and then escape. If she wanted to stay, she could. But if Galphus could kill Smutt then he would have no hesitation in killing them, Thomas thought as he settled down.

Kate didn't speak. There was no sign of welcome in her heart. It was if Thomas didn't matter. All she could think of was the pyx of *Gaudium* that eluded her. She wrapped the knife in her coat, a thought crossing her mind as to why the Druggle didn't ask for its return. It was then, as Galphus's voice spoke in her head, that she realised. It was for her to kill Thomas. Kill him and it will be yours, the voice said, changing to sound like the cry of the wasp.

236

Kate waited. She counted the seconds in her head and kept her eyes closed for fear of what she would see. Demurral appeared to her. He was smiling, hooded and radiant. Opening one eye, she looked to Thomas. It appeared he slept, his head lolled to his chest as he groaned with sleep-talk.

Kill Thomas and the *Gaudium* will be yours, Galphus said in her mind. She tried not to listen. The pain in her stomach grew to a fever. It spun her guts, knotting them ever tighter as her hands shook. The *Gaudium* began to radiate upon the stool. The pyx glowed and shone brightly. It sung sweetly like the call of a blackbird that only she cold hear. She knew it wanted her to be close by and would only be complete when it was held in her hand.

'It would be worth his life,' a voice said.

Kate looked around her. She could see no one.

'Galphus is right in what he said,' the voice spoke again.

Kate looked up. There, hanging from the beam above the cage, was a large spider. It smiled at her and spoke again. 'Just take the knife and it will soon be over,' it said cheerfully. It spun its web and then descended upon a silver thread that glistened in the moonlight. 'I will watch you, tell him how well you've done. Quickly girl, get it done.'

Kate stood to her feet and looked at the spider. 'He's my friend, my brother,' she said.

'I ate all my sisters,' the spider said. 'Hard at first, then it gets better.'

'But we said . . .'

'Words, girl. Think of yourself, what you want.' The spider dropped towards her.

Kate couldn't take her eyes from the creature. It was black and gold with red-tipped feet and the size of a bird. Upon it crawled a multitude of other tiny spiders, all the same in size and colour. They dangled from it so it looked like a Christmas bauble. The spider came closer until it rested upon her shoulder. Kate didn't move as it spun a web about her face. It felt as if this was what should be done.

'Here,' said the spider as it suddenly nipped her neck. 'Take this from me it will give you strength.'

Kate could feel the bite. It pinched her quickly. She lifted a hand to knock the spider from her, but it had gone. She pulled the threads of sticky web from her face and watched as they dissolved upon her fingers like strands of angel hair. Then she looked to Thomas. He slept bitterly. His breath was laboured, as if he was running. His hand twitched to fight all around him.

Kate moved closer and closer, knife in hand. She steadied herself, her eyes looking from Thomas to the pyx and back again. She bit her lip, hoping he would forgive her for what she would do. She thought his life was worth less than the *Gaudium* – all she had to do was what Galphus had said, kill Thomas and it would be hers. From all around in the dark shadows came a multitude of voices: her mother, Kitty who had drowned on the long rocks, the hanged man they had watched as he swung from the gibbet . . . Their spirits panted heavily, mumbling the same words: *'Do it . . . Do it . . . Do it . . .'*

She raised the knife, looking for a place to strike him quickly. She reached out to take hold of his hair to hold his head back and slice the neck. The voices sung like a dark choir and stamped their feet in the black that surrounded them. The blade glinted in the light. She held it like a key to gain what she desired. There was no sense of fear, no swelling of guilt. Thomas had to die. Gently she stroked his head and grasped the locks of hair within her fingers. Taking the knife she drew it back, ready to strike.

'THOMAS!' screamed a voice from outside the cage.

Kate jumped back and let go of him as the spectre of the girl appeared before her.

'THOMAS!' the ghost screamed again, hoping he would hear. 'SHE WILL KILL YOU!'

Thomas stirred from his sleep and opened his eyes. 'Kate,' he said as he looked at her. 'What were you going to do? A voice called me . . .'

Kate held the dagger in her shaking hand and stared at it.

'He wanted me to,' she said awkwardly. 'Said he would give it to me if you were dead.'

'Give you what?' he asked as he got to his feet.

'The *Gaudium*, that's all I need,' Kate said.

There was a swirling of crinoline as the ghost wafted through the cage and into the room. Thomas could see her clearly. 'Look, Kate,' he said.

'She called you, saved you. She is a ghost.'

'Galphus has poisoned her,' the spectre said. 'It will kill her if she has more.'

'What do you know?' screamed Kate. 'You've never had *Gaudium* . . . I want more now . . .'

In a sudden burst of anger, she ran at Thomas with the knife. He grabbed her arm as it thrust towards him and twisted it until she broke her grip. She kicked and punched, not wanting to let go. He threw her to the floor and took the knife.

'Leave it Kate,' he said as he pushed her away. 'You're gripped by the madness.'

'I want it all, I want it now,' she said as she stalked him like a mad cat.

'Stay back and leave me be,' Thomas said.

Kate lunged again, trying to claw his face and rip out his eyes. He held her back with one hand and then without hesitation struck her with a single blow. Kate fell to the floor like a corpse dropping from the gallows.

Thomas looked down at her and sobbed. The ghost of Lady Isabella came into the cage and stood by him.

'Look what I have done,' he said as he stooped to pick her from the floor.

'She did it to herself,' the ghost said gently. 'You must get from this place and bring her to Pallium's house. There is a secret way of escaping from Salamander Street. The only way. I will show you.'

'How can we get from this place?' Thomas asked.

'Wait until you hear the clock strike midnight and then you will be free. I will come for you then.'

In a swirl of foxgloves and meadow grass, Lady Isabella vanished from the room. Thomas held Kate in his arms and waited for the clock to strike.

# The Green Man

THE bugler stood on the roof of the carriage and called the hounds. From the door of the Black Shuck Inn came the travellers. Ergott followed on at a distance, wand in hand and a small leather bag draped about his shoulders. The coach had been decked in sprigs of holly and upon the door had been painted a rough cross inscribed with signs and symbols long since forgotten. Bounding in the dirt were the hounds, their barks echoing from wall to wall. The innkeeper quietly passed words with Barghast, who handed him a small bag of silver coins. The man nodded in appreciation and stepped back from the coach.

'For the inconvenience,' Barghast whispered to him, hoping that the money would ease his conscience and cover the deaths of his fellow travellers. They both turned and looked to the freshly dug earth beneath the oak tree.

'I'll keep an eye on them,' the innkeeper said. 'Make sure they stay in the grave.'

'And a shilling for Carsington to ease his wounds,' Barghast replied.

'Not that he'll need it now he is Lord of the Manor,' the

innkeeper said as the hounds barked and the sun dimmed behind the high hill.

Beadle ran down the steps towards the carriage as Raphah walked slowly behind, looking at the clear evening sky in great expectation of the journey. The mist of hound-breaths rose up and then vanished in the cold night air. Far to the east the moon rose from the sea.

Raphah had wrapped himself in one of Bragg's old coats. It was far too big but was warm as toast and was just like a huge blanket. He carried the bag he had found in the cave and inside was the Chalice. In his mind he had already decided that this would be taken to his village – a sufficient replacement for the loss of the golden Keruvim that now lay at the bottom of the Oceanus Germanicus. He studied the holly sprigs and strange signs that adorned the coach. The driver saw him looking and tutted mournfully.

'Why have you done this?' Raphah asked.

'We go through the great forest,' said the driver slowly. 'We make one stop to change horses and then we are off again. London by dawn, if we get through.'

'And should we not get through?' he asked.

'Sometimes it is difficult,' the driver said with a smile that contorted his face, as if he wanted to speak the full truth but could not. 'You've seen what is happening. Since the sky-quake and the coming of the comet all kinds of beasts seem to be roaming the world. Only last week a coach was set upon by beasts with red flaming hair dressed in armour.' The driver spoke as if he didn't believe his own words. 'All that was left was splinters – not one man left alive.'

'Filling his head with stories?' Barghast asked.

'Only saying what went on,' the man replied.

'And we'll be protected by these?' Barghast asked, pointing to the holly sprigs and crude pictures daubed upon the carriage.

242

'Best not travel without them – then we can say we did what we could.' The driver pulled up the collar of his coat and double charged the blunderbuss. 'Will be an *interesting* journey and one I will be glad to end. Billingsgate Dock an hour before eight and I'll be done'.

'London,' Barghast said with anticipation in his voice. 'Not the kindest of places.'

'I hope to find my friends before they are found by Demurral,' Raphah said.

'Demurral – an old fox and twice as cunning,' said Barghast. 'You are wiser than I thought.'

'We are all here for a purpose. I feel as if another hand plays us like a card. None of this has come by chance.' Barghast stepped inside the coach. 'You travel above?'

'Beadle insists upon it,' Raphah replied. 'Said he could escape if the beast attacks again. Didn't want to tell him he'd been sharing a table with the creature.'

'Better to share a table than your mind. I take hope that soon the beast will be dead.' Barghast drew close to Raphah so that no one would hear what he would say. 'When I put Bragg to the earth, I took a handful of soil and held it to my face. I wanted to know what it would be like. You will never know how I have waited for that time.'

'Carriage!' screamed the coachman as he cracked the whip for the off.

The yard burst into sudden life as the gates of the inn were thrown open. Lady Tanville took her seat, followed by Ergott. He looked even sourer faced, and his lips pouted like a fat trout. Beadle clambered up the steps of the coach and onto the roof. He took his place behind the luggage and beckoned Raphah to follow as a large owl flew overhead.

'There is one thing,' whispered Barghast. 'Should Ergott be transformed, he must be killed and killed quickly. I fear that he searches for your friends and that he knows who you are.'

Within the minute the coach was under way. The horses jumped and clattered, as if they knew what was to come. Around their feet the hounds barked as the mist from the vale wisped about their feet.

Raphah took his place by Beadle's side and pulled the coat around him to keep out the approaching night. From the off, the bugler kept the blunderbuss at the ready and held a sprig of holly in his hand. As they left the inn and made their way to the road to London, all kept silent.

'He's near,' Beadle said. 'I can always tell when he is near.'

'Demurral?' asked Raphah, not surprised by what he heard. 'I too can see his work in all that has happened. He will be a day behind. We can get to London, find them and be on our way. Let us pray that we are protected from what is to come.'

In the carriage, Ergott sat quietly and stared at Lady Tanville. He tried to smile and show warmth in his manner. She replied by looking coldly, staring at him with her piercing eyes. Barghast sat back in his cape and laughed to himself, quite pleasured by the entertainment of their mutual anger.

'So how will you search for the lost children?' he asked Ergott to distract him.

'I am to meet someone and together we will seek them out. My dowsing rods will take me to where they are. That shall not be a problem,' he said.

'Then what will you do when you find them?' Barghast said as he teased with the wolf whistle, every now and then putting it to his lips.

'They will be returned to their rightful place and all will be well,' Ergott said.

'And if they should not want to go?' Barghast asked.

'There will be no doubt of that. I have been asked to recover many things and never have I failed in my duty.' He stopped speaking and looked at Lady Tanville as he thought of some-thing to say. 'You look for something. I could find it for you – for free, gratis and with no charge.'

'I know where to look and I know what I am looking for. I don't need splinters to find it for me.'

'You sound as if you are a sceptic, Lady Chilnam. Could I give you a demonstration of my abilities?' Ergott asked as he took the pipe from his pocket and stoked it with an even stronger brew.

'Let him entertain us while we journey,' Barghast said, rais-ing his eyebrow. 'It is a long way to London and the night will soon be upon us. Continue, Mister Ergott, and I assure you we'll both be enthralled.'

'Very well,' said Ergott as he sucked upon the pipe and took from his travel bag a small silver cup. 'First of all, I take some-thing that belongs to the one I seek and tear from it a small por-tion.' Ergott took a piece of cloth from his pocket and dropped three threads within the cup. 'Then we add some fine wine and a powder, the secret of which I am not at liberty to say.'

'You said you weren't a magician, Mister Ergott, and yet you act like one,' Tanville sniffed.

'On the contrary, Madam. This is a science and not magic,' Ergott said as he took a small flask of wine, poured some into the cup and then sprinkled it with some white powder that looked like a pinch of salt. 'Finally I place this lens upon the cup and concentrate my intention upon it.'

'And what happens next?' Barghast asked politely as Ergott took the lens from his pocket and sealed it upon the rim of the cup.

'This!'

There was a fizzing within the cup as Ergott's brew effer-vesced momentarily and then became still.

'Look!' he said as he held out the cup. 'All I need to know will be shown to me.'

From within the cup, the deep red of the wine cleared instantly. It shimmered like a looking glass glazed with snow. They could all see the view of a town as if from the eye of an eagle or other bird that soared high above. Ergott held the cup in one hand and with the other took his wand and held it above.

'Is this the town?' he asked the cup, keeping an eye upon the movement of the wand. In turn the wand bowed to the cup touching the rim. 'Show me more,' Ergott said as the vision then changed to that of something looking down from the rooftop. 'Is this the street?' he asked. Again the wand responded and touched the rim. 'And more,' he said to the cup. The scene changed to that of the front door of a house. 'Is this the house?' he asked, and before he could even finish the question the wand had tapped the rim.

'But how do you know which street and in which town?' Tanville asked.

'Simple,' he replied. 'I ask the wand and it will show me. Right for yes and left for no. It is just a process of elimination. I take a map of the city and hold the wand above and within the hour will have the place they are hiding.' He unfolded a map of London and dowsed the wand across it as the carriage rolled back and forth.

They didn't speak for the rest of that evening. Ergott sat in the candlelight dowsing the map and making notes as he went. It was as if he sat in a cloud of vapours that clung to him and made the carriage lamp dim.

Lady Tanville dozed. She thought of Isabella and how she would be returned to the castle, her portrait turned to face the wall and kept from roaming the night. In her mind she looked from her bedroom window across the gardens to the gate beyond. She tried to count the yew trees that grew in each avenue of flowers and formed peculiar boxed hedges. In her counting, sleep came to her quickly and she closed her eyes.

Barghast kept watch. He looked to Ergott and spied the map, keeping note of where Ergott had looked upon the page. He saw that in several places he had scored it with a cross, marking where he thought the wand had told them the children were hidden.

The carriage drove on into the night. Leaving Peveril, the road dropped from the hills and went towards the great forest. To the east was a vast lake and to the west a deep marsh. The road was straight and well metalled. Upon the mile stood a row of small houses. Beadle counted them as they went by. Each one was the same. A small chimney sat on a tiled roof, two windows and a door upon each front and a fire lit within. They were the houses of the road-makers. Built to mark the way, they gave Beadle a feeling of being safe. He snuggled contentedly in his coat, knowing he was never more than a mile from them.

By the time they had driven for five hours, the horses became weary. The road was overwhelmed by a wall of high trees that stood like ancient pillars before them. Branches reached up into the sky and rattled in the wind like sabres. It was as if they were speaking to them, telling them to turn back and go another way.

Beadle held on to Raphah's arm, hoping to be reassured that all was well. Raphah slept soundly. The coach slowed to walking pace as the bugler called the hounds in close. The forest rustled with noises from within. Eyes stared at them from the darkness as the horses pranced nervously.

The last mile-house was now some way behind. Beadle turned back and looked at the fading glow from the window – a sign of a welcome fire now disappearing into the night. A cold draught blew against his face and rattled the branches of a nearby oak. There was a distant creak and the splitting of a limb as a branch fell unseen. The horses gained pace, not by command but by their own desire. It was as if they knew something was there, something was watching. They quickened their gait until the carriage rocked as if at sea. The hounds followed, their yelps silenced as they kept guard. They ran on, not wanting to cry out, hoping to keep step, not wanting to fall behind.

Ahead, the forest grew thicker. The road was darkened by overhanging branches that formed an impenetrable tunnel against the night sky. The coach rattled over broken stones that crunched like skulls beneath the wheels.

Beadle wrapped himself against the dark. He hated it more than anything he knew. For Beadle, the dark was full of fear, not that he knew why; it had always been the same. He would see things in the shadows; tufts of grass would become monsters, hanging branches the limbs of dead men. It was as if the creatures that inhabited the night had freedom to haunt his very soul. He couldn't resist; he was helpless.

Hour after hour, as the coach went on, Raphah slept. Beadle peered out occasionally from his hiding place. He wanted to keep completely covered so that nothing could touch him, snatch him from the carriage and drag him away. The forest moaned and chirped. Eyes flashed from dark places, lit by the coach lamp as it went by. The driver kept on, the bugler at his side, the hounds nearby.

Beadle thought he must have fallen to sleep. In his dream he saw Demurral on his horse, cantering through the night. Not stopping, not waiting, always going on. Day and night went by. The sun rose and set. Demurral continued on.

It was the slowing of the wheels that woke him from his sleep. He could hear the squeaking of the cork against the metal rims as the carriage slowed and slowed. He pulled the coat from his face and looked out. The thick black of the forest that had covered the land like a cowl had thinned to a sparse wood.

Beadle could see the moon high above him. It lit many paths through the trees. He stood up and looked ahead. Far in the distance he could see the staging post where the horses would be changed. They would rest for a while and then be off again. The hounds began to bark and chatter, signalling a brief mark of civilisation in the realm of the forest. A spiral of smoke went up into the night air. Beadle could smell burning pine that scented the damp wood as the wind rustled the leaves from tree to tree.

'The Green Man,' the coachman shouted as they drew closer. He turned the horses towards a large stable built onto the side of a chalk house that glistened with old flints. 'Half the hour and then we set pace.' He shouted as two men came from the dwelling, torches in hand, to welcome them.

It was only in passing that Beadle noticed the black horse tethered to the door of the barn. He gave it but a fleeting thought as he noted its huge size and deep mane. He pushed Raphah in the ribs, waking him from his sleep, and together they left the carriage and followed Barghast and the others into the house.

Beadle took a piece of flint from the outer wall and unthinkingly put it into his pocket. They were all welcomed and stood by a warm fire that lit the room. Each was served by a young girl and given small beer and bread and cheese.

On the hearth wall was the head of a man carved in wood. He had a growth of beard that swept about his face and turned to oak leaves. Within the beard were birds and animals, each carved to an unbelievable likeness. Beadle stared at the face of the man whose warm eyes looked upon them all.

'Is this the Green Man?' he asked the girl as she filled his cup again.

''Tis he,' she said as she turned and went away.

The minutes went quickly by. The fire was warm and took the chill from their bones. Outside the horses were changed and harnessed and the hounds made ready. It was Lady Tanville who first noticed that Ergott was not with their company. She looked about the room and couldn't see him, nor could she remember him coming from the coach.

'You look troubled,' Beadle said.

'Did you see Ergott?' she replied.

'He's not here,' Barghast said, and he went outside to look for Ergott.

From the side barn, he cold hear voices in conversation. He walked quietly towards them, his steps parlous and slow. Ergott stood by the barn door, his back to the night and his breath snorting in grabbed staccatos. He nodded and mumbled as Barghast attempted to hear what was being said.

Ergott stopped and turned as if he knew Barghast was there. 'Cold night, Barghast,' he said, and he stepped from the barn and into the light of the tallow torches that sparkled against the flint and chalk walls.

'You alone?' Barghast asked as he looked into the empty barn.

'Quite. And you?' he asked.

'We make ready. It's time to leave,' Barghast said. He looked into the darkness of the barn and then walked towards the coach, expecting Ergott to follow on.

The carriage took on its guests as the bugler called the hounds and the driver made ready. There was a sense of foreboding as they all took their places. Nothing was said, but there was urgency in their ways. The driver looked towards the road and the dark forest beyond. Raphah looked down upon the yard outside the Green Man. He looked for Beadle and wondered what kept him from the journey.

The house stood like a chalk-flint chapel. Its walls glowed in the light of torches that appeared to have been placed in a circle against the approaching forest. Beadle sat by the fire in the empty room, a small mug of beer in his hands. He roasted his feet against the side of a burning log and thought of Whitby. Outside he could hear the calling of the hounds and knew in his heart he should soon stir and be on his way.

The fire reminded him of the scullery where he had lived those many years. He would sit by its hearth, drink beer and dream. He would be alone with his own thoughts, wrapped in a ragged blanket and with a plate of cheese. Snatching that most pleasant of moments when Demurral slept and the house was silent, he would be very happy. He would steal a log from his master just for the occasion. Fire made him feel that way, fire and beer. Beadle pulled the chair closer for a final warm, knowing he would soon have to stand and make ready for the off. It was like the morning, when the bed keeps you to sleeping and begs you not to welcome the world. Just another minute, he thought to himself, hearing the baying of the coach hounds.

'Beadle . . . Beadle . . .' whispered a voice from the shadows behind him. Beadle knew it well. It was the voice of Demurral.

For what seemed to be a lifetime, Beadle stood before the fire unable to move. He fidgeted in his pockets, turning a piece of string in his fingers as he slowly began to twist his head to where the voice had spoken. In his heart he hoped someone would walk in and break whatever spell was over him. Outside he could hear the coachman making the final preparations.

The voice spoke again. 'I followed you, Beadle. Told you I would never let you go. My journey is your journey – it's you who has led me to the place. From each other we can never escape,' it said darkly.

Beadle took courage from his beer and turned. There in the shadows was a tall hooded figure. Its face looked sallow and had the covering of a growth of grey stubble. Its eyes shone from beneath the dark hood. He knew he need not ask its name. It was Demurral.

'Will you travel with me to the city?' Demurral asked.

'How did you get here?' Beadle replied.

'Followed you. Watched you, and the Ethio. Know you too well,' he said slowly.

'I travel another way now, master,' Beadle replied, knowing in his heart he would have to run. From the yard he heard the bugler call the hounds again and Raphah shouting his name.

'Don't think of running – I'll only follow you wherever you go,' Demurral said as he reached out for him. 'One day you'll have to face me. I know Raphah has the Chalice of the Grail, and it's mine, Beadle. Get the cup and you will live, betray me and you will die.'

Without thinking, Beadle threw the dregs of his beer in Demurral's face and set off to run. He crashed into the door, fell upon the stone steps and into the mud, and scrabbled to his feet. Demurral was close behind, ordering him to stop. The horses bolted at the commotion. The lead mare reared up and then set off in flight as if she knew who was chasing her.

Raphah was thrown from his seat, slipping on the footplate behind the luggage rack and gripping on as the coach bolted forward. The hounds gave chase as Beadle ran behind as fast as he could, Demurral getting ever closer.

# 24

# Deus Ex Machina

MIDNIGHT came with the chiming of a clock. It crept ino the warehouse through a broken window high in the roof. Thomas stood barefoot and listened to the first strike, which seemed to come from a street close by. He sighed desperately as he looked down at the boots he had cut from his feet. Kate had not stirred since she had attacked him. He knew not whether she slept or feared opening her eyes to the world. Since the ghost of Isabella had gone, he had picked at the lock with the knife. His fingers were now numb with cold and his hands were sore, bruised and bleeding with his desire to escape. Thomas looked at the pyx of *Gaudium* and then to Kate. He twisted the knife into the lock repeatedly, his hands frantic to pull the tumblers and be free before Galphus returned.

Upon the final strike of the clock, all was silent. Thomas waited for the coming of the ghost. Kate stirred from her sleep as if she was being called by a voice she knew.

'Beadle!' she screamed, sitting upright. She held her head, where the blood pounded, it felt to Kate, as if it were being cleaved in two with an axe. 'I saw Beadle . . . Demurral is going to kill him!'

Thomas didn't reply as he stuck the knife into the lock yet again and attempted to prise it from the clasp.

'It was Beadle,' she insisted. 'He is coming for us – Demurral knows we are here – he knows Galphus – can't you see, Thomas? It was all a trap.'

'*Gaudium*, that's what's speaking. Your ghost said she'd be back at midnight and I'm still waiting.'

Kate held her swollen face as the pain throbbed. 'You hit me,' she said as she looked up at him.

'You would have killed me,' he replied.

'I need the *Gaudium* – you don't understand. It opens your mind to see things and be someone else.'

'From what I have seen it captures your soul and turns you into a murderer,' Thomas snarled, prepared to hit her again. 'We've been together for years. Thicker than blood – that's what you said. Yet you would have killed me given half the chance.'

'Galphus said . . .'

'Said many things and told many lies – how do you know the bottles are not empty? Makes you see things, does it? What was Beadle doing, then?'

'He was running through a wood – a dark place, wicked and black. Demurral was there,' she said, and then stopped and looked about her as if the dream continued in the air. 'I cannot see a way for us to go. Demurral's wish will be fulfilled.' She spoke as if all hope had gone.

There was a sudden chill as a winter breeze blew through the room. The floor, sprinkled with crisp leaves and the petals of foxgloves, became like a forest, as if the cage were in the open air. The night was full of sound. Within the centre of the cage a thick black mist began to swirl. It spun in a dark vortex until the floor could not be seen. There was the crackling of fire and the spitting of burning twigs. Smoke billowed from the centre of a whirlwind within a whirlwind that hugged the floor like a spinning platter.

'It's Isabella . . .' Kate said nervously.

'She's late,' Thomas said as a tumbler slipped within the lock. 'Don't need a ghost to set me free.'

'But you do need one to show you the way to freedom,' Isabella said as she appeared from the whirlwind. All fell silent. The leaves scattered themselves upon the wooden boards. Isabella folded her arms and stared at Thomas. 'Galphus has sent his men for you, they are coming.'

'Then I will have to work to free us from this place,' he said.

'And then?' Isabella asked as a ghostly woodmouse ran from the folds of her skirt and disappeared before them.

'I'll fight. No one will take me and Kate, no one.'

'Then be quick, the guards are on the first landing,' Isabella said as she vanished from the cage and reappeared suddenly by the door.

Thomas slipped the knife into the lock again and tipped the final lever. The door sprang open. Kate got to her feet and staggered towards him, her wits twisted. She dizzily reached for Thomas to help her, all the time keeping her eye on the pyx. Thomas, knowing her intentions, took the pyx. He snatched it from the table and pushed it into his pocket. 'Better I keep it,' he said, and he dragged her towards the warehouse door.

Kate shrugged, in the mist of the *Gaudium*, knowing it would be worthwhile to wait her time. The *Gaudium* was safe, she thought, for now anyway.

'Then how do we get out?' Thomas asked the ghost, expecting some *deus ex machina* to come to their aid and solve an apparently unfathomable complexity.

'You may escape but you will never be free of Salamander Street, only if Galphus wants you to be,' Isabella said. Her skin began to change like that of a chameleon. Thomas could see the dirty paint of the wall. Isabella faded. The scent of the wood began to vanish and she slipped from view.

'Gone . . . Tricked again,' Thomas said as he searched the gloom for any sign of her.

'Quickly!' Isabella said as she appeared behind them. 'The Druggles are coming for you. This way.' She pointed to a painted window much like the one that was in the tower.

'Rather take my chance with the Druggles,' Thomas said, thinking this to be a trap and remembering what Smutt had said. He grabbed the warehouse door and pulled it open. A Druggle swung at him with a thick cudgel. It clattered against the frame, splintering the wood.

'DO SOMETHING!' Kate screamed suddenly, pulling the hair from her head with her skeletal hands.

Thomas kicked at the Druggle, knocking him back across the landing.

'Bolt the door,' Kate shouted as the *Gaudium* made the whole world tremble and shudder and the face of the Druggle sneered at her like a rat. 'Do something!' she shouted again, searching the room for Isabella.

Thomas struggled with the door, pushing it with all his might as the Druggle beat it with the cudgel.

'Isabella!' Kate screamed hoping to see the ghost.

Isabella appeared beside Thomas, her hands clasped behind her back.

'Open the door when I tell you,' she shouted above the sound of the beating cudgel.

Thomas turned to her as he pressed his shoulder against the door. The sweat rolled down his face as anger welled from within. Isabella stood rigidly still, her eyes fixed on the doorway.

'Now!' she shouted.

Thomas jumped back from the door just as the Druggle beat

at it yet again. It swung violently open, knocking him from his feet and pushing him into the room. The Druggle stepped inside, and seeing Thomas on the floor began to smile.

'I told you I would see to you later,' he said as he stepped towards him and beat the cudgel against his hand. 'Now we'll see what will happen to you.'

The Druggle had no realisation of the presence of the ghost. Isabella stalked him from behind, only visible to Kate and Thomas. Within a pace he lifted the cudgel to strike Thomas a blow to the legs. Isabella vanished for a second, disappearing through the floor. The warehouse began to shake, struck by a violent tremor. The Druggle stopped and looked as if he couldn't understand what was happening. Thomas smiled; he knew what was to come.

In a lightning crack the floor exploded from beneath, and a gust of wind blew through the boards. Dust and dead mites were scattered into the air, showering all in a thin vapour of dead skin. Another crack of light exploded from the ceiling, instantly dazzling the Druggle. He stumbled back, taking hold of the wall for comfort. It was then that Isabella appeared to them all. Kate cowered to the floor, covering her face for fear this was another hallucination of the *Gaudium*. Thomas looked upon the sight and hid his eyes with his hands; fear stopped him from staring at the visage of the creature that stood above him. The Druggle didn't move. His eyes opened as wide as his dry mouth, holding his face in a lopsided smile. Terrified, he dropped the cudgel from his limp fingers as he stumbled on weak feet.

The lad gagged and choked upon his own spittle as fear gripped his throat and made him incapable of gulping it back. He slowly lifted his hand as if to point at the creature that defied belief.

Isabella had been transformed. Gone were the pretty dress

and foxgloves. Gone the crinoline and laced-ruff neck. Now she stood, dark and sinister, a human snake that stared upon her victim through eyes of fire. Instantly she spat out her tongue to catch the lad who stood and trembled. It shot blood-red from her mouth, tipped with the heads of other dead. It was skull-laced and stank of death. Her long rat's tail cast itself about his feet, pulling him to the floor as he fell backwards. The lad clawed for the entrance, gripping the gaps between the beams as Isabella slowly drew him towards her. He began to scream. He hollered, blank and empty and utterly feeble. He had not the strength to scare a mouse. The words dropped from his lips and summonsed no one.

Isabella coiled through the air as if to strike. The lad rolled like a dog upon the floor, waiting for the attack. Then in a fit of madness he twisted from her grip, jumped to his feet and fled. He ran into the wall so hard he smashed the plaster, which fell in pools of dust about him. He screamed the scream of a bed-wetter. His throat tightened to a breaking drum as he grabbed his sodden pants and ran from her.

As the dust settled they heard the Druggle running down the wooden stairs whelping like a pup. Isabella was again transformed and smiled at them.

'How?' asked Thomas as he lowered his hands.

'I did nothing, 'twas all in your minds – you saw what you wanted. You haunted yourselves,' Isabella said as she smoothed her wig and made straight the ruff upon her pure, lead-white neck.

'But I saw . . .' Thomas said

'What you wanted,' she replied.

Kate said nothing. She had seen Thomas smile at Isabella. It was a smile he had once given to her. She knew what it meant and the *Gaudium* knew her envy all too well.

'There's a way across the roof into the factory and then

down to the street. It's the only way – follow me,' Isabella said as she made off. Kate stumbled mindlessly behind, not thinking of where she would go. Reluctantly, Thomas followed, casting back his glance to the door.

'Wait,' he said, and he ran back to the door to the stairs and stacked the wooden boxes against it. 'We need more time.'

Isabella waved urgently for him to follow. Thomas watched as she went to the window. There was no sign of any physical movement; it was as if she had no feet but just glided without friction. She beckoned him again as she stood by the window. 'This is the one,' she said. 'There is a stairway on the other side, it'll take you across the roof.'

'And you?' he asked, as Kate drudged behind in her melancholy.

'I'll see where they are and come back to you,' Isabella said in her shrill voice.

'And tell Galphus?' he asked, still not sure of the ghost's heart.

'It's a chance you take. I'll come and find you. There is your escape – take it,' she said with a smile. With that she was gone, vanished like a spring mist.

'Come on, Kate. You'll have to go faster,' Thomas said as he kicked open the window and stood upon a gantry high above the roofs of Salamander Street. He could see the lights of the city going on forever, glistening against the cold.

They took to the steps in the cold night, Thomas shutting the window and slipping the lock. He followed Kate across the wooden pathway that ran across the leaded roof. It glistened in the frost, grey, cold and bitter. Thomas thought it was like the whole of the factory had been encased in sour pastry. It was the frozen skin of a vast skeleton, which traced the way of the eaves. The gantry led on by the tower along the east of the factory. Far away, Thomas could see the masts of ships. He thought of Crane and the *Magenta* – he would be there, some-where, very close. They turned the corner and the scaffold took them to another window. Isabella stood graciously waiting.

'This way. They look for you in the factory. The guards have gone to wake Galphus,' she said as the window opened by itself.

Once inside, Thomas knew where they were. To the right was a flight of stairs. Two floors below he knew would be the front door, and by its side was the room Galphus used as his laboratory.

'Isabella, a favour – and one which I trust you for. Please, I need to know if there are any Druggles in the doorway below,' Thomas said, and he reached out to touch her hand.

Kate saw it all. It simmered in her as the *Gaudium* whispered in discontent. The ghost vanished from sight and then quickly returned.

'Gone,' she said. 'I have waited for this for so long.'

'Kate, you have to keep up,' Thomas said. 'We'll get to the door and I'll get the key. Galphus keeps it in the desk in the room at the side. Then we'll be gone.'

'I think I'll die, I need some . . .' Kate said.

'It'll kill you, Kate. Isabella said,' Thomas replied.

'What does she know?' she whispered like a cauldron hag at Beltane.

Thomas walked swiftly on. Isabella glided ahead, and Kate struggled to keep up. Everything within her felt as if it were wizened and arid. In her mind she saw herself as an old barren women, frail and decrepit. The *Gaudium* whispered to her again as she bided her time, waiting for the moment to steal it from him.

The way was clear. The Druggles could be heard far away as they beat the Dragon's Heart. Thomas looked to his bare feet, thankful he had cut the boots from them before he escaped.

At the turn of the landing, just before the entrance to the

factory, was the door to Galphus's laboratory. It stood slightly open. A shaft of amber light came through the crack from a candle upon his desk. Thomas looked to Isabella. Again she disappeared in the blink of an eye and then was manifest again.

'He's not there, the room is empty,' she said as she smiled at Thomas.

Kate shook with a tremor of disdain and sniffed the air as Thomas pushed the door slowly open and peered inside.

'I'll get the key,' he said confidently, nodding to Isabella.

Stepping inside the room, he went to the desk by the wall. For the first time he noticed the thousands of glass jars that lined the shelves to the ceiling. The higher he looked the more he saw, until at their zenith was a single jar wrapped in cobwebs. Isabella appeared beside him as Kate stood in the hallway, arms folded and frowning.

'Look,' said Isabella. 'What are they?'

'Got nothing in them, just empty jars with writing on,' he said.

'Open that one,' Isabella said pointing to the highest one as if giving a command.

Thomas obeyed. Climbing the shelves like a ladder, he took the jar from the shelf and read the name that was written upon it. 'Andreas Lib . . . av . . . ius,' he said, stumbling upon the last name as one self-taught. With that he jumped to the floor and began to slowly prise open the cork stopper. The jar spun in his hands as if it were alive. It burnt his fingers and danced from his grip. The stopper popped from the jar and an ear-splitting bellow shrieked through the room, as if invoked by the name Thomas had spoken.

'Comenius – lux – en – tenebris – ereptor – occisor!' The strange voice screamed from the jar like the hissing of a cooking pot. As it hollered, an effervescence of green mist oozed from the lid over Thomas's fingers.

The ghost of Isabella recoiled, dimming in colour and shrinking before his eyes. She was like a fading candle out of wax, the wick burnt to the end.

'Spirit,' she gasped as the mist rolled about their feet like an ebbing tide. 'LAST WORDS – HELD IN DEATH!' she grunted. 'Go to Pallium's room – I will see you there. This is too much for me – too much death, too much sorrow.' The ghost looked to the floor as inch by inch she unwillingly vanished. 'They take my portrait – it is gone from the wall . . . They take me.'

Isabella spoke harshly, her voice coarse and brutal as if it were another who spoke through her. Kate cowered in the doorway as she waited her moment. The *Gaudium* whispered again. It spoke secrets, opening her eyes to its visions. She looked at Thomas with scorn and saw the way he smiled at Isabella. She thought how death was a garment that suited the spectre and one that would suit Thomas well.

# Flibbertigibbet

BEADLE gripped the back of the carriage with his fingers. He hopped, skipped and jumped upon the mud as the carriage gained pace. Raphah grasped his wrists, holding them tightly so his friend wouldn't fall, then quickly plucked him from the mud and dragged him onto the coach. Whatever had feared Beadle was now etched on his face.

'Where were you?' Raphah asked.

'Demurral,' Beadle said, eyes wide, as he rubbed his face with dirty hands. 'The Green Man – Demurral was waiting.'

'You saw him?' he asked.

'More than that, he spoke to me,' Beadle mumbled, unable to comprehend what had happened to him. 'He follows us, Raphah, has done all this time. Said that I had led him to you. Everywhere we have been, Demurral has been a step behind. He speaks of a cup, the Chalice of the Grail – said we have it.'

Raphah looked to the bag that was strung about his neck. 'That we do,' he said as he opened the bag and gave Beadle a glimpse of the Chalice. 'It's a beggar's cup.'

'Magic?' Beadle asked, quietened by its presence.

'Deep magic. Without the need to cast a spell or kill a chick-

263

en. *Magic* that was won by blood and nail.' Raphah carefully wrapped the vessel and placed it within the bag. He looked behind to the dark trail. Stark thick limbs of dead trees cut in across the path. Here the forest was at its darkest. The lamps of the coach lit the night. Forest creatures moaned and howled, the velvet black hiding all from human eyes. By the coach the hounds pressed on, never failing to keep pace.

They said no more. Both knew that Demurral wasn't far behind, and his presence stalked them in the night. Beadle looked back constantly, tired eyes searching the pitch for any sign. The wind rushed through the trees and rattled the branches. He begged the wheels to keep turning. *Faster, faster* . . . he urged them on in his mind, fearful they would stop. The mud grew thicker. It clung to the wheels and slowed their progress. From here on, the horses couldn't canter; they walked, wading through the mud, dragging the carriage behind which lurched and creaked like a storm-tossed ship. The hounds kept to the soft earth of the forest. They howled as they ran, all wanting to take the lead as if they knew a great evil was following their path.

Raphah slept fitfully, constantly aware of Beadle's great agitation. He was conscious too of the growing warmth of the air. The cold frost had long gone and the night was now still. It also smelt dreadfully. Hanging in the air was a thickening mist with the odour of damp, rotting fur. He sniffed as the mist grew thicker and coated the earth like a blanket.

He could not count the hours, but watched the moon cross the sky from east to west. Raphah looked to where the comet had hung like a Damoclean sword. He counted the stars as they travelled on and wondered how they hung upon the firmament. He had spent many nights as a boy looking at the stars. Now, far to the north and wrapped in a blanket, he was thankful that they reminded him of home. His mother had said when

264

he looked at the moon he would see her face, and that she would stand upon the mountain above the village and look up. In the moon they would share a meeting. Raphah lifted his hands to the sky and closed his eyes. He knew she would do the same and that in Riathamus they would be made one.

The carriage rolled on, the road becoming smoother and metalled. The woodland gave way to high hedges and open fields that slumbered from hill to hill as they journeyed south. The horses clattered as they cantered, sometimes slowing to a trot and then speeding on. Hounds ran quietly behind, their voices stilled by familiar roads.

Beadle looked behind, wary that in the night Demurral followed. He wanted to speak, but feared the trees would hear his words and they would tell of his passing.

'He's near,' Beadle said to Raphah as the coach rolled from side to side. 'I can feel him, he's watching us.'

'Then we shall give him the fight he so desires,' Raphah said.

'Can't we just give him the Chalice and be done with it?' Beadle asked.

'If he wants it, then he will have to snatch it from my dead fingers,' Raphah said, nestling the bag closer to him. 'It should not be kept in the world of men.'

The carriage went on as the hours passed. Beadle kept watch, convinced that he saw all manner of beasts staring from the high hedges. The moon set behind the hills and the night became as dark as a locked vault. Stride by stride the horses slowed their pace until the carriage crawled on.

'Can't see,' said the coachman, as with one hand he held the lamp above him. 'You'll have to go ahead,' he said to the bugler reluctantly as he shivered in the cold.

The bugler leapt from the driving plate to the ground and summonsed his hounds. Taking hold of the collar of the lead horse he walked ahead, blunderbuss in hand. All he could see was the broken stones beneath his feet that cut through his thin soles.

'All's well,' he said every few yards until they had gone half a mile. One by one the hounds began to shiver. Their hair stood stiffly on end and dog after dog began to moan. Their growls began softly, tenderly, like the calling to a young pup. Then as they went further down the lane, their voices changed. Each hound sounded discontent, joining the chorus as their fear grew. The bugler tried to calm them, calling them by name until they clustered tightly around him. He knew they could feel a presence close by – someone or something was near.

A large, lean dog with a severed ear came to him and nuzzled its head into his leg and pawed him as they walked on together. It growled a guttural growl and then, reaching up on its hind legs, wailed like a dying child.

'What can you see, Hugo?' the bugler asked the hound as it continued to cry, biting at the air, snapping at the darkness and bristling its fur as it leapt back and forth.

'Steady ahead,' he said nervously to the coachman. 'Something's up . . .'

The coachman kept a tight rein. He could feel the horses pulling against the hot metal bits. They snorted wildly, wanting to break free of their bridles and run off into the night. It was as if they were being stalked from the hedgerow, that some great beast followed.

The road dipped towards a bridge. Though the driver couldn't see this he knew it to be there. Years of driving the road had ingrained each turn and twist upon his mind, and although blind to what was ahead, he knew that the bridge was there. From then on the trees and hedgerows would vanish and there would be open heath for twenty miles. At the ridge of the next hill they would see the distant lights and smell the fragrance of the city – London.

The bugler walked on. His hounds stayed near and the horses blustered in the slow pace. With every step he looked behind as the hounds' barks grew louder.

It was then that a sudden, vociferous blast of light, brighter than the sun, exploded before the carriage. High to the right, a large sycamore was blown from the ground. Its branches scattered across the road as it ripped itself from the mud and crushed the earth beneath it. Several hounds were thrown through the air and strewn forlornly across the road. The bugler was knocked from his feet and fell to the mud, and the horses stood petrified.

The coachman looked into the dark night, still seeing the brightness of the explosion burning into his head.

Raphah pulled the blanket from his face and gouged the splinters from the back of his neck. Beadle cowered, not daring to move as a burning torch was held before the coach.

Lady Tanville held on to Barghast, who peered through the wooden shutter to see a man on horseback approaching through the gloom.

'STAND!' shouted the man. He held a tallow lamp and pointed a pistol at the coachman's head. 'DELIVER YOUR MONEY OR I'LL TAKE YOUR LIVES!'

His words echoed like the explosion. They were harsh and cold; he cared not for them or what he would do.

'ONE MOVE AND MORE GUNPOWDER!' he shouted again.

The bugler stumbled around beneath him, abandoned by his dogs and unable to see as the flash had blotted out the world. Clumsily he picked his way like his lost dogs through the dirt and fumbled with the blunderbuss.

'We have no money – we are just travellers,' cried the driver as he tried to make out who stood before him.

'No one journeys without the fare,' said the highwayman as

he approached the carriage. All around, the sound of the frightened hounds faded in the distance. 'I'll take all you have and be gone. No one will get hurt, just cooperate.'

There was a yelp of a hound as Hugo leapt from beneath the carriage and took hold of the man by the leg. The hound pulled at his boots as he bit and twisted, spinning in the air as he held fast with his teeth.

'Damn the dog!' the highwayman shouted.

'Hugo, no!' yelled the bugler, clambering blindly to find his hound.

There was a click, then a flash and a sudden crack. The dog fell to the floor, dead. The highwayman calmly slid the gun into a saddle holster and pulled another from his belt.

'No need to kill my Hugo,' the bugler cried as he touched his hand from stone to stone to find his pet.

Raphah looked down from the carriage. In the lamplight he could make out the shape of a large-framed man sat upon a jet-black horse. He wore a riding cape, and his face was obscured by a silk scarf that covered his mouth.

'Blagdan?' asked the coachman, as if he knew the man's voice.

'Who asks me that?' the highwayman said, pointing his gun at the bugler who grovelled beneath him. 'It is I and I am proud to say that I will take every penny you carry and make your journey lighter – Blagdan, the most wanted man in England, nothing to lose and all the world to gain.' He laughed as he spoke. 'Who or what are *you*?' he said as he looked up at Raphah.

'He's a traveller, got no money, on his way to London,' interrupted the driver, who held his calloused hands to his face.

'Then I'll have him do me a trick,' the man said as he kicked the coach door. 'Get yourself down and let me see you dance. In fact, I would have you sing me a song. Sing well or I'll shoot you dead, and doubtless no one will ever mourn your passing.' Blagdan looked to the driver. 'Better you be going – I'll spare your life this time but be sure to tell the magistrate it was me.'

The coachman leapt from his seat and ran across the bridge as the bugler stumbled on, half-blind.

Raphah stepped down from the carriage and stood on the ground before him. 'I'm not a puppet or a jester and I won't dance for you,' he said calmly.

'Saw a bear dance once, he didn't complain,' Blagdan said as he pulled the hammer of the pistol. 'And where I'm from, a bear has more right to live than the likes of you.'

'Leave him,' said Lady Tanville from inside the carriage. 'I have something you can take that is worth more than watching the lad dance.'

Blagdan stopped and turned as if to listen intently to the voice. 'A woman?' he asked merrily, unable to see within the coach, as his thick chin rubbed against the collar of his coat.

'I'll dance and sing for you,' said Raphah, 'but leave her alone.'

'You had your chance. I'd rather dance with the woman. Hold my horse. If it's not here when I've finished I cut off your ears and post them through your mouth.' Blagdan spat the words as he got down from the horse and went to the carriage door.

'Don't do it, don't open the door. It's not what you expect,' Raphah pleaded.

Blagdan laughed as he belted his pistol and took a long, slender knife from inside his coat.

'Keep it shut, boy,' he said blithely, gripping the door handle and giving it a slow twist.

'It's not worth your life,' Raphah pleaded. The coach rocked from side to side as if someone was desperate to escape. Raphah let go of the horse and stepped quickly away from the carriage.

Beadle wrapped himself within the blanket, not wanting to see what he knew would come.

'You little tiger – can't wait to see me?' Blagdan shouted as he undid the buttons of his coat.

It was the last thing he ever said. The door to the carriage was blasted from its hinges. Blagdan fell backwards as the door smashed his face and Barghast leapt from within. The villain was gripped by the throat. He screamed momentarily. By reflex, he fired the pistol into the air. Barghast scragged him back and forth with the strength of ten men. He pulled his throat until he breathed no more. Blagdan was dragged to the ground as the remaining hounds scattered.

'Leave him,' shouted Raphah as Blagdan was dragged away. Barghast stared back, his eyes unwilling to give up his prey.

'Barghast, no!' screamed Lady Tanville as he pulled the body of the man towards the heath. Far in the distance, the screams of the coachman cried out as he ran into the night.

All fell deathly still. Lady Tanville stepped from the coach.

'The explosion knocked Ergott from his seat. He still sleeps,' she said.

From out of the darkness, Barghast stumbled back towards the coach. He came quickly from the shadows and into the light of the lamps. As he walked, he wiped the blood from his mouth. His eyes swept from side to side before focusing on Raphah and then on Beadle.

'I couldn't help it,' he said as he bent to the ground and picked up Blagdan's pistol from the dirt. 'Shoot me now, Raphah – let me taste death.'

'It would be no use, Barghast. This is not the time or the place and our troubles are not yet over, are they, Beadle?'

Beadle looked to the ground. 'Not yet,' he whispered, as if he didn't want to speak.

'What does he mean?' Barghast asked.

'Demurral follows us. He was at the Green Man. You are now a part of the mystery, Barghast, and you too, Tanville. We should have been more plain in our journey.'

Tanville Chilnam looked at Raphah as if she didn't understand. 'Demurral?' she asked.

'A magician and a thief, a collector of trinkets that he thinks will bring him power,' Barghast said. 'I took from him a piece of the true Cross. I heard that he even searched for the Keruvim – it was I who told him of its presence. I had been offered the Keruvim in Paris. It was enough to pay the ransom of a king and I had no reason to have such a device. I told Demurral in exchange for the true Cross.'

'You?' Raphah asked. 'I am the guardian of the Keruvim. A guardian who lost it to the sea.'

'Then it cannot be charmed by fish and will never be seen again,' Barghast said.

'Never,' repeated Raphah.

'So why does he still pursue you?' she asked.

'Why do you search for a lost portrait?' Raphah replied.

'Because I have to. It has to be taken home before it does more harm.'

'And Demurral seeks that which in his hands will cause harm. It is his intention to kill me. Whilst I am the guardian of the Keruvim, its power is within me. If I am killed then he will have his desire and the power of God will be his.'

'And he wants to kill Thomas and Kate and turn them into begging spirits,' Beadle said.

'And this is your journey?' she asked.

Beadle nodded, a smile on his face as if he knew what she would say.

'Then we travel together. This is not by chance that we have met. I now know that my quest lies in Salamander Street. In the carriage, Ergott dowsed for the hiding place of the children. I

271

looked upon his map whilst he slept – there is no such place as Salamander Street, it doesn't exist. Yet Bragg had business there with a man named Galphus.'

'Salamander Street is the road for which I search,' Barghast said. 'It is the last road I shall walk and if it is your destination then it is mine also.' He looked at them and smiled. 'I fear that a greater hand plays each one of us. Salamander Street cannot be found easily, only those invited will find the way.'

'Bragg was invited,' Tanville said. 'He was to take that cup to the man called Galphus.'

'Galphus?' asked Barghast as Raphah listened. 'The man is an alchemist, a dabbler, and if he has the key to Salamander Street, then a greater force possesses him.'

# Tatterdemalion and Galligaskins

IT was only a matter of minutes before they reached the alleyway that led from the factory to Salamander Street. It appeared to twist and turn less than it had before – no longer a labyrinth in which they would be lost, but an avenue that led them to a destination.

'She's pretty,' said Kate as she tramped morbidly, her shoulders sagged and hunched.

'Who?' Thomas asked, knowing well who Kate meant.

'Isabella. I saw the way she looked at you in the factory. She's pretty, even for someone who's been dead a hundred years.'

'Doesn't she frighten you?' Thomas asked.

'Frighten?' Kate said in a voice that attempted to be soft and warm. 'I'm not sure . . .' She paused and shook her head. It was as if something was clinging to her skull, something dark, miserable and black. 'Thomas, please, I need to have some *Gaudium* . . . Just a drop, let me moisten my lips.'

'It'll kill you. You heard Isabella. It's poison,' he replied.

'Not if you've tasted it. It's like honey and cream and it does things to your head, good things.'

'And makes you want more,' Thomas replied as he watched her warily. Kate appeared to hunch even further, clutching her guts and moaning slightly as if in pain.

'Thomas, I need some – now.' She looked at him pitifully, her eyes pleading. 'Please Thomas. I will die without it, that's what Galphus said, said I would die if I didn't have one drop every day. What does a ghost know about it? She's dead.' Kate spoke quickly as she took a smouldering breath.

'She's seen things you haven't,' he said tersely.

'She tried to kill me, drag me into her world, that's what she wants to do. That hag wouldn't care if I were dead. That's what she wants, someone to share that picture and live in that rotting copse of stinking trees.'

'A ghost couldn't do that,' Thomas protested.

'Isabella tried to,' she insisted as she stumbled on, falling over every tiny stone.

Kate didn't finish what she had to say. The sound of running echoed through the passageways like a pack of dogs pursuing them through the night. The shouts of several Druggles chilled their steps as the beating of the Dragon's Heart spread news of their escape through the factory. Thomas grabbed Kate by the hand and pulled her onwards. He ran faster, dragging her along the hidden lanes as the din of those who gave chase came ever closer.

'I can't run,' she said as she pulled against him.

'You have to, Galphus will take you,' he pleaded, dragging her on.

Kate thought for a moment. 'Leave me,' she said. 'Galphus has more *Gaudium* – he'll give it to me.'

'I can't – won't,' Thomas snapped. 'Always together – remember?'

'That was then, this is now. Leave me. You get away, find Crane and come back.'

Thomas thought for a moment as the sound of the beating footsteps came closer still.

'Look,' he said pulling the *Gaudium* from his pocket. 'Run with me and you can have a drop,' he said as he ran from her.

Kate followed. She ran faster than before, somehow managing to keep pace with him. Thomas pressed on, not knowing which way to flee. He turned every corner and followed his heart. From somewhere in the darkness the voices got closer.

'They'll have us if we don't get faster,' he pleaded.

Kate slumped against the wall of the narrow alley and shrugged her shoulders. She stopped and looked around. In the light of the tallow lantern that hung from the stone wall, she saw the cuts to Thomas's bare feet. 'Let's not go on. Take the *Gaudium* and die, be with Isabella . . . We'll never escape. Can't you feel it? Can't you understand? This isn't the real world, it's all an illusion. We're already dead and this is hell. Galphus is the devil and this is our punishment. That's why you can't get away from Salamander Street.'

'I'll not believe it. This is life and we're alive.'

'The *Gaudium* told me . . . We are dead. Dead as nails in a coffin lid,' she said earnestly as she stared at him.

There was a rushing sound from the alleyway as the sound of heavy footsteps beat on the stone. It was as if a thousand feet ran towards them. Thomas snatched Kate from the path, pulled her into a small ginnel and held his hand across her mouth to shut up the words. She struggled to be free as a herd of Druggles rushed by, staves in hand.

'See,' he whispered. 'They know we have escaped. If you want us to be killed just keep being the knave.'

'I want the *Gaudium*,' she said, not caring what was heard of her.

From over the wall they could hear the harping of music and the rolling of barrels. Thomas peered from their hiding place and listened for the Druggles. They had gone. Looking up, he saw the light of the inn above the wall. Even higher was the meeting place of the roofs that blocked out the night. Holding on to the tallow lamp, Thomas hoisted himself on top of the wall. He bent down and as he twisted grabbed Kate by the arm and began to pull her to him. 'Climb, Kate,' he whispered as she scrambled towards him.

'Why?' she asked.

'Just do it.'

Kate was pulled upwards until she sat with him on the wall. She looked at him and held out her hand. Thomas jumped to the ground on the far side of the wall and landed in a narrow yard of three brick walls and a doorway into the Salamander Inn.

A fiddle played and lilted the music back and forth. The door stood unlocked, releasing the sound of many drunken voices.

'We have to take the chance,' Thomas said. 'Will you do it?'

'*Gaudium* . . .' she replied, as if to sign the deal. 'Then I'll come.'

Thomas hesitated for a moment. He could feel the pyx in his pocket. It burnt against his hand as if he held a hot coal.

'One drop?' he asked, knowing she would drink the lot given the chance.

'One drop,' she replied as a smile lit her face.

He took the pyx, unscrewed the lid and tipped it upon her hand. A large golden drop the size of several sorrowful tears dripped out. It fell upon her skin with a hiss. Kate licked it quickly as she closed her eyes and held her hand to her mouth. She said nothing. Every thought she had ever had rushed through her mind, and she slumped to the floor. Her eyes burst with a rainbow of colours as the world around her shimmered and the music from the Salamander Inn danced like butterflies before her face.

'Gobwash and turdyguts.' Kate groaned with a shuddering smile that looked as if it brought new life to her. 'Can you see it?' she asked.

'What?' replied Thomas as he looked about.

'The music. I can see every note, it dances in the air.'

Thomas looked again. He could see nothing and hear nothing but the dull jangling of the violin and the stamping of many feet in time with its rhythm. From the noise within, it was obvious to him that the beer-house was full of people and a grand bacchanalia was taking place within its walls. The shouts of drunken men echoed from the doors and windows. Here were the people who lived clustered around the inn – men like Pallium, all indebted to Galphus, dangling like puppets.

'We need to find Isabella,' Thomas said as he listened against the door of the inn.

'You'd like that, wouldn't you?' Kate leered. 'Find Isabella, fancy that . . . Thomas in love with a pouting milksop.'

'She wants to help us escape from this place,' Thomas insisted.

'She knows as little as I do,' Kate said boldly as she pushed against the door to go in. 'She wants to kill us both.'

'Galphus . . .' Thomas said.

'I care not,' Kate snorted.

With that she pushed open the door and shielded her eyes as the sharp light beat against her. A plume of thick blue smoke swelled out like a giant wave. It stank of heavy tobacco and beer and in Kate's eyes was laced with strings of fine diamonds that danced like snakes upon the breeze.

The noise was intense. A babble of men grunted and groaned in some foreign language. They cared not for the two who stepped in from the cold night. Their entire gaze was fixed on a pair of fighting birds that danced and squawked upon the floor at the centre of the inn. No one seemed to notice the barefoot lad and dishevelled girl who edged their way slowly into the room.

In the corner was a fire that spat wood sparks from the grate into the crowded room. A small bench was perched on the hearth. Thomas nodded for Kate to take a seat. He looked for Druggles. To a man, everyone who crowded around the fighting birds was a drunk. They slopped mugs of beer upon the floor, filling them from ornate pot barrels set upon tables. No one paid for their drink, all appeared to be free. They sang raucously, blind to Thomas and Kate as they cheered on the fight.

Thomas could see that the door to the street was bolted. He took two mugs of beer from a table and pushed his way through the crowds to the fire. Kate held her head in her hands and stared at the flames. She didn't notice his return, her eyes oblivious to the world.

'Drink this,' he said as he handed her the mug.

She sipped the beer that washed against her nose like warm froth. Kate smiled at him and then reached out and touched his face.

'Thomas,' she said as if they were just met. 'What are we doing here?'

'Drink it and then we leave,' he said above the cries of the dying bird as the victor plucked the feathers from its neck.

The men began to argue, angered by the lack of fight in the vanquished bird. A small vixen-like man grabbed another by the throat and began to peck at him with his fists. The two began to fight and roll about in the beer and sawdust that covered the floor. Thomas stood before Kate as more men joined in.

Suddenly, a hand grabbed him by the shoulder.

'Thomas,' said Pallium. 'I'm glad to see you alive. I heard that you were dead – thought Galphus had killed you.'

'What would you care?' Thomas said, pushing Pallium from him. He stepped back, grabbing the fire-iron as he stared at Pallium.

'Quickly,' Pallium said. 'I know you cannot trust me, but I am with you. Crane needs your help, he is in serious trouble. Galphus betrayed him.'

'More lies?' Thomas asked as the fight went on about them.

'I can get you from this place. Kate needs to be free from Salamander Street. She will die if she stays here. It is only a matter of time.'

Thomas looked at him as if every word he spoke dripped from his lips like vile slather.

'Trust me,' he pleaded. 'Galphus has me gripped by the *Gaudium* – just like Kate. I have to do what he says. Now I want to be free.' Pallium looked ashen and drawn. He nibbled on his fingertips and ducked behind the high back of the oak settle as the fight came closer.

Kate had returned to the fire. Her mind was lost in the embers. From above her she felt the wafting of a spider as it stirred the air upon its thread. She looked up and watched it fall helplessly from the mantel into the flames. Thomas looked at her and in that moment decided what to do.

'Get us from this place, Pallium. Let this not be a trick or I'll kill you.'

'I'll take you to Jacob Crane, that I'll promise and it will not be a trick.'

'How can we trust you?' Thomas asked him.

'You can't,' he said, 'but I am the only hope you have of escaping the Druggles.'

Thomas grabbed Kate and pulled her to her feet and from her dream. Pallium turned and ran to the door. Thomas followed, his hand clasping Kate's as the small vixen-like man was beaten upon the head with a dead chicken.

'Crane needs you both,' Pallium pleaded, out of breath as he ran ahead. 'He is in much distress.'

They left the Salamander Inn and trotted along the street to Pallium's house. The sound of the Dragon Heart could be heard chiming far away. It echoed through the roof-capped streets and chased the dust and dirt through the alleyways.

Kate murmured his words as she ran on. To her left and right she saw faces peering from frosted windows. They were all the same: meagre, sombre and pinched. They had large eyes that stared not at her, but into her. She felt that they all knew who she was and why she was running. She began to weep.

As they turned the corner the stink of the street began to grow even worse. They knew that they were near to where Pallium lived. The road became darker with no tallow lamps. Pallium ran ahead, waddling like a mother goose in baggy pants.

The door to the house stood open. Pallium looked for the key in his pocket and then went inside. Kate and Thomas followed.

'Do you have *Gaudium*?' she asked him.

'Only enough for the day, only enough for me,' he chirped happily as if he owned the world. 'Quickly, there could be Druggles – they know you have escaped and will be searching for you.'

'Why does Galphus keep people here?' Kate asked.

'It isn't Galphus, but Salamander Street. Don't you understand? We are all kept here by who we were before. Victims of our wicked hearts.' Pallium laughed.

'Before?' Thomas asked. 'What do you mean, *before*?'

Pallium pulled on the tie that hung loose around his scrawny neck. Taking the key he locked the door and sighed as if in deep contentment. 'Before I came here I was a businessman. Had many things but wanted happiness. I fell in love and she brought me here. I thought this would be the perfect place but it became a prison.'

'Then escape,' Thomas said.

'I don't want to. This is a prison of my own making. Everyone here in Salamander Street would never want to leave. Our desires are fulfilled. Mine is the desire to hold gold coins in my hand, to count them one by one and never be able to spend them. That is pure joy – *Gaudium*!' he exclaimed. 'Galphus has his own vice. He could no more set Jacob Crane free than I ever could.'

'Jacob is still here?' Thomas asked.

'He is closer than you think,' Galphus said as the door to the parlour opened and three Druggles stepped into the hallway. In their hands they carried two sets of manacles. Galphus looked to Pallium and nodded in thanks.

'Greatly appreciated,' he said to the man as he handed him a vial of *Gaudium*.

'I will kill you,' Thomas said as the Druggle wrapped his wrists in the metal straps and twisted the bolt into the lock. 'You promised me, Pallium.'

'I promised you would see Jacob Crane, and that you will – immediately.

Kate didn't even realise she was being restrained. She looked to Galphus like a begging dog, holding out her hands as her eyes followed the *Gaudium* into Pallium's pocket.

'For me?' she asked him, her fingers trembling.

'Not yet, my pretty girl, but there will soon come a time when you can have as much as you want and in return all you will give me is a breath.'

Pallium banged against the wall of the stairs and as he did the oak panel appeared to split in two and slide open. He took the lamp from the table and lit the way. The Druggles followed, then Kate and Thomas and finally Galphus.

The stone stairs slipped quickly below ground. The scent of the river ebbed through the sewer as a stiff breeze blew cobwebs about their heads.

'See,' Pallium said, 'he hadn't gone far at all.' Pallium hammered upon a thick black door that blocked the passageway a yard from the stairs. It was a narrow place, just wide enough for a man to stand shoulder to shoulder with another.

Pallium turned the lock, opened the door and stepped inside. The cell was larger than they had thought. It was lined with dripping stone and at the far wall was a wooden bed. On each side of the door was an oil lamp that hung precariously from a wooden spittle-rod. They gave a bright light that found every corner of the room.

'More guests,' Galphus said as he pushed them inside.

It was then that Thomas saw Jacob Crane. He was manacled, crestfallen and bitter.

'Keep your eyes from me,' he said to Thomas. 'Don't look on a man cheated for greed.'

'You sold us for pieces of silver,' Thomas shouted at him. He lashed out at Crane with his feet.

A Druggle knocked him to the ground and held him in the stench with his black, red-laced boot.

'I sold nothing – I saw you buried and dead, came looking for you. Galphus said you were in the grave – fell from a window. My only sin was believing he would save my ship.'

'Very true, Jacob, very true,' Galphus said, laughing to himself. 'I enjoy to lie, it is far the most exciting thing to do. When you lie you have to remember what you have said and it is a great test for the memory.'

'Crane speaks truth?' Thomas asked.

'What is truth?' Galphus replied. 'If you mean he presented the facts then it would be correct. He never sold you to me. I took you. Took you because I wanted to. It was Smutt who fell from the tower – sent to fly by a Druggle – how exciting.'

'Now you have us what will be done?' Crane asked, all forlorn.

'Your fate is not yet decided. I know a man who would like to see Thomas again and someone is on their way to take him to Whitby. You, my friend . . .' Galphus sighed. 'As for Kate, her fate is sealed with mine and she will stay. Tell me, Jacob. You're a man who always has loved power. How does it feel for it now to be such vainglory? You have the rest of the day to consider. At nightfall we will come for Kate and then she will set out upon her journey.'

# Blatherskite

'CHILDREN? Names?' Ergott complained as Barghast held him by the neck and pushed him back in his seat of the carriage. 'I don't know their names.'

'Then how will you find them?' Raphah asked as the coach rolled slowly on.

'With the dowsing rod – what else?' Ergott grumbled as he folded away the map and slid the wand back into his pocket. 'I don't need a name to find a child, all I need is something that belongs to them.'

'Then who employed you?' Lady Tanville asked.

'A friend of my uncle's. Is that such a crime?' Ergott sank back into the smoke-stained leather and frowned. 'I am a dowser, I care not for who employs me.'

'And who would that be?' Barghast asked.

'A priest,' Ergott said in a matter-of-fact way as he took the pipe from his pocket.

'Demurral?' asked Raphah.

'Could be. The name seems familiar. I am not sure if I can remember.'

'Then let me be a lightning bolt to your memory.' Barghast

grizzled angrily. 'Do you know where to look for the children?'

'Why such an interest? It is as if you have a stake in my venture.' Ergott lit his pipe to fumigate them from his presence.

'And Bragg?' Tanville asked.

'He's dead. You three saw to that and then covered your tracks. I would see a magistrate, were there one nearby, and have you all hanged. Capital offence – murder.' Ergott was silent for a moment and looked at them as he blew purple smoke from the side of his mouth. 'I was employed by Demurral and what of it? He asked me to find two urchins that had escaped his care. I had to bring them to Whitby and I would be paid. He said they were in the hands of a villain called Jacob Crane. Is that so important?'

'We are satisfied by what you said,' Tanville said in a serene voice. 'We thought that you were a changeling and the one who killed Mister Shrume. Your answer was good enough for us not to believe that any more.'

Lady Tanville nodded as she spoke and smiled politely as the carriage rocked from side to side. An uncomfortable silence fell upon the gathering that lasted for several miles.

'Beadle drives well,' Ergott said eventually to break the silence. No one replied. 'London will be soon, within the hour at least,' he said again, hoping to illicit an answer.

'At least,' said Lady Tanville as the carriage slowed upon the hill.

Beadle drove on. The light of dawn breaking upon the Hampstead trees and the road that led across the heath. Ahead was the city that tugged upon the Great North Road, pulling them on. London came suddenly. Fields gave way to houses that soon surrounded one another. Already the streets were full of people making their way to the city. From east and west, those who had fled the sky-quake were returning slowly. Many pushed their handcarts filled with all they had, others drove carriages piled high with mattresses, vagabonds and crying children.

Beadle had never seen anything like this before. He wiped the sweat from his brow as he pulled the horses on a closer rein. They knew the journey and needed no encouragement. For the first time he could see the battered dome of St Paul's, reaching to the sky like a broken egg. Far away, small fires spiralled columns of smoke into the cold morning air. Above the Thames a November mist clung to the water margin. Beadle began to sing tunelessly. He quickly forgot the night. The sight of Demurral faded, somehow the day brought no fear.

Beadle allowed the horses to lead them on. He sat, wrapped in the coachman's blanket, and wondered about his fate. Upon the mile, Raphah would call up to him as he asked his welfare. Each shared hope. In the morning light there was a hint of bitterness. Beadle didn't want the journey to end. As the coach trundled down the Hampstead road, London lay before him. It was like he was journeying into a new world and all would be well.

Eventually, as they drove through beaten streets of Camden and then Holborn, the horses stopped where they had always stopped. Beadle looked up at a cold grey building, its walls drab and scarred. The front of the coaching inn was peppered with marks from the comet and its torn thatch hung like an old hayrick. No one came to greet them. All was quiet; the street was empty but for the horse dung and several rogues who drank on the steps of the demolished church opposite the inn.

Beadle jumped from the driving plate and opened the carriage door. About his shoulders he had the coachman's jacket. Three sizes too big, it hung like a sack. He didn't care – everyone could see that he had driven the coach. In due course a small woman peered around the door and looked at him suspiciously. She flaked the paint from the wood with her long fingers. All Beadle could see was her one staring eye. The other was covered in a black patch strapped to her head so tightly that it looked like a ridge in her skin. She didn't speak but examined each of them intently, as if she knew why they had arrived.

Reluctantly she opened the door and gestured for Beadle to step closer. Beadle walked towards her as the others in the carriage watched.

'Where's Mister Gervais?' she asked.

'Left me in charge. He had urgent business elsewhere,' Beadle said proudly as he pulled the man's coat about his shoulders.

'Better come in, and bring them with you,' she said, and nodded to someone inside. Raphah and the others stepped from the coach. The inn door opened fully and a young boy ran to the carriage and led the horses through a narrow gateway at the side.

Ergott clutched his bag as his wand danced in his pocket. Barghast and Lady Tanville followed him inside as Raphah looked down the road to a small park surrounded by tall iron railings.

'Thought they'd be more than this. How can I make a living with just you three? No one here but you, the entire place to yourself,' she said to Ergott as he stood dumbfounded and she picked her nose.

'Times are difficult, since the coming of the comet,' Barghast tried to answer before she stormed on.

'Don't mention that to me. Madness everywhere. Just look at that dog, quiet as a mouse and then when the moon comes out, becomes like a madman.' The woman pointed to a small terrier in the corner of the room and then called it to her. 'Ziggie, come here.' The dog looked at her from its place by the fire and grunted to itself. 'Ziggie . . .' The dog didn't move but rolled over by the fire and roasted its belly.

'Well behaved,' Ergott joked as he sat in a dusty chair by the narrow wooden stairway that led from the dark hall to a darker landing.

Ziggie looked at him and sniffed. The hackles on the back of its neck stood rigid. It bared its teeth and gave a guttural growl.

'You have made a friend,' Barghast teased as the dog spun to its feet and began to bark.

'That I have,' he said as he stood and looked at the woman. 'I take it I have a bed and a room of my own?'

'You sleep by the fire,' she said to Beadle. 'You come with me,' the woman grunted to the others as she walked up the stairs to a landing of rooms above. As they turned the corner to the stairs they saw a gallery of rooms that looked down upon the hall. Set in a frame of oak panels were several doors. She opened one door after another, not giving any sign as to who should sleep in each. Finally she looked at Raphah.

'Do you sleep in a bed?' she asked.

'I sleep wherever you would like me to,' he replied.

'The street is a fine place, but then you wouldn't pay me.' She looked at him as he smiled at her. In his heart he wanted to laugh at her foolishness. 'Do you mind him sleeping here?' she asked Barghast.

'In fact I would suggest he shares my room,' he said. 'I have three beds and a fire and we wouldn't want to overburden you with work.'

The woman nodded and looked at Barghast as if he were demented. She pulled up her corset and ruffled her skirt as she wiped her hand under her sweated arms.

'Suggest you open the window,' she said as a borborygmic convulsion rumbled in her guts. With that, she left them alone and disappeared down the stairs to appease her barking dog and find Beadle.

Ergott quickly shut the door to his room without speaking.

The bolt was slid swiftly and the mortise double-locked.

'He needs to be guarded. I suspect he knows the way to Salamander Street,' Barghast whispered. 'I will take the first watch. We must keep him near at all times. Be ready, both of you.'

Raphah slept for the hour as Barghast watched through the narrow opening of the door. He could hear Beadle chuntering to himself by the fire. Every so often the dog would moan as if bored by what he said. Ergott's room was silent. The morning came and went and the afternoon faded and darkness fell as Barghast waited. Several cases were delivered one by one to Lady Tanville by a tawdry youth who looked as if he would die mounting the stairs. By the time the evening came, Barghast like all the others had begun to doze. He sat in the chair propped against the wall and rested his head upon his arm. The journey had taken life from them all. In the hallway below, Barghast could hear the sound of Beadle snoring.

On the landing there was a sudden clink of metal as a latch dropped. Like a waiting fox, Barghast was woken from his dreaming. He listened intently as a booted footstep clattered against the board. Raphah woke without being called and stared at the door. Barghast motioned for him to be silent as he kept watch. The footsteps came closer. Barghast could see the shadow of a man cast black in the lamplight, the long coat and booted legs spread across the floor. The man came closer. Through the crack in the door, Barghast could just make him out as he looked over the landing to the hallway below. Raphah sneaked across the room and peered over his shoulder as together they watched the shadow get closer.

A small-framed man in a frock coat and clean riding boots sauntered slowly along the landing. They could neither make out a single feature nor see his face. It was only when he got to the door of their room that the figure turned to face them, and then Raphah recognised who it was.

Tanville Chilnam had cropped her hair, discarded her ladies' travelling clothes and dressed as a man. She wore the attire of a country squire: yellow waistcoat, silk tie and canvas pants. As she turned she tapped gently upon the door.

'Surprised?' she asked in a whisper as she pushed the door open and went in. 'Thought I would dress for the occasion, now I'm in London I don't have to be so . . . provincial.'

Raphah didn't speak. He signalled for her to sit by the fire as they waited for Ergott.

The wait was quickly over. In the hallway below, an old clock chimed nine of the clock. It rattled with each note as the spring recoiled and clattered against the case. Beadle chuntered in his sleep. The dog gave a sudden yelp as if woken from a dream of chasing rats. The door to Ergott's room opened.

Ergott stalked along the corridor, arms outstretched, diving rod in hand. It bobbed and danced in his fingers as if it had a life of its own, and Ergott obediently followed. He gave no notice to the narrow opening of the door to Barghast's room. His mind was focused on the dowser in his hand. The wand led him onwards as if it were a hound that pursued its prey in the dark of the night.

Ergott scurried down the stairs, jumping them three at a time, and skipped across the hall.

'The chase is on,' Barghast said as he and Raphah sprang to their feet and dashed along the landing, with Tanville running behind. 'When we get to the streets, keep to the shadows. I will go ahead – he won't see me.'

As they watched Ergott run across the hall, all that clothed him began to disappear. Thick black fur sprung from his shoulders, and what were once hands became black paws. He fell to the floor by the fireplace and writhed in agony. Beadle woke from his sleep. The dog began to bark frantically as the man contorted before him. Ergott screamed as if in severe pain.

'Blatherskite!' Beadle exclaimed as the sight of the transformation sent him and the dog hiding in the shadows.

The changing Ergott looked up, his face contorted. He growled as he breathed, seething painfully. The transformation from man to beast was quickly over. The wand vanished from sight.

Beadle hid behind a large potted plant, not daring to step from the shadows. Then the scullery door creaked open and there was a shriek and a scream as the hosteller saw the lion by the fire. She raised her hand to her face and fell backwards, panting like a lamb about to be slaughtered.

'*Slabberdegullion!*' she shrieked, as if it were the last word she would ever say. With much ceremony she fainted: she twisted on her heels, spun several times and then crashed to the floor in a fat heap.

Ergott growled loudly and leapt towards the door. He smashed against the wood as the door came open and he slithered into the street, vanishing in the darkness. The front door slammed behind him.

Raphah and Tanville followed quickly. 'See to her, Beadle,' Raphah said as they left the inn for the cold of the night. Once outside, they caught a fleeting glimpse of the creature running in the shadows that fell from the eaves of the broken houses.

They set off on the chase, keeping to the shadows. Ahead they could hear Ergott growling as he ran back and forth through the empty streets. Somewhere nearby was Barghast, hunting the creature as he ran through the shadows.

Slowly they managed to track Ergott from a closer distance. He kept to the wide streets and walked in the middle, away from the shadows.

Within the hour they had walked half of London and Ergott stood before a large wall of cut stones. Raphah and Tanville hid themselves behind a stack of handcarts that had been made ready for a morning market that never came. The road had opened to a large square; on one side was a building with a large tower that looked out over the city. It looked like a prison or an old fortress.

Ergott suddenly transformed, the dowsing wand appearing in his hand. He walked backwards and forwards along the wall. The dowsing rod danced in his hands and it took all in his power to stop it leaping towards the wall.

'Lubberly louts and flouting milksops,' he shouted, his words of frustration echoing around the square. 'It has to be here . . . They have to be here . . .'

Then he stopped and looked along the wall. Far to the right was a small arched door the size of half a man. The dowsing wand led him closer. Raphah and Tanville watched as he walked towards it and turned the handle. Before he entered, he read the sign that was embedded in the plaster. They heard him laugh as he stooped through the entrance and quietly closed it behind him.

Barghast appeared from the shadows. He panted, out of breath, a broad smile on his face. 'It is behind the wall – Salamander Street. I have been up on the roofs and it is here, though it cannot be seen with the eye. My journey is done, Raphah. Can you believe it?'

'It comes to us all. I pray we will find Thomas and Kate.'

There was a clatter of horses' hooves as a black mare cantered along the road and into the square. The rider wore a long black cloak; his long white hair was tied back. He wore a parson's collared shirt and sea-boots. The man jumped from the horse and looked about him. He surveyed the square and waited as if making sure he had not been followed.

Raphah was not surprised by the man he now stared at from the shadows. He turned to Barghast, who nodded to him as if he too had seen the man and knew who he was.

The man left the horse and slipped through the door.

'*Demurral*,' Raphah said. 'He has been with us all the way.'

'Then they are all in this together,' Barghast said.

'So why send Ergott if he knew where they would be?' Raphah asked.

'To make sure the job would be done. He couldn't leave it to chance. Every step of our journey has been followed intently. We are expected to follow and the door will be open to us,' Barghast said.

'What business does he have here?' Tanville asked.

'Kate and Thomas. He said he would never let them go. Something binds him to them. He would have had them killed. Slaughtered like innocents. If they are here then their fate is sealed.'

'Not if we take them from him,' Tanville said, and she pulled a dandy gun from her pocket. 'We shall each endure our fate in Salamander Street and I shall have an advantage when I meet with Galphus.'

One by one, they crept across the square to the small wooden door. Raphah looked at the plaque above it. *The Eye of the Needle* – he read the scrawled letters plastered into the wall.

Barghast smiled as he stooped through the entrance. 'I know I will not see this place again, Raphah. You have been a good and unlikely companion. Whatever comes to pass, I pray that we will stand together when the sun rises in the east.'

'A sure and certain hope,' Raphah said quietly as he closed the door behind him and shut out the light of the hunter's moon.

# The Jobbernol Goosecap

*A*thick slime trickled across the ceiling before it dripped to the floor by Crane's feet. Thomas and Kate huddled together in the corner to keep warm. Thomas thought how unnaturally cold she was – it was as if she was made of ice, or that death itself had already taken hold of her and the heart that warmed had stopped beating. She had tried to smile with her blue lips and muttered something in her stupor, and Thomas thought how she was no longer the Kate he knew. She had gone, without the chance for him to say goodbye. All he now embraced was a cold skin, an empty bag, a wrinkled carcass.

'I let you down,' Crane said, his shoulders drooped and head lowered. 'Should have known things were not that easy. All the time, I could think of nothing but Salamander Street. Even on the ship I could hear the word in my head. When the priests seized the ship this was the first place I thought of to run to. We were tricked, well deceived.'

'We can escape,' Thomas said, his breath a cold vapour.

'It's gone from me, Thomas. Something has taken the will. With every day in this place I have resigned myself more to what will come. Wouldn't be right to cheat fate. Payment – it's payment for all that happened in Whitby.'

'I feared you Jacob,' Thomas said. 'The very mention of your name made me quake in my boots. But you're the man, Jacob. The man we all wanted to be.'

'It was just a lie, I can see it now. Strip everything away and here I am. There is nothing here to be proud of, nothing at all.' Crane's voice sounded strained. He panted, as if each word were coated in broken glass.

'I won't wait to die, Jacob. And I won't let them kill you and Kate. That's what Galphus will do, kill us all. I've seen what the man does. He takes the moment of death and puts it in a jar. He'll not take me, the old shite-a-bed.'

Crane laughed. He rattled the manacles that held his wrists to the long metal chain that was coiled about his feet and braced to a metal ring wedged in the cobbled floor.

'Think we could take 'em?' he asked.

'We could die trying.' Thomas replied.

'Wait until I say the word, and then . . .' Crane paused and looked at Kate. 'He's killed her with the *Gaudium*, Thomas. I've seen it before. If all else fails, run and leave us both. Take the *Magenta*. There is a drinking house by the river, the Devil's Inn, and close by is *The Prospect of Whitby*. If I have counted the days rightly then tonight is the feast of St Sola the Hermit. All my men will gather at the inn. Tell them my fate and take sail. With me dead the revenue men will auction the ship. Steal it before it can be sold and head for France. Will you do this for me?'

'I won't leave you,' Thomas replied.

'You'll do what I say and have done with it. Would be stupid for us all to die, and Galphus will get what he deserves before he takes me. Whatever happens I promise he will not kill her. Even if I have . . .'

Crane's words were cut short. There was a jangling of a key

in the lock and a bright light crept in through the cracks around the door. Muffled voices moaned and groaned from the far side and as the door was pushed open, Pallium and several Druggles stepped into the cell.

'Galphus requests your company,' Pallium snivelled, wiping more slug trails from his nose and across his sleeve. 'I am to take you to him, all of you.'

Thomas thought how he looked thinner than before. It was as if he were being eaten from inside, as if something took a pound of flesh every day and consumed him by the minute.

They were taken without fuss. Crane was held by a long chain and a metal hoop on a long pole was placed around his neck as he was walked ahead of the rest. A Druggle carried Kate. Unaware of her condition, in her blissful slumber she lolled from side to side. Through several tunnels and then out across a cold yard they were taken into the back of a large house that stood near to the factory, just away from the Salamander Inn. Thomas could hear the constant singing just like the time before. He thought of the warm fire and Pallium's deceitful words.

Along a bare passageway, they were taken into what was once a drawing room. In the centre of the room was a long, narrow table. By its side were a bell jar and other primitive equipment, and near to the table was a wooden chair fitted with wrist-locks and strands of copper wire. Above the ornate fireplace was Isabella's picture.

The grime of a hundred years had been cleaned from the paint. Within the bars across the pciture, Isabella stood proudly in death, looking down upon them. About the frame was wrapped more copper wire and hanging from it were pieces of teeth and bone. A small writ dangled from the frame; Thomas could make out an inscription on the parchment and could see the red wax seal that bound the spell.

Kate was taken and placed in the chair. Her head was

strapped to the high back and her hands and feet callipered to the wood. Crane was tethered like an old horse to the door; what was left of the chain was wrapped around him and tied to the large chair that he had been forced to sit upon. Thomas stood by the door, a Druggle holding him with the chain of the manacle.

No one spoke. Pallium stood by the raging fire that gulped the chimney and sucked and seethed air into the room. They waited. The clock on the mantel chimed the quarter, the half and then the hour. They still waited.

From the far end of the house the tap, tap, tap of a cane and footsteps could be heard – it was Galphus. He walked proudly, hitting the tip of his cane against the floorboards to match every step he took. Galphus entered the room.

Thomas held back his laughter as he looked at him. Galphus had changed his attire. Gone were the day clothes of a dandy. Now the man dressed in a black silk gown that billowed as he walked. On his head he wore a tiger skull with silver teeth and emerald eyes; his hands were covered in red silk gloves and on his feet were Persian shoes that curled at the toes.

Galphus smiled at Kate. He tapped the cane several times on the floor and then looked into the crystal ball.

'All is well,' he said smugly. 'The doors to Salamander Street have been opened and the trap is set.' Galphus looked at Pallium before he spoke again. 'We have visitors, Mister Pallium, you know what to do.'

Pallium turned and was gone. A Druggle followed him from the room.

'I feel I must explain,' Galphus said as he looked at Thomas. 'This has all been an elaborate hoax on my behalf. Please do not feel let down but I have to say that I actually work in concert with an old friend. Obadiah Demurral. I believe you are familiar with him?' Galphus asked.

Thomas nodded, keeping tight-lipped.

'Obadiah and I are brothers in a fraternity. We are bound by sworn oaths. My life has been set on the discovery of the soul and capturing its essence on death. His has been to find the nature of God and tame it for our use. If it hadn't been for you then we would have succeeded in our task and the world would be a better place. When you escaped Whitby we first thought our task would never be complete. Then my crystal showed me that someone you knew well was still alive and it gave us hope. The Ethio has travelled far to find you all and as we speak he is just about to walk on Salamander Street – look for yourself.'

Galphus thrust the crystal towards Thomas. He could see the face of Raphah edged in the darkness. Quickly it changed to the face of Demurral and then, just as it was about to fade, Thomas saw the head of a black dog. Its eyes glowed red, its teeth were bared and white as it spat and growled.

Galphus laughed. 'That is another of our companions – a man who can change from man to dog in the twinkling of an eye. He was the bait to bring your friend to us. With every day he gave him another clue as to who he was. Calmly and cleverly he waited his time. Every night he met with Obadiah and told him the good news. Every day, he brought them another step closer to us.'

'He won't be cheated by you. Raphah knows Riathamus – he can speak to him,' shouted Crane.

'Then Riathamus can sit and listen to his screams as we steal the lad's soul and capture his final words. Not mortal words, Thomas, but the words of an angel. Your friend has lied to you. He is not a man but a Keruvim. That Ethio is the keeper of secrets that would explode our mortal minds like a spiked cannon if we knew. Soon, Obadiah and I will have all of his power and more. When I take his soul from him he is bound by eternal oath to utter a name so powerful that it is the key that will open time and heaven forever.'

298

'And what of us?' Crane asked.

'What do you think, my pirate friend? Shall I set you free or take you to your ship and burn you upon it?'

'Do what you want with me but let them go,' Crane shouted.

'Never. Spoil my enjoyment? Since I was a child that picked the wings from a butterfly, I have delighted in times such as this. I would no more set them free than cut off my right hand.'

'Set them free or as Riathamus is my witness I will sever your hand and dip it in wax and it will light my way to bed,' Crane said.

'Spirit,' Galphus said as he banged his cane against Isabella's portrait. 'How much room do you have in that world of yours?'

'Don't torment me, Galphus,' a shrill voice said from somewhere very near. 'Let me from this prison.'

'I would invite Captain Crane to join with you and Thomas as well, they could keep you company.' Galphus laughed.

'Then let me from this place and I will take them to be with me,' the ghost of Isabella replied. The picture rattled upon the wall, the teeth and bones jangling like Christmas merriments.

'Did you hear that? She would take you with her and my problems would be solved. Sadly, that will not be so. I must await Obadiah. But first I shall prepare my dearest Kate. She is the screaming bait that will lead the Keruvim rushing to bring her salvation.'

Galphus looked at Kate as he spoke. Behind her was a handle connected to a large wooden box that resembled a hurdy-gurdy. He saw Crane stare at the device. 'If you are wondering what this machine can do, it takes a charge like lightning and forces it to travel along the copper threads and then into the metal bracelets upon her wrist.'

Galphus took a hat made of goose feathers from the mantle and threaded more copper wire within each quill.

'A Jobbernol Goosecap,' he said pleasingly. 'Placing this on the head adds to the charge and takes her life. Her screams should be enough to bring him here. When he comes to this place he shall find his own death. Living and dying becomes a matter of turning the handle.'

Galphus signalled for the Druggles to hide themselves and make ready. Thomas frantically eyed Crane, as if to ask him what to do. He sat rigidly still. He was frozen and icy to the bone, unable to move. His teeth chattered and rattled his jaw. Thomas couldn't move or think a single thought.

'Hurt her, Galphus, and I will give you thrice the pain and it will pleasure me to do so,' Crane said as he rattled the chains that held him fast.

'You sound like an old ghost, a Bard's King, dead and futile. How can you hurt me, chained like that?' Galphus asked, taunting the man.

With that, Galphus thrust his cane into the floorboards. A sudden bright light shone from the crystal and cast a vision upon the high ceiling. There, played out before them, was the scene of Raphah's approach. It looked as if the whole of Sala-mander Street was cast on the plaster above their heads. Raphah walked side by side with two others, whilst stalking them in the shadows was a red-eyed beast, a dog so terrible that Thomas turned his face from the sight of the creature.

Along the cobbled road they walked, the creature always a few feet behind them, lurking in the thick black shadows. Thomas saw Raphah turn as if he realised that something fol-lowed. He could see him speak but could not hear the words.

Isabella began to scream as she rattled the bars of her prison, desperate to be free of the picture and walk in the world of men. As she appeared, captured by the frame, she looked up. There on the ceiling, dressed as a man, she saw Tanville. Isa-bella shrieked her name again and again and shouted a warning.

Tanville looked about her, as if she could her the calling of her name from far away. Galphus smiled, knowing that the screams of the spectre would draw them quickly. He took the handle of the machine and slowly began to turn it the way of the sun. It whirred and groaned like it would give song, and the copper threads began to spark. Kate was pricked from her sleeping as the first jolts of lightning shot through her fingers. She twitched in spasm and her back arched. Galphus turned the device even faster.

Kate began to howl like a dying cat as sparks burst from her forehead and the blue essence of her departing soul shimmered above her. Thomas jumped to his feet to intervene but a Druggle stepped from the shadows and with a blow from his cudgel knocked him to the floor.

Crane shouted and kicked out with his feet as the whole room became like a night in Bedlam, spitting with madness and writhing with insanity.

Galphus laughed, a smile on his face. It was like he had woken to a great remembrance of some incredible feasting. He gave no attention to the pandemonium, the crying, shouting and wailing that was all about him. Kate's pain oozed from her with each breath that she snatched from the air.

In the vision from the crystal, they saw Raphah begin to run towards the house. The crystal followed his every step, watching him as he ran. It chased him like an eagle's eye following a mouse through the cornfield. On and on he raced. He panted his breaths as he looked to each building to spy out the sound that in his heart he knew to be Kate.

From outside they all could hear Pallium shouting. He hollered like a Judas, calling Raphah by name, in words that betrayed them more than a kiss. It was then that the crystal eye turned to reveal the thoughts of the beast, shining through its eyes and seeing what it saw.

There in the street far behind Raphah was an older man.

With every step he aged a day, as if the centuries chased him from afar. What was once vital and alive was now crumbling and aged. Barghast was transforming as the dirt of the street sullied his boots and the air he breathed speeded his death.

He fell behind, slowing to a walking pace, unable to keep up with the lad ahead. The beast made ready, tracking him from the shadows. It waited as he took several faltering steps and then stopped for breath.

In the light of the tallow lamps they saw the man smile and wave for the other to go on and find Kate. Barghast sat upon an empty barrel, his hair turning bright white and falling to the floor strand by strand. As he had walked Salamander Street, the curse upon him was broken. He bent slowly and picked a handful of dirt from the ground and held it in his hand. Barghast stared at the rooftops that hemmed in this tiny world. He was delighted that he had taken such feeble steps along Salamander Street. Even as the frailty of age took hold of his bones and tepid blood coursed in his veins, he gave thanks.

Then, giving no warning as it lurched from the blackness, the dog leapt for him. The hell-hound took Barghast by the throat. There was a spinning of flesh and in the vision upon the ceiling Thomas thought that he could see two beasts fighting. He could hear their cries as they battled to death, tearing at each other. For the briefest of moments he thought he saw a lion's head and then, from just outside the house, came the sound of a single shot.

The aura upon the ceiling faded as a shadowed figure stepped into the room. Even Galphus himself gasped in its presence.

'Just in time,' he said with a hint of nervousness as he tussled a lock of hair in his fingers. 'I am so glad that you could make it, Parson Demurral.'

# A Republic of Heathens

IN a dazzling moment, as if the sun had exploded, the street echoed with the shot from the pistol. Lady Tanville stood perfectly still, her eye still gazing along the line of the barrel. The dog lay dead, blood seeping from its ears and from the small bullet hole through what had been its eye. In death it was silent, and before her eyes the corpse began to change to that of Ergott.

Raphah turned as he ran, taking a final glimpse of Barghast as he lay in the mud. He rushed up the flight of stone steps and as he passed Pallium he stared at him eye to eye. It was as if a friend was greeting him. Pallium held open his arms and welcomed him to the house, ushering him onwards towards Kate's cries. It was then, as Raphah took his first racing steps into the long hallway, that he felt an intense sense of foreboding. A dart of anguish blasted through his spirit, telling him to turn away. As he cast a look back, he saw the large varnished door closing behind him and Pallium sniggering in the lamplight.

Ahead, Kate's screams and the whirring of the electrometer billowed from the room. Without hesitation or concern for himself, he dashed in. A thin hand grabbed him by the throat and threw him with the strength of a hundred men towards the fireplace.

'Raphah,' the voice said.

'Demurral?' he replied.

Raphah looked about the room. Thomas and Crane sat against the wall, and Kate was strapped into the chair by the fire. Galphus nodded and the Druggles stepped from the shadows as Thomas jumped to his feet to welcome his friend.

'Take him,' Galphus said, as if he were calling a dog.

Raphah was snatched from the floor and dragged to his feet as Demurral began to laugh.

'How things change. I knew that Riathamus would not have you dead so quickly. It was easy to bring you all here. I had Ergott follow Beadle from the day he left Whitby. Does anyone ever notice a dog? Beadle did well for me,' Demurral said. Then he pulled the bag from Raphah and looked inside at the Chalice.

'Beadle?' Raphah asked. 'Did well for you?'

'Not that he knew it, but I knew he would find Thomas and Kate. I wasn't sure if the magic would work on Crane and that my suggestions to bring them to Salamander Street would be heard. Obviously all was well. New friends always impress Beadle. He would have searched them out no matter what. Meeting you was a gratuity, a bonus. All I had to do was follow on behind. Ergott kept me informed. As for Beadle, when I have done with you I will make sure whatever ounce of life he has left will become a misery.'

'So it *was* you. And we walked into your trap,' Raphah said.

'It was me on the road *and* it was me in the cave. Bragg knew too much and had to die. He found out that Ergott had devoured Mister Shrume and wanted him for his own. Promised him the Grail – which I believe is carried in your bag. The others were just food for dear Ergott. His appetites are insatiable . . . '

'But it's over – Raphah told us . . . ' Thomas said.

'You were lied to. It is never *over*, Thomas. It is not just I who seek the desires of our hearts – there are many people who would like to see heaven overthrown. It is time for a new nation and an old order to take power. A republic of the damned. Goodness and mercy are things of the past. Our desires are all that matter. Think of it, Thomas, think of you and Kate as the key to a better future for the whole world.'

'Don't think you'll be killing them, Demurral,' Crane shouted.

'Jacob Crane, how peculiar. Is that a chain I see around your neck? I thought you were a man of action, one who would never be caught, and here you are trussed like a Christmas turkey.'

'A matter of coincidence,' Crane replied. 'But should I ever be free from these chains I shall cut the gizzard from your throat and serve it for breakfast.'

'And hell shall freeze over,' Demurral replied as he looked at Kate. 'Do we have the *Magenta*?' he asked.

'Still in the dock,' Galphus replied. 'Taken without a fuss.'

'Ready to sail?' Demurral asked. 'So you believed the priest and the scoundrels we had paid to take your ship, Jacob? Taken in by a fallen cleric, how quaint.'

Galphus paused and looked around him. Kate stared at him through eyes that bulged with the pain of the electrodes.

'I . . . only have the Druggles and they have never sailed such a ship,' Galphus said.

'Why do you only have Druggles? Is there not a man who can sail amongst them?' Demurral asked.

'The people think the *Magenta* to be carrying the plague,' Galphus replied. 'But,' he said quickly, 'it is prepared to sail and everything is ready at Dog Island.'

Crane cast a look to Thomas and gave him a sly wink and half a smile. 'The ship, wait until we are on the ship,' he said in a whisper.

Demurral turned, his stare telling them to be silent. 'Did you think you had won? Escaped? Free to live your life as you desired?' he shouted. 'I could not rest in the grave until I have seen this day.'

'What will you do to us?' Thomas asked.

'What I should have done days ago, had an angel not interfered with things. Meddling wingless wonder, fit for hell. Take the manacles from them and bind them, Galphus. Bind them tightly for we take them all to Dog Island. Then our work will be complete. Pallium,' Demurral shouted. 'This is not the place to take Kate's life, that shall be kept for Dog Island. Go and find Mister Ergott, he should have made a feast of Raphah's companions.'

They heard the door open and Pallium step into the street. This was followed quickly by a scream and the clattering of the handle. Pallium rushed back along the hallway and into the room.

'The man is dead,' he said, shuddering at the sight he had witnessed. 'Shot in the eye . . . and . . .'

He did not say another word. Tanville Chilnam pushed Pallium into the study, holding the pistol to his back. She looked about the room. There was Galphus dressed in his finery. A girl was strapped in a chair with a goose wing-hat upon her head. A man was chained to the door and a lad skulked nervously by his side.

'I've come for Isabella,' she said as she pointed the gun at Galphus's head. 'The picture was stolen from my family and I seek its return.'

Demurral looked at her and laughed. 'My dear girl, if that is what you are,' he said through his teeth, 'the picture is all a part of what I seek to do. Once I am finished I will gladly give it to you.'

'But he'll kill them first,' Raphah said.

'The picture *and* your guests,' she demanded, knowing in an instant that they had to be set free.

'A request too far,' Demurral replied. 'I would suggest that you do the honourable thing and shoot me as you shot Mister Ergott – for I will not let them go.'

Tanville Chilnam clicked the hammer of the pistol and took aim. All that Demurral could do was smile. Galphus gulped nervously as the moments seemed to last for a lifetime.

Thomas noticed the woman swallow, and the scarf around her neck quivered slightly as her eye flickered from Demurral to the picture of Isabella. The ghost hung to the bars, staring out like a lost child.

'Kill him, Tanville!' she screamed from within the confines of her prison.

'No!' shouted Crane. 'Leave that to my men – they wait this night for *The Prospect of Whitby* – let them kill him. Remember, tell Beadle – *The Prospect of Whitby*.'

For a brief instant she looked at him. Lady Tanville licked her lips and then, as her hand slightly trembled she pulled the trigger. Again the gun exploded. The shot blasted from the pistol and instantly hit Demurral in the chest, sending flecks of blood and linen cloth across the room. He reeled backwards, clutching the wound. Then with his right hand he thrust his fingers into the skin, burrowing them deeper.

Demurral gave a sudden and sharp cough as if he cleared his throat of a fishbone. He shook his head, pulled his fingers from the wound and dropped the lead shot to the floor.

'I am beyond dying,' he said like a man tired of the day. 'It will heal. I am a curser of God and cannot be destroyed until he himself comes for me.' As Demurral spoke, the blood stopped in its flow.

'Take her,' Galphus shouted to the Druggles, who appeared from the shadows and took hold of Tanville. 'See she causes no more trouble. This has to be done tonight. In the morning, I will test her to see if she has a soul.'

'And so you shall,' Demurral said, looking closely at Kate. 'To the ship and then to Dog Island. Nothing shall end this day until I command it.'

Like a forlorn caravan of wastrels, Raphah, his companions and Isabella's portrait were bound and marched from the house and into the street. An old carriage was drawn up by the door. It filled the width of Salamander Street from wall to wall, and its flaking black-lacquered doors could barely open to allow them inside. Thomas was pushed to the roof and tied like an old hen to the luggage rail. When all were gathered in, the carriage took flight.

Four horses charged on, rolling the coach from side to side as it scraped against the houses. They were garbed in funeral black and each was plumed about the head with the blackened tail of a cockatrice. The coachman whipped the horses to go faster. Ahead was a solid wall.

Thomas covered his face as they drew closer, the sound of the tumbling wheels clattering against the cobbles. 'Stop!' he screamed to the coachman, who turned to him and grinned as the coach sped towards the wall. 'No . . .' Thomas screamed again as the first horse vanished through the solid stones as if it were a ghost.

The coachman turned and slapped him with the back of his hand. 'Keep silent,' he squealed in the voice of a mouse, from a man the size of a mountain.

There was a long silence. The noise of the street had gone, the glow of the lamps vanished. Suddenly there was a whooshing of the breeze as the night sky blazed above. People stopped and stared as the coach was driven madly towards the dock. Soon it turned towards the Thames. Salamander Street was left far behind. Thomas could smell the stink of the sewer that ran through the city. Far in the distance, he could see the masts of several ships rising from the water. There was the *Magenta*, tall and bare, still tied to the quayside.

The horses slowed as they shivered and jumped along the road. Thomas remembered how he had once seen a funeral coach take a man from the town and climb the cliff path to the high church above the harbour. It had slithered through the streets, drawn by horses just as these, dark and bringers of death. Twice it had circled the church, then thrice and then for a fourth time. The coffin had been lead-braced and made of holly. 'Four times round the church,' Thomas said out loud, 'four times to keep the man dead . . .'

'Bed?' asked the coachman. 'There will be no bed.' He laughed again, his teeth black like rotted potatoes.

At that the coach stopped and the doors opened. On the *Magenta*, a crew of grey Druggles waited impatiently for their master. Galphus led the procession from the quayside and onto the ship. A crowd of sultry women gathered and looked on.

'Prisoners of the King,' shouted Demurral as he strode behind, kicking out at Thomas. 'Stop your staring and be about your business. We can't be late,' he shouted to Galphus who married himself with his cane. 'She will not wait for us, not tonight.'

The many eyes gave no heed to what he said. They stared and stared as Thomas and the others were quickly taken below deck and the ship made ready. Three small boats, each with oars and a small mast, pulled the ship into the tide. It creaked and groaned as the fingers of the current took hold and pulled it against the breeze.

Crane felt the ship move beneath his feet and smiled. He looked around his cabin. All seemed familiar and yet different. The door was locked. Galphus sat in Crane's chair and glared, his eyes blood-red. Propped against the wall by his desk was the picture of Isabella. The spirit was nowhere to be seen. All that was present was her outline against the canvas. On the deck above, they could hear Demurral shouting to the Druggles as they attempted to steer the ship to Dog Island.

Salamander Street was deathly still. Lady Tanville Chilnam looked out of the upper-floor window of Galphus's house. The room was bare, but for a leather-backed chair placed close to the fire. A single candle burnt on the mantel. Outside the door a Druggle waited. Lady Tanville held the empty pistol in her hand. No one had thought to take it from her when they had pushed her from the room and bundled her up the stairs. She had heard the carriage take flight as the horses raced from the street. Now she was alone, she thought of what she could do.

In the light of a nearby house, Tanville Chilnam could see Ergott's body lying in the mud. She felt no concern for what she had done. Her mind was numb, she was unconcerned with his death. Tanville mused on this again and again, unable to feel any compassion.

All she could feel were the pangs of betrayal and the irritation of being locked in the room. For several seconds she searched the street to see where Barghast had fallen. Tanville thought him to be dying, the curse on his life broken by the dust on which he walked. In the last moments of his life she had watched him age. Wrinkle crept upon wrinkle as he had withered before her eyes.

Now in her prison she searched for him again. She needed to know if he was really dead, for she needed to escape.

She could see the shadow of the Druggle that crept in under the door, lit by the storm lantern he held in his hand. The house was silent and as quiet as the street outside. From somewhere very near she heard the creaking of an old door. There came a sudden rush of footsteps that pounded against the stairs. The Druggle had not the time to shout out. He gave a muffled scream and dropped the lantern. Tanville heard it roll down each step – first the glass cracked in its case and then smashed. The body of the Druggle slumped against the door, which in time opened slowly.

A bloodied, frail hand slowly appeared around its edge and then the face of Barghast. He was old and near to death. He wheezed and coughed as he reached out to her. 'Quickly,' he said breathlessly. 'You have to leave this place and find Raphah.'

Tanville took hold of him as she led him step by step along the landing and down the steps. Flames from the broken lamp licked against the walls. They passed quickly, listening to the creaking of the house as the fire took hold.

'You'll have to leave me,' Barghast said, his face now that of an old, old man without teeth or hair. 'I die a happy man.'

'But not here,' she demanded. 'Not in this place.'

Tanville pulled him to the door. His pace was slow, laboured and painful. She looked back to the flames that now grew brighter, filling the house with thick black smoke that spiralled in the draught. High above she could hear the beams spit and crackle as the roof burst into bright red flame. The thatch exploded like sulphurous tinder and lit the sky.

As they stumbled down the flight of stone steps to the mud-died street, Barghast fell to the floor.

'Leave me,' he said in an aged melancholy.

Ignoring him, Tanville dragged him further as the windows of the house exploded with flames, showering the street with shards of glass. She found shelter in the narrow alleyway that led to the factory. From far away they could hear the clanging of the Dragon's Heart as the Druggles beat out the warning of the fire.

'I die here,' Barghast said calmly as his flesh began to fall from his bones. 'This shall be my resting place.' With that, he held out his hand to reach for someone Tanville could not see. Barghast smiled as if he stared into the face of a long-lost companion. 'I will not turn you away, I know who you really are,' he said to whoever stood invisibly before him. Then he turned to Tanville and opened his eyes and whispered his final words. 'Tell Raphah . . . not a beggar . . . but a king . . . He will know what you mean . . .'

Barghast slumped to the floor, his flesh crumbling. Tanville held his hand as it became a jumble of bones.

From the factory the sound of a human stampede drew closer. Taking a final look at Barghast, his skull now glowing in the flames, Tanville began to run. Something inside her led the way as if a voice within her heart told her every turn of the road ahead.

In the distance she could see The Eye of the Needle. It grew smaller as she ran towards it and became a simulacrum of what it was. The door diminished in size with her every step, disappearing before she could reach it. Behind, she could hear the Druggles chasing her. The echo of their footsteps became like the thundering of the sky.

The doorway shrunk and shrunk until it was the size of a small window. Tanville grabbed the now tiny handle and pushed open the door. It faded away until it was a mere vapour of what it was before. Tanville dived through the fading aperture and smelt the London street. Just as she managed to squeeze herself through, the portal finally disappeared.

# 30

# Dog Island

TAKING Demurral's tethered horse, Tanville Chilnam made her way back to the lodging house. Beadle slept by the fire, his face covered in an old hankersniff coated in snotty blisters. The dog slept fitfully by his feet. Tanville woke Beadle gently; her face gave away her concern and her meagre smile told him what had gone before.

'Raphah?' he asked rubbing his eyes wearily.

'Taken . . .' she replied. 'By ship to Dog Island with Thomas and Kate *and* Jacob Crane.'

'And Barghast?'

'Dead.' She spoke the word softly, unable to tell him all that had happened. 'So is Ergott. He was the beast,' she said with a glance that Beadle knew meant she had killed him. 'Demurral was also there. It has all been a trap. It was his desire to capture them and in that he has succeeded.'

'Never,' he exclaimed angrily as he threw a lump of wood into the fire. 'We should go and bring them back. We can't give up on them, Tanville.' Beadle fidgeted with his hands in a frustration that shivered its way from his fingers to the tips of his toes. He shook like a wet dog and his jowls wobbled furiously.

'Did Crane say what would be done?' Beadle asked.

' He said, "Remember, tell Beadle – *The Prospect of Whitby*." I have no idea what the man meant.'

Beadle looked into the flames as he thought. 'He meant to tell you that his men were at the Devil's Inn, by the Thames at Wapping – that is the place where *The Prospect* is always birthed. It's a collier brig, a ship – the *The Prospect of Whitby* . . . Smugglers, murderers and hob-smackers. A landmark if ever there was one,' he said excitedly. 'His men will be there – that's what he meant. He knew I would understand, the old dog knew . . .'

Beadle could not contain himself. He danced a jig upon the hearth and kicked the embers of the fire about the stone tiles.

'Dog Island is just at the turn of the river. It'll be quicker by land. I have heard so many stories of the place I could take you there blindfold,' he said, bubbling eagerly. 'Let's steal a horse and make for the place.' Beadle laughed as he dipped his hand in the cold ash bucket by the side of the fire and, taking a handful of powder, smeared it upon her face. 'Can't be having you looking like a lass. Keep your gob shut and let me speak and then we'll keep our throats. Dog Island!' he exclaimed again as he danced and danced.

They left the lodging inn and set off into the night. Demurral's horse took them through the darkened streets. Beadle gripped himself to Tanville's waist as the horse trotted on.

A column of burning smoke lit the night sky above the walled bastion of Salamander Street. On they went by the river until the streets became narrow and dank. They smelt of the nearby marshes and the midden heaps that were piled at every crossroads. Butchers shops soon gave way to fishmongers' yards until the door of every house was edged in sea-cable. Sale-makers and sextant-sellers filled their windows with goods for sale. Quadrants, chronometers and brass sea compasses hung from door eaves, watched over by fat women with calloused legs.

Tanville covered her muckied face with the brim of her hat as they passed the gangs of seafarers huddled by the torches that lit the street. To her right, she could hear the tide beating against the walls as the river ran quickly to Dog Island.

'Wapping,' Beadle said as they had gone another mile. 'Soon be at the Devil's Inn.'

Tanville twisted the wet leather of the horses' reins in her fingers. She had seen many years come and go. Now the providence of her family was held in her young hands. She looked at their reflection as they walked by the large windows of a sail shop. In the light of the tallow she could see Beadle clutching at her waist and hanging on for dear life. They rode on, the streets filling with people like the dregs washed in by a dark tide.

Ahead was the Devil's Inn. It was a small dark building, nondescript and vague in the shreds of fog that crept from the river through the landings and steps along the riverside. Outside the inn was an old cart stacked with empty barrels. It was surrounded by a mass of people. Some drank from flagons of beer whilst others picked pockets and drew on clay pipes.

As the smog rolled about them it brought from the river the stench of the sewer. Tanville Chilnam was overcome by the smell. She put her hand to her face and gulped back the desire to cough. She felt that every eye and face had turned towards her. There in that small part of England were the faces of every nation under the sun. As they drew closer the horse became more wary. It slowed in its gait, reluctant to go on. Several times it threw back its head and snorted the air as its ears twitched.

'Don't look at them,' Beadle said as he closed his eyes. 'If they look at you, they'll know we shouldn't be here.'

'Then how will we find Crane's men?' she asked as they got from the horse and started to walk.

'No need to look any further,' a voice said from the doorway of the inn. 'If it's Crane you want then you can talk to me.'

Tanville looked at the man. He filled the frame of the door with his gigantic hulk. He had a small beard and dark eyes that stared at them. Wrapped in a thick coat, he looked out of place, almost from another time. Beadle jumped from the horse and vanished in the fog. Chilnam dismounted and looked at the man.

'Why do you want Crane?' he asked, not realising he spoke to a girl.

'I have to find the crew of the *Magenta*,' she replied as Beadle hid behind the horse and pretended to look at its feet.

'No such vessel,' the man said. 'There was once, but now she has gone for good. Why does a young lad like you want to see a rascal like Crane?'

'Because he's in danger and as we speak the *Magenta* sails down the river to Dog Island and tonight he is not captain of the ship.'

The man snatched her suddenly by the arm and dragged her inside the inn. Without a single word, he pulled her through the inn and onto a large wooden balcony that overlooked the river. A long bench ran the length of the wall and to one side were a set of wooden steps down to the water. Three iron braziers that burnt sea coal and wood lit the gallery, crackling and spitting against the fog. By each were huddled a group of men. They were tattered and forlorn, bearded and dishevelled. From where she stood, Tanville Chilnam could smell each one.

'He's after Crane,' the man said, and he laughed. 'Says the Captain is in danger and that the *Magenta* sails down the river.'

'Who do we talk to, Mister Abel?' a voice asked.

'Lady Tanville Chilnam,' she replied quickly as she looked for Beadle.

'A lass?' one asked scornfully. 'Dressed like a boy and it's a lass?'

'Would you let your daughter upon these streets?' Tanville asked. 'Not one of you would ever dare – if you had any love for your family.'

'Then why did they let you, my *lady*?' asked one.

'They didn't. All my family are dead and I the last one. It was I who decided to come – what did I have to lose?'

Before she had finished speaking, Beadle was dragged from where he had been hiding in the pub. He was gripped by the ear and squealing like a pig.

'Look what I have found,' said the smuggler as he threw Beadle on to the gallery. 'If I am right then this is Beadle of Baytown, Demurral's pet lamb. Seen him many times licking around his master's rump . . .'

'Strange you should come together,' the voice said.

'We *are* together, Mister Martin,' Beadle said, knowing the voice well. 'Travelled from Whitby and met in the carriage.'

'And Demurral?' he asked.

'He has the Captain, Thomas and Kate,' Beadle said as the man twisted his ear.

'It's a trick,' said another.

'Kill them,' said yet another, as dark swirls of mist blew across the balcony.

'Truth,' Tanville shouted as she stepped towards Martin. 'Your master is captured by Demurral and is being taken to Dog Island. You can let him be killed or help us find them.'

'Crane told us to come here tonight – the night of the Feast of Sola the Hermit. Strange you should appear in his place,' Martin said as he rubbed his chin and spat into the river.

'And he told me where you would be found. *The Prospect of Whitby*, Crane said. Remember, *The Prospect of Whitby*.'

'And there she is as always,' Martin replied, pointing to an old ship tied on to the landing rail at the bottom of the flight of wooden steps. 'Not much of a ship – but with the *Magenta* gone our only way home.'

Mister Martin stopped and looked up the river. His eyes peered through the gloom. The water was edged in the mist that formed a grey mantle. In the distance were the billowing white sails of a brig. It sailed slowly and somewhat cumbersomely as the tide took hold of its boards and brought it nearer.

'Look,' he said in amazement as he pointed for them all to see. 'She's right – the *Magenta*.'

Like a floating gallows, the *Magenta* came closer and closer. The tide ran fast and the ship rolled in the wake.

'I told you it was the truth. Believe me. Crane is being taken to Dog Island by Demurral and will surely be killed.'

'Then it will be our business to be catching them,' Martin said as he drew a small telescope from his pocket and looked through it. 'Quickly – six of you take the rowboat, the rest come by land.'

His words went unquestioned. Six of them ran down the flight of wooden steps to a long rowboat that was tied at the water's edge. Without ceremony they raised the oars and pushed from the land into the river. One man called the pace as they quickly set out from the Devil's Tavern and rowed ahead of the *Magenta*. Within the minute, Tanville had lost sight of them. They had merged with the dark waves and the shadows of the far shore and were gone.

'You two can stay here,' Martin said as he looked at her and Beadle. 'This is our business.'

'It's also mine,' Tanville said as she pushed Martin away. 'If I don't go with you then I shall make my own way and Beadle will be with me. Demurral has something that belongs to me and I want it back.' Tanville wanted to say more, to tell them about the portrait and the misery it had brought to so many.

She wanted to tell them of her father's dying wish, the betrayal of her mother and the loss of everything that Tanville Chilnam held as being precious. She wanted to speak of a castle that once rang out with laughter and now stood like miserable sackcloth in the border fells. Tanville Chilnam would have chattered for hours of all that had been good in her life and the misery that had befallen her. Instead, like the dour walls of her castle she kept silent.

She stared at Mister Martin, her eyes angry and bright, her face set like stone. He thought for a moment, as he looked her up and down.

'Very well – so mote it be. And if you die – don't blame me . . .'

The *Magenta* rolled in the tidal wave that washed it like a lump of flotsam along the Thames. Obadiah Demurral adjusted the long white collar of his priest's shirt and folded it neatly into his waistcoat. From his place on the bridge of the ship he could see the faint lights on either side of the river. They moved with the tilting of the ship and reminded him of the harbour at Whitby. Demurral gulped the air like a fish on the sand. He paced the deck, jittery and excited, and looked to a dark outline in the bend of the river. On the near shore was the Devil's Tavern; its lights shone brightly, set against the walls of the warehouses that flanked each side. He gave no heed to the rowboat that beat ahead of him. His hand shivered in the cold of the night and, looking around once more to see all was well, he went below deck.

The steps led to the door of what was once Crane's cabin. Demurral knocked with the tip of his long white finger. The handle was turned from the inside and Galphus smiled to welcome him. Demurral thought that the man looked nervous – *strange for an alchemist*, he thought, as he nodded and looked at Crane and then to Raphah.

'Boy,' he said politely to Raphah. 'In the time I have known you I have never told you why all this has come to pass. I am troubled that I should even think such a thought, but something in my mind tells me I should at least inform you as to why your life will be taken.'

Crane moved uncomfortably. The leather bands were tight around his wrists; his chains had been exchanged for horse bonds that burnt his hands.

'Why do you have to kill any of us?' Raphah asked.

'Was it not Riathamus who took the first life in the Garden? Did he not kill an animal to clothe the man who ate from the Tree of Life? Did he not want blood and desire sacrifice at all times? If those are the ways of Riathamus, then why cannot we demand the same? It began with blood and shall end with blood . . . Your blood. You three are the divine proportion – each of you chosen for this purpose. A Keruvim for the Angels, a boy for Adam and a girl for Eve. In all creation there is a meaning, even in your dying.'

'Take of me what you want,' Raphah replied as he smiled at him. 'I don't fear death or what is beyond . . . And as for Riathamus his demands are mercy, not sacrifices.'

'We shall see. Your redemption is in my hands. I will be your judge and your jury.'

'And Thomas and Kate – what of them?' Raphah asked.

'I will fill the Chalice with seven drops of blood from each of you. Not one of you are spoiled or tarnished by life – that is the way it must be. The Grail has more power within it than the Keruvim. It has the force of heaven, and to think you brought it to me.'

'Then do it now, here and now, Demurral, but let me die fighting and not hog-tied,' Crane shouted and spat.

'Patience, Jacob, patience,' Demurral said as he smirked. 'I have waited many years for this moment and will not have it taken from me so quickly. Since the beginning of time mankind has waited to overturn the reign of the Almighty. Think it a privilege that you should witness this at first hand. You are a guest at the destruction of Riathamus. It is my second chance,' he snarled at Raphah. 'He should have killed me when he had the chance. Doesn't he sicken you that he allowed me to bring you here? Don't you feel abandoned by him? And yet you still give him glory?'

There was a sudden rustling of the wind that rattled the windows of the cabin and blew the papers across the chart stand. All felt strangely cold as Raphah raised his eyes from the floor and talked slowly. It was as if a voice had taken his and spoke for him. 'I tell you this, Obadiah Demurral. Before the crowing of the cockerel, you shall be gone from this world. Your flesh shall hang like rags from your bones for it is a foolish man who falls into the grip of a jealous God.'

# A Pocketful of Stones

THE derelict quayside of Dog Island stuck into the river like a broken finger. To one side was a swathe of marsh that crowed and croaked with the sound of every wetland creature that had walked the earth. In the stillness of the night the screeches echoed and carried, distorted into grotesque calls by the wind. The water slopped against the side of the *Magenta*. Here, away from the tide, it stank of the London foul that frothed on the surface in a thick brown scum.

The vagabond procession were dragged one by one from the ship along the quay and towards a small mound surrounded by a circle of densely planted silver birch. A shale path led like a long white finger through the tall reeds to drier land. It rose up, away from the river, but even there were signs that the tide had washed through the grass in flood.

Demurral led the way, dancing like a small child, skipping every other step. Behind, the weary Galphus walked on, followed by twelve Druggles who hemmed in their guests. Thomas was bound like the others. Around his wrists were leather straps that he rubbed back and forth to loosen as he walked.

For most of the mile they walked they said nothing. Thomas

looked at the far-away dock. He could see the masts of ships on the other side of the island. To the west was the city. Lighting the sky blood-red was a fire and a pillar of cloud. In the distance, far along the path, he could see even more Druggles. They lined the shale walkway, lanterns in hand that shimmered in the growing breeze. Two held an arch of holly branches high above their heads as they walked through.

Demurral bowed serenely, dropping to one knee and nodding his head. In his hand he held the Grail Cup. Soon they all walked up the stone steps, through the copse that surrounded the hill. Once they were at its shallow summit they were pushed into a circle that was cut in the goose-eaten grass and marked by chalkstone. Thomas could see the village of Greenwich and the burnt hulk of the *Lupercal*. It sat like burnt ribs at the southern tip of Dog Island. Three masts cast moon shadows on the water. The entire world seemed to be cut with silver and black shadows that lined each contour as if they had been drawn by hand.

Thomas looked at Jacob and then Raphah. Kate was slumped on the ground, her body shaking. She sobbed and moaned as two Druggles hung Isabella's portrait to a low bough of a larch tree. It hung out of place, incongruous in the landscape, as Isabella stared from her prison screaming at her captors.

Demurral and Galphus bowed to each other as they silently walked the circle. Druggles in turn bowed to them as they went by. It was as if they had all become the workings of some gigantic living clock. When Thomas looked he realised they had each been placed at points in time: he at the ninth hour, Crane the third, Raphah the sixth and Kate at midnight. In the centre of the circle was a burning pot. It flamed and smoked with acrid incense that blew about them in the changing wind. Demurral walked the circumference and then stopped next to Kate.

A Druggle stepped from the shadows without command and stood before the cauldron. He ripped open the front of his shirt to expose his flesh as he faced the river. His eyes spoke of *Gaudium*. Thomas could see the look of complete and utter glee on his face: the fixed grin, the quivering lips and sniffing nose.

Galphus thrust his cane into the earth and called out as Demurral took a knife from his coat and one by one cut the strands and charms from Isabella's picture. Immediately she broke free, jumping from the frame, and there, for all to see, the doorway to her world opened. The vortex from the painting roared like a thundering whirlpool as it sucked the air from the world. It rattled the branches of the trees as if its power would suck the stars from the firmament. Isabella ran to Kate and danced around her as Kate held out her tethered hands as if to be cut free.

Demurral cut her cheek with the knife and dribbled seven drops of blood into the Grail Cup. Crane stiffened with rage, tightly bound to the trunk of a wizened birch tree. He could not move from his place, his hand clasped together by leather straps and tethered to the trunk.

'No more, Demurral,' he shouted. 'I will see you dead before you cut another.'

Slowly and purposefully, Demurral went to Thomas and then Raphah. Before he cut each one, he looked to Jacob Crane and smiled. Galphus stared into the crystal, glancing frequently to Demurral as if for some sign of what should happen now.

When Demurral had gathered the twenty-one drops of blood he stood in the centre of the circle and raised the Cup to the sky. Far to the south there was a crack of thunder. From the river bubbled a silver mist that crawled from the water and followed the path of a small inlet.

They could all see it drawing closer and closer as the wind blew through the rattling branches above their heads.

'She comes,' Galphus said, looking deeper into the crystal. 'She comes, Demurral.'

Demurral looked into the crystal. In the swirling mist he could see a dark figure striding through the mist-laden fields towards the hill.

'Who do you summon now?' Crane shouted above the wind.

'Your fate and my future, Jacob Crane. Cover your eyes and look not on the form of the Queen of Heaven. Soon you will stand in the presence of Hertha and you will die.'

'Fear her not,' shouted Raphah. 'All that comes is a demon from hell, sold to the world as the mother of God. What you will see in her eyes, Demurral, is the brimstone that will consume you both.'

There was a sudden deathly silence. All was still as the wind ebbed from the branches. Isabella walked slowly back to her picture frame and hid within the glade. It was as if she could sense what was to come. She smiled at Thomas from behind a ghostly yew tree.

From around the hill came a pleasant whispering. It was like the call of dawn birds but uttered on the lips of a thousand excited children. From every tree then came the hissing of serpents and the rattle of snakes. Then it came.

Gathering speed as it flew, a dark silhouette broke through the branches of the trees that covered the hill. It landed by the outer circle and, taking the form of a large fox, ran to the centre. Without hesitation, it dived through the skin of the Druggle who stood waiting as if he knew this would be his fate and welcomed it gladly. For several moments it vanished completely within him and then appeared again, a heart in its hand.

'Demurral,' said the voice of the woman as she transformed from the fox to human form. 'Is all prepared?'

'All is well. The blood is in the Cup and the divine principle is set. The seconds tick and our clock is ready.'

'Then we shall steal time and the kingdom of heaven,' Hertha said, wiping her hands upon her green velvet dress. 'The gate is open, I see. And the child, Isabella, does she suspect?'

'All is well,' Demurral said again, as if they were the only words he dare utter.

'Then let us chime the timepiece and bring an end to this all,' Hertha said.

'It will not end here,' Raphah said.

'Ah, Raphah . . . My brother has spoken of you many times. A thorn in the flesh born of righteousness. What angel shall you conjure to stop us tonight?' she asked. 'I have it on good authority that Raphael shall not appear as he searches for Tegatus in the depths of the sea. Tonight, *Raphah-the-healer*, it is you and I who shall decide the fate of the world. Think of it. What began long ago shall be completed here.'

'You shall be sent to a place from which you will never escape,' he shouted.

'And you, you will beg me to let you die. All of you mean nothing to me,' Hertha raged as she threw the remnants of the bloodied heart into the fire.

'My Queen,' Demurral begged. 'The time has come, it is an hour from morning.'

'The last one ever – how glad will I be to never see a sunrise,' she said. She walked towards Kate and, lifting her head, kissed her cheek. 'You will be the first to welcome death.'

'Not as long as I live,' Crane shouted. 'I fear no witch from hell.'

Crane looked defiant, his eyes bold as he held back his head. He feared no one. Hertha twitched as she thought and then suddenly pulled the crystal stick from the ground and, leaping the circle, smashed it upon his head, knocking him to the ground.

'See,' she said as she panted her breath. 'I fear no man. Take him from this place and drown him in the river.'

The Druggles took Crane's bindings from the tree and dragged him across the circle towards the path through the trees. He could not resist, the flow of blood from his head blinding his eyes. He stumbled and fell as Demurral kicked him for a final time.

'How things change, Jacob,' Demurral said as he disappeared into the wood. 'How things change . . .'

Hertha clicked her fingers. Demurral and Galphus turned like two dogs.

'Take his place, Galphus,' she commanded. 'It needs a soul to be in his place, the timepiece will soon chime. Cut the bindings from the others, they need to stand freely in their death.'

With that Druggles cut the bindings on Thomas and Raphah. Hertha snatched the Grail Cup from Demurral's fingers and began to spin and spin. She whirled like a mad dervish. It was as if with every turn the earth moved with her. The trees began to whirl about them, and Thomas could not stand as the vortex of Isabella's portrait opened up once more and began to pull them all towards it.

Hertha laughed as she danced around and around, her long red hair trailing like a comet about to smash to the earth. Raphah looked up at the swirl of stars above them and from far away could hear Crane's tormented cries. Galphus gripped his cane and trembled as from all around him the souls of the dead were sucked from the earth towards the golden frame that hung from the tree.

Thomas could see Kate as she got to her feet as in the swirling mist. Isabella came to her side. For a moment Kate looked at him and then fell back towards the vortex. From within the Chalice blood began to flow, covering the ground beneath them as the hill spun in time and space like the whirring of a clock. The Druggles ran into the dark wood, leaving them alone.

'Raphah,' Thomas screamed. He felt his skin begin to dry and the life flow from him as a purple haze surrounded him. 'Kill her . . .'

The world stopped as if time had ceased. Hertha stared at Thomas. He looked and saw her feet had changed to those of a ram. She moved towards him and with one hand suddenly gripped his throat. He screamed as he choked his breath. Kate ran as fast as she could and grabbed at Hertha. They began to fight, the girl holding the demon by her hair and beating at her with her fists.

Demurral stood motionless, as if paralysed, as Thomas kicked at the creature. Raphah seized the moment and grasped the Chalice from her fingers. Galphus came towards him, cane outstretched, and from far away they could all hear the cries of a mob.

'Leave me, boy!' she screamed as Thomas dug his nails into her face and Kate pulled her to the ground. From Hertha's back, two small wings arose from the flesh. They fluttered and beat like those of a small bat that in the night air began to grow hideously.

'She's getting away!' Thomas screamed as Demurral finally broke himself from his fear and jumped towards him.

Kate spun on her heels to see Isabella's ghost grab Demurral and throw him to the floor. Hertha broke free of Thomas and lunged for the Grail. Thomas, without thinking, hit her about the face harder than he had punched anyone before.

Hertha looked at him, stunned by the blow. She turned to Kate, who stood close to the open portal. With a sudden jab she pushed Kate towards the vortex. Kate stumbled and tripped, falling towards the inner glade as the world within sucked her closer. In a second she was gone, transformed between worlds and never to return. Thomas rushed to her as she held out her hand. He grasped her fingers that in a moment were pulled from him as Hertha dragged him back. Thomas saw Kate's last smile. The *Gaudium* had lost its power in her death. She was like she had always been – his Kate Coglan and no other.

Raphah lifted the Chalice into the air and shouted in his tongue as loud as he could, calling the names of the angels. Hertha laughed as she pushed Thomas away.

'I have heard all those names before, boy,' she said as she reached for the Cup.

In a single breath Raphah uttered the unutterable and screamed the hidden name of G–d. '*Shaddai– El–Aadonai . . .*' he said again and again. The dirt beneath him began to awaken and the powers and principalities of the earth stirred beneath his feet like the rising of a volcano.

Demurral pushed the bucket of fire and incense from its stand and spilt the hot coals at Raphah's feet. The ground began to burn about him as fire leapt to consume him.

'Die, Ethio!' Demurral screamed as a wall of red flames encircled him.

Raphah recited the true name again and again. With every word the fire retreated as the ground trembled.

Hertha was beaten back by the flames. They burnt brightly, consuming the grass beneath her feet and chasing between her cloven hooves. The uttering of the Name filled the night air and called across the marshes. It was as if a power had been unleashed upon the world. It came in the sound of raindrops that beat against the river and fell from the sky like silver pearls. The whole of nature twisted within itself as birds and fowl flew in spirals like black clouds over the city with one mind.

Hertha was silenced. She looked up in wonder as she dropped her hands to her side and sighed.

It then happened so quickly that no one saw Thomas as he grabbed the cane from Galphus. With all the anger and pain that he had ever known – all the hatred that he had for the world, all the misery of his heart – he thrust it like a spear through Hertha's chest, piercing her cold, cold heart.

At first she just stood silently and looked at the crystal set on the black-lacquered rod. She giggled, as if this could never have happened.

'An angel,' she said softly. 'Can only, when killed by love . . .' Hertha turned to Thomas and smiled at him. 'You set me free. I take from you and you from me. I have no bitterness . . .'

Thomas let her speak no more. 'Shut it, witch,' he said, and he pulled the cane from her and pierced her again, watching her fall to the ground at Raphah's feet as she began to burn in the flames.

Galphus and Demurral began to pace slowly backwards towards the pathway. Raphah could see Galphus look for the Druggles – they had all to a man vanished and ran as the fire took hold.

'Now we are equal,' Raphah said. 'Two stand against two.'

'Thou shalt not kill,' Demurral murmured as he saw Thomas holding the cane in his hand.

'You know not the meaning of the words you say. They roll from your lips like lies and please no one,' Raphah said. He held the Chalice towards him as if to summon the powers from within.

'THOU SHALT NOT KILL!' shouted Crane as he stumbled, beaten and bruised, towards the circle with a pistol in each hand, followed by Tanville Chilnam and Beadle. 'BUT I CAN!'

He gave them not a moment longer as he fired both barrels towards them. Galphus raised his hands and the lead burst through the palm of his hand and into his face. Demurral turned to run and screamed in fear. The lead sped by and smashed against a tree, missing him by an inch.

Thomas waited no longer. He thrust the cane through the air like a spear, striking Demurral in the leg. He fell to the floor, bleeding from the wound. Thomas walked towards him, not listening to the shouting of his companions. All seemed like a dream. The trees beat against each other as he picked a burning coal from the ground. He felt no pain, no burning of his skin as his hand blistered and bubbled.

'I have known you since the day you were born,' Demurral bleated. 'I am the keeper of a secret you now must know. Your father didn't drown, Thomas. I am your father . . . Your mother worked for me, she loved me. Believe me – *I* am your father . . .'

'My father is in heaven and that you know,' Thomas said as he calmly placed the burning ember in Demurral's waistcoat. 'If I cannot see you burn in hell, then I shall see you burn upon the earth.'

Demurral began to smoke as the flames took hold. He screamed and screamed as if consumed by a fire within. Thomas turned from him and walked away. There was another shot as the Shadowmancer was relieved of his misery. Beadle stood on the outer edge of the dark wood, clutching the pistol he had taken from Jacob Crane. He looked at his master, a tear trickling down his cheek, and knew the world would not be the same again.

Beadle put the pistol on the ground and picked seven small round stones from the path. He looked at each one and without speaking put them in the pocket of his frock coat.

# Chilnam Castle

THOMAS sat on the bench by the fire. He looked at the stone lintel that spanned the width of the room and held up the enormous chimney and the fireplace within. In the grate burnt a holly log. It sparked and spit as it was heated on the coals. Above the fireplace was the portrait of Isabella. It was where it had always been, the bars now taken from the frame, the canvas bright and full of colour. Since the return of the painting to the castle, Isabella had not been seen. Beadle had said that she would no longer come from within, not now that she had Kate to keep her from walking the world of men.

Thomas thought of all that had gone before and none of it made the slightest sense. The world had not changed – all that was lost was Kate. His hand was well healed, the skin mended and his pride restored. The thoughts of that far-away night had slipped from his mind as if in the telling they had faded to a dream.

Thomas had spent the month walking in the forest and gardens of the castle. Since the *Magenta* had put in to winter at Berwick, he longed for the summer and the promise of sailing with Jacob Crane to take Raphah to Africa. In the long nights

332

Raphah had told him of what would come as they journeyed south: fish that would fly from the sea, breezes so warm that they would burn the skin and nights under the stars as the sea rocked them to sleep. All this was far away from the border castle and the Northumbrian gales that blew from the fell.

Tanville Chilnam sat at the long table that ran the length of the Great Hall and folded a red banner in her hand.

'They said they would be back by Christmas and that is three days from now,' Thomas said as he stacked the fire with more logs.

'Jacob said he had to be with Raphah, it was the only way they would be safe,' she said.

'But why did they take Beadle?' he asked.

'To see Whitby for the last time and help dispose of the Chalice,' she replied.

The door slowly opened and a small face peered within.

'I should have gone with them,' Thomas said half-heartedly as he looked to his scarred fingers and remembered the fire that had consumed Demurral.

Then the door swung open and Beadle, Raphah and Jacob Crane stepped within.

'Thomas,' said Crane, and he opened his arms to be greeted.

'The Chalice?' Thomas asked.

'Buried where no one will find it and in the place where it was taken from,' Raphah said as he came into the hall and beat the cold from his coat.

'The chapel at Bell Hill?' Thomas asked.

'It's now but a ruin,' Crane said. 'We found the chamber beneath an old stone where the Templars had placed the Grail Cup. Think of it, a mile from Demurral all that time and it took Mister Bragg to find it.'

'Why not take it to Africa?' Thomas asked, as Raphah warmed by the fire.

'Who would think to look for the Cup of the King a mile from the sea in a ruin by an old farm? There will come a time in this world when people will run after legends as if it is those that have the meaning of life. Best to keep these things from foolish men who look for comfort in that which is hidden. It will be safe there.'

'And what of the power that Demurral sought?' Lady Tanville asked.

'There will be others and in a time to come another Keruvim will take my place,' Raphah said, as if the battle would rage forever in the hearts of men. In the high rafters above them an owl screeched its song as it waited for night.

'Raphah, what will I say when I face the King?' Thomas asked his friend.

'Love will cover a multitude of wrongs and when you stand before him you will not stand alone. Each of us shall have an advocate to speak for us. In that you will have no fear and no concern. As summer turns to autumn we do not grieve the passing.'

Thomas looked to the painting, his eyes searching for some sign of Kate. There, for the first time, he noticed that within the image another face could be seen. On the canvas, standing to the side of Isabella, was the face of his lost friend.

In some strange way, Kate's face had been etched within the canvas as bright as Isabella's. From above the fireplace she smiled at them with eyes that followed their every step.

Raphah saw Thomas looking at the picture. 'She's not there, Thomas,' he said, placing a hand upon his shoulder. 'Isabella and Kate have gone on to a far kingdom.'

'Do you believe all of that?' Thomas asked.

'How can you say that after all we have seen?' Crane replied as he pulled the bench closer to the fire and sipped brandy from a cup. 'Even I have no excuses. There is more in the land of men than I dare admit.'

'But where are they?' Thomas asked again.

'I don't know until I go there myself, but what I do believe is that they are alive,' Raphah said.

'If I could see them, touch them, I could believe and my soul would rejoice,' Thomas said. 'But my heart doubts. Then when I hear you speak, I can believe again.'.

'Did you see all what I saw, Thomas?' Raphah asked.

'Yes, everything.'

'Then hold that as the truth.'

'And Demurral, is he really dead?' Thomas asked as he looked to the burn upon his hand.

'Forever . . .'